The Complete Warrior's Mindset Collection (Vol. 4)

Politics & The Prince
— Governing the State and the Self

A Modern Translation

Adapted for the Contemporary Reader

Aristotle | Niccolò Machiavelli

Translated by Tim Zengerink

Table of Contents

Preface - Message to the Reader

What If You Could Help Rebuild the Greatest Library in Human History?

Thousands of years ago, the Library of Alexandria stood as the crown jewel of human achievement — a sanctuary where the collected wisdom of every known civilization was gathered, preserved, and shared freely.

And then, it was lost.

Through fire, conquest, and the slow erosion of time, humanity lost not just books — but ideas, dreams, discoveries, and stories that could have changed the world forever.

Today, the Library of Alexandria lives again — and you are invited to be a part of its restoration.

Our mission is simple yet profound:

To rebuild the greatest library the world has ever known, and to translate all timeless works into every language and dialect, so that no seeker of knowledge is ever left behind again.

By joining our movement to rebuild the modern Library of Alexandria, you become part of an unprecedented mission:

- **Unlimited Access to the Greatest Audiobooks & eBooks Ever Written:**

  Instantly explore thousands of legendary works—Plato, Shakespeare, Jane Austen, Leo Tolstoy, and countless more. All instantly available to read or listen, placing a complete literary universe at your fingertips.

- **Beautiful Paperback & Deluxe Editions at Printing Cost**

  Own any title as an elegant paperback, deluxe hardcover, or stunning collectible boxset—offered to you at true printing cost, delivered straight to your door. Build your personal Library of Alexandria, crafted for beauty, built for durability, and worthy of proud display.

- **Fresh Translations for Modern Readers—in Every Language & Dialect**

  Enjoy timeless masterpieces reimagined in clear, contemporary language—no more outdated phrases or obscure references. Alongside the original versions, we're tirelessly translating these classics into every language and dialect imaginable, ensuring accessibility and understanding across cultures and generations.

- **Join a Global Renaissance of Literature & Knowledge**

  You directly support expanding our library, publishing deluxe editions at true cost, translating works into all global languages, and bringing humanity's greatest stories to people everywhere. By joining today, you're not just preserving a legacy of masterpieces; you set in motion a powerful wave of literary accessibility.

Become a Torchbearer of Knowledge.

Join us for free now at **LibraryofAlexandria.com**

Together, we will ensure that the light of human wisdom never fades again.

With gratitude and a shared love of knowledge,
The Modern Library of Alexandria Team

Visit:

www.libraryofalexandria.com

Or scan the code below:

Introduction

Leadership Between Philosophy and Power:
The Warrior as Statesman

The warrior is not only a figure of combat, but a steward of order. To lead effectively, the warrior must understand not only how to conquer, but how to govern—how to stabilize power, maintain harmony, and construct institutions that endure. In The Complete Warrior's Mindset Collection (Vol. 4), we bring together two of the most influential texts ever written on governance and leadership: Aristotle's Politics and Niccolò Machiavelli's The Prince.

These two works could not be more different in tone or method. Aristotle, the Greek philosopher and scientist, presents a systematic, idealistic vision of the city-state, grounded in ethics and civic virtue. Machiavelli, writing in the chaos of Renaissance Italy, offers a ruthless guide to acquiring and keeping power in a volatile political world. And yet, when read together, they provide a powerful and complete portrait of the warrior-statesman's mindset.

Aristotle teaches how to build a stable and just society. Machiavelli teaches how to survive and rule in a dangerous one. One is normative, the other descriptive. One outlines what ought to be; the other describes what often is. Together, they give the reader a full-spectrum understanding of leadership that spans principle and pragmatism, vision and maneuver.

This introduction explores how both thinkers view the nature of rule, the moral challenges of leadership, and the balance between personal virtue and public effectiveness. It is not a matter of choosing between them, but of integrating their insights—so that the modern warrior can remain principled without being naïve, and strategic without being cynical.

Aristotle:
The Architecture of Just Rule

In Politics, Aristotle examines the foundation of the polis—the city-state—as the highest form of community. For him, the purpose of political life is to cultivate virtue and enable human flourishing. A good government does not simply maintain order; it creates the conditions for excellence in its citizens.

Aristotle classifies governments based on who rules and whether they rule for the common good or their own advantage. Monarchy (rule by one), aristocracy (rule by a few), and polity (rule by the many) can each be virtuous when directed toward the common welfare. Their corrupt forms—tyranny, oligarchy, and democracy (in his pejorative sense of mob rule)—arise when leaders prioritize personal gain over collective well-being.

Crucial to Aristotle's political theory is his belief that ethics and politics are inseparable. The just ruler must be a virtuous person—prudent, courageous, moderate, and just. Education is therefore a political necessity. Without cultivating reason and virtue in citizens, even the best constitutions will collapse.

For the warrior-leader, Aristotle offers several profound lessons. First, he asserts that political power is not about domination, but stewardship. Second, he emphasizes the importance of the middle class and the dangers of extreme inequality. Third, he argues that law, not men, should rule—because law is reason freed from passion.

Aristotle's ideal leader is both philosopher and citizen, both thinker and actor. He must not only win battles but guide the moral trajectory of the state. In this sense, Aristotle is the blueprint for the ideal warrior-statesman—someone who sees leadership as a noble discipline requiring both inner character and civic responsibility.

Machiavelli:
Power, Fortune, and the Necessity of Force

While Aristotle builds from principles, Machiavelli builds from observation. The Prince, written in 1513, is a brief but explosive manual for rulers seeking to gain, consolidate, and retain political power. Set against the backdrop of fragmented Italy and foreign invasions, Machiavelli dispenses with illusions. He offers not moral aspiration, but strategic realism.

The central premise of The Prince is that politics is not governed by ideal virtue, but by the shifting tides of fortune, perception, and necessity. The successful ruler must learn to navigate these forces with cunning, flexibility, and decisiveness. Virtue (virtù), for Machiavelli, is not moral goodness but effective action—strength, boldness, and the ability to adapt to changing conditions.

Machiavelli shocks many readers with his claims: that it is better to be feared than loved if one cannot be both; that rulers must be willing to use deception; and that the appearance of virtue is often more important than virtue itself. Yet beneath the surface, his purpose is not to encourage evil, but to defend political stability.

He argues that moral purity in politics is often a trap. If a ruler clings to goodness in a world of wolves, he will be destroyed. To preserve the state, the prince must sometimes act against faith, charity, or honesty. But these actions are justified if they prevent chaos and protect the realm.

For the warrior-leader, The Prince is a powerful counterweight to idealism. It warns against naïveté, against trusting enemies or being trapped by rigid principles. It insists that survival requires strategy, perception management, and the courage to act when others hesitate.

But Machiavelli is not simply ruthless. He also respects order, unity, and national pride. His admiration for Roman virtues and citizen militias reflects his belief that lasting power must be grounded in civic strength. In this sense, he complements rather than contradicts Aristotle.

Virtue and Victory:
A Unified Philosophy of Rule

Reading Aristotle and Machiavelli side by side is not a clash of opposites—it is an education in complexity. It reveals that leadership requires multiple lenses:

- Aristotle teaches us to govern the self and create just institutions.
- Machiavelli teaches us to read the world and act decisively under pressure.

One without the other is incomplete. A purely moral leader may be ineffective in crisis. A purely strategic leader may destroy what he rules. The warrior's mindset must therefore include both: the strength of principle and the sharpness of strategy.

Both thinkers also affirm the need for discipline. Aristotle sees discipline as the path to virtue. Machiavelli sees it as the backbone of power. Neither believes that strength comes naturally. It must be cultivated through learning, reflection, and struggle.

Finally, both understand that leadership is about stability—not only of territory, but of the soul. The leader must maintain control not only over events, but over himself. In this, we see the true fusion of their thought: a political theory that begins with the mastery of the mind.

Welcome to The Complete Warrior's Mindset Collection (Vol. 4). May Aristotle strengthen your sense of justice and purpose, and may Machiavelli sharpen your sense of timing and reality—so that you can lead with wisdom, act with courage, and navigate the balance between what is right and what is necessary.

Politics

Aristotle

Book 1

Every state is a type of community, and every community is formed with the aim of achieving some good. Humans always act to get what they believe is good. If all communities aim for some good, then the state or political community, which includes all other communities, aims for the greatest good. It does so to a higher degree than any other community.

Some people believe that the roles of a statesman, king, head of a household, and master are the same, and they only differ in the number of people they control. For instance, a master rules over a few people, a head of a household rules over more, and a statesman or king rules over even more, as if there were no difference between a large household and a small state. The distinction made between a king and a statesman is this: if the government is run by one person, he is called a king, but if citizens take turns ruling according to the rules of political science, then he is called a statesman.

However, this is a mistake. Governments differ in nature, which becomes clear if we break things down into their simplest elements. Just as in other sciences, in politics we must break things down into their basic parts. We should examine the basic elements that make up the state so we can understand how different types of rule differ from one another, and whether we can reach any scientific conclusions about them.

Anyone who looks at things from their very beginning, whether it's a state or anything else, will see them most clearly. First, there must be a union between those who cannot exist without each other—specifically, male and female so the race can continue. This union happens not by choice but because humans, like animals and plants, have a natural desire to leave behind something of themselves. There must also be a union between the natural ruler and the natural subject so that both may survive. For the one who can think and plan is naturally meant to be the ruler, and the one who can use their body to carry out these plans is naturally meant to be the subject, or the slave. Therefore, the master and the slave have a common interest. Nature has clearly distinguished between a woman and a slave, as she makes everything for a single purpose and not for many. But among barbarians, there is no distinction between women and slaves, as they have no natural rulers. They are a community of slaves, both male and female. That's why poets say, "It is right for Greeks to rule over barbarians," as if they believe that barbarians and slaves are naturally the same.

From these two relationships—between man and woman, and between master and slave—the family emerges. Hesiod is correct when he says, "First, a house, a wife, and an ox for plowing," as the ox is the poor man's slave. The family is a natural association created to meet people's everyday needs, and the members of the family are called 'companions of the cupboard' by Charondas and 'companions of the manger' by Epimenides the Cretan. When several families unite to achieve more than just daily survival, the first community formed is a village. The most natural form of a village seems to be a colony from the family, consisting of children and grandchildren who are said to be raised 'on the same milk.' This is also why early Greek states were originally ruled by kings because they were governed by kings before coming together as states, just like the barbarians today. Each family is ruled by the eldest, and so in these family colonies, a kingly form of government existed because they were all related by blood. Homer says, "Each man gives law to his children and wives," because in ancient times people lived apart from one another. Therefore, people say the gods have a king, because they imagine the lives of the gods to be like their own.

When several villages unite to form a complete community that is large enough to be nearly or entirely self-sufficient, a state comes into existence. It starts because of basic needs but continues for the sake of living a good life. So, if the earlier forms of society are natural, then the state is also natural because it is the end goal of those earlier forms. A thing's nature is its end goal. For example, the fully developed form of a person, a horse, or a family is its true nature. Furthermore, the final purpose of something is the best, and being self-sufficient is the highest goal.

Therefore, it's clear that the state is a creation of nature, and man is naturally a political animal. A person who lives outside the state by nature and not by accident is either a bad person or someone above human society, like the "tribeless, lawless, heartless one" that Homer condemns. Such a person is a natural outcast, like a piece removed from a game of checkers.

It is obvious that man is more of a political animal than bees or other social animals. Nature does nothing in vain, and man is the only animal with the gift of speech. Mere sounds, like cries of pleasure or pain, exist in other animals too, as they can sense pleasure and pain and communicate it to each other. However, speech allows us to express what is useful or harmful, just or unjust. It is human nature to have a sense of good and evil, right and wrong, and it is the sharing of these values that creates families and states.

The state is also naturally more important than the family and the individual, because the whole is always more important than its parts. For example, if the whole body is destroyed, there will no longer be a foot or hand, except in name, like a stone hand. The parts are defined by their function, and when they lose their function, they lose their true nature. This proves that the state is natural and more important than the individual because a person cannot be self-sufficient alone. A person is like a part of a larger whole. Someone who cannot live in society or who doesn't need society because they are completely self-sufficient is either a beast or a god. They are not part of a state. Humans have a natural social instinct, and the person who first founded the state was the greatest benefactor. When a person is fully developed, they are the best of animals, but without law and justice, they are the worst. Injustice with power is dangerous, and humans are born with weapons—intelligence and virtue—that can be used for both good and evil. Without virtue, a person becomes the worst of all animals, full of greed and violence. Justice is the bond that holds a state together, and the administration of justice is what creates order in political society.

Since the state is made up of households, we must first understand how a household is managed before we can understand the state. The parts of household management correspond to the people who make up the household, and a complete household consists of both slaves and free people. To understand household management, we must start by examining its simplest parts: master and slave, husband and wife, and parent and children. We need to consider what each of these relationships is and should be. There is also the part of household management known as acquiring wealth. Some say this is the same as household management, while others say it is a major part of it. We will need to consider the nature of this as well.

Let's first talk about the relationship between master and slave, looking at both practical life and how we can understand this relationship better. Some people think that mastering slaves is a science and that running a household, controlling slaves, and political or royal rule are all the same. Others argue that ruling over slaves is unnatural and that the difference between slaves and free people exists only because of laws, not nature, and is therefore unjust.

Property is a part of the household, and the skill of acquiring property is part of the art of managing a household. No one can live well, or live at all, without the basic necessities. Just as workers need tools for their work, managing a household requires its own set of tools. Some tools are lifeless, like a rudder, while others are living, like a lookout on a ship. In the household, a servant is like a living tool. Property is a tool for maintaining life. A slave is a living possession, and property consists of many such tools. A servant is an instrument that comes before all other tools. If all tools could do their own work, obeying or anticipating the will of others, like the statues of Daedalus or the tripods of Hephaestus that "walked by themselves into the assembly of the gods," then master craftsmen wouldn't need assistants, nor would masters need slaves. However, the tools we use for production are different from the possessions we use for action. For example, a shuttle is used to make something else, while a bed is only used for its function. Life is about action, not production, and the slave's role is to assist in action. A possession is part of something else, and the part fully belongs to the whole. In the same way, a possession fully belongs to its owner. The master is only the master of the slave; he does not belong to the slave. But the slave belongs entirely to his master. Therefore, a slave is someone who, by nature, belongs to someone else. A possession is an instrument of action, separate from its owner.

Is there anyone naturally meant to be a slave, for whom slavery is both good and right, or is all slavery against nature?

The answer is clear based on both reason and experience. It is necessary and beneficial for some to rule and others to be ruled. From birth, some people are marked for leadership, and others for following.

There are different types of rulers and subjects. The rule is better when it's over better subjects. For example, ruling over humans is better than ruling over wild animals because the work done by better workers is always better. Wherever one person rules and another is ruled, they are doing something together. This distinction exists in all living creatures, and it comes from the way the world is organized. Even in non-living things, like music, there's a guiding principle. But let's stick to living things. Every living creature is made of both soul and body, with the soul naturally ruling and the body naturally following. To understand nature, we have to look at things that are in their best form, not those that are corrupted. So, we must study someone who has both a healthy body and soul, for only in such a person will we see the correct relationship between the two. In people who are in bad shape, the body may seem to rule the soul, but this is not natural.

In living creatures, we can observe two kinds of rule. The soul rules over the body like a master over a slave, while the intellect rules over desires in a more balanced, constitutional way. The soul's rule over the body, and the mind's rule over desires, is natural and beneficial. When desires rule over the mind, it's always harmful. The same is true of animals in relation to humans. Tame animals are better off when ruled by humans because humans help them survive. Likewise, men are naturally stronger, and women weaker. Men are meant to rule, and women to follow. This principle applies to all human beings.

When there's a big difference between two things, like between soul and body or humans and animals, the lower kind is naturally a slave. This is especially true for people whose only role is to use their bodies and who can't do anything better. It's good for them, just like it's good for all lesser beings, to be ruled by a master. A person who belongs to someone else and who can understand reason but can't fully grasp it is a natural slave. On the other hand, animals can't even understand reason. They follow their instincts. The way we use slaves and tame animals is similar—they both serve life's basic needs with their bodies.

Nature seems to want to make a clear difference between the bodies of free people and slaves. Slaves should be strong for hard labor, while free people should be upright and fit for political life. But this doesn't always happen. Some people have the souls of free people but the bodies of slaves, and others the opposite. If people were as physically different from one another as humans are from statues of gods, everyone would agree that the weaker class should serve the stronger. And if this is true for the body, it's even more true for the soul. However, we can see physical differences easily, but differences in the soul are harder to see. It's clear that some people are naturally free, and others are naturally slaves. For those meant to be slaves, this is both beneficial and just.

Still, those who disagree also have a point. The words "slavery" and "slave" can mean different things. There is slavery by nature, and then there is slavery by law. The law I'm talking about is the idea that anything taken in war belongs to the victor. But many legal experts reject this idea. They don't think that one person should be a slave simply because another person is stronger. Philosophers also disagree on this point. The confusion comes from the fact that people often link power with virtue. They think that the strong should rule because they are better in some way. So, this debate about slavery is really a debate about justice. One side thinks justice is about goodwill, while the other thinks it's about the rule of the strongest.

If we look at these arguments separately, the view that virtuous people should rule is strong. But the other side believes that the law justifies slavery in war. However, they also admit that this only works if the war itself is just. No one would agree that a person who doesn't deserve to be a slave should be one simply because they were captured in war. This is why Greeks don't like calling other Greeks slaves; they reserve that term for barbarians. In reality, they are talking about natural slaves. Just like nobility, there are two kinds of slavery—one that is natural and one based on law.

Greeks think of themselves as noble everywhere, but barbarians are only noble in their own lands. In a play, Helen says, "Who would call me a servant, when I am descended from the gods on both sides?" This shows how they link freedom and nobility to good and bad. They think good people come from other good people, just like animals give birth to animals. But nature doesn't always make this happen.

So, there is some truth to both sides. Not everyone is naturally free or naturally a slave. In some cases, it is clear and right that some people should be slaves and others masters. When this relationship is natural, both benefit. The master and the slave are like parts of the same body. But when slavery is based only on law and force, the relationship is not beneficial.

From these points, it's clear that the rule of a master is not the same as the rule in a political system. The rule over free people is different from the rule over slaves. The head of a household rules like a king because there is only one leader. In a political system, free and equal citizens share power. A master isn't called a master because of any special skill, but because of who he is. The same applies to slaves and free people. However, there could be a skill in mastering slaves and a skill in being a slave. For example, a man in Syracuse taught slaves how to do their daily tasks for money. This kind of knowledge could even include skills like cooking. Some tasks are more necessary, while others are more honorable, like the saying goes: "slave before slave, master before master." But these kinds of knowledge are low-level skills.

There is also a skill in being a master, which is about using slaves effectively. This skill isn't particularly great, as the master only needs to know how to give orders that the slave must carry out. This is why wealthy people have managers to take care of their households while they focus on philosophy or politics. The skill of acquiring slaves, however, is different from the skill of ruling them—it's more like hunting or warfare. That's enough about the difference between masters and slaves.

Now let's explore property in general and the skill of getting wealth. We've already said that a slave is a kind of property. The first question is whether getting wealth is the same as managing a household, or just part of it. If it's part of it, is it like how making shuttles is part of weaving, or how casting bronze is part of sculpture? These two aren't the same: one provides tools, while the other provides the materials. For example, wool is the material for weaving, and bronze is the material for statues.

It's easy to see that managing a household is different from getting wealth. The household manager uses the things that wealth-getting provides. There is some debate about whether getting wealth is part of household management or a separate skill. If wealth-getting is about finding where wealth can be obtained, and there are many types of property and riches, then is farming and providing food part of wealth-getting or a separate skill? There are many types of food, which is why there are many types of lives for both animals and humans. Different creatures live in ways that suit the food they eat—some are social, some live alone, and they all live in ways that help them find the food they need.

Humans also have many different ways of living. The simplest are shepherds, who live quietly and get their food from their animals. They follow their flocks wherever they go to find food, living a wandering life. Others live by hunting, which can take many forms. Some are bandits, while others live by fishing in lakes, rivers, or seas, or by hunting birds and wild animals. Most people get their food from farming. These are the basic ways of living for people who don't rely on trade. There are shepherds, farmers, bandits, fishermen, and hunters. Some people combine two jobs, like a shepherd who is also a bandit or a farmer who is also a hunter. People adapt in whatever way is necessary to survive.

It seems that nature gives all living things the basic necessities of life. Some animals bring forth their young with enough food to last until they can care for themselves. Oviparous and viviparous animals are examples of this. Viviparous animals, for example, produce milk to feed their young for a time. Similarly, we might say that plants exist to provide food for animals, and some animals exist to provide food and materials for humans. If nature makes nothing incomplete or pointless, it seems that she made all animals for the sake of humans. Therefore, in one sense, war is a natural way of acquiring what we need, including hunting wild animals and forcing those meant to be ruled into submission. War of this kind is naturally just.

There is one kind of wealth-getting that is part of household management. This involves finding or providing what is necessary for life and what is useful for the household or the state. These are the elements of true wealth. There is a limit to how much property is needed for a good life, even though the poet Solon said, "No limit has been set on wealth." But there is a limit, just like there is for all other arts. The tools of any craft are never unlimited in number or size.

Wealth can be defined as the tools needed for managing a household or a state. So, we see that there is a natural way of acquiring wealth, which is practiced by household managers and statesmen, and what is the reason of this.

There is another type of skill for getting wealth, and it's often called the art of making money. People commonly think that wealth and property have no limit because of this idea. This skill is closely related to what we've already talked about, but they're not exactly the same. The one we talked about before is more natural, while this one is learned through experience and skill.

Let's start by looking at this question with the following points in mind:

Everything we own can be used in two ways. Both uses are related to the thing, but they're not the same. One is the correct, main way to use it, and the other is a secondary, less proper use. Take a shoe, for example. You can wear it, or you can trade it. Both are uses of the shoe. If someone trades a shoe for food or money, they're using it, but that's not what it was made for. Shoes weren't created to be traded. The same is true for all things we own. The art of trading applies to all of them, and it began because some people had too little while others had too much. This shows that retail trade isn't a natural part of getting wealth. If it were natural, people would stop trading once they had enough. In the first community, which is the family, this art wasn't needed, but it became useful when society grew. Families originally shared everything. Later, when families divided, different parts had different things, so they had to trade for what they needed. This kind of barter is still used by some nations today. They trade just for life's basic needs, like exchanging wine for money. This kind of trade isn't part of the art of making wealth and isn't against nature. It's simply needed to meet people's natural needs. The more complex kind of exchange came from the simpler one. When people from one country started depending on those from another, they traded things they had too much of for things they needed. This led to the use of money, because it was hard to carry goods around. People agreed to use something useful in itself and easy to handle, like iron or silver. At first, its value was measured by weight and size, but later they put a stamp on it to avoid the trouble of weighing and to mark its value.

Once money was used, a new kind of wealth-making arose from the simple barter of necessities—retail trade. It probably started as something simple but became more complex as people learned where and how to make the biggest profit. Since money was now involved, people thought the art of making wealth was mostly about dealing with money. They believed that the goal was to collect money, thinking riches only meant having lots of coins. Since the art of getting wealth and retail trade dealt with money, people assumed money itself was wealth. But others argued that money isn't really wealth. It's just something we agree on. If people stopped using it, it would be worthless, and it's not something we need for life's necessities. A person could have lots of money and still starve, like King Midas, who, according to the story, wished for everything he touched to turn to gold. But even though he had a lot of gold, he couldn't eat any of it.

So, people look for a better understanding of wealth and how to get it than just collecting money, and they're right to do so. Natural wealth and the natural way of getting wealth are different. In their true form, they are part of managing a household. Retail trade, however, is about creating wealth through exchange. It's focused on money since money is used for trade and is the measure of that trade. There's no limit to the riches that can come from this kind of wealth-getting. Like how there's no limit to health in medicine or to achieving the goal in other skills, the goal in this kind of wealth-getting—riches—also has no limit. The art of managing a household, though, does have a limit. Its goal isn't to get unlimited wealth. So, in one way, wealth should have a limit, but in reality, people try to collect as much money as possible. The confusion happens because these two types of wealth-getting are so closely related. The tools used are the same, even though the way they're used is different. In one case, the goal is to collect as much as possible, and in the other, there's another purpose. This makes some people think that managing a household is all about collecting wealth, and their whole focus is either to increase their money or, at least, not lose it. This attitude comes from people being focused only on living, not on living well. Their desires are endless, so they want the means to meet their desires to be endless too. People who want to live well focus on getting the means to enjoy their lives. Since they believe that enjoyment depends on wealth, they focus on collecting money. This leads to the second kind of wealth-getting. Since their desire for enjoyment is excessive, they look for ways to create an excess of enjoyment. If they can't satisfy their desires with wealth-getting, they try other ways. They use their abilities in ways that go against nature. For example, courage is meant to inspire confidence, not to make money. Neither is making money the goal of a general's skill or a doctor's skill. A general aims for victory, and a doctor aims for health. Yet, some people twist every skill and quality into a way to make money. They believe money is the goal, and everything else should help them achieve that.

We've now talked about the unnecessary kind of wealth-getting and why people desire it, as well as the necessary kind of wealth-getting, which is part of managing a household and is focused on getting food. This kind of wealth-getting has limits, unlike the other kind.

We've answered the question of whether getting wealth is the responsibility of a household manager or a statesman. The answer is that wealth is something they use, but it isn't their main task. Just as political science doesn't create people but uses them as nature made them, so nature provides people with resources like land or the sea for food. This is where the job of the household manager begins. He has to make use of what nature provides, like a weaver uses wool. He doesn't make the wool but needs to know what kind is good and useful. If this weren't the case, we wouldn't know why getting wealth is part of managing a household while medicine isn't. After all, people in a household need to be healthy, just like they need to live. The answer is that the household manager does need to think about health in one way, but it's really the doctor's job. Similarly, wealth is considered by the household manager, but in a limited way, as part of a natural system. Nature provides the means of life, and the manager must use them, like food coming from plants and animals.

There are two kinds of wealth-getting. One is part of managing a household, and the other is retail trade. The first is necessary and respectable, while the second, which involves trading things for money, is often criticized because it's unnatural. Usury, or charging interest on money, is the most disliked form of wealth-getting because it takes money and makes more money from it, rather than using it for trade. Money was made to help trade, not to grow by itself. The word "interest" means the birth of money from money, and it's called this because it's like money giving birth to more money. This is why usury is seen as the most unnatural way to get wealth.

We've talked enough about the theory of getting wealth. Now, we'll move on to the practical part. It's not beneath philosophy to talk about these things, but actually doing them is not a noble or pleasant task. The useful parts of wealth-getting involve knowing which livestock—like horses, sheep, or oxen—are most profitable and where they'll thrive. A person should know which animals give the best return and which do better in certain places. Then, there's farming, which includes planting crops, keeping bees, raising fish or birds, or any animals that are useful to humans. These are the main parts of the natural way of getting wealth.

The second way, involving exchange, has several parts. The most important is commerce, which includes shipping, transporting goods, and selling them. Commerce can differ in safety and profitability. Then, there's usury, and finally, there's work for hire. This can involve either skilled mechanical arts or unskilled physical labor. There's also a middle ground between natural wealth-getting and exchange. This includes industries that make money from the land, like cutting timber or mining, even though they don't produce food. Mining itself has many branches, since there are different things to dig out of the earth. I've now covered these different ways of getting wealth in general. Going into more detail might be helpful in practice, but it would also be tedious right now.

The jobs that are the most respected involve the least amount of luck. The least respected jobs are those that wear down the body the most, and the most servile jobs are those that use the body the most. The least noble jobs are those that don't require much skill or virtue.

There are many books on these subjects, like those written by Chares of Paros and Apollodorus of Lemnos, who wrote about farming and planting. Others have written about different parts of wealth-getting. Anyone who's interested in these things can read their works. It would also be useful to gather stories of how individuals became wealthy because that information can help those who care about the art of making wealth. There's a story about Thales of Miletus and a clever way he made money. It's said he knew by studying the stars that there would be a big olive harvest that year, so during the winter, he used a small amount of money to rent all the olive presses in Chios and Miletus. When the harvest came and many people needed presses, he rented them out at a high price and made a lot of money. He showed that philosophers can be rich if they want to be, but that's not their main goal. His plan was a monopoly, something that's used often by cities when they need money. They control the supply of certain goods.

There's also the story of a man in Sicily. He used money deposited with him to buy all the iron from the mines. When the merchants came to buy, he was the only one selling. Without raising the price too much, he made a 200 percent profit. When Dionysius heard about it, he told the man to take his money and leave the city because he thought the man's way of making money was a threat to his own interests. Like Thales, this man figured out how to create a monopoly. Statesmen should know about these things because cities often need money and have to use clever ways to get it, just like households do.

We've talked about how household management has three parts: managing slaves, which we've already discussed, being a father, and being a husband. A father and husband rules over his children and wife, but these roles are different. A father's rule is like that of a king, and a husband's rule is like that in a government. Even though there are exceptions, the male is naturally better suited to command than the female, just as an older person is superior to a younger one. In most governments, citizens take turns ruling and being ruled, since everyone is considered equal. But when one person is in charge and another is being ruled, we try to create a difference by using titles and signs of respect, like the story of Amasis and his foot-basin. The relationship between men and women is like this, but here the inequality is permanent. A father's rule over his children is royal because it's based on love and the respect that comes with age. That's why Homer called Zeus the "father of gods and men," since he was king of them all. A king is naturally above his subjects, but he should be related to them, just as a father is to his children.

It is clear that managing a household focuses more on people than on getting material things. It also values human excellence more than wealth, and the virtues of free people more than the qualities of slaves. A question might come up: can a slave have virtues like self-control, courage, or justice, or do they only have physical and servant-like qualities? And no matter how we answer, there's a challenge. If slaves do have virtues, how are they different from free people? But, on the other hand, since they are human and can reason, it seems wrong to say they don't have virtues at all.

The same question can be asked about women and children. Should women be considered brave, just, and self-controlled? Should children be called self-controlled or not? In general, we can ask whether natural rulers and natural subjects have the same virtues or not. If both need to have noble qualities, why does one always rule and the other always follow? And we can't just say it's a matter of degree because the difference between ruler and subject is a difference in kind, not just in amount.

It seems strange to think that one person should have virtue and the other shouldn't. If a ruler is unjust and lacks self-control, how can they rule well? And if a subject lacks self-control and is cowardly, how can they follow orders well? It's clear that both need to have some virtues, but they need different types of virtues, just like there are differences among natural subjects. The very makeup of the soul shows us the way. One part of the soul naturally rules, and another part naturally follows. The ruler's virtues are different from the subject's virtues. The ruler's virtue is based on reason, while the subject's virtue comes from following.

This same principle applies to almost everything. Most things in nature involve some form of ruling and following. But the type of rule is different: a free person rules over a slave in a different way than a man rules over a woman or an adult rules over a child. Even though all of them have the same parts of the soul, those parts work differently. The slave doesn't have the ability to make decisions. A woman has this ability, but it doesn't carry authority, and a child's ability is immature. So, the virtues should be different too. Everyone should have some virtues, but only the ones needed for their role.

This means the ruler should have complete moral virtue because their job requires a high level of skill. Rational thought is that skill. The subjects, on the other hand, need only the amount of virtue that fits their role. So, moral virtue belongs to everyone, but the self-control of a man and a woman, or the courage and justice of a man and a woman, are not the same. As Socrates said, a man shows courage by leading, while a woman shows courage by following. This applies to all other virtues too. If we look at them closely, we'll see that they aren't the same for everyone, even though some people say virtue is just about having a good attitude or doing the right thing. They're mistaken. It's much better to think, as Gorgias did, that virtues should be listed separately for different types of people.

Different groups of people have different qualities. As the poet said, "Silence is a woman's glory," but that's not a man's glory. A child is still growing, so their virtue isn't just for themselves, but also in relation to adults and teachers. In the same way, a slave's virtue relates to their master. We said earlier that a slave is useful for daily needs, so they only need enough virtue to keep them from failing in their duties due to fear or lack of self-control.

Someone might ask if this means that craftsmen, too, need virtue, since they can fail in their work due to lack of self-control. But there is a big difference. A slave shares in their master's life, while a craftsman is more distant. A craftsman only reaches excellence if they become like a slave. The lower types of craftsmen have their own kind of slavery. Slaves exist by nature, but not shoemakers or other craftsmen.

So, it's clear that a master should be the source of the slave's virtue. The master should do more than just give orders; they should teach the slave how to do their duties. This is why it's wrong to think that masters shouldn't talk to their slaves and should just command them. Slaves need guidance even more than children do.

This is enough on this subject. The relationships between husband and wife, parent and child, their virtues, what's good and bad in their relationships, and how to pursue the good and avoid the bad will be discussed when we talk about different types of government. Since every family is part of a state, and these relationships are part of a family, the virtue of each part must match the virtue of the whole. Women and children must be educated with the state in mind because their virtues affect the state. They do matter because children grow up to be citizens, and women make up half of the free population in a state.

We've said enough about this for now. What's left to discuss can be covered later. With this part of our inquiry finished, we'll start on a new topic. First, we'll look at different ideas of a perfect state.

Book 2

Since we are trying to figure out what type of civil society is the best for people who have the freedom to live however they want, it's necessary to look at the governments of states that are known to be well-managed. If there are any other states that people say are properly run, we should note what is right and useful about them. And if we point out where they have failed, it's not to act like we know everything. It's because there are big problems with all the systems that already exist, which is why I've taken on this task. We will start with the part of the subject that naturally comes first. The members of any state must share everything in common, share some things but not others, or share nothing at all. Clearly, sharing nothing in common is impossible, because society itself is a kind of community. The first thing necessary for that is a common place to live—the city—which must be one, and every citizen must have a share in it. But in a well-founded government, is it better to make everything shareable, or only some things but not others? For example, citizens might share their wives, children, and property, as in Plato's Republic, where Socrates says this should be the case. Which should we prefer—the customs we already have, or the laws Socrates suggests?

Now, having wives in common brings many difficulties, and the reasons he gives for structuring society this way don't seem logical. It also wouldn't achieve the goal he aims for. He hasn't given any specific directions for how it should work either. I agree with Socrates' idea that a city should be as unified as possible, but if you reduce it too much, it stops being a city, since a city must have a lot of people. If we go too far, we will shrink a city into a family, and a family into one person. We admit that a family is more unified than a city, and one person is more unified than a family. If this is the result, it's clear it should never be put into practice because it would destroy the city. A city isn't just a large group of people; it must have different kinds of people. If everyone were the same, it wouldn't be a city. A city and a confederacy are two different things. A confederacy is valued for its numbers, even if everyone in it does the same job. This is because a confederacy is created for mutual defense, like adding weight to tip the scale. This difference is the same between a city and a nation when people don't live in separate villages but all together like the Arcadians.

Now, there are different ways in which a city can be united, and keeping a balance of power between these is where its safety lies (as I have mentioned in my treatise on Morals). Among free and equal people, this balance is necessary because not everyone can govern at the same time. People can govern for a year or some other period, meaning that everyone takes a turn in office. It's like if shoemakers and carpenters were to switch jobs, instead of always working in the same trade. But it's obviously better for them to keep doing their own jobs. Similarly, in civil society, it would be better for the same people to continue governing where possible. But where it's not possible, as nature made all men equal, it's only fair—whether the administration is good or bad—that everyone gets to take part. In such cases, the best approach is to rotate leadership, letting people take turns submitting to those who are in office. In time, they will switch, being both governors and the governed, as if they were different people taking on different jobs.

From this, it's clear that a city can't be unified in the way some propose. What they claim would be the city's greatest good would actually be its destruction, which cannot happen because the good of anything is what preserves it. Another reason it's clear that making a city too unified is not for the best is that a family is more self-sufficient than an individual, and a city is more self-sufficient than a family. Plato also thinks that a city exists because its members can provide for themselves. If this self-sufficiency is desirable, then the less unified the city, the better.

But even if we agree that it's best for a city to be as unified as possible, that doesn't mean it will happen if everyone says, "This is mine," or "This is not mine," as Socrates suggests as proof of a city being united. The word "all" is used in two ways. If it means each individual, then what Socrates proposes will nearly happen because each person will say, "This is my son, my wife, my property," and so on. But if wives and children are shared in common, they won't say that individually. Instead, everyone will say it together, which is misleading because the word "all" is used in both a distributive and collective sense. This causes confusion in reasoning. So, for everyone to say the same thing is theirs in a distributive sense would be ideal but impossible. In the collective sense, it wouldn't help the unity of the state. There's also another problem. When something belongs to many, it's taken care of the least. People care more about what is specifically theirs than about what is shared with others. They pay less attention to it than they should. People are often more careless about things they share responsibility for than about their own personal tasks, just like how a family is often worse served by many servants than by a few.

If every citizen in the state had a thousand children, but none of them were considered their individual child, then all the children would be neglected. Whenever any citizen acted well or badly, everyone might say, "This is my son," or "This is someone else's son," and in this way, they wouldn't know whose child it was. Which do you think is better: for everyone to say, "This is mine," when they might apply it to two thousand or ten thousand people, or for someone to say, "This is mine," in our current forms of government where one man calls another his son, another calls him his brother or nephew, and each cares for him according to their relationship? It's better for someone to be a nephew in his private capacity than a son in the shared manner Socrates describes.

It would also be impossible to prevent people from realizing they are brothers, sisters, fathers, or mothers to each other. From the natural resemblance between parents and children, they would know their relationship, just like writers tell us happens in some parts of the world. For example, in Upper Africa, wives are shared in common, but they still give their children to their real fathers based on their likeness to them. Some animals, like certain mares and cows, also give birth to offspring that look so much like the male that it's easy to tell which one fathered them, as with the famous mare Just in Pharsalia.

Additionally, people who propose this kind of shared community can't easily avoid the problems that come with it, such as accidental or intentional harm, quarrels, and insults. It would be wrong to treat your father or mother or close relatives this way, but these problems happen more often among people who don't know how they're related to each other. When they do happen among these people, they allow legal consequences. But when these issues arise among close family, those legal actions are not possible. It's also absurd for those who suggest a shared community to forbid people who love each other from fully indulging in their desires, while not restraining them from the passion itself. This includes the most improper relationships, like between a father and son or a brother and brother. Preventing relations between close family members, not because of the intensity of the pleasure, but because of the relationship itself, is ridiculous.

It would make more sense for farmers to share wives and children than for soldiers to do so because there would be less love among them, and these people should be under the law to follow it and not seek change. Overall, a law like this would do the opposite of what good laws should, which is what Socrates aimed to establish with his rules about women and children. We believe that friendship is the greatest good a city can have because it prevents civil strife. Friendship in a city is something Socrates praises above all else. He says it is the effect of true friendship, as Aristophanes explains in the Erotics, where he says those who love each other intensely wish to be one and the same person, blending into one soul. But if this happens, one or both of them would have to disappear.

In a city that shares everything, the bond of friendship would be weak because no father can say, "This is my son," or no son can say, "This is my father." Just like how a little sweetness gets lost when mixed with a lot of water, family ties would fade away in such a society.

The names and roles that come with family would be lost. It wouldn't matter if a father had any regard for who he called his son or brothers for those they call brothers. There are two things that make people care about and love their children: knowing they are their own and knowing they should be the focus of their love. Neither of these would happen in a shared society.

Switching the children of farmers with those of soldiers, and the reverse, would only cause more confusion, no matter how it's done. The people who move the children will always know where they came from and who they gave them to. This increases the chances of harm, inappropriate love, fights, and similar problems. For example, those who are taken from their real parents and given to the soldiers won't call each other brother, son, or father. The same thing would happen to soldiers placed among farmers, and everyone would be afraid of acting inappropriately toward someone they might be related to.

Next, let's look at how property should be handled in a state with the best form of government. Should property be shared or not? This is a separate question from what we discussed about wives and children. Should property stay separate, as it is now everywhere, or should both possessions and their use be shared in common? Another option is for the land to have individual owners, but for the produce to be gathered and used as common property, as some nations do today. Or should the land be shared, and should it be farmed in common, with the produce then divided among individuals for personal use, as is said to be practiced by some barbarians? Or should both the land and its produce be shared? When the citizens aren't the ones farming, it's easier to settle. But when those who farm also have a shared right to the land, there can be problems. There might not be an equal amount of work done compared to how much people consume. Those who work hard but get little will certainly complain about those who do less but take more.

Overall, sharing everything between people is difficult, and this is especially true when it comes to property. We can see this in new colonies, where settlers often have conflicts over minor things and even fight over trivial matters. We also see that the slaves we most often punish are the ones who do the common chores for the household. So, sharing property has these and other problems.

But the way of life we have now, especially when guided by good morals and fair laws, is far better because it combines the benefits of both shared and private property. In some ways, property should be somewhat shared, but overall, it should stay private. When everyone focuses on their own property, there will be fewer complaints. This will also encourage people to work harder to improve their private property. Then, through virtue, they will help each other according to the saying, "All things are common among friends." In some cities, traces of this custom can be seen, showing it's not impossible, especially in well-governed cities. In these places, some things are shared while others are private. In Sparta, for example, people share each other's slaves, as if they were their own. They also share their horses, dogs, and sometimes even food when traveling.

So, it's clear that it's best for property to be private, but for its use to be shared. It's up to the lawmaker to figure out how to make this happen. There's also great satisfaction in feeling like you own something. It's natural for people to have affection for themselves, and though being selfish is often criticized, it's natural. We don't mean someone who simply loves themselves, but someone who loves themselves more than they should. In the same way, we criticize those who love money, yet everyone loves both money and themselves. It also brings pleasure to help friends, companions, and those we're connected to through hospitality. This is impossible without private property.

In a society that's too unified, these opportunities are lost, and two key virtues—modesty and generosity—are also lost. Modesty is about respecting other people's relationships, and generosity depends on private property. Without private property, no one can be generous or do noble deeds because generosity is about giving away what belongs to you.

The system of shared property seems appealing at first because of its appearance of kindness and friendship. It might give someone the impression that it will create a strong bond between everyone, especially when people criticize the problems in society today, like disputes over contracts, fraud, perjury, and flattery of the rich. But these problems don't come from private property; they come from human vices. In fact, people who share everything are more likely to argue than those who have private property. There are fewer examples of conflict in shared-property systems only because so few people live that way. It's important to note not only the problems avoided by sharing property but also the benefits lost. When everything is considered, this way of life turns out to be impractical.

We should assume that Socrates made a mistake because the idea he started with was wrong. We agree that a family and a city should be united in some ways, but not completely. If a city goes too far in becoming just one, it will no longer be a city. There's also a point where a city could still be called a city but would be so close to not being one that it would be worse than nothing. It's like trying to make all the voices in a choir sound like one, or reducing a whole verse to just one word. The people should be united as a community, as I've said before, through education. At Sparta and in Crete, their lawmakers made property and public meals common to everyone. But anyone who thinks they can make their city excellent and respectable by introducing education alone is mistaken if they don't also shape it with good manners, philosophy, and laws.

Anyone trying to establish a government where goods are shared should look at the experience of many years, which would show whether or not this idea is helpful. Almost everything has already been discovered, but some things have been forgotten, and other things, though known, haven't been put into practice. This would be even more obvious if someone could see such a government actually

32

working. It would be impossible to create such a city without breaking it into separate parts, like public meals, neighborhoods, and tribes. Here, the laws would only prevent the military from working in agriculture, which is what Sparta tries to do.

Socrates hasn't told us (and it's not easy to say) how the government should deal with individual people in a state where goods are shared. His citizens will mostly be people from different jobs, but he hasn't decided what to do about them. Should the farmers' property be shared or should each person have their own part? Should their wives and children be shared too? If everything is shared equally, what will set them apart from the military? What would they gain from accepting the rule of the military? Why would they do it unless they follow the wise idea of the Cretans, who allow their slaves to have everything except physical training and the use of weapons?

If these people don't have their property in common like other cities, then what kind of community would there be? In one city, you would end up with two separate groups opposing each other. Socrates makes the military the guardians of the state and the farmers, artisans, and others into citizens. But all the arguments, accusations, and problems that he says ruin other cities would be present in his city too. Socrates also claims they won't need many laws because of their education, only laws for basic things like streets and markets. However, he only focuses on educating the military and ignores everyone else.

Socrates makes the farmers pay a tax in exchange for owning property, but this would likely make them more troublesome and rebellious than the Helots, Penestae, or other slaves. He doesn't say if he would take care of these details, like their government, education, and laws. It's not a small issue and not easy to figure out how to organize these things while still keeping the military community intact.

Also, if wives are shared but property is kept separate, who will take care of household matters with the same care that men give their farms? The problem wouldn't be fixed by making both property and wives common. And it's absurd to compare humans to animals and say that the connection between a man and a woman should be like that of animals, which don't have family relationships.

Socrates's plan for government is risky because he suggests keeping people of the same rank in office forever. This can lead to rebellion even among people with little power, but especially among those with courage and a warrior mindset. It seems necessary for him to arrange his community this way because he believes that God mixed a small bit of gold into some people's souls, which stays with them from birth. He says some people are born with gold and others with silver, while farmers and artisans have brass and iron.

Even though Socrates denies happiness to the military, he says that a lawmaker should make all citizens happy. But it's impossible for a city to be happy unless all or most of it is happy. Happiness is not like numbers adding up to a certain sum, where none of the parts contain happiness on their own. Happiness must be in every individual, just like certain qualities belong to every whole thing. And if the military isn't happy, who else would be? The artisans and common people doing low-level jobs certainly aren't happy. The state Socrates describes has these problems and others that are just as serious.

This is also true in his later work on laws, so it makes sense to briefly consider what he says about government there. In that work, Socrates only deals with a few aspects of government in detail, like how to share wives and children, how property should be handled, and how the government should run.

He divides the people into two groups: farmers and soldiers. From these, he picks a third group to be senators and run the city. But he doesn't say whether the farmers and artisans will have a say in government or whether they'll have weapons and join in wars. He thinks that women should also fight in wars and be educated like the soldiers. As for other details, his work is filled with ideas unrelated to government. When it comes to education, he only talks about how the soldiers should be educated.

In his book about laws, he mainly focuses on laws, and he says little about the actual government. The system he wants would create more of a shared community than any other city, but it ends up being similar to the first system he described. Except for shared wives and goods, both systems are set up the same way. In both, the citizens have the same education, don't do menial work, and eat together in public meals. The only difference is that in one system, the women eat separately, and there are a thousand soldiers. In the other system, there are five thousand soldiers.

All of Socrates's arguments are impressive, clever, and full of new ideas. But it's probably too much to say that all of them are true. As for the number of soldiers he mentions, we have to admit that he would need a huge country, like Babylon, to support five thousand idle men, plus even more women and servants. Anyone can make up whatever plan they want, but it should at least be possible.

A lawmaker should consider two things when making laws: the land and the people. It's also wise to think about the neighboring states if the community is going to have any kind of political relations with them. They need to know how to defend themselves, not just in their own country but in other countries too. Even if someone chooses not to engage in public or private life, they still need to be a threat to their enemies, both when defending their land and when attacking others.

We might also consider if people's property could be divided up more clearly than Socrates suggests. He says that everyone should have enough to live moderately, as if someone had said they should live well, which is a broader idea. A person can live moderately and still live miserably at the same time. He should have proposed that people live both moderately and generously because if you don't balance these two things, either luxury or poverty will follow. These are the only two ways people use their money. We can't say that a person's fortune makes them kind or brave, but we can say that they are wise and generous, which are qualities related to their money.

It's also strange to make property equal without thinking about the increasing number of citizens. Leaving that uncertain, as Socrates does, assumes that things will work themselves out depending on how many women are childless. But this is not the same as how things happen in real cities. In real cities, no one goes without because the property is divided among everyone, no matter how many there are. But in Socrates's system, property can't be divided, so if there are too many people, some will have nothing at all. It's more important to control the growth of the population than to regulate property, and in doing so, you have to consider children who will die and women who will be barren. Ignoring this, as is done in many cities, leads to poverty, and poverty causes rebellion and crime. Phidon of Corinth, one of the oldest lawmakers, thought that families and the number of citizens should always stay the same, even if the amount of land they originally received didn't match their numbers.

In Plato's Laws, the situation is different. We'll talk later about what we think is best in these matters. Plato also didn't explain how the rulers should be chosen from the common people. He says that like wool is made into different threads, some people should govern, and others should be governed. But if Plato allows their property to increase fivefold, why doesn't he allow the country to grow in the same way? He should also think about whether his system of assigning houses will work. He gives two houses to each person, but it's not practical for someone to live in two houses.

He wants his government to be something between a democracy and an oligarchy, which he calls a polity. This is because it will be made up of soldiers. If Plato wanted to create a state where everything is more shared than in any other state, he's given it the right name. But if he meant for it to be the next best state after the one he described earlier, it isn't. Some people might prefer the Spartan system of government or another system that better achieves an aristocracy.

Some people say the best government is one that combines parts of all other types of government. That's why they praise Sparta. They say Sparta's government includes elements of oligarchy, monarchy, and democracy. The kings represent the monarchy, the senate represents the oligarchy, and the ephors, who are chosen from the people, represent the democracy. Others say the ephors have absolute power and that the common meals and daily life represent the democracy.

Plato says in his Laws that the best government is one that mixes democracy with tyranny, but no one else would call that a real government, and if it is, it would be the worst possible kind. Those who suggest mixing many types of government have a better idea because the most perfect government is one made up of many parts. But Plato's government shows no sign of a monarchy, only oligarchy and democracy. He seems to favor oligarchy, as seen in how he assigns the magistrates. Choosing them by lot is common in both oligarchy and democracy, but requiring that a rich man must be a member of the assembly, while others are left out, leans toward oligarchy. Plato also tries to ensure that most of the rich will hold office, and the rank of officials will match their wealth.

The same idea applies to how the senate is chosen. The election process favors an oligarchy. Everyone must vote for the first-class senators, then the same number from the second class, and then from the third class. But the lower classes aren't required to vote for the third and fourth classes. Only the first and second classes must vote for the fourth. He thinks this will create an equal number of senators from each class, but he's wrong. The majority will always be from the upper classes and the wealthiest people. This is because many of the common people won't be required to attend the elections and won't bother showing up.

It's clear that this state will not be a mix of democracy and monarchy. We will explain this further when we discuss this type of government in more detail. There's also a big risk in how the senate is chosen because the elected senators get to choose the others. If even a small group of people decide to work together, they can always control the election. These are some of the ideas Plato suggests in his book about laws.

There are also other types of government that have been suggested by private individuals, philosophers, or politicians. These come much closer to the governments that have been established or that exist today, unlike Plato's two systems. These suggestions don't include sharing wives and children or having public meals for women, but instead, they focus on the rules that are absolutely necessary.

Some people believe that the first goal of a government should be to manage private property well. They say that ignoring this leads to all kinds of conflicts. For this reason, Phaleas of Chalcedon suggested that the fortunes of the citizens should be equal. He thought this would be easy to do when a community is first set up, but it would be more difficult in one that has been established for a long time. However, he still believed it was possible by making the rich give marriage gifts but never receive them, while the poor would always receive but never give them.

But Plato, in his Laws, thinks that some differences in wealth should be allowed, as long as no one can have more than five times the amount of the poorest person, as we've already mentioned. Lawmakers who try to enforce these rules often forget something important. While they limit how much property someone can own, they also need to control how many children people have. If the population grows beyond what the available resources can support, the law would have to be changed. Even after the law is changed, many people would still end up poor. This shows how easy it is for those trying new ideas to make mistakes.

Some of the ancients understood that having some equality in wealth could help strengthen society. For example, Solon made a law, as did others, to stop people from owning as much land as they wanted. Similarly, there are laws that prevent people from selling their property, like in Locri, unless they can prove they suffered some serious misfortune. People were supposed to hold onto their inherited property. When the Leucadians broke this custom, it made their government too democratic, because it was no longer necessary to have a certain amount of wealth to be a magistrate. However, if wealth is distributed too equally, it could allow people to live in luxury, which might be too much. On the other hand, if it's too little, it could force people to live miserably. So, it's clear that lawmakers shouldn't aim for total equality, but instead, should find a balance.

Even if someone could divide up property so that everyone had enough, it wouldn't be enough to fix the problem. What matters more is that citizens share the same values, and that can't happen unless they are properly educated under the law. Phaleas might say that's exactly what he proposed, with both equal property and a single system of education. But he didn't explain what kind of education he meant, and even if there's only one type of education, it might teach people to be too focused on gaining honors or wealth, or both.

It's not just inequality in wealth, but also inequality in honors, that can cause unrest. The common people will cause trouble if wealth is unequal, while those with higher ambitions will rebel if honors are too equal.

"Both good and bad should not be treated the same."

People don't only commit crimes because they need the basics, like food or warmth (which Phaleas thought equal wealth would solve). They also steal to get what they want or to experience pleasures they wouldn't otherwise be able to afford. What solution is there for these three types of wrongdoing? First, to prevent stealing out of need, everyone should be given enough to live on, but they should also need to work for more. Second, to stop people from stealing to get luxury items, temperance should be encouraged. And third, those seeking pleasure for its own sake should look for it in philosophy, while everyone else will need to rely on other people for help.

Since people commit the worst crimes because of ambition, and not just to meet basic needs, no one tries to become a tyrant just to stay warm. That's why the highest praise goes to the person who kills a tyrant, not just a thief. Phaleas's system might help prevent minor crimes, but it wouldn't stop greater ones.

Phaleas was also very focused on creating rules to perfect the internal order of his city, but he should have done the same for its neighbors and foreign nations. When planning a government, it's important to think about military needs, so the city isn't defenseless in case of war, but Phaleas didn't mention that at all. Property should not only be distributed in a way that meets the city's needs, but also in a way that prepares it for external threats.

The amount of wealth shouldn't be so large that it tempts stronger neighbors to invade, but it shouldn't be so small that the city can't defend itself against equal powers. Phaleas didn't address this at all. It's true that it's better for a city to be rich than poor. A good rule to follow is to have enough wealth that a more powerful neighbor wouldn't bother attacking you, but not so much that they think it's worth the effort. This is like when Autophradatus wanted to besiege Atarneus, but Eubulus told him to think about how long it would take to capture the city. He advised him that even if it took less time than planned, it wouldn't be worth it, so Autophradatus gave up the siege.

It's true that equal wealth can help prevent conflicts, but not by much. People with great talents will resent being treated as equals with the rest of society. Because of this, they are often quick to start conflicts or rebellions. People's greed has no limits. While they may start by wanting just a little more, their desires grow and grow until they want everything. Many people live only to satisfy these endless desires.

The real solution isn't to focus on making everyone equally wealthy, but to stop good people from wanting more than what's theirs, and to prevent bad people from getting what doesn't belong to them. This can be done by keeping them in lower positions and ensuring they aren't treated unfairly.

Phaleas didn't do a good job with his idea of equal property because he only applied it to land. A person's wealth includes more than just land—it also includes slaves, livestock, money, and other possessions. There should be either equality in all of these things, or clear rules about them, or they should be left completely unrestricted. It also seems that Phaleas wanted to create a small state because he intended for all craftsmen to work for the public and not be considered citizens. If all public workers are to be owned by the state, this should be done like it was in Epidamnum or as Diophantus once organized it in Athens. From these points, anyone can judge whether Phaleas's plan was well-thought-out or not.

Hippodamus, the son of Euruphon of Miletus, invented the idea of designing city layouts and was the one who planned the division of the Piraeus. He was always looking for attention and seemed to live in an eccentric way. He had long hair, dressed in flashy clothes, and wore a heavy cloak even in the summer. He wanted to be known as an expert in many subjects and was the first person, without being involved in politics, to ask what the best form of government was. He designed a state with 10,000 citizens, divided into three groups: craftsmen, farmers, and soldiers. He divided the land into three parts, one for religious purposes, one for public use, and one for private citizens. The land for religious purposes was for supporting worship, the public land was for the soldiers, and the private land was for the farmers.

He also thought there only needed to be three kinds of laws, which would deal with assault, property damage, and death. He suggested that there should be a special court of appeal where cases could be reviewed if someone thought they were judged unfairly elsewhere. This court would be made up of older men chosen for this task. He also proposed that judges shouldn't cast their votes in the usual way. Instead, they should use a tablet to say whether they thought someone was guilty or not. If they found someone guilty of one part of the charge but not the other, they could write that on the tablet too. Hippodamus didn't like the usual way of deciding cases, which forced judges to make a decision one way or the other. He also made a law that anyone who came up with a good idea for the city should be rewarded, and that the children of soldiers who died in battle should be educated at the city's expense. This law hadn't been suggested by any previous lawmaker, though it is used now in Athens and other cities. He wanted the magistrates to be chosen from all three groups he mentioned earlier. The magistrates would be in charge of public matters, as well as taking care of strangers and orphans.

These are the most important points of Hippodamus's plan. However, some might question his decision to divide the citizens into three parts. The craftsmen, farmers, and soldiers all make up one community, but the farmers don't have weapons, and the craftsmen don't have either weapons or land, which makes them almost like slaves to the soldiers. It's also impossible for everyone in the community to share in the most important jobs, like generals or protectors of the state. These roles must go to the soldiers, who would hold the highest offices. But since the other two groups wouldn't have a part in the government, why would they care about it?

It's necessary for the soldiers to be stronger than the other two groups, and this won't be easy unless they outnumber them. If the soldiers do outnumber the others, why should there be any other groups at all? Why should these other groups have a right to elect the magistrates? Also, what role do the farmers play in this system? Craftsmen are needed because every city needs them, and they can live by working in their trade. If the farmers were providing food for the soldiers, then they would be a part of the community. But in Hippodamus's system, the farmers are supposed to own private property and work it for themselves.

If the soldiers are supposed to work the land assigned to them for their own support, then there would be no difference between a soldier and a farmer, which Hippodamus didn't intend. If someone else is supposed to farm both the private property of the farmers and the common land for the soldiers, this would create a fourth group in the city. This group would have no part in the government and would likely be hostile toward it.

If someone suggested that the same people farm both their own land and the public land, then there wouldn't be enough food to support two households. The land wouldn't produce enough for both the farmers and the soldiers, and all this would lead to chaos.

I also don't agree with his method of handling legal cases, where he wants judges to divide up a simple case into parts. Instead of being judges, they would become arbitrators. When a matter goes to arbitration, several people usually discuss it together, but this doesn't happen when a case goes before judges. In fact, many lawmakers make sure that judges can't share their opinions with each other. Besides, what would stop confusion in court when one judge thinks a fine should be one amount, and another thinks it should be something else? One might propose a fine of twenty minae, another ten, another less, and another even less. In this way, they would all disagree, with some giving the full amount asked for and others giving nothing. How could their final decisions be settled?

A judge wouldn't be lying if they simply found someone guilty or innocent, as long as the case was fair. The judge who acquits someone isn't saying they shouldn't pay a fine at all, but that they shouldn't have to pay the full fine of twenty minae. However, a judge who finds someone guilty would be lying if they sentenced them to pay twenty minae when they believe the fine should be less.

As for rewarding those who suggest something useful for the city, this sounds good in theory, but a lawmaker shouldn't actually make it a rule. It would encourage informers and likely cause unrest in the city.

This suggestion raises even more questions. Some people wonder whether it's helpful or harmful to change the established laws of a country, even if it's for the better. For this reason, it's hard to say whether this idea would be useful or not. We know that it's possible to suggest improvements to both laws and government for the common good. Since I've mentioned this subject, it's worth exploring a little further because it's a difficult issue.

It might seem better to change the laws since it has been helpful in other fields. Medicine, for example, has advanced beyond its original methods, as have gymnastics and other arts. So, we can be certain that the same is true in the art of government. History shows us that the old laws were often too simple and primitive. For example, the Greeks used to carry swords in the city and bought their wives from each other. All the old laws that we still have are quite basic. In Cuma, there was a law about murder that said if a person could get a certain number of their relatives to testify against someone, that person would be found guilty.

In general, everyone should aim to follow what is right, not just what is traditional. The first people on earth, whether they came from the ground or survived some disaster, probably had little understanding or knowledge, as is said about early humans. It would be foolish to continue following their rules. It's also wrong to keep written laws unchanged forever. Just like in other fields, in politics it's impossible to write everything down perfectly. When we put things in writing, we have to use general terms, but every situation is different and unique. This shows that some laws can be changed when necessary.

However, looking at the issue from another angle, we see it's something that requires great caution. If the benefit of changing the law is small, it might be better to leave things as they are because making it too easy for people to change their laws can have bad consequences. It's often better to overlook some mistakes made by lawmakers or officials because the harm of changing the law could be worse than the benefit.

The example from other fields is misleading because changing a law is not the same as improving a craft. A law gets its strength from tradition, and that takes time to build. If we make it too easy to change the law, we weaken its authority. This brings up another question. If we are to change laws, should we change all of them? Should this happen in every government or just some? Should one person decide or should many? These are important differences, and for now, we'll leave this issue and explore it more at another time.

There are two main questions to consider about the government in Sparta and Crete, and in almost all other states: First, do their laws create the best government possible? Second, is there anything in the way the government is set up or run that stops it from following the original plan? In a well-organized state, it's agreed that people should be free from hard labor. But it's not easy to figure out how to make that happen. For example, the Penestae often revolted against the Thessalians, and the Helots frequently rebelled against the Spartans. The Helots were always looking for a chance to take advantage of any trouble that might weaken Sparta. However, this didn't happen with the Cretans. One reason is that although the Cretans were often at war with neighboring cities, none of those cities were willing to support the revolters because they had their own slaves to worry about. But in Sparta, there was constant hostility between them and their neighbors, such as the Argives, Messenians, and Arcadians. The first rebellion of slaves against the Thessalians happened while they were at war with their neighbors, the Achaeans, Perrhaebians, and Magnesians.

In my opinion, managing these slaves is always a difficult task. If you are too lenient, they become arrogant and think they are equal to their masters. But if you treat them harshly, they will hate you and plot against you. It's clear that no one has figured out the best way to deal with slaves yet.

Letting women have too much freedom in society is also harmful to the government and the city's well-being. A man and his wife are two parts of a family, and if you think of the city as divided in two, you'd expect the number of men and women to be equal. So, in any city where the women are not under proper rules, you could say that half of the city is not following the law. This was the case in Sparta. The lawmaker focused on making the men warriors, and he succeeded in that, but he completely ignored the women. The women lived without restraint, indulging in luxury and improper behavior.

Because of this, wealth became highly valued in Sparta, especially when men were influenced by their wives. This has happened to many brave and warlike people, except for the Celts and other nations that openly practiced male relationships. The first mythmakers probably had a reason for pairing Mars, the god of war, with Venus, the goddess of love, because nations like these are often either devoted to the love of women or to male lovers. In Sparta, the women held a lot of influence, which led to many decisions being made by them. It doesn't matter whether the power is in the hands of women or in the hands of those they control—the outcome is the same.

This boldness of the women wasn't helpful in everyday matters, and if it were useful, it would be in war. But even in war, the Spartan women were a huge disadvantage. This was proven during the Theban invasion, when they didn't contribute at all and caused more trouble than even the enemy did.

The reason Spartan women had so much freedom can be traced back to the long time the men spent away on military campaigns against the Argives, and later against the Arcadians and Messenians. When these wars ended, the men had learned a disciplined, military way of life and were prepared to follow the laws of their lawgiver. However, we are told that when Lycurgus tried to make the women follow his laws, they refused, and he gave up trying. It may be said that the women were to blame for this, but we're not focusing on blame here. The question is what is right and what is wrong. And when women's behavior isn't properly controlled, it not only brings disgrace to the state but also increases the desire for wealth.

Another issue was the unequal distribution of property. Some people had far too much, while others had too little, which led to land being concentrated in the hands of a few. Lycurgus made it shameful to buy or sell land, which was a good idea. But he allowed people to give away or bequeath their land, which caused nearly the same problems. It's estimated that almost two-fifths of the land was owned by women because they often inherited property and brought large dowries into marriages. It would have been better to limit what women could inherit or own, either giving them nothing, a small amount, or a set portion. As it stands, anyone can make a woman their heir if they want. And if someone dies without a will, the legal heir can give the property to anyone they choose.

Because of this, although the land is capable of supporting 1,500 cavalry and 30,000 infantry, the number of soldiers has dropped to less than a thousand. This clearly shows that the system was poorly managed, as the city couldn't withstand even one major crisis and was ruined because there weren't enough men.

It's said that during the reign of the ancient kings, foreigners were given citizenship to prevent a shortage of people while Sparta fought long wars. It's also believed that Sparta once had a population of 10,000. Whether this is true or not, it's clear that having more equal property helps increase the number of people. The law that was meant to encourage large families didn't fix this inequality. Lycurgus wanted the Spartans to have as many children as possible, so he made laws to encourage this. For example, a man with three children didn't have to stand night guard, and a man with four children didn't have to pay taxes. But it's clear that if the land was divided in such a way, having more people would only lead to more poverty.

Lycurgus also made mistakes with how he set up the ephorate (a council of five elected officials). These ephors were responsible for making important decisions, but they were chosen from the general population. This meant that a poor person could be elected and easily bribed. There have been many examples of this in the past, including the recent events in Andros. These corrupt men tried to bring down the city, and because their power was so great, almost tyrannical, the

---

kings were forced to flatter them, which weakened the state. This turned Sparta from an aristocracy into more of a democracy.

The ephorate is the main support of the state, because people feel reassured knowing that they could be chosen for the highest office. Whether this was Lycurgus's plan or just happened by chance, it has helped the state. It's important for every part of the government to support the rest to keep it stable. This is why the kings always act to protect their honor, the wise and good protect the senate, and the common people support the ephors, since they come from the people.

It's good that the ephors are chosen from the whole community, but the way they are selected now is ridiculous. The ephors are in charge of judging the most important cases, but since anyone could be chosen by chance, they shouldn't rely on their own opinions. Instead, they should follow written laws or customs. Their lifestyle is also too lenient, while others in the city live too harshly. Because of this, some secretly break the laws to enjoy life's pleasures.

There are also problems with how the senators are selected. If they were truly trained in every human virtue, they could be very useful to the government. But even if they were good men, it could be debated whether they should remain judges for life, since the mind ages just like the body. However, since the senators weren't raised in such a way that they could be trusted to always do good, their power puts the state at risk. We know that senators have been guilty of taking bribes and showing favoritism in many public matters. It would have been much better if they were held accountable for their actions, but they are not.

Some might say that the ephors act as a check on all the magistrates, and it's true that they have a lot of power in this area. But I believe they shouldn't have as much control as they do. Additionally, the way the senators are elected is very childish. It's also wrong for people to campaign for an office they want. Everyone should serve in whatever role they are fit for, whether they want to or not. Lycurgus's goal was to fill his government with ambitious men seeking honors, which is why the senate is filled with men like this. However, most crimes are committed because of ambition or greed.

We can discuss whether kings are necessary for the state another time, but for now, it's clear that kings should be chosen based on their character, not in the way they are currently selected. Lycurgus himself didn't expect to make all his citizens perfectly honorable and virtuous, which is clear because he didn't trust them. He sent people who were in conflict with each other on the same mission, believing that their rivalry would keep the state safe.

The common meals, or public dinners, were also not well organized at first. These meals should have been provided at public expense, as they are in Crete. In Sparta, however, everyone was required to contribute their share, even if they were too poor to afford it. This had the opposite effect of what Lycurgus intended. He wanted these public meals to strengthen the democratic part of the government, but in reality, they excluded the very poor. Their ancestors warned that not allowing the poor to join the common meals would lead to the ruin of the state.

Others have criticized the laws about naval affairs, and they have a point. The head of the navy was almost set up as a rival to the kings, who were the generals of the army for life.

There's also another problem with Sparta's laws, which Plato pointed out in his Laws. The whole system was designed for war. It's great for making them good soldiers, but it's not good for anything else. The state's survival depended on war, but its downfall began with its victories because the Spartans didn't know how to do anything but fight. They thought that the things people fight over are better gained through virtue than through vice, and they were right. But they wrongly valued those things more than virtue itself.

Sparta's finances were also poorly managed. The state was practically worthless, even though they were involved in major wars. They raised funds in a careless way. The Spartans owned a lot of land, but they didn't hold each other accountable for paying their share. The result was the opposite of what Lycurgus intended: the state was poor, and the citizens were greedy. These are the main problems with the Spartan government.

The government of Crete is similar to Sparta's in many ways, though it's worse in some areas. Overall, it's a less well-thought-out system. In many ways, Sparta's system was modeled after Crete's, and usually newer systems improve on the old ones. It's said that when Lycurgus finished being the guardian of King Charilaus, he traveled and spent time with his relatives in Crete. The Lycians were a colony of the Spartans, and the early settlers there adopted the laws they found in Crete. Those who live nearby still follow the laws first set up by Minos.

Crete is in a position that naturally makes it the ruler of Greece, as it is surrounded by the sea. It's not far from either Peloponnesus or Asia, where Triopium and Rhodes are located. Minos used this position to control the sea and the surrounding islands, conquering some and settling others. He eventually died in Camicus while trying to capture Sicily.

There are several similarities between Sparta and Crete. The Helots farm the land for the Spartans, and domestic slaves do the same for the Cretans. Both states have common meals, though the Spartans used to call them andreia instead of psiditia, like the Cretans do, which shows where the custom started. Their governments are also alike in other ways. The ephors in Sparta have the same role as the kosmoi in Crete, though there are five ephors and ten kosmoi. The Spartan senate is the same as the Cretan council. There was once a king in Crete, but that position was later removed, and the kosmoi became the commanders of the army.

In both states, everyone has a vote in the public assembly, but this assembly can only confirm decisions already made by the council and the kosmoi.

Crete managed the public meals better than Sparta. In Sparta, each person had to provide their own share, and if they couldn't afford it, they lost their rights as citizens. But in Crete, the public meals were paid for by the community. All the grain, livestock, taxes, and contributions from the slaves were divided up to meet the needs of the gods, the state, and the public meals. This way, everyone, including men, women, and children, was supported by a shared fund. The lawmaker also made sure that people ate modestly, believing this was good for the citizens. He also tried to keep the population from growing too large by encouraging the love of boys, which reduced the connection with women. Whether this was a good or bad idea can be discussed another time. But it's clear that Crete's public meals were better managed than those in Sparta.

The system of the kosmoi was even worse than that of the ephors. It had all the problems of the ephorate, plus some of its own. In both states, it's uncertain who will be elected. But Sparta has an advantage because everyone is eligible, which gives all citizens a stake in the government's success. This makes everyone want to protect the state. In Crete, however, the kosmoi are chosen from certain families, and the senate is selected from the kosmoi. The same criticisms of Sparta's senate apply here. The senators have too much power, especially since they serve for life, and their decisions aren't guided by written laws but by their own judgment.

The fact that there are no revolts, even though the people don't have a say in the government, isn't proof of a well-run state. The kosmoi don't face the same opportunities for bribery as the ephors, because they live on an island far from those who might corrupt them. But the way they handle problems is foolish and tyrannical. It's common for fellow magistrates or private citizens to conspire against the kosmoi and remove them from office. The kosmoi are even allowed to resign before their term ends, which would be fine if it were done by law, but it happens at the whim of individuals, which is not a good practice.

Worst of all, the kosmoi often cause chaos by disrupting the legal system. This shows what kind of government they really have—it's not so much a government as it is lawless power. It's common for the leaders to gather their supporters and some of the common people, then rebel and fight against each other. What's the difference if a state is destroyed all at once through violent means or gradually falls apart over time until it's no longer the same government?

A state like this would always be vulnerable to attack from a stronger enemy. But as I mentioned earlier, Crete's location protects it, since it is free from foreign invaders. That's why the domestic slaves in Crete remain quiet, while the Helots in Sparta are always rebelling. The Cretans stay out of foreign affairs, and it's only recently that any foreign troops have attacked the island. When they did, it quickly became clear that Crete's laws were ineffective.

That's enough for now about the government of Crete.

The government of Carthage seems to be well-organized and, in many ways, better than others. In some aspects, it is similar to Sparta, and in other ways, to Crete, though there are many differences. One of the great things about their system is that even though the people have a role in the government, it has stayed stable. There have been no major revolts from the people, and it hasn't turned into a tyranny either.

Carthage shares some features with Sparta, such as having public meals for groups of friends, similar to Sparta's Phiditia. They also have a group of 104 magistrates, similar to Sparta's ephors, but chosen with more care. In Sparta, any citizen can become an ephor, but in Carthage, they are picked from the best families. There are similarities between the kings and senates of both governments, though Carthage's method of selecting kings is better. They don't limit the position to just one family, and they don't base it on age. Instead, they choose the most capable person, even if they are younger than other candidates. This is important because, in Carthage, the kings have a lot of power, and if they are not competent, they could harm the state, as has happened in Sparta.

In Carthage, their government is a mix of aristocracy and democracy, and some parts lean towards democracy, while others tend to create an oligarchy. For example, if the kings and senate agree on something, they don't have to bring it to the people for a vote. But if they disagree, the people get to decide. The people not only hear what the senate has approved, but they have the final say, and anyone can speak out against any proposal. This is different from other places where such freedom of speech is not allowed.

The five officials who elect each other hold a lot of power. They choose the 100 top magistrates, and their influence lasts longer than any other officials because they hold power before and after their term. This makes the government more like an oligarchy. But since they are elected based on merit and can't take bribes, they help preserve the aristocracy.

In Carthage, all cases are decided by the same magistrates, unlike in Sparta where different cases go to different courts. This system helps keep things stable. However, Carthage's government is slowly shifting from aristocracy to oligarchy because of the belief that officials should not only be from good families but also be wealthy. People think that if someone is poor, they won't be able to handle the responsibilities of office or devote enough time to public duties.

Choosing wealthy people for office makes the government lean toward oligarchy, while choosing capable people makes it more aristocratic. In Carthage, they consider both wealth and ability when selecting officials, especially for the highest positions like kings and generals. But this approach has its problems. The lawmaker should have ensured that capable citizens wouldn't be forced to do anything beneath them and would always have time to serve the public, both in office and as private citizens. If wealth becomes the main requirement for holding office, important positions will soon be bought and sold, leading to corruption. Riches would become more important than virtue, and the love of money would dominate the city. What those in power value becomes what all citizens strive for. When virtue isn't honored, an aristocracy can't thrive.

It's likely that those who buy their way into office will use their power to make money. It's unreasonable to think that a good but poor person would want to make money in office, but a bad person wouldn't want to do the same, especially to recover their costs. For this reason, the government should be made up of people who are capable of supporting an aristocracy. It would have been better for the lawmaker to ignore the poverty of good men and make sure they had enough free time to focus on public duties while in office.

It's also a mistake to let one person hold multiple offices, which was allowed in Carthage. A job is best done when one person focuses on it. It's the lawmaker's duty to make sure this happens, not to allow one person to do several jobs, just like you wouldn't expect the same person to be both a musician and a shoemaker. In a large state, it's better and fairer to let more people share in the government, because when different tasks are given to different people, things get done better and faster. You can see this in both the army and navy, where people take turns leading and following orders.

But because Carthage's government leans towards oligarchy, they avoid its bad effects by appointing some common people to run the cities and make their fortunes. This helps fix the problem and keeps the government stable, but it's still risky. The lawmaker should have set up the government so that revolts couldn't happen in the first place. Right now, if a major disaster struck and the people turned against their rulers, there would be no way to restore order through the laws.

These are the most important things about the governments of Sparta, Crete, and Carthage that deserve praise.

Some of the people who wrote about government never actually took part in public life. They lived as private citizens. We've already discussed what's important in their works. Others were lawmakers, either in their own cities or hired to fix the governments of foreign states. Some only wrote laws, while others designed the entire system of government. Lycurgus did both, as did Solon, who saved Athens from becoming a complete oligarchy and prevented the people from falling into slavery. He brought back the ancient democratic system, and each part of it was well-balanced to fit with the rest. In the senate of Areopagus, there was an oligarchy; in the election of officials, an aristocracy; and in the courts of justice, a democracy.

Solon didn't change the basic structure of the government, either the senate or how officials were elected. But he gave the people a lot of power by putting them in charge of the courts, and some people criticize him for this, saying it disrupted the balance he was trying to create. By allowing the people, chosen by lot, to judge all cases, Solon had to appeal to their power, which eventually led to the pure democracy we see today.

Both Ephialtes and Pericles reduced the power of the Areopagus, and Pericles introduced pay for those who served in the courts. Every leader who wanted to be popular gave more and more power to the people until the government became what it is now. It's clear that this wasn't Solon's original plan, but it happened by chance. The people had won the naval battle against the Medes, and that victory made them feel powerful. They followed populist leaders, even though they were opposed by the better citizens.

Solon believed it was necessary to give the people the right to choose their officials and hold them accountable. Without this, they would have been slaves and enemies to the wealthier citizens. However, he limited the elections to those who had a certain amount of wealth. Officials had to be chosen from those worth 500 medimni, those called zeugitae, or those of the third census, who were called horsemen. The fourth class, made up of craftsmen, couldn't hold office.

Zaleucus was the lawgiver for the Western Locrians, and Charondas of Catana created laws for his own city and for other cities in Italy and Sicily that were founded by the Chalcidians. Some claim that Onomacritus, a Locrian, was the first to write laws, and that he did so while studying the prophetic arts in Crete. They say Thales was his companion, and that Lycurgus and Zaleucus were his students, and Charondas was a student of Zaleucus. But this timeline doesn't add up. Philolaus, from the Bacchiadae family, was also a lawmaker in Thebes. He was very close to Diocles, an Olympic victor, who left Corinth because of an inappropriate passion his mother had for him. Diocles moved to Thebes, and Philolaus followed him. They died there, and their graves can still be seen. They were buried facing each other, but Diocles's tomb doesn't look toward Corinth because of his hatred for his mother's feelings. Philolaus's tomb does face Corinth, and that's the reason they both lived in Thebes.

Philolaus made laws about many things, including adoption, which he created to preserve the number of families. Charondas didn't make many new laws, except for one about perjury, which he was the first to address specifically. His laws were written with more care and elegance than any others we have today.

Philolaus introduced the law for the equal distribution of property. Plato created the idea of shared women, children, and property, as well as public meals for women. He also made a law about not getting drunk, so people would stay sober at their banquets. He created a rule for military exercises so that people would learn to use both hands equally, believing it was important to make both hands useful.

As for Draco's laws, they were created when the government was already in place. The only thing that stands out about them is their harshness and the extreme punishments they imposed.

Pittacus made some laws, but he didn't design a whole system of government. One of his laws stated that if a drunk person hit someone, they should be punished more severely than if they were sober. He didn't excuse bad behavior caused by drunkenness, but instead focused on the good of society. Andromadas of Rhegium was also a lawgiver for the Chalcidians in Thrace. Some of his laws, such as those about murder and inheritance, still exist, but there's nothing particularly original in them.

And that's enough for now about the different types of governments, both those that exist and those that have been proposed.

Book 3

Anyone who wants to understand government and its different types should start by asking, "What is a city?" There is disagreement about this. Some say the city did something, while others say it wasn't the city, but the oligarchy or tyranny. The city is the main focus of politicians and lawmakers in everything they do, and a government is how the people living in the city are organized. Since a city is made up of different parts, we first need to understand what a citizen is because a city is made up of citizens. So, we need to figure out who should be called a citizen and what makes someone a citizen, because this isn't always clear. For example, someone who would be considered a citizen in a democracy might not be one in an oligarchy. We're not talking about people who become citizens through special honors, but only those who have a natural right to it.

Living in a city doesn't automatically make someone a citizen. Visitors and slaves live in cities, too, but that doesn't make them citizens. Having certain legal rights, like being able to use the courts, also doesn't make someone a citizen. People from other countries can sometimes do that through agreements, but they still aren't considered full citizens. Often, visitors need the protection of a patron to use the courts, showing that they aren't fully part of the community. The same applies to children who aren't yet registered as citizens or to old men who are no longer able to serve in the military. We consider them citizens in some ways but not fully because they either aren't old enough or are past the age of service. The situation is similar for people who are banished or who have lost their honor. The clearest sign of being a full citizen is having a role in the judicial or executive parts of the government.

Some government roles are temporary, meaning that a person can't hold the position twice or must wait a certain amount of time before doing so again. Other roles, like being a juror or a member of the general assembly, aren't limited in this way. Some might argue that these aren't really offices or that these citizens don't play an important role in the government, but that's wrong. It's silly to say that people who hold the most power in the state don't hold office. This is just a disagreement about words. There's no general term that covers both jurors and assembly members, but we can call it an indefinite office. I believe that people who can hold these offices are citizens. This is the best description of what it means to be a citizen.

Everyone should also understand that parts of different things that belong to different groups become less and less similar the more they change. We can see that governments come in different forms, with some being flawed and others as good as possible. It's obvious that governments with many flaws are much worse than those without them. I will explain what I mean by flawed governments later. The role of a citizen also changes depending on the form of government. In a democracy, a citizen has all the rights that come with being a citizen, but in other forms of government, this isn't always the case. In some states, the people have no power, and there is no general assembly. Only a few selected men make decisions.

In different governments, different people handle different types of cases. For example, in Lacedaemon, contracts are handled by the ephors, and the senate judges murder cases. In Carthage, specific magistrates decide all cases. We can adjust our earlier definition of a citizen because, in some governments, the role of a juror or assembly member is not indefinite. Specific people are chosen for these roles, and all or some citizens are chosen as jurors or assembly members.

They may deal with all public business or just specific issues. This helps clarify what a citizen is. A citizen is someone who has the right to participate in the judicial and executive parts of the government. A city is simply a group of these people, large enough to manage all the needs of life.

In general, people say a citizen is someone born to citizen parents on both sides, not just on the mother's or father's side. Some take this even further and ask how many generations back their ancestors were citizens, like their grandfather or great-grandfather. But some people question how the first generation of a family could prove they were citizens if this definition were used. Gorgias of Leontium made fun of this by saying that just like a mortar is made by a mortar-maker, a citizen is made by a citizen-maker. This explanation is too simple. If citizens were defined this way, it would be impossible to apply it to the founders of cities, who couldn't claim citizenship through their parents. It's even harder to figure out the rights of those who became citizens after a political revolution. For example, in Athens, after the tyrants were overthrown, Clisthenes added many foreigners and freed slaves to the citizen rolls. The question wasn't whether they were citizens but whether they were legally made citizens.

Some people even wonder if someone can be a citizen if they weren't legally made one, as if an illegal citizen and someone who isn't a citizen at all were the same. But we see that some people rule unjustly, yet we still consider them rulers, even if they aren't ruling justly. Since we defined a citizen as someone who holds certain offices, it's clear that someone who was made a citizen illegally is still a citizen, but whether this was done justly or unjustly is a different question.

It's also been debated what counts as the actions of the city. For example, when a democracy replaces an aristocracy or tyranny, some people refuse to honor their contracts, claiming that the agreement was with the tyrant, not the state. There are other similar issues, like if a government official made an agreement based on force rather than for the common good. In a democracy, the actions of officials are considered the actions of the state, just as they are in an oligarchy or tyranny.

It's important to ask when we can say a city is the same and when it has become something different. It's not enough to just look at the location or the people. These things can change, and people can live in different places. A city can be defined in many ways, so the question can be answered in many ways. If people live in the same place, when do we say they are living in the same city or that the city is the same? It doesn't depend on the walls. For example, Peloponnesus could be surrounded by a wall like Babylon, which enclosed many nations rather than just one city. Some people in Babylon didn't even know it had been captured for three days. We'll figure out the right time to answer this question because the size of a city and whether it should include more than one group of people are things politicians should know about.

Another question is whether a city stays the same while the same group of people lives there, even though some die and others are born. For example, we say a river or spring is the same even though the water is always changing. But when a revolution happens, do we say the people are the same but the city is different? If a city is a community, and the type of government changes, it seems like the city must also be different. Just like we would call a tragic chorus different from a comic one, even if the same performers were in both. In the same way, if the type of government changes, we say the city is different, just as the same hands can play different musical harmonies. So, when we say a city is the same, we are really talking about the government that's in place, no matter what name it has or who lives in it. But whether it's right to dissolve a city when the government changes is another question.

Given what's been said, we should now consider whether the same virtues that make someone a good person also make them a good citizen or if they are different. To answer this, we need to first give a general description of the virtues of a good citizen. Just like sailors are part of a crew, citizens are part of a city. Sailors have different jobs—some row, some steer, and some are in charge of the equipment—but they all share one goal: the safety of the ship. In the same way, citizens may have different roles, but they all care about the safety of the community because the citizens make up the state.

Since there are different types of governments, it's clear that what makes a good citizen in one type of government may not be the same in another. This means that a citizen's virtue can't be perfect. We call someone a good person when their virtues are perfect, so a good citizen doesn't necessarily have the same virtues as a good person. This can be proven by looking at the best-organized states. It's impossible for a city to be made up entirely of excellent citizens. Everyone should be good at their own job, but not everyone can have the same qualities. It's impossible for all citizens to have the same virtues. A city is made up of different parts, just like an animal is made up of a body and soul, and a family includes a man and woman, and property includes a master and a slave. Since a city is made up of all these different parts, it's clear that the virtues of the citizens cannot all be the same. The person leading the dance is different from the other dancers.

It's clear that the virtues of a citizen aren't all the same. But can a good person also be a good citizen? We often say someone is an excellent leader and a wise and good person. Prudence is necessary for anyone involved in public affairs. Some people believe that those who are going to rule should have a different education than other citizens, like how the children of kings are taught how to ride and fight. As Euripides says, "Teach me what the state requires." This suggests that rulers need a special education.

If we agree that the virtues of a good person and a good ruler are the same, and a citizen is someone who obeys the ruler, then the virtues of a good citizen and a good person can't always be the same, though they might be the same for some citizens. The virtue of a ruler must be different from the virtue of a regular citizen. Jason once said that if he were no longer king, he would waste away because he didn't know how to live as a regular person. It's important to know how to command and how to obey. Being able to do both well is the mark of a good citizen.

If the virtue of a good person is only about being able to command, but the virtue of a good citizen is about being able to both command and obey, then these virtues are not the same. It seems that both the ruler and the follower need to learn their roles separately, but the citizen must know how to do both. In a household, the master doesn't need to know how to do the servant's work but just benefits from the servant's labor. Doing that work would be beneath him. I mean that regular family duties are the work of a slave.

There are different types of slaves because there are different kinds of work. Artisans, for example, make their living with their hands, and these kinds of workers include all mechanics. In some states, these people were not allowed to take part in the government until democracies were established. It's not proper for an honorable person or anyone involved in public life to learn these kinds of jobs unless they need them for personal use. If this distinction isn't maintained, the line between master and slave would disappear. But there is another kind of government where men rule over their equals and other free people. We call this a political government. In this type of government, men learn to command by first learning to obey, just like a good horse general or army commander learns their duty by being under someone else's command. This is true in any part of the army. As the saying goes, no one knows how to command unless they've been commanded first.

The virtues of rulers and followers are different, but a good citizen must have both. A good citizen should know how free people should rule and be ruled, and this is also the duty of a good person. If the justice and self-control of the ruler are different from those of the free person who is being ruled, then the virtues of a good citizen must also be different from the virtues of a good person. The virtues must change in these two situations, just like the courage of a man is different from the courage of a woman. A man who had only the courage of a woman would seem like a coward, and a woman who spoke as much as a man would seem like a gossip.

The household duties of men and women are also different. The man's job is to earn a living, while the woman's job is to manage the household. Leadership and understanding of public affairs are virtues unique to rulers, though both rulers and those being ruled need other virtues. However, those being ruled don't need to worry about ruling—they just need to have the right beliefs. They are like flute makers, while the rulers are the musicians who play the flutes. This is enough to show whether the virtues of a good person and a good citizen are the same or different, and how they are sometimes the same and sometimes different.

There's still some debate about who really counts as a citizen. Are only those who can participate in the government truly citizens, or do mechanics and workers count too? If people who don't have a say in running the city are still considered citizens, then not all citizens can have the same virtue. But if we say these workers aren't citizens, where do we place them? They aren't just visitors or foreigners. Maybe it doesn't cause a problem if they aren't citizens, since they aren't slaves or freedmen either. It's true that not everyone needed for a city to function is a full citizen, just like boys aren't citizens in the same way adults are. Boys are citizens, but not fully—they aren't old enough yet. In the past, some societies made mechanics either slaves or foreigners, and this is still true today in some places. The best-organized cities often don't allow mechanics to be citizens. But if mechanics are allowed to be citizens, then we can't expect the same virtue from every citizen, only from those who aren't doing servile work.

People who work for one master are slaves, and those who work for money are mechanics or hired workers. So, it's clear what their position is. In some places, mechanics and hired workers must be allowed to be citizens, but in others, like aristocracies, they can't be. In aristocracies, honor is based on virtue, and it's impossible for someone living as a mechanic or hired worker to practice the same virtues. In an oligarchy, hired workers also aren't citizens because offices are based on wealth. But mechanics might be citizens since many of them are rich.

Thebes had a law that no one could participate in government until they'd been out of trade for ten years. In some places, laws invite foreigners to become citizens, and in some democracies, the child of a free woman is also considered free. The same happens with children born outside of marriage. But this usually happens because there aren't enough citizens being born regularly. As the population grows, cities first stop giving citizenship to children of slaves, then to children of free women, and eventually, only those whose parents are both free are considered citizens.

There are clearly different types of citizens, and a person is most fully a citizen when they share in the honors of the state. Achilles, in Homer, complains that Agamemnon treats him like a dishonored stranger. A stranger or visitor is someone who doesn't share in the honors of the city. When the right to be a citizen isn't clear, it's done to protect the residents of the city.

From what's been said, it's clear whether the virtue of a good man is the same as that of a good citizen or not. In some places, they are the same, but in others, they aren't. This doesn't apply to all citizens, but only to those who lead or are capable of leading in public affairs, either on their own or with others.

Now that we've established this, we can consider whether only one form of government should be used or if there should be more. If there should be more than one, how many should there be, and what should they look like? What are the differences between them? A form of government is the way a city is organized, especially the offices that hold the most power. The government always holds this power. The way power is shared in a city is what makes up the government. In a democracy, power is in the hands of the people. In an oligarchy, power is held by a few. So, we can say that these governments are different, and the same is true for others.

First, we should determine why a city exists and explore the different types of leadership people accept in society. I've already mentioned in my writing on household management that humans are naturally social creatures. When people don't need help from others, they still want to live together, mostly because it makes life more pleasant for everyone. This desire for a better life is something all people feel, both as individuals and as a group. But it's not just a choice—they also come together to survive. People will even endure hardships just to keep living, because life is naturally sweet and desirable.

It's easy to describe the different types of government. I've already done so in other writings. The authority of a master, though useful for both the master and the slave, is mainly for the master's benefit. The slave benefits only indirectly—if the slave is lost, the master's power ends. The authority a man has over his wife, children, and household is different. This type of leadership benefits those being governed, or at least benefits everyone equally. It's like how a doctor or a coach works for the good of the patient or athlete, not for themselves. Sometimes the doctor or coach might benefit, but that's just a bonus—it's not the main goal. The same goes for political governments that aim to maintain equality among citizens. In these governments, it's fair to take turns leading. In the past, it was normal for citizens to take turns serving the public, expecting that others would do the same for them when their turn came. But now, people want to stay in power all the time so they can keep benefiting from holding office, as if being in charge solves all problems.

It's clear that governments aiming for the common good are rightly established and truly just. Governments that only aim for the good of the rulers are based on wrong principles. They're more like a master ruling over slaves, while a city is a community of free people.

Now that we've covered these points, we can look at how many types of governments exist and what they are. First, we'll talk about their good qualities, because once we know those, it'll be easy to see their flaws.

Every government has a supreme power that controls the entire state. This power must be held by either one person, a few people, or many people. When this power is used for the common good, the state is well-governed. But when the power is only used for the benefit of the one, few, or many who hold it, the state is poorly governed. If the people making up the state are truly citizens, they must share in the benefits of government. When one person governs for the common good, we call it a monarchy. When a few people govern for the common good, we call it an aristocracy—this might be because they are the best citizens or because it's the best system for the city. When many people govern for the common good, we call it a republic, though this term can apply to other governments too. These terms make sense because it's easy to find one or a few very capable people, but it's almost impossible to find a large group where everyone is equally good. The only virtue that can exist in large numbers is courage because it comes from strength in numbers. In these kinds of states, military power will always play a major role in the government.

The corrupt versions of these governments are as follows: a monarchy can turn into a tyranny, an aristocracy can become an oligarchy, and a republic can turn into a democracy. A tyranny is a government where one person rules for their own benefit. In an oligarchy, only the rich are considered, and in a democracy, only the poor are. None of these corrupt forms have the common good in mind.

We need to explain these forms of government more clearly because they can be difficult to understand. If we want to truly understand their principles, we can't just look at their surface features—we need to dig deeper into their true nature. A tyranny is a monarchy where one person has absolute power over the entire community and every person in it. An oligarchy is where the rich hold power, and a democracy is where the poor have control.

But here's the first problem with these definitions: what if the majority of the people in a democracy are actually rich? Or what if the poor are fewer in number, but because of their strength or skill, they control the government? This raises the question of whether our definitions are correct. Also, what if the majority of the people are rich but hold power as a group? What if the minority are poor but they still hold power? Our definitions seem to miss something.

It's clear that whether power is in the hands of the many or the few might just be a matter of chance. What really matters is that when power is in the hands of a few, it's an oligarchy, and when it's in the hands of many, it's a democracy. This is because there are always more poor people than rich people. So, it's not just the number of people in power that defines these governments—it's whether the people in power are rich or poor. When the rich are in charge, it's an oligarchy, and when the poor are in charge, it's a democracy. And, as we've said, there will always be more poor than rich, which leads to constant competition between wealth and liberty for control of public affairs.

Let's now figure out the limits of oligarchy and democracy and what justice looks like in each. All people have some idea of justice, but they only get part of it right. They often don't fully understand what is absolutely just. For example, equality seems just, and it is, but only among equals. Inequality also seems just, but only among those who are unequal. People often overlook this and make bad judgments because they only think about what's good for themselves. Most people are bad judges of their own cases.

Justice relates to people, so we need to make distinctions between different kinds of people just like we do with things. I've talked about this more in my work on ethics. People often agree about equality when it comes to things, but they disagree about equality among people. This is because they are judging their own cases, and people aren't good at judging what's fair for themselves.

If society were only about keeping property safe, then people's rights in the city would be based on their wealth. Those who support oligarchy would be right—someone who contributes just a little shouldn't have the same rights as someone who contributes much more. But society isn't just about preserving life or property—it's about living well. If it were just about staying alive, then a city could be made up of slaves or even animals, but this isn't the case. These creatures don't share in the happiness of the city, and they don't live according to their own choices. A city isn't just an alliance for defense or trade. If that were true, then trade alliances between different nations would make them into one city, but that's not how cities work. For example, Tyrrhenians and Carthaginians have trade agreements, but they don't share a government or work together to improve each other's morality. They only care about preventing harm and ensuring fair trade. But a lawmaker who wants to build a city that's more than just an alliance needs to focus on making the citizens virtuous.

A city is different from an alliance for protection because its main goal is to make its citizens good and happy. If the citizens aren't virtuous, then the city is just an alliance for survival, like any other agreement between groups of people. Law is just an agreement to do justice to one another, but it's not enough to make everyone in the city good.

If we built a wall around two cities like Megara and Corinth, they still wouldn't be one city, even if the people could marry each other and trade freely. A city isn't just a group of people living close together. A true city forms when people come together not just for survival, but to live well. They join with their families and raise their children together to create a community that helps everyone live the best life possible. That's why cities have social gatherings, religious ceremonies, and celebrations to build friendships and connections. These activities help make life better and happier for everyone.

A city is a community of families and villages working together to live well and independently. It's not just about living together—it's about living the right way. Those who contribute the most to this goal should have more power in the city than those who are equal in wealth and freedom but are less virtuous. From this, we can see that in any argument about government, each side has some part of the truth.

It might also be a question where the highest power should be placed. Should it be with the majority of people, the wealthy, a group of the best people, one person better than the rest, or a ruler with complete control? No matter which one we choose, there will be some issues. For example, should the poor be in charge just because they are the majority? If that happens, they might divide the wealth of the rich among themselves. Is this wrong? It might not be, if the top power has decided it's fair. But what good is it to say something is the height of injustice if this isn't one of those cases?

If the majority takes everything from the few, it's clear the city will collapse. Virtue doesn't destroy what's virtuous, and what's right shouldn't ruin the city. So, a law that allows this can't be right, just as a tyrant's acts can't all be wrong. If someone has absolute power, they force others to follow their commands, just like how the majority can overpower the rich.

Is it fair, then, that the rich, who are the few, should hold the highest power? What if they are just as guilty of stealing from the majority? That would be as unfair as the other case. It's clear that any behavior like this is wrong. So, should those who are better than the rest have the power? But does this mean that all the other citizens will live without honor, never sharing in the city's leadership?

The city's offices are its honors, and if one group is always in charge, the rest will be without honor. Should we give power to one person who is the best fit for it? This would shrink the power even more, leaving even more people unhonored. Some might argue that a person shouldn't have the highest power but that the law should, because a person is controlled by many emotions.

But if the law creates a government of the best or a democracy, will it help in solving these problems? The issues we've mentioned will still happen.

Other points will be discussed separately, but it seems important to prove that power should belong to the many rather than the few who are considered better. We should also explain what doubts might arise. Even if no individual in the majority is fit for the highest power, when they come together, they may actually be better qualified than the few. This is not true for each one separately, but for the group as a whole. It's like how public meals are better than those prepared by just one person. Since they are many, each person brings a bit of wisdom and virtue. When they combine, they're like one person with many hands, feet, and minds. In this way, the collective understanding and morals of the group are better.

For example, the public is the best judge of music and poetry because some people understand one part and others understand another. Together, they understand the whole thing. Important people are different from the majority, just like how beautiful people are different from those who aren't, or how good paintings collect the best parts of different people into one image. Even if the separate parts, like an eye or hand, are better in real life, the whole picture is more beautiful.

But if this difference exists between every group of people and the few who are important, it might be unclear whether this is always true. In fact, it's clear that, for some groups, it isn't true. The same could be said for animals. In what way are some men different from animals? Nothing stops this from being true in some places. So, the doubt we mentioned can be settled like this: the free citizens who make up most of the people should have power in some areas. However, since they are not wealthy and don't always act with virtue, it's not safe to trust them with the highest offices in the state. They might do wrong either because of dishonesty or because they don't know better.

Still, it would be dangerous not to give them any power or role in the government. If there are many poor people who can't take part in their country's honors, there will be many enemies of the state. So, they should be allowed to vote in public assemblies and decide cases. This is why Socrates and other lawmakers gave them the power to elect officers and examine their conduct after their term. But they weren't allowed to be magistrates themselves. When the majority is gathered together, they have enough wisdom for these tasks. By mixing with those of higher rank, they help the city. Sometimes things that aren't good by themselves are better when mixed with others.

However, there is a problem with this form of government. It seems like the person who can cure someone who is sick should be the best judge of who should be hired as a doctor. But this person must be a doctor himself. The same goes for any art or skill. A doctor should report his work to another doctor, and the same is true for other professions. Doctors, for example, can be divided into three groups: those who make the medicine, those who prescribe it (like how an architect plans while a mason builds), and those who understand the science but don't practice it.

These groups exist in other arts as well. We respect the opinions of those who understand the principles of a skill, even if they don't practice it. The same applies to elections. Choosing the right person in any skill is the job of those who know that skill. For example, mathematicians should choose the best in geometry, and sailors should choose the best in steering. Even if some people know something about certain arts, they don't know more than the professionals.

So, based on this, neither the election of officers nor the review of their work should be given to the majority. But maybe this isn't entirely right. If the people aren't completely unskilled, even if each person knows less than experts, when they come together, they might know better, or at least not worse. Besides, in some arts, the worker isn't the only one who can judge the work. For example, the person who lives in the house might be a better judge of it than the builder. Similarly, a ship captain knows more about the steering equipment than the person who made it, and someone hosting a meal knows more about it than the cook.

This seems to solve this problem, but another one arises: it seems strange to give power to people with average morals instead of those with excellent character. The power to elect and judge is very important, and in some places, it's given to the people. The public assembly is the highest court, and they make decisions in all public matters, judging all cases without regard to their social standing or age. But treasurers, generals, and other high officials are chosen from people with wealth and honor.

This difficulty can also be solved in the same way. The power is not in the individual assembly members but in the assembly as a whole, which includes the council and the people. The whole group, including the senator, adviser, or judge, shares the power. For this reason, it's right that the majority should have the greatest power because the people, council, and judges are made up of them. Together, they have more wealth than any one person or small group who holds high offices. This resolves the issue.

The first question we asked shows clearly that the highest power should be in well-made laws. The magistrates, whether one or more, should decide cases where the laws can't be specific. After all, it's impossible for laws to cover every possible situation. But we haven't yet explained what these best laws should be. This is still open to debate. The laws of each state will reflect the state itself, either good or bad. It's clear that good governments will have good laws, while bad ones will have bad laws.

In every art and science, the goal is always something good, and this is especially true in founding a society, where the goal is justice.

Justice benefits everyone. Most people agree that justice involves some kind of equality, and philosophers agree on this when talking about morals. They say justice means giving equal things to equals. But we need to know how to decide what things are equal and unequal. This is a difficult question that requires the wisdom of a politician.

Some people might say that government jobs should go to the best person in each category, as long as they are similar to others in every other way. Justice gives different things to people based on their merits. But if this is true, then someone's looks, height, or similar qualities could be reasons to give them more rights. This is clearly absurd. In music, the best flute player doesn't get the best instrument because he's from the best family. His playing won't be better because of that. The best flute should go to the best player.

To make this clearer, let's say there is a great flute player who isn't from a good family and isn't very attractive. Family and beauty are more valuable than musical skill, but the best flutes should still go to the best player. Strength and size shouldn't outweigh virtue. The point is that claims to office shouldn't be based on just any advantage. For example, being fast or slow doesn't make someone more or less qualified for government, even if it matters in a race. What matters for government offices is having the skills useful to the state.

So, it makes sense that people with family, wealth, and independence should compete for these offices. A city can't be made up only of poor people, just like it can't be made up only of slaves. If people like this are necessary, then people who are just and brave are also important. No state can survive without justice, and it can't be happy without bravery.

It seems necessary, then, for the establishment of a state, that most, if not all, of these details are thoroughly examined. Virtue and education have the strongest claim to be considered the key to making citizens happy, as we've said before. Since people who are equal in one way aren't necessarily equal in all ways, and those who are unequal in one way aren't unequal in all ways, it follows that any government based on such a principle is flawed.

As we've already said, all members of the community will argue over who should hold office; and they may be right in some ways, but not in all. For example, the rich argue that they should lead because they have the most land, and since the right to land is shared by the community, their wealth is seen as dependable. Free men and those from noble families also dispute who should hold power, as they see themselves nearly equal. These men argue that their heritage gives them a higher status than those from obscure backgrounds, as honorable ancestry is respected everywhere. It's also reasonable to think that descendants of virtuous men will be virtuous too, as noble birth is seen as the source of virtue. This is why virtue itself has the right to claim power. For instance, justice is a virtue so essential to society that all other virtues must come second.

Now, let's see what the majority has to argue against the few. They might say that, collectively, they are stronger, richer, and better than the few. But if it happens that the rich, the noble, and the good all live in the same city, like the majority, will there still be a reason to argue over who should govern, or will there not? In any community we've mentioned, there's no argument over who holds supreme power; as the communities differ, so do the ruling groups. In one state, the rich rule, in another, the virtuous do, and each rules based on their own customs. But what happens when all these different groups live in the same city at the same time? If the virtuous are very few in number, what should we do? Should we prefer the virtuous due to their abilities if they are capable of governing? Or should we choose them if they almost make up the entire state?

There's also a debate over the claims of those who argue they should govern due to their wealth or family status. They don't have a strong defense, since, based on their argument, if one person is richer than all the others, that one person would have the right to govern everyone. In the same way, one person from the best family would claim the right over others based on family merit. Likewise, in an aristocracy, the same argument might apply to virtue—if one person is more virtuous than all the others, then that person should rule. By the same logic, while the majority believes they should rule due to being stronger, if a small group is stronger than the majority, then the smaller group should rule instead.

All of this shows that none of these principles can fairly justify the right to supreme power, and no one can claim that all others must obey them. For those who claim to rule based on virtue or wealth, they might have objections, because it's possible that the majority can sometimes be better or richer than the few, not as individuals, but collectively.

To address the question some people have raised: should a legislator create laws that serve the best part of the citizens or the majority, in the circumstances we've discussed? The fairness of something lies in its equality, so what is equally right will benefit the entire state and every citizen.

In general, a citizen is someone who shares in governing and is also willing to be governed. This varies in different states, but the best system is one where a man can live a virtuous life, both publicly and privately. But if there is one person or a very small group who are extremely virtuous—so much that the virtue of the majority cannot compare—such a person or group shouldn't be considered part of the city. It would be wrong to treat them as equals to those who are so inferior to them in virtue and ability, as they would appear god-like compared to ordinary men. This shows that laws must be designed for those who are equal in nature and power. These exceptionally virtuous men are not subject to laws, for they are like a law unto themselves. It would be absurd to try to subject them to the penalties of the law. As Antisthenes said, when the lions were asked to share equal power with the hares, they refused. This is why democratic states use ostracism—to keep equality their main goal. They force those who become too powerful in wealth, influence, or other areas to leave the city for a time. As the story goes, Hercules wasn't taken aboard the ship Argo because of his superior strength. Those who dislike tyranny and criticize the advice Periander gave to Thrasybulus should realize that Periander's suggestion wasn't without reason. The story goes that Periander didn't say anything to the messenger sent to consult him. Instead, he simply struck down the tallest ears of corn in the field, reducing them to the same height. The messenger relayed this back to Thrasybulus, who understood the message—that he should eliminate the city's leading men. This isn't just helpful to tyrants; oligarchies and democracies also use similar tactics. Ostracism works in a similar way, by restraining and exiling those who grow too powerful. Even powerful governments, like Athens, imposed their will on places like Samos, Chios, and Lesbos after gaining control of Greece, violating previous agreements. The King of Persia also often suppresses the Medes and Babylonians when they try to regain their past power. Every government, even the best-run ones, keeps this principle in mind—some for private gain, others for the public good.

This is also seen in other fields, like the arts. A painter wouldn't draw an animal with a foot that's too large, no matter how beautiful it is otherwise. A shipbuilder wouldn't make one part of a ship larger than it should be. The leader of a band won't let someone who sings louder than everyone else dominate the performance. In the same way, a monarch might act in line with free states to maintain his own power, just as they do to benefit their own communities. When there's a recognized difference in the power of citizens, the idea behind ostracism is politically just. But it's better for a legislator to create a system from the start that doesn't need such measures. If problems arise later, they should fix them with careful correction. However, ostracism was often used improperly, not for the community's benefit but as a weapon for causing conflict.

It's clear that in corrupt governments, ostracism is partly just and useful to the individual, but it's also evident that it isn't entirely fair. In well-governed states, there's doubt about its usefulness—not because of differences in strength, wealth, or connections, but when the superiority lies in virtue. In that case, what should be done? It doesn't seem right to exile such a person, but it also doesn't seem right to govern them, as that would be like trying to share power with Zeus. The only natural solution is for everyone to submit to the leadership of those who are truly virtuous and allow them to rule as kings forever.

It seems now appropriate to change our focus and look into the nature of monarchies. We've already accepted that monarchies are one of the valid forms of government. Let's consider whether a monarchy is suitable for a city or country focused on the happiness of its people or if another form of government would be better. First, let's determine whether monarchy is of one type or several. It's easy to see that there are many kinds and that governments don't all operate the same way. In Sparta, for example, the king's power is mostly regulated by law and isn't absolute in all matters. When the king leaves the state, he becomes the army's general and oversees religious affairs. In essence, the king there is more of a general, not to be held accountable for his actions, and his command is for life. He doesn't have the power of life and death except as a general, as we see in their military expeditions, something Homer describes. For example, when Agamemnon is insulted in council, he controls his anger, but on the battlefield, he has the power to say:

"Whoever I find avoiding the fight Will soon be prey for dogs and vultures, for I control death."

This is one type of monarchy, where a king rules as a general for life, and the position can be hereditary or elective. Another type is found among some barbarian tribes, where kings hold near-tyrannical power, though they are still bound by laws and customs. Since barbarians tend to be more submissive to authority, especially in Asia compared to Europe, they tolerate despotic governments. This is why their governments are tyrannical, but stable, as they are customary and legal. Their guards, like those in monarchies, are citizens, unlike tyrants, who rely on foreign guards. The monarch rules according to the law over willing subjects, while a tyrant rules arbitrarily over unwilling subjects. So, one king is guarded by citizens, and the other guarded from them.

These are two types of monarchy. Another type is the aesumnetes, which was an elective tyranny found in ancient Greece. This differs from barbarian rule not because it wasn't based on law, but because it didn't follow the traditional customs. Some aesumnetes ruled for life, others for a specific time or purpose, like Pittacus of Mitylene, who was elected to deal with exiles. Alcaeus, the poet, criticized the Mitylenians for making Pittacus their tyrant, praising him while he destroyed a misguided people. These governments are despotic because they are tyrannies, but since they are elective and over a free people, they are also monarchies.

A fourth type of monarchy existed in the heroic age, where free people accepted kings according to the laws and customs of their time. Those who benefited society—through their skills in war or the arts, or by organizing people—became kings of willing subjects and established hereditary monarchies. They were primarily generals and oversaw sacrifices, except for those performed by priests. They also acted as supreme judges, and sometimes took an oath while doing so, swearing by their scepter.

In earlier times, kings had absolute authority over everything, both public and private, but over time, they gave up some of these powers, and people took others. In some states, kings were left with only the right to preside over sacrifices. Even those who retained the title of king were reduced to being commanders of foreign wars.

These are the four main types of kingship: the first, from the heroic age, ruled over a free people with clearly defined rights. The king was a general, judge, and high priest. The second type is barbarian, an hereditary despotism governed by law. The third is the aesumnetic, an elective tyranny. The fourth is the Lacedaemonian, which is essentially a hereditary generalship. A fifth type of kingship exists where one person has supreme authority over everything, just as a city or state governs its public affairs. Just as a master rules over his household, this king rules over the entire city or state.

The different types of monarchies can basically be reduced to two main forms, which we'll look at more closely. The last one mentioned, and the Lacedaemonian form, are the two extremes. The others fall in between these two, having more power than the Lacedaemonians but less than an absolute monarchy. The main questions can be reduced to two points: one, whether it's good for a general's position to be held by one person for life and whether it should be limited to specific families or open to everyone; and two, whether it's good for one person to have total control over everything or not. However, discussing the position of a Lacedaemonian general is more about creating laws for a state than considering the nature and benefits of its constitution, since every state appoints generals. So, we'll skip that topic and focus on the second part, which is the structure of the state itself. This is something we need to look at in detail and address any questions that come up.

The first thing we need to consider is this: is it better to be governed by a good person or by good laws? People who prefer monarchy believe that laws can only speak in general terms and can't address specific situations. This is why they think it's foolish to follow written rules in any science. In Egypt, for example, doctors were allowed to change the treatment prescribed by law after the fourth day, but if they did it sooner, they took a risk. This shows that a government ruled by written laws isn't always the best. However, general rules are necessary for those who govern, and these rules are much better if they come from people who are free from emotions than from those who are naturally affected by them. Laws have this quality, while emotions are natural to the human soul. But someone might argue that a person would be a better judge of specific situations. So, a king would need to be a lawmaker, and his laws should be made public, but only the reasonable ones should have authority.

The question is whether it's better for the community to be governed by every worthy citizen, as happens now when public assemblies act as judges and advisors, making decisions on specific cases. For example, it's clear that one individual, no matter who they are, is less wise than the collective judgment of the whole community. Just like a large feast is better than one person's portion, the judgment of many people is often better than one. The larger group is also less likely to be corrupted because of its size, just like water is less likely to be polluted if there's more of it. An individual's judgment can be clouded by anger or other emotions, but it's unlikely that a whole community would be misled by anger. Furthermore, if the people are free, they will do nothing against the law except in cases where the law doesn't apply. And while what I'm about to suggest may be rare, if most of the state's citizens happen to be good people, and they have to choose between one uncorrupt ruler or many equally good rulers, isn't it clear that they should choose the many? However, divisions can occur among the many, which can't happen with just one. The answer to this is that all of them should be motivated by virtue just like the one good ruler would be.

If a government of many good people is called an aristocracy, and a government of one is called a monarchy, then it's clear that people should choose an aristocracy over a monarchy, especially if the state is powerful and there are enough good people to form it. This is probably why the earliest governments were usually monarchies—it was hard to find many virtuous people, especially since the world was divided into small communities. Also, kings were often chosen as a reward for the benefits they brought to society, and these actions were usually performed by good men. But when a large number of virtuous people appeared, they no longer accepted one person's superiority. Instead, they sought equality and established free states. Later, when people became corrupt, they treated public property as their own, which likely led to oligarchies. In these systems, wealth became the qualification for power, and government positions were reserved for the rich. These oligarchies eventually turned into tyrannies, and these, in turn, gave rise to democracies. Tyrants' power weakened because of their greed, and the people became strong enough to establish democracies. As cities grew, it became more difficult for them to be governed by anything other than a democracy.

But if someone prefers a monarchy, what should be done about the king's children? Should his family continue to rule? If his children turn out poorly, it could be harmful to the state. Some might say the king will prevent his unworthy children from succeeding him, but that's hard to guarantee and would require more virtue than is typically found in human nature. There's also the question of how much power a king should have. Should he have enough force to compel those who refuse to follow the law, and how should he maintain his authority? If he governs according to the law and does nothing against it, he will still need some power to enforce the law. This issue isn't too hard to solve, though: the king should have enough power to be stronger than any individual or large part of the community, but weaker than the whole community. This is why the ancients gave guards to aesumnetes, or tyrants, when they appointed them, and someone advised the Syracusans to give Dionysius only the number of guards he requested.

Next, we'll consider the absolute monarch, who does everything according to his own will. A king who follows laws that he must obey doesn't create any specific form of government by himself, as we've already said. In any state, whether aristocratic or democratic, it's easy to appoint a general for life, and many people entrust the administration of their affairs to a single individual. This is the case in Dyrrachium and similarly in Opus. Absolute monarchy, where the entire state is under the control of one person, seems unnatural to many. It doesn't make sense for one person to rule over citizens who are equal to him. Nature suggests that those who are equal in merit should also be equal in status. Just as it would be harmful for people with different physical constitutions to follow the same diet or wear the same clothes, it's harmful for those who are equal in virtue to be unequal in rank. This is why people should take turns ruling and being ruled, as this is the purpose of law—law creates order. And it's better for law to govern than for one citizen to do so. Even if some individuals are given supreme power, they should act as guardians and servants of the laws. But it's unfair for one person to hold supreme power when all are equal.

It's also unlikely that one person can make better judgments than the law in cases where the law cannot be specific. The law sets down the best general rules, leaving the application of specifics to the magistrate's discretion. Additionally, the law allows changes if experience shows there's a better way to do things. Those who believe the supreme power should rest in reason would entrust it to the laws and to God, but those who give it to a man hand it over to a wild beast, as human desires can sometimes overpower reason, even in the best people. This is why law represents reason without desire.

The argument about the arts seems flawed. It's said that a sick person shouldn't rely on books for treatment, but instead, trust experienced doctors. Doctors act according to reason and aren't swayed by friendship; they earn their money by curing the sick. In contrast, those who manage public affairs often act out of hatred or favoritism. As proof, when a sick person suspects their doctor of foul play, they might turn to books for a cure. Even doctors themselves call on other doctors when they fall ill, and those who teach gymnastics train with others in the same profession. This shows that those who seek justice look for a balance, and law provides that balance.

The moral law deals with higher principles than the written law, and the supreme magistrate is more trustworthy than the written law, even if he is inferior to the moral law. But since one person can't oversee everything, the supreme magistrate must employ several assistants. So why not do this from the beginning instead of appointing just one person? Besides, if, as we've already said, a virtuous person is fit to govern, two virtuous people are better than one. For example, Homer says, "Let two go together," and Agamemnon wished for "ten such faithful counselors." Even now, there are specific magistrates with the authority to decide cases where the law doesn't apply, and no one doubts their role. Since laws cover some things but not everything, we must ask whether it's better for the best person or the best law to govern. After all, it's impossible to make laws for every situation humans might face.

No one denies that there should be someone to decide cases that fall outside the law's reach. But we argue that it's better to have many such people rather than one. Although everyone who judges according to the law makes just decisions, it seems ridiculous to suggest that one person can see better with two eyes, hear better with two ears, or act better with two hands and two feet than many people can with many eyes, ears, hands, and feet. Absolute monarchs today have many eyes, ears, hands, and feet by entrusting power to their friends. If they aren't friends of the monarch, they won't act as he wishes. But if they are friends, they are also friends of his government. A friend is an equal, and if the king thinks such people should govern, then he believes that his equals should also govern. These are some of the common objections raised against monarchy.

It's likely that what we've said applies to some people but not to others. Some people are naturally suited to be ruled by a master; others by a king; and others are citizens of a free state, just and useful. But tyranny and other corrupt forms of government aren't natural, as they go against nature. It's clear that among equals, it's neither fair nor right for one person to rule over all, whether there are no laws and his will is the law, or even where laws exist. Nor should a good person rule over other good people, or a bad person over other bad people, unless in a very specific way, which we will explain, though we've touched on it already. Next, we will determine which people are best suited for a monarchy, which for an aristocracy, and which for a democracy. A monarchy is best for people who are naturally inclined to submit their civil government to a family known for its virtue. An aristocracy is best for those who are naturally inclined to be ruled by free men whose superior virtue makes them fit to manage others. A free state is best for a warlike people, naturally inclined to both govern and be governed by laws that allow even the poorest citizens to share in the honors of the state based on their worth.

But if a whole family or an individual stands out in virtue, excelling beyond all others, then it's right for them to hold kingly power, or for the individual to be king and ruler of all. This principle aligns with the foundation of all governments—whether aristocratic, oligarchic, or democratic—which seek to place supreme power in the hands of those with merit. And, as we've already said, it wouldn't be right to kill, banish, or ostracize someone for their superior merit. It wouldn't be right either for such a person to only hold power in turn. It goes against nature for the highest to ever become the lowest, which would happen if such a person were governed by others. So the only solution is to let them continuously hold supreme power. This is the conclusion we reach regarding monarchy in different states, and whether or not it benefits them.

Since we have said that there are three types of regular governments, the best one will naturally be the one that is led by the best people. This could be a government where one person, one family, or a group of people stand out in virtue and are capable of both governing and being governed in a way that makes life most pleasant. We've already shown that the virtue of a good man and that of a citizen in the best government are the same. It's clear, then, that the same qualities that make a person good would also make a government—whether it's an aristocracy or a kingdom—well-established. Therefore, it's education and morals that are almost entirely what make someone a good person. The same traits make a good citizen or a good king.

Now that we've discussed these details, we'll move on to consider what kind of government is the best, how it naturally comes about, and how it is set up. It's important to carefully examine these questions.

Book 4

In every art and science that deals with a whole subject and not just parts of it, it's the job of that art to decide what fits best with that subject. For example, in exercise, it's important to choose the right kind of exercise for a particular body to help it function best. A body that is naturally strong and perfect needs the best exercises, and it's also important to choose exercises that will work for most people. This is the role of the gymnastic arts. Even if someone doesn't want to become an expert in these exercises, it's still necessary for the teacher to be an expert if they're going to train others. We see this same principle in other areas like medicine, shipbuilding, and tailoring, as well as all other arts. This shows that it's the same art or science that should find out which form of government is the best and which matches what people would ideally want, without any outside interference. It should also find which type of government is best suited for different types of people, as some may not be able to handle the best form of government. This means that a lawmaker, or someone who understands politics well, should not only know about the best form of government but also know what type of government fits certain situations.

There's also a third category—an imaginary one—that the lawmaker should be able to recognize if it ever comes up. They should be able to see how such a government would start and how to keep it going for a long time. This could happen if a state doesn't have the best form of government or if it's missing something important, or if it only has part of what it needs. Additionally, it's important to know what kind of government works best for all cities. Most writers on this subject, even if they talk about it in interesting ways, don't describe how to make it work in practice. It's not enough to understand what's best; it must also be possible to put it into action. The system should be simple and something that everyone can achieve. Some people only focus on the most complicated forms of government. Others prefer to criticize the government they live under and praise the greatness of another state, like Sparta or others. But a lawmaker should create a government that fits the current state and mindset of the people it will serve, so they will be willing to follow it. Changing an existing government's mistakes can be just as difficult as forming a new one. It's as hard to recover something you've forgotten as it is to learn something new. Therefore, anyone aiming to be a lawmaker should also know how to correct the errors of an established government, as we've already mentioned. But this is impossible for someone who doesn't know how many different forms of government exist. Some people think there's only one type of democracy and one type of oligarchy, but this isn't true. It's important for everyone to understand how different these governments are and where their differences come from. It's also essential to know which laws are best and most suitable for each type of government.

All laws should be made to match the state they govern, not the other way around. Government is the way power is distributed within a state, especially when it comes to magistrates—how they are selected and where supreme power is placed, and what the main goal of the state is. Laws are something different from the government's structure. Their job is to guide the actions of the magistrates in carrying out their duties and punishing wrongdoers. Therefore, it's clear that lawmakers should understand both the number and the types of governments that exist. It's impossible for the same laws to work for every type of oligarchy or every type of democracy because both of these governments have many different forms, not just one.

Since we have divided regular governments into three types—the monarchy, aristocracy, and free states—and shown that each has its extremes, we now need to examine them more closely. Monarchies can turn into tyrannies, aristocracies into oligarchies, and free states into democracies. We've already discussed aristocracy and monarchy because deciding what form of government is best involves looking closely at these two, as they are both based on virtue. We've also explained how monarchy and aristocracy differ from one another and what it means for a state to be ruled by a king. Now we must examine the free state, as well as other forms of government such as oligarchy, democracy, and tyranny. It's clear which of these extremes is the worst, and which comes next after that. The worst excess comes from the best and most virtuous form of government. The name of king may remain, but if a king takes more power than he should, tyranny results, which is the worst possible form of government, being the opposite of a free state. The next worst is oligarchy because it differs a lot from aristocracy, and the least bad is democracy. One previous writer said that of all the excellent forms of government, like a good oligarchy, democracy was the worst, but of all the bad forms, democracy was the best.

I believe that all these types of states have fallen into excess at some point, and that the writer should not have said that one oligarchy was better than another but that it was just not as bad. We won't get into that question right now. First, we'll examine how many different types of free states there are, since democracies and oligarchies have many forms. We'll also look at which of these is most suitable and desirable after the best form of government, and whether there is another form similar to a well-established aristocracy. We'll also look at which form works best for most cities and which is best for specific groups of people. Some people might prefer an oligarchy over a democracy, and others the opposite. After this, we'll discuss how someone should go about establishing either a democracy or an oligarchy. Finally, once we've covered all the important points, we'll try to explain what causes governments to become corrupt or stay stable, both the things that apply to all governments and those that are unique to each type, and the main causes behind them.

The reason there are so many types of governments is that each state is made up of many different parts. First, we see that all cities are made up of families. Among these families, some people are rich, some are poor, and others are in the middle. Among both the rich and poor, some people are used to fighting and others are not. We also see that some common people are farmers, others are merchants, and others are craftsmen. There is also a difference among nobles in terms of their wealth and the status they live with, like how many horses they own, since horses can only be kept by the very wealthy. This is why, in the past, cities whose strength came from cavalry often became oligarchies. They used their cavalry to fight against neighboring cities, like the Eretrians, Chalcidians, and Magnetians, who lived near the Meander River, as well as many others in Asia.

In addition to differences in wealth, there are differences in family background and merit. If there are any other distinctions that make up the city, we've already talked about them when discussing aristocracy, where we considered how many parts a city must have. Sometimes all these different groups share in the government, sometimes only a few do, and other times more.

It's clear, then, that there must be many forms of government that differ based on their specific makeup because the parts that make them up are different from one another. Government is about how the magistracies of the state are organized, and the people share power among themselves, either by force or according to some common equality, like poverty, wealth, or something they both share. There must be as many forms of government as there are different ranks in society, depending on the superiority of some people over others and their different circumstances. These seem to fall into two main types, like the winds—the north and the south. All the other forms are variations of these. In politics, we have the government of the many and the government of the few, or democracy and oligarchy. Aristocracy can be seen as a type of oligarchy because it's also a government of the few. What we call a free state can be considered a type of democracy. In the same way, people see the west wind as part of the north and the east wind as part of the south. Some people also think there are only two types of music—the Doric and the Phrygian— and they group all other music under one of these names. Many people look at governments in the same way. But it's more practical and more accurate to divide governments the way I have—into two main categories: those based on sound principles, which can have one or two forms, and those that are excessive forms of the first. We can compare the best form of government to the most harmonious music, oligarchy and tyranny to more violent tunes, and democracy to soft and gentle melodies.

We shouldn't define a democracy as some people do, saying it's simply a government where the majority of the people have the supreme power. Even in oligarchies, the majority can have supreme power. Nor should we define an oligarchy as a government where power is in the hands of a few. For example, if there are thirteen hundred people in a community and one thousand of them are rich and do not allow the three hundred poor people to have any say in the government, no one would call this a democracy, even though the rich are the majority. Similarly, if the poor, even though they are fewer in number, gained power over the rich, no one would call this an oligarchy just because a few poor people hold power.

Instead, we should say that a democracy is when power is in the hands of the free citizens, and an oligarchy is when it's in the hands of the rich. Usually, this means that in a democracy, the many will have power, and in an oligarchy, the few will, because there are usually more poor people than rich. If power were given based on size or beauty, as they say it is in Ethiopia, then it would still be an oligarchy because few people are large or beautiful.

What we've said so far isn't enough to fully explain these forms of government, though. There are many types of both democracies and oligarchies, so the matter needs more thought. For example, we can't say that a government is a democracy if a few free people hold power over the many who aren't free, like in Apollonia, Ionia, and Thera. In these cities, power is held by a few wealthy families who founded the colonies. Also, if the rich were in the majority, as they once were in

Colophon before the Lydian war, this wouldn't make the government a democracy just because there were more rich people.

A democracy is when the majority of free citizens, including the poor, hold power. An oligarchy is when the wealthy and noble families, being fewer in number, control the government. Now that we've shown there are different forms of government and explained why they exist, we'll move on to show that there are even more variations and explain what they are and why. Let's start with the principle we've already discussed. Every city is made up of different parts. If we were trying to categorize different species of animals, we'd first look at the parts every animal has, like sensory organs, and the parts needed to eat and digest food, like the mouth and stomach. We'd also look at the parts needed for movement. If these were the only parts an animal had, and there were differences between them, like different types of stomachs and sensory organs, the combinations of these parts would make up the different species of animals.

The same thing is true for governments. A city is made up of many different groups, as we've said before. One group provides food, which includes farmers. Another group is made up of craftsmen who do manual work, which is essential for a city to function. Some work on basic needs, while others focus on luxuries and pleasures. Another group includes traders—those who buy, sell, and transport goods. Then there are the hired laborers who do various jobs. The next group is made up of soldiers, who are just as important as the others because, without them, the city would be defenseless and vulnerable to invaders. A city that can't defend itself isn't really a city because a true city is self-sufficient, unlike a slave who depends on others. So, when Socrates, in Plato's Republic, says a city is made up of four groups—weavers, farmers, shoemakers, and builders—he's speaking well but not quite correctly. He then adds more groups, like blacksmiths, herdsmen, merchants, and traders, as if a city exists only for necessity and not for happiness, or as if a shoemaker and a farmer are equally important.

He doesn't mention soldiers until later when he talks about expanding the city's territory and the need for war. Even among the groups he does mention, or in any group of people, there must be someone to distribute justice and resolve disputes between individuals. If the mind is more important than the body, then the things that benefit the mind should be more valued in the city than basic necessities like war or justice. You can also add wisdom and council to this, which fall under civil leadership. It doesn't matter if these jobs are done by different people or the same person, like someone who is both a soldier and a farmer. So, if the judge and council member are considered parts of the city, then the soldier must be as well.

The seventh group is made up of those who perform public services at their own expense; these are the rich. The eighth group includes those who fill the various offices of the state, without whom the city couldn't survive. It's necessary to have people who can govern and hold office in the city, whether for life or in rotation. The roles of senator and judge, which we've already discussed, are the only ones left. If a city is going to be happy and just, it needs citizens who are capable of managing public affairs. Many people believe that one person can do multiple jobs, like being both a soldier and a farmer or craftsman. Some also believe that the same people can serve as both senators and judges.

However, a person can't be both rich and poor at the same time, so the most obvious way to divide a city is into the rich and the poor. Most of the time, the rich are the few, and the poor are the many. These two groups are the most opposed to each other, and depending on which one is stronger, the city will either become a democracy or an oligarchy.

Now that we've discussed the causes of different governments, let's explain the different types of democracies and oligarchies. This should be clear from what we've said already. There are many types of common people and many types of nobles. Among the common people, there are farmers, craftsmen, and traders who buy and sell goods. There are also sailors, some who fight in wars, some who trade, some who transport goods and passengers, and others who fish. In some places, like Tarentum and Byzantium, there are many fishermen; at Athens, there are galley captains; at Aegina and Chios, there are merchants; and at Tenedos, there are those who rent out ships. We can also include those who live by manual labor and have little property, meaning they have to work to survive. Then there are those who aren't fully free citizens, and other types of common people.

Nobles are distinguished by their wealth, family background, talents, education, or some other excellence. The purest form of democracy is based on equality. In this kind of democracy, the law ensures that the poor aren't more controlled than the rich and that neither group holds supreme power. Instead, both groups share power. If liberty and equality are the main goals of democracy, as some say, then a democracy is at its strongest when all parts of the government are equally open to everyone. Since the people are the majority and their votes determine the law, this form of government is called democracy. This is one type of democracy. Another type allows magistrates to be elected based on a small property requirement, with everyone who meets it eligible for office. However, if someone's wealth drops below the requirement, they lose the right to hold office.

Another type allows any citizen who isn't dishonorable to participate in government, but the laws still hold the highest authority. Another type allows every citizen to participate, regardless of their wealth, and in this case, the people, not the laws, hold power. This happens when decisions are made by a majority vote rather than by following laws, and it occurs when demagogues influence the people. In democracies where laws govern, demagogues have no role, and the best people hold the highest offices. But when the people hold power, demagogues thrive because the people act as a collective ruler, not as individuals.

Homer criticized the rule of many, but it's unclear if he meant the type of government we're talking about or one where each person rules individually. When the people hold this kind of power, they want complete control and don't want to be limited by laws. This is when flatterers gain favor. There's no real difference between this type of democracy and a monarchy under a tyrant. Both rulers act the same way and have absolute power over people better than themselves. The decrees in such democracies are like the edicts of tyrants, and the demagogues are like the flatterers of tyrants. The greatest similarity is the way the demagogue and the people support each other. The demagogue leads the people, and the people give him power. As a result, the people's votes, not the laws, control the government. Demagogues bring all issues before the people because they influence the people's opinions, and the people follow their lead. The people enjoy accusing magistrates and use these accusations to weaken all offices.

So, we can say that this kind of government, which is a democracy in name but not a true free state, is flawed. When the laws don't hold power, there is no free state. The laws should rule over everything, and the magistrates should handle any issues that the laws don't cover. If a democracy is to be considered a free state, it's clear that a government where all power rests in the votes of the people cannot truly be called a democracy, because its decisions aren't general or based on the law. This is how we can describe the different types of democracies.

There are also different types of oligarchies. One type is when the right to hold office is based on a certain property requirement, so the poor, even if they are the majority, have no say in the government, while everyone who meets the requirement participates in public affairs. Another type is when officials are chosen from among people of modest wealth. If these officials come from the general population, the government leans toward an aristocracy. But if they come from a specific group, it's an oligarchy. Another form of oligarchy is when power is held by an inherited nobility. The fourth type is when power is in the hands of a few, and they aren't controlled by laws. This form of oligarchy is similar to a monarchy that becomes a tyranny, and it's also like the form of democracy we just described. This type of oligarchy is called a dynasty. These are the different forms of oligarchies and democracies.

It's important to note that sometimes a free state, where the laws hold power, might not be democratic. However, because of the customs and traditions of the people, it might function as if it were a democracy. On the other hand, a government with more democratic laws could function like an oligarchy, especially after a change in the government. People don't change easily and are attached to their old customs. Change happens gradually, so the old laws remain while power shifts to those who brought about the change.

From what has been said, it's clear that there are many kinds of democracies and oligarchies, as I have listed. In a democracy, either all the people I mentioned will have a share in the government, or only some will, and others will not. When farmers and those with moderate wealth hold the power, they will govern according to laws because they have to work for a living and don't have much free time for public business. They will create good laws and only call public meetings when necessary. They will also allow anyone who reaches the wealth requirement set by law to share in the government. Anyone who qualifies will have a role in the government. If some people are excluded, it would become an oligarchy, but not everyone has time to attend unless they have enough to live on. This is why this form of government is a type of democracy.

Another type of democracy is when officials are elected, and anyone is eligible, as long as there's no reason to disqualify them based on birth, and they have time to participate. In this type of democracy, the law holds the most power, because those attending public assemblies are not paid. A third kind of democracy is when all free citizens have the right to take part in the government, but they won't accept it for the same reasons mentioned before. So, here again, the law will hold the supreme power. The fourth type of democracy arose later when cities grew larger, and public revenue increased. At that point, even the poorest citizens were allowed to take part in public affairs because they were paid to do so. These poorer citizens had more time to attend public meetings since they didn't have personal wealth or businesses to worry about, unlike the rich, who often didn't attend. This resulted in the poor holding the most power, instead of the laws. These are the different types of democracies, and these are the causes that led to them.

The first kind of oligarchy is when most of the citizens have moderate property, which gives them enough time to manage public affairs. Since they are a large group, it's only natural that the laws, not individuals, hold the highest power. They are far from a monarchy and don't have enough wealth to ignore their personal business, and they are too many to be supported by the public. So, they will decide to be governed by laws, not by each other. But if only a few people in the state have large amounts of wealth, then a second type of oligarchy will form. Those with the most power will believe they deserve to rule over the others. To make this happen, they will include some people interested in public affairs. Since they aren't strong enough to govern without laws, they will create laws to help them. If the few rich people become even more powerful, the oligarchy will change into a third kind. They will pass laws allowing them to control all government offices, passing them down from father to son. As their wealth and influence grow, they will oppress others even more, and this will eventually lead to a monarchical dynasty where individuals hold all the power, not the laws. This is the fourth type of oligarchy, similar to the last type of democracy I mentioned.

There are also two other types of government, a democracy and an oligarchy, that people often talk about. These are usually considered part of the four types of governments. People count them as monarchy, oligarchy, democracy, and a fourth type they call aristocracy. There is also a fifth type, which is often called "the state." But because this type is rare, those who try to list all the types of governments usually miss it. Plato, in his Republic, also mentions only four types of government.

An aristocracy, as I talked about earlier, is rightly called so. This is a government where the best people, who follow the most virtuous principles, are in charge, not just people who have good ideas. In this type of government, a person can be both a good citizen and a good person, which isn't always true in other forms of government. In some governments, people are only considered good in relation to that particular state. Some other governments are also called aristocracies, but they differ from both oligarchies and free states. In these aristocracies, both the rich and virtuous share in the administration, which is why they are given the name aristocracy. In governments where virtue isn't a main focus, there are still good and honorable people. A state like Carthage, which values the rich, the virtuous, and all citizens, can be considered a form of aristocracy. When a state only values the virtuous and the citizens, like in Lacedaemon, this is a virtuous democracy. These are the two main types of aristocracies after the first, which is the best type of government. There's also a third type, which is when a free state leans toward the rule of a few people.

Now, we will talk about what is called a free state and about tyranny. The reason I discuss the free state here is because, like aristocracies, it seems like a good system, but to be honest, both have moved away from being truly perfect governments. They are both deviations from other forms, as I mentioned earlier. Tyranny is mentioned last because it is the least like a proper government. But since my goal is to discuss all forms of government, I will talk about tyranny when the time comes.

Now, I will explain what a free state is, and we will better understand it by comparing it to oligarchy and democracy. A free state is really just a mix of both. People often call a state that leans toward democracy a free state, and a state that leans toward oligarchy an aristocracy because the rich are usually from well-known families and have a good education. They also have things that others commit crimes to get, which is why they are considered honorable and important.

Since aristocracy aims to give the best citizens the most power, people say oligarchy is made up of the most worthy and honorable individuals. It seems impossible for a government where good people hold power to have bad laws, and it's just as unlikely that a government with bad leaders will have good laws. A government is not well-structured just because it has good laws. It's also important to make sure the laws are enforced. A sign of a well-structured government is one that makes sure its laws are followed and that those laws are suited to the people who live under them. If the laws are bad, they still need to be obeyed. This can happen in two ways: the laws can be the best for a specific state or the best in general.

An aristocracy is likely to give the honors of the state to virtuous people because virtue is the focus of aristocracy, while wealth is the focus of oligarchy, and freedom is the focus of democracy. What most people approve of will prevail in all three types of government. What seems good to most members of the community will prevail. What we call a "state" prevails in many communities that aim to balance the interests of the rich and the poor, as well as wealth and freedom. The rich are often considered to be in the same category as the worthy and honorable. Since freedom, wealth, and virtue are the three main things valued in a state (and the fourth, family rank, comes from virtue and wealth), it's clear that the combination of rich and poor creates a free state. But all three—freedom, wealth, and virtue—lcan more toward an aristocracy than any other form of government, except for a true aristocracy, which holds the highest rank.

We have already explained that there are forms of government different from monarchy, democracy, and oligarchy, and we've shown how they differ from each other. We've also discussed aristocracies and states, and it's clear that they are quite similar to each other.

Next, we'll explain how a government called "the state" comes about alongside democracy and oligarchy, and how it should be structured. We'll also show where democracy and oligarchy differ from each other and how a state can combine parts of both.

There are three main ways to mix two forms of government. First, you can combine the rules of each. For example, in an oligarchy, the rich are fined if they don't show up as jurors, but the poor aren't paid for attending. In a democracy, the poor are paid, and the rich aren't fined if they don't show up. These practices, which are common to both, are suitable for a free state, which is made up of both types of citizens. This is one way to combine them. Second, you can create a middle ground between the two systems. For example, in a democracy, there is either no wealth requirement to vote or a very low one, while in an oligarchy, only those with a high amount of wealth can vote. Since these two systems are opposites, a free state can establish a middle ground between them. Third, you can adopt different laws from each system. In a democracy, officials are often chosen by lot, while in an aristocracy, they are elected. In one system, the choice is based on wealth, while in the other, it is not. A free state or aristocracy can take ideas from both systems, using elections from the oligarchy and removing the wealth requirement like a democracy.

The best sign of a successful mix between democracy and oligarchy is when people can call the same state both a democracy and an oligarchy. Those who speak this way do so because both systems have been combined well. This is true for all balanced systems—elements of both sides are present. In Lacedaemon, for example, some say it's a democracy because of the many ways it follows that system. For instance, rich and poor children are raised the same way, and the poor can access the same education as the rich. As adults, they are treated equally, and at public meals, everyone gets the same food. The rich also wear clothes that the poorest person can afford. In their two highest offices—the senate and the ephorate—everyone has the right to participate. Others say Lacedaemon is an oligarchy because of certain things it follows from that system, like choosing officials by vote and not by lot, and only allowing a few people to judge serious cases.

A state that successfully combines two systems should resemble both and neither at the same time. It should have the strength to maintain itself from within, not relying on external factors. By this, I mean that it shouldn't depend on the goodwill of its neighbors, as even a poorly governed state can be left alone by others. Instead, every member of the state should be committed to maintaining its constitution without any desire to change it. This is the way a free state or aristocracy should be structured.

Finally, let's discuss tyranny. Although there isn't much to say about it, we need to include it since we listed it among the different forms of government. At the start of this work, we looked into the nature of kingship and discussed in detail what a true kingship is, whether it benefits the state, how it should be set up, and how it works. We also mentioned two types of tyranny, which are somewhat similar to kingship because both are established by law. In some barbarian societies, they elect a king with absolute power, and in ancient Greece, there were similar leaders called sesumnetes.

These two systems are different, though. Some kings only have limited power under the law and rule over people who willingly accept their leadership. Others rule as tyrants, governing according to their own desires. A third type of tyranny, which is the most properly called tyranny, is the exact opposite of kingship. This is the government of one person who rules over his equals and superiors without being held accountable. His goal is his own benefit, not the benefit of the people he governs. Because of this, he rules by force since no free people would willingly accept such a government. These are the different types of tyrannies, their principles, and their causes.

Now we move on to explore what type of government and way of life is best for most communities, not focusing on the perfect virtue that only a few can achieve or an education that only those with great natural abilities and wealth can have. We are not talking about imaginary ideas, but rather about a way of life that most people can reach and a government that most cities can establish. The aristocracies we've mentioned are either too perfect for most states to maintain or so similar to the state we are about to examine that we will treat them as the same thing.

Our views on this topic must follow a basic principle: if what I said in my work on ethics is true, then a happy life comes from a constant practice of virtue. If virtue is about finding the middle ground, then a life lived in the middle is surely the happiest, and this middle ground can be reached by everyone. The same balance between good and bad in a person must also exist in a state because the government is the life of the city. In every city, there are three types of people: the very rich, the very poor, and those in the middle. If we agree that the middle is best, it's clear that in terms of wealth, the middle ground is the most desirable. People in the middle are more likely to follow reason. The very rich, very strong, very noble, or very wealthy often don't follow reason well, just like the very poor or very weak. The rich tend to be arrogant and commit crimes because of their excesses, while the poor often become mean and deceitful. Neither group is likely to take part in the offices of the state, which hurts the state overall. The rich and powerful are not willing to be ruled, and this starts early in life when they are raised without being taught to follow rules. The poor, on the other hand, are so focused on their lack of wealth that they live in a way that is too lowly.

In a city like this, where there are only masters and slaves, not free citizens, one group will hate the other, and there will be no possibility of friendship or unity in the political community. Friendship is essential in a community because we don't even travel with our enemies. A city should be made up of equals as much as possible, and this happens when most of the people are in the middle class. This means the best city will be made up of those who naturally belong to the middle class. These people will also be the most secure because they won't desire the property of others like the poor do, and others won't want to take what they have, like how the poor want to take from the rich. This way, they can live without fear of being plotted against or needing to plot against others. This is why the philosopher Phocylides wisely wished for the middle class, as it brings the most happiness.

It's clear that the most perfect political community comes from people in the middle class, and the best states are those where the middle class is the largest and most respected group, bigger than both the rich and the poor combined. If this isn't possible, the middle class should at least be larger than either group on its own, so it can balance the state and prevent either extreme from gaining too much power.

The greatest happiness for citizens is to have a moderate and comfortable amount of wealth. If some people have too much and others have nothing, the government will either fall into the hands of the poorest people or become a strict oligarchy. In extreme cases, it can even lead to tyranny, which often comes from a wild democracy or oligarchy. However, when the members of a community are roughly equal in status, tyranny is rare. We will explain this more when we discuss how states change.

The middle class is the best because it is the least likely to cause rebellions and unrest. Larger states are also less prone to these problems because they have more people in the middle class. In small states, it's easier to have extremes where most people are either very rich or very poor, leaving little room for the middle class. This is why democracies tend to last longer and are more stable than oligarchies. However, even in democracies, if there aren't enough people in the middle class, the poor can become too powerful, leading to problems and the collapse of the government.

As evidence of what I'm saying, we can look at the best lawmakers in history. They have often come from the middle class, such as Solon, as we can see from his writings, and Lycurgus, who wasn't a king, and Charondas, among others. What I've said explains why many free states have changed into democracies or oligarchies. When the middle class is too small, the larger groups—whether the rich or the poor—take control of the government. This leads to either a democracy or an oligarchy.

Moreover, when the rich and poor fight with each other, and one side wins, they don't set up a free state. Instead, they create a government that favors their side, making it either a democracy or an oligarchy.

Those who conquered Greece often set up democracies or oligarchies based on the governments of their home cities. They didn't think about what was best for the conquered state, but rather what was familiar to them. This is why governments that put power in the hands of the middle class are rare. Only a few conquerors have recognized the value of this group, and most cities don't aim for equality. Instead, people want to either rule or be ruled when they are conquered.

Now that we've explained what the best state is and why, it will be easier to understand which governments are the best among the many that exist. There are different types of democracies and oligarchies, and we can see which are better or worse based on how close or far they are from the best possible government. The best is the one closest to the ideal middle ground, while the worst is the one furthest from it. However, different governments might be better for different situations, so a government that is worse in general might still be the best for certain purposes.

After discussing this, we should now explain which form of government is best for different groups of people. The first rule is that those who want to keep the current government should always outnumber those who want to change it. Every city is made up of both "quality" and "quantity." By "quality," I mean things like freedom, wealth, education, and family background. By "quantity," I mean the number of people. It's possible that quality might be found in one group in the city, while quantity is found in another. For example, there might be more poor people than rich, or more people from unknown families than from noble families. However, the numbers should not outweigh the quality. These elements must be balanced, because if the poor outnumber the rich too much, a democracy will form. If the farmers have more power than others, it will be a democracy of farmers. The kind of democracy depends on which group is the largest. If the majority are farmers, it will be a democracy of farmers, which is the best kind. If the majority are craftsmen or hired workers, it will be the worst kind of democracy. The same applies to any other group.

When the rich and noble have more influence because of their status than they lack in numbers, an oligarchy will form. The type of oligarchy depends on the nature of the ruling group. Any lawmaker who wants to create a stable government should focus on the middle class. Whether it's an oligarchy or a democracy, the laws should be designed to support this group. If the middle class outnumbers both the rich and poor combined, or at least one of them, it will bring stability to the state. There's no risk that the rich and poor will team up against the middle class, because neither group wants to help the other.

Anyone who wants to build the most stable government should rely on the middle class. The rich and poor won't want to take turns ruling because of their mutual distrust. In contrast, the middle class can act as a fair judge for both groups, which is why it's often the best group to hold power.

Those who aim to create aristocratic governments often give too much power to the rich and end up tricking the common people. This creates real harm in the long run, as the actions of the rich are often more destructive to the state than those of the poor.

There are five key areas where the rich try to unfairly undermine the rights of the people: public assemblies, state offices, courts, military power, and athletic training. In public assemblies, they make the meetings open to everyone but only fine the rich for not attending, or they fine others very little. For state offices, they allow the poor to opt out but don't give the same option to those who meet the wealth requirement. In the courts, they fine the rich for not serving, but fine the poor either very little or not at all, as was the case under the laws of Charondas. In some places, every enrolled citizen had the right to attend public meetings and serve as jurors, and if they didn't, they faced a heavy fine. This fine made people avoid getting enrolled so they wouldn't have to serve.

The same approach applies to military service and athletic training. The poor are excused if they don't have weapons, but the rich are fined if they don't have them. The rich are also fined if they don't attend their training sessions, while the poor face no penalty. As a result, the rich make sure to have weapons and attend training, while the poor do neither. These are the sneaky tricks used by oligarchical lawmakers.

In contrast, democracy does the opposite. In democracies, the poor are paid to attend meetings and serve in court, while the rich are not. This shows that the best way to combine these practices is to extend both the payments and the fines to everyone in the community. Then, everyone would participate, whereas now only some do.

The citizens of a free state should be those who serve in the military. It's not easy to say exactly how much wealth a citizen should have, but the rule should be that the number of people who qualify for citizenship should be larger than those who don't. The poor, even if they don't hold office, will be content as long as they are left alone to manage their property. However, this isn't always easy because those in charge may not always act kindly.

In times of war, the poor usually don't fight unless they are provided with food. When they are fed, they are willing to fight. In some states, power is given not only to those currently serving in the military but also to those who have served in the past. For example, in Mali, only former soldiers held office, and all their officials were veterans.

The first states in Greece that replaced monarchies were military governments. At first, the power was with the cavalry because, back then, armies relied on horsemen. Heavy-armed foot soldiers were useless without proper training. The art of military tactics wasn't known to the ancients, so their strength was in their cavalry. As cities grew larger and foot soldiers became more important, more people gained freedom in the city. This is why what we now call republics were once called democracies. Early governments were either oligarchies or monarchies because there were so few people in each state. It would have been impossible to find enough middle-class people to form a government, so the few who were used to following orders accepted being ruled.

We've now shown why there are so many types of governments and why they differ. There are more kinds of democracies and oligarchies than one might think. We've also discussed their differences, their origins, and which form of government is best, both in general and for specific groups of people.

We will now continue to look at different types of governments and how each one works, starting with their key principles. There are three important things that a careful lawmaker must consider in every state. If these three things are properly managed, the state will be happy. These three things also cause one government to differ from another. The first is the public assembly. The second is the officers of the state—who they should be, what powers they should have, and how they should be chosen. The third is the judicial system.

The job of the public assembly is to make decisions about war and peace, forming or breaking alliances, passing laws, deciding punishments such as death or banishment, and holding officials accountable for their actions while in office. These powers can be given to all the citizens, or just some of them. They can be given to one official, to a group of officials, or split among different groups. When all the power is given to all the citizens, this is a democracy because democracy is about equality.

There are several ways to delegate these powers to the citizens. In one way, the citizens take turns in making decisions, as was done by

Tellecles of Miletus. In another method, a council made up of different officials handles these decisions. People don't meet together unless they are making new laws, discussing a national issue, or hearing proposals from officials. Another method is for the people to meet as a group to make laws, discuss war and peace, and check the behavior of officials, while the rest of the public business is managed by different officials who are chosen by vote or lot. In a fourth method, everyone discusses every issue in public meetings, where the officials cannot decide anything on their own but can only give their opinions first. This method is used in the most direct form of democracy, similar to how power is distributed in strict oligarchies or tyrannies.

These are the different ways public business can be conducted in a democracy. When the power is held by only part of the community, it's an oligarchy, and there are different customs for this too. If officials are chosen from those with moderate wealth, and there are many such people, they will follow the law carefully. When everyone with the required wealth can participate, it's an oligarchy, but one based on fair principles. In another type, a few people are chosen to make decisions, and they govern according to the law. This is also an oligarchy. When officials are elected from among themselves, and their positions are passed down to their sons, allowing them to override the laws, this is a stricter form of oligarchy.

In some cases, different groups make decisions on different matters, like war and peace, while another group checks the behavior of officials. This type of government is either an aristocracy or a free state. In other cases, some officials are chosen by vote, others by lot, and they may come from either the whole population or just a selected group. When both voting and drawing lots are used, it's partly an aristocracy and partly a free government. These are the various ways the power to make decisions is divided in different governments, all following some version of these rules.

It benefits a democracy, where the people hold power even over the laws, to hold frequent public meetings. It's also a good idea for democracies to follow the example of oligarchies in their court systems, where they fine people for not attending when they're supposed to. In a democracy, they should reward poor people for attending public assemblies. The best decisions will come when both the citizens and the nobles discuss things together. If only part of the citizens are involved in the council, an equal number of nobles and citizens should be chosen, either by vote or by lot. If the common people outnumber the nobles, either not all of them should be paid for attending, or they should be reduced by lot.

In an oligarchy, it's a good idea to include some common people in the council, or to set up a court, as some states do, where officials called pre-advisers or guardians of the laws propose laws for the council to approve. This way, the common people can have a role in public affairs without causing disruption. The people can also be allowed to vote on proposals, but they can't suggest new laws themselves, or they can offer advice, but the final decision rests with the officials. It's also important to follow the opposite practice of democracies, where the people are allowed to forgive someone but not to condemn them. In an oligarchy, forgiving is left to a few people, while condemning is left to the public. This is how the power to make decisions is handled in different governments.

Now, let's consider how officials are chosen. This is an important part of government, involving many aspects: how many officials there should be, what their duties are, and how long they should serve—whether six months, a year, or longer. Some officials may be allowed to serve multiple terms, while others may not be allowed to serve more than once. It's also important to decide who can be chosen as an official, who will choose them, and how they will be chosen. We need to explore all these options and figure out which ones are best for different types of governments.

It's not easy to say who exactly should be called a "magistrate" (an official). Governments need many people to fill different roles, but not everyone chosen by vote or lot should be considered a magistrate.

Priests, for example, are different from civil officials. Other roles, like choregi (who organize festivals) or heralds (messengers), are also chosen, but they aren't the same as magistrates. Civil officials are those who take part in making decisions or enforcing the law, and those who hold positions of authority, especially those who command others, are most properly called magistrates.

But deciding who qualifies as a magistrate is less important than figuring out which offices are necessary for a state, how many offices there should be, and which ones, though not necessary, would still benefit a well-governed state. This is important for all states, large or small.

In large states, each office should be given to one person, as there are enough people to fill these roles, and everything is done better when one person focuses on one task. In smaller states, however, one person may need to take on multiple roles because there aren't enough people to spread the work around. Smaller states may need the same officials and laws as larger ones but won't need to use them as often. So, it's sometimes necessary for one person to handle multiple roles in a small state without causing problems.

If we could figure out how many officials are necessary for each city and how many, though not essential, would still be useful, we could better determine how many roles one official could manage. We also need to know which courts should handle which issues in different places and what matters should always be handled by the same official. For example, should market inspectors handle cases of improper behavior if they happen in the market, while another official handles them elsewhere, or should the same official handle them everywhere?

In different types of governments, should the officials be the same or different? In an aristocracy, for instance, offices are given to those who are well-educated; in an oligarchy, they are given to the rich; and in a democracy, they are given to free citizens. The types of officials may also change depending on the needs of the state. In some cases, officials need great power, while in others, only small power is needed.

There are certain officials who belong to specific types of governments. For example, pre-advisers are not needed in a democracy, but a senate is necessary. The senate's job is to prepare bills for the people to vote on so they can focus on their own lives. When the senate is small, the government tends to lean toward an oligarchy. The power of the senate is reduced in democracies where the people handle all the business themselves in public meetings. This happens when people have enough money or are paid to attend, making them free to meet often and decide everything themselves.

Officials who control the behavior of boys or women are only found in aristocracies, not democracies. After all, who can stop poor women from going out in public? Such officials also don't exist in oligarchies because the women there are too delicate to be controlled.

Now that we've discussed this, let's talk more about how magistrates are chosen, starting from the basics. Magistrates are chosen in three different ways, and all the variations come from these. The first difference is in who gets to appoint the magistrates. The second is in who is appointed, and the third is in how they are appointed. Each of these three can be done in three ways. Either all the citizens can appoint the magistrates, or some of the citizens, or only a specific group of citizens chosen based on wealth, family, or virtue. They may also be chosen by vote or by lot. These methods can be combined in different ways, with some magistrates chosen by part of the community and others by the whole community.

There are also different ways to elect magistrates. In a democracy, all magistrates are chosen by all the people, either by vote or by lot, or some are chosen by vote and others by lot. In a free state, not all the magistrates are chosen by the whole community, but some are chosen by part of it, either by vote, lot, or both.

In an oligarchy, some officials may be chosen from the whole population, while others are chosen by vote, some by lot, and others by both methods. In a free aristocracy, some officials are chosen from the whole population, and others from a specific group, either by vote or lot. In a strict oligarchy, officials are chosen from a certain group of people, and this is done either by lot or vote, or both. Choosing from the whole community is not part of this type of government.

In an aristocracy, the whole community should choose magistrates from a specific group of people, and this should be done by vote. These are the various ways magistrates can be chosen, based on the type of government. What is best for each government and how the offices should be set up, along with the powers each official should have, will be discussed in detail later. When we talk about the powers of a magistrate, we mean what specific duties they are responsible for, like handling finances or enforcing the laws. Different magistrates have different powers, just as the role of a general in the army differs from that of a market inspector.

Now we turn to the judicial part of government, which we will divide into three parts just like we did with the officials. These three parts are: who the judges will be, what cases they will handle, and how they will be chosen. When we talk about "who," we mean whether the judges will be chosen from the whole population or just certain people. By "what cases," we mean how many different courts there will be. By "how," we mean whether the judges will be chosen by vote or by random selection (lot).

First, let's decide how many different courts there should be. There are eight main types. The first court is for reviewing the actions of officials after they leave office. The second is to punish those who harm the public. The third handles cases where the government is involved. The fourth is for disputes between officials and private citizens who appeal fines placed on them. The fifth court handles cases involving large contracts. The sixth deals with cases of murder, including different types like premeditated murder, accidental killing, and justified killing, where the fact of the crime is accepted but whether it was legal is debated.

There is another court in Athens called the Court of Phreatto, which handles cases where someone who has fled because of a murder wants to return. This kind of case happens rarely and only in very large cities. The seventh type of court deals with cases involving foreigners, whether it's a dispute between two foreigners or between a foreigner and a citizen. The eighth and last court handles small cases, like those involving sums of money between one and five drachmas, or a little more. These smaller cases should also be settled by law, but not by a large group of judges.

Without going into details about murder cases or cases involving foreigners, let's focus on the courts that deal with the community's main affairs, which, if not managed well, can cause unrest or revolts in the state. These cases must be handled by all the citizens, or by some citizens selected for this purpose, either by vote or by lot. Some judges may be chosen by vote for certain cases and by lot for others. This means there will be four types of judges. The same number of types also applies if judges are chosen from only part of the population. For example, all judges may be chosen from part of the population by either vote or lot, or some by vote and some by lot, depending on the case.

Different groups of judges may also be combined, meaning that judges from the whole population or from part of it, or both, can sit together in the same court. These judges may be chosen by vote, by lot, or by both methods. That covers the different kinds of judges.

The system where all citizens judge all cases is most suited for a democracy. The system where only certain people judge all cases fits an oligarchy. The system where the whole population judges some cases and specific people judge others is best for an aristocracy or a free state.

Book 5

We have now covered everything we planned to discuss. Next, we need to look at what causes changes in governments, how these changes happen, and what types of changes occur. We also need to understand what leads to the downfall of each type of government and which systems they are most likely to shift into. Additionally, we will examine what actions help preserve governments in general and which steps are useful for preserving specific types of governments. Furthermore, we will discuss how to fix corrupt governments, either as a whole or in specific cases.

First, we should establish this principle: many governments claim to support justice and equality but fail to achieve it, as we've already discussed. Democracies emerge because people think that if they are equal in one area, like freedom, they must be equal in all areas. Oligarchies arise from the belief that if some people are unequal in one thing, like wealth, they should be unequal in everything. As a result, those who are equal in some ways try to gain equality in all things, while those who are superior in some ways try to get even more. This drive for more creates inequality. Most governments, while having some understanding of justice, are largely mistaken, and when one side doesn't get the share of power they expect, they become rebellious. However, those who truly have the most right to rebel, the people of the highest virtue, are the least likely to do so because they are genuinely superior.

There are also people from well-known families who refuse to be treated as equals because they believe their noble lineage makes them better than others. These attitudes are the main sources of rebellion. There are two main types of changes people might try to make to a government: either they want to replace the existing system with a different one, such as turning a democracy into an oligarchy or the other way around, or they are fine with the current system but want to take control for themselves, either by concentrating power in the hands of a few or one person. People also argue about how much power a government should have. For example, if a government is already an oligarchy, they may want to make it more purely oligarchical, or the same goes for a democracy. People may also want to either expand or reduce the government's powers, or make specific changes like adding or removing a certain office, such as how Lysander tried to end the king's rule in Sparta, or how Pausanias tried to eliminate the ephors. In Epidamnus, one part of the constitution changed when they replaced the philarchi with a senate.

At Athens, all magistrates must attend court at the Helisea whenever a new magistrate is created. The power of the archon in Athens has an oligarchical nature. Inequality is always a cause of rebellion, but this doesn't happen when those who are unequal are treated in a way that corresponds to their inequality. For example, monarchy is unequal when exercised over people who are equals. In general, it is the desire for equality that causes rebellions. There are two kinds of equality: one based on number and one based on value. Numerical equality is when two things are the same in terms of parts or amount. Value-based equality is proportional, like how four is twice as much as two, and two is twice as much as one. This kind of equality is based on ratio.

Now, while everyone agrees on what is absolutely just, people argue over proportional value. Some believe that if they are equal in one thing, they should be equal in everything, while others believe that if they are superior in one thing, they should be superior in everything. This is how democracies and oligarchies mainly arise. Nobility and virtue are found in only a few people, while the opposite traits are found in the majority. You won't find hundreds of noble or virtuous people, but you will find plenty of the others. Building a government based entirely on either of these equalities is wrong, and history proves this. None of these governments have lasted because if something is wrong from the start, it will eventually fail. This is why, in some cases, numerical equality should prevail, and in others, equality in value should be considered.

However, democracy is generally safer and less prone to rebellion than oligarchy. In an oligarchy, rebellion can arise from two causes: either the ruling few conspire against each other, or they plot against the people. In a democracy, rebellion usually occurs only against the few who want exclusive power. There's hardly ever a case of the people rebelling against themselves. Also, a government made up of moderately wealthy people is more like a democracy than an oligarchy and is the most stable of all types.

Since we're looking into the causes of rebellions and political changes, we should start by identifying the main factors that lead to them. These can be broadly divided into three main categories. First, we must understand the situations that make people start rebellions. Second, we must consider the reasons for these rebellions. Finally, we need to examine how political conflicts and tensions begin between different groups.

The main reason people want to change the government is what I've already mentioned: people who want equality are always ready to rebel if they see that others they consider their equals have more than they do. Similarly, those who want superiority over others will rebel if they feel that those beneath them have the same or more. Whether their reasons are fair or not, those who feel inferior will rebel to become equal, while those who feel equal will rebel to become superior. People will start rebellions for the sake of gaining profit or honor, or to avoid shame or losing wealth, either for themselves or their friends. The original causes that lead people to seek these things can be categorized into seven main factors, though they could be more. Two of these are the same as already mentioned but affect people in different ways. For example, profit and honor lead to conflict, not just to gain these things for themselves, but when they see others, whether justly or unjustly, hoarding them. The other causes are pride, fear, a desire for distinction, contempt, and an imbalanced growth in some part of the state.

There are also other causes that, in different ways, lead to political changes, such as election rigging, negligence, lack of citizens, and extreme differences in circumstances.

The impact of poor treatment and the pursuit of profit on causing rebellion is almost obvious. When leaders are arrogant and try to take more than their position allows, they cause conflict, not just among themselves but also with the state that gave them their power. Their greed is aimed at either private property or state property. The desire for honor also causes rebellion when people see others being honored while they themselves are not. When honors are given or denied unfairly, either by giving someone too much or not enough, it leads to rebellion. Excessive honors can also lead to rebellion if one or more people become more powerful than the state can handle, leading to a monarchy or dynasty. This is why some places, like Argos and Athens, use ostracism to prevent this. But it's better to avoid this kind of power imbalance when founding a state than to try to fix it later.

Those who commit crimes will rebel out of fear of punishment, just as those who expect to be harmed will rebel to prevent it, like in Rhodes, where the nobles rebelled because they feared the new laws that would be passed against them. Contempt also causes rebellion and conspiracies, such as in oligarchies where many people have no share in government. The wealthy in democracies may also rebel, thinking they can improve their position through the same means that caused the downfall of democracies in places like Thebes, Megara, Syracuse, and Rhodes, where poor administration and disorder led to rebellion.

Rebellions can also be caused by imbalanced growth. Just as a body should grow proportionally to stay in harmony, a government should grow in balance. If one part grows too much, it disrupts the system, like a foot growing to four cubits while the rest of the body stays small. This kind of imbalance can change the government into something else, especially when the imbalance occurs without being noticed, like when the number of poor people grows in democracies or free states.

Rebellions can also happen by accident. For example, after the Median War, many of the nobles in Tarentum were killed, which led to a free state becoming a democracy. The same thing happened in Argos after Cleomenes, the Spartan, killed many citizens, forcing the state to grant citizenship to many farmers. In Athens, after battles reduced the number of nobles, more common soldiers were selected from the citizen rolls during wars with Sparta, which also weakened the power of the aristocracy. Sometimes, revolutions happen even in democracies, though this is rarer. When the rich increase in number or gain more property, these democracies can become oligarchies or dynasties.

Governments can also change without rebellion when people of lower status unite. For example, in Hersea, the mode of election was changed from voting to lots, allowing common people to take power. Negligence can also lead to political changes, as happened in Orus when outsiders were allowed into high office, ending the oligarchy of the archons and turning the government into a democratic free state.

Sometimes, small unnoticed changes can lead to large political shifts over time. In Ambracia, for instance, the property census was initially low, but over time it became irrelevant, as if a small change was as good as none. States composed of different groups are also prone to rebellions until their differences are merged. No city can be built from just any group of people, nor can it do so at any given time. This is why republics that either start with different people or later include neighboring groups are the most prone to rebellion.

For example, after the Achaeans and Traezenians founded Sybaris, the Achaeans grew more powerful and expelled the Traezenians, leading to the saying about Sybarite wickedness. Similar disputes occurred in Thurium between the Sybarites and their allies, and in Byzantium, new citizens who were caught plotting against the state were forced out by the army. The same thing happened in other places where outsiders were brought into the citizenry. These situations often cause conflict because one group assumes superiority over the other due to their origins or status.

In oligarchies, many people feel mistreated because they are excluded from honors, as we've mentioned. In democracies, it's often the most prominent citizens who feel resentful because they don't receive more than an equal share with others who are not their equals.

Even the layout of a city can lead to unrest if the geography divides people, as in Clazomene, where those living in one part of town fought with those on the island, or in Athens, where citizens in the Piraeus were more supportive of democracy than those in the city center. Just as a small stream can disrupt a line of soldiers, even small disagreements can lead to rebellion. However, nothing leads to rebellion more than the tension between virtue and vice, followed by the divide between rich and poor. These are the most powerful sources of conflict.

Conflicts in governments don't usually start because of small matters, but they often come from small beginnings. Major disagreements arise from these small issues, especially when they involve people of high status in the government. For example, in ancient Syracuse, a government was overthrown because of a personal quarrel between two young men in office over a romantic relationship. One of them, while away, had his mistress seduced by the other. To get back at him, he convinced his friend's wife to live with him. Soon, the whole city picked sides, and the government collapsed. This shows how important it is to stop these disputes early before they grow, as small problems can lead to major consequences. Disputes between prominent people often involve the entire city. In Hestiaea, after the Median war, two brothers fought over their father's estate. The poorer brother, angry that the wealthier one had hidden some of their father's money, got the common people on his side, while the wealthier brother rallied the upper class. In Delphos, a wedding-related quarrel led to a series of seditions. The bridegroom, scared off by a bad omen on his way to the wedding, fled without marrying the bride. Her relatives, feeling insulted, secretly planted sacred money in his pocket while he was making a sacrifice, then accused him of sacrilege and killed him. In Mitylene, a dispute over inheritance led to a major conflict and a war with the Athenians, during which Paches captured the city. Timophanes, a wealthy man, left behind two daughters, and when Doxander was tricked out of arranging their marriages for his sons, he started a rebellion and encouraged the Athenians to attack.

A similar conflict over inheritance happened in Phocea between Mnasis and Euthucrates, leading to the Sacred War. The government of Epidamnus also changed because of a quarrel over a planned marriage. One man had arranged to marry off his daughter, but the archon, who was the father of the groom, punished him for an unrelated offense. The insulted father then joined forces with others who had been left out of the government and overthrew it.

A government can shift into an oligarchy, democracy, or a free state when certain groups in the city gain more power or influence, such as when the Areopagus court in Athens gained great influence during the Median war, which strengthened their control. On the other hand, the navy, made up of common people, secured the victory at Salamis and boosted the power of the democratic faction. At Argos, the nobles gained credit after winning the Battle of Mantinea against the Spartans and attempted to overthrow the democracy. In Syracuse, after the common people won the war against Athens, they changed the government into a democracy. In Chalcis, after the people overthrew the tyrant Phocis and expelled the nobles, they took control of the government. The same happened in Ambracia, where the people expelled the tyrant Periander and took power.

In general, whenever a person, group, or institution is responsible for making a state powerful—whether they are private citizens, officials, a particular tribe, or any segment of the population—they often become the cause of disputes. Either others envy them for the honors they've received, or they themselves are no longer satisfied with the equality they once had. Conflicts also arise when opposing groups, such as the rich and the common people, grow closer to each other in power. If one side is clearly stronger, the weaker side won't risk a confrontation. That's why those who are superior in virtue and excellence don't usually cause rebellions—they are too few in number to challenge the many.

In general, revolutions and changes in government happen in two main ways: either through force or through deceit. If by force, the ruling powers are compelled to submit to the change, and if by deceit, the people are initially tricked into agreeing to a change in government and are later forced to stick with it. For example, the Four Hundred in Athens misled the people by claiming that the King of Persia would provide money for the war against Sparta. After deceiving the people, they tried to keep control of the government. In some cases, people are first persuaded and later agree to be ruled.

We should now look at what these causes lead to in different types of governments. Democracies are most prone to revolutions because of dishonest leaders. They may target wealthy individuals, forcing them to band together for protection since common fear unites even enemies. These leaders also turn the common people against the wealthy, which can be seen in many states. For instance, in Cos, the democracy fell because of corrupt leaders, as the nobles formed a coalition. In Rhodes, leaders bribed the people, causing them to refuse to pay the trierarchs what they owed. The trierarchs, burdened by lawsuits, conspired together and overthrew the democracy. A similar thing happened in Heraclea, where, after the city was founded, the influential citizens were mistreated by the leaders. They left the city but later returned and destroyed the democratic government. In Megara, democracy was overthrown in a similar way. Leaders confiscated property to gain wealth and exiled the nobles until a large group of exiles returned, defeated the people in battle, and set up an oligarchy.

A similar event occurred in Cumae, where Thrasymachus destroyed the democracy. If you look at other cities, you'll find that revolutions happen for the same reasons. Leaders trying to gain favor with the people either divide the property of the wealthy, force them to spend it on public services, or exile them so they can confiscate their wealth. In earlier times, when the same person acted as both leader and general, democracies often turned into tyrannies. This was the case with most ancient tyrannies. In those days, leaders gained power not through speeches but through military action. Now, with the art of public speaking, leaders are more often skilled orators than generals, so they are less able to become tyrants, though there are a few exceptions.

Tyrannies were more common in the past because certain magistrates were given broad powers, such as the prytanes in Miletus, who held control over many important matters. Additionally, cities were smaller, with most people living in the countryside and working as farmers. This gave leaders in the city a chance to become tyrants if they were good at war and could gain the people's trust by opposing the rich. This was how Pisistratus in Athens rose to power by opposing the Pedieis, and how Theagenes in Megara became tyrant after slaughtering the cattle of the rich. Dionysius also became tyrant by accusing Daphnaeus and other rich men, earning the people's trust through his enmity with them.

A democracy can also change into something entirely new if there's no system to regulate how magistrates are chosen. If elections are controlled by the people, then leaders, eager to gain power, will do everything they can to make the people more powerful than the laws. To prevent this, magistrates should be chosen by tribes rather than by the people at large. These are the main ways that democracies experience revolutions and the causes behind them.

There are two main causes of revolutions in oligarchies: one is when the people are mistreated, making them ready for rebellion, especially if one of the oligarchs becomes their leader. This was the case with Lygdamis, who became tyrant of Naxos. Revolutions also arise when the wealthy, who are excluded from power, feel wronged.

In some cities like Massilia, Ister, and Heraclea, those who were left out of government kept fighting until they gained a share. First, the older brothers were included, then the younger ones. In some places, fathers and sons were not allowed to hold office at the same time, and in others, only the eldest brother was allowed in power. In these cases, the oligarchy became somewhat like a free state. At Ister, the government changed into a democracy, and in Heraclea, instead of being ruled by a few, the government was expanded to include six hundred citizens.

In Cnidus, the oligarchy was destroyed when the nobles fought among themselves because too few people held power. Only one member of a family, usually the eldest, could hold office at a time. The people took advantage of this division and chose one of the nobles as their leader, eventually gaining control.

In Erithria, during the rule of the Basilides, although the city thrived under their leadership, the people grew dissatisfied with power being held by so few and changed the government. Oligarchies can also fall because of internal conflicts among their leaders. Some demagogues flatter the ruling few, as Charicles did with the Thirty Tyrants in Athens, or Phrynichus did with the Four Hundred. Others flatter the people to gain power, like the state-guardians in Larissa, who flattered the people because they were elected by them.

This happens in oligarchies where officials are not self-elected but chosen from wealthy or prominent families by the soldiers or the people, as was the custom in Abydos. If the judicial power isn't controlled by the ruling party, demagogues may side with the people in legal cases, which can lead to the downfall of the government, as happened in Heraclea in Pontus. Oligarchies can also be weakened when some try to concentrate power into even fewer hands. In these cases, those trying to maintain equality must appeal to the people for support.

Oligarchies are also prone to revolution when the ruling class spends too much on luxuries. These individuals may seek to become tyrants themselves or support others in doing so, as Hypparinus supported Dionysius in Syracuse. In Amphipolis, a man named Cleotimus brought in a colony of Chalcidians and used them to stir up conflict with the rich. In Aegina, a man who brought a lawsuit against Chares attempted to use the case to change the government.

At times, oligarchs will start disputes to cover up theft from the public or to fight against those who try to expose them. This happened in Apollonia in Pontus. However, if the members of an oligarchy remain united, the government is harder to overthrow without outside interference. Pharsalus is an example of this, where, despite being a small city, the people maintained power through wise governance.

An oligarchy can also collapse if it creates another oligarchy within itself. This happens when the government is controlled by a few, but not all members share equally in power. For instance, in Elis, the general government was controlled by a small group, but out of this group, a senate of ninety members was selected, holding their positions for life. Their election process ensured that power stayed within certain families, much like the senators in Sparta.

Oligarchies are vulnerable both in times of war and peace. During war, they may rely on mercenaries instead of citizens, and these mercenaries' commanders may seize power, as Timophanes did in Corinth. If they appoint multiple generals, it could lead to the establishment of a ruling dynasty. In some cases, oligarchies are forced to give more power to the people because they need their help in wars.

In times of peace, distrust among the oligarchs may lead them to rely on mercenaries and their general, who may end up controlling both sides, as happened in Larissa when Simos and the Aleuadae had the most influence. A similar situation occurred in Abydos during the rule of political clubs, like the one led by Iphiades.

Oligarchies can also fall apart when one group becomes too dominant or when there are conflicts over lawsuits or marriages. For example, in Eretria, Diagoras overthrew the oligarchy of the knights because of issues related to marriage. A similar sedition occurred in Heraclea when someone was condemned by the courts, and at Thebes when a man committed adultery.

Although the punishments in these cases were just, they were carried out in ways that caused unrest. At Thebes, for instance, enemies tried to publicly humiliate Archias. Oligarchies have also fallen when people could no longer tolerate the despotism of the ruling class, as in Cnidus and Chios.

Sometimes changes happen gradually in free states or oligarchies where senators, judges, and officials are chosen based on a certain wealth requirement. Initially, only a few people may meet the requirement, but as the city grows wealthier, more people can participate in the government, leading to a shift in power. These changes can happen slowly over time or more rapidly, depending on circumstances.

These are the types of revolutions and seditions that occur in oligarchies, and the causes behind them. Both democracies and oligarchies can sometimes change not into completely different forms of government, but into variations of the same form, such as shifting power from the law to the ruling party, or the reverse.

Revolts can also happen in aristocracies because only a small number of people hold power, just like in oligarchies. This makes aristocracies similar to oligarchies, even though the reasons for this power imbalance might be different. Problems are more likely to occur when most people are confident and believe they are equal in ability, such as in the case of the Partheniae in Sparta. They were the descendants of citizens who conspired against the state but were caught and sent to found the city of Tarentum. Trouble can also arise when highly respected individuals are dishonored by others who have gained more power than they have, even though they are equally capable. For example, Lysander was disgraced by the Spartan kings. Revolts also occur when an ambitious person can't rise to power, like Cinadon, who led a conspiracy against the Spartans during the reign of Agesilaus.

Moreover, issues arise when some people become too rich and others too poor, which is especially common during wars. This happened in Sparta during the Messenian War, as described in a poem by Tyrtaeus called "Eunomia," where some people wanted the land divided because they had been impoverished. Conflicts also occur when someone of very high status wants to increase their power and rule alone. This seemed to be the case with Pausanias in Sparta during the Median War and Anno in Carthage.

Both free states and aristocracies often fail when there isn't a clear structure for running public affairs. This happens because the balance between democratic and oligarchic elements is not properly managed. In aristocracies, the problem also comes from a lack of balance between virtue and power. States that lean more toward oligarchy are called aristocracies, and those that lean toward democracy are called free states. Free states are more stable because the broader the foundation of a government, the more secure it is. It's always better to live in a place where equality is emphasized. However, when the rich are given special status, they often try to dominate others. In general, whichever direction a government leans, that's where it will end up. A free state will become a democracy, and an aristocracy will become an oligarchy, or the opposite may happen. For instance, if the poor feel mistreated, they will side with the opposite faction, and an aristocracy may turn into a democracy, or a free state into an oligarchy. The only truly stable government is one where everyone has the equality they deserve and where people fully possess what belongs to them.

This is what happened in Thurium. The magistrates were originally elected based on a high property qualification, but the requirement was lowered, and more courts were created. However, because the nobles owned most of the land against the law, the government leaned too much toward oligarchy, allowing them to take advantage of the rest of the people. Eventually, the people, strengthened by their experience in war, overthrew their rulers and expelled those who owned more than their fair share. Aristocracies, which are essentially free oligarchies, often face problems when the nobles try to seize too much power, as in Sparta, where property is concentrated in the hands of a few. The nobles have too much freedom to make alliances as they please. For instance, the city of the Locrians was ruined because of an alliance with Dionysius. Their government was neither a democracy nor a well-balanced aristocracy.

Aristocracies tend to collapse slowly, as we've seen with other forms of government. This happens when small, seemingly insignificant changes gradually lead to larger ones. Once a minor issue is treated lightly, something more important will be more easily changed, until the entire structure of the government is destroyed. This happened in Thurium, where the law required soldiers to serve for five years. A group of young, ambitious soldiers, who were well-regarded by their officers, despised the officials in charge of public affairs. They believed they could change the law so they could remain in the military indefinitely, knowing the people would elect them. The magistrates, called counselors, initially resisted this change but eventually agreed to it, thinking that if they allowed this law to be changed, they would retain control over other public matters. However, when they tried to prevent further changes, they found they had no power to stop them, and the government turned into a ruling faction of those who had introduced the changes.

In short, all governments can be destroyed from within or from external forces. External threats arise when neighboring states have opposing policies, or even when a powerful state far away is at odds with their system. The Athenians and Spartans serve as examples of this. The Athenians overthrew oligarchies when they were victorious, and the Spartans did the same with democracies. These are the main causes of revolutions and conflicts in governments.

We now need to consider how governments can be preserved, both in general and in specific types of states. First, if we understand the causes of a government's downfall, we can also understand the means of preserving it, since opposites produce opposite results. Destruction and preservation are opposites. In well-ordered governments, it's especially important that nothing is done against the law, and this is particularly true with small matters. Small violations can gradually destroy a state, just as small expenses can drain a person's income over time. The mind is often deceived by this faulty reasoning: if each small part is insignificant, then the whole is also insignificant. But while each part may be small, together they add up to something significant.

The first step is for the state to prevent small violations from occurring. Second, people should not trust those who try to deceive them with false claims, as they will eventually be proven wrong by the facts. The various ways in which this deceit happens have already been discussed.

Aristocracies and oligarchies often last not because their systems of government are strong but because their leaders are wise in dealing with both those who hold power and those who do not. They avoid harming those who aren't involved in government and instead offer important roles to the most influential among them. They also avoid offending those who seek honor and refrain from taking individuals' property. For those who are in power, leaders treat each other as equals. This desire for equality is both just and convenient for those of the same status. If many people share power, democratic principles can be useful, such as limiting how long someone can hold office. Rotating leadership ensures that all people of the same rank have their turn, which prevents any one person from gaining too much power. This method helps prevent both aristocracies and democracies from turning into dynasties because leaders don't hold power long enough to cause significant harm.

Governments are sometimes preserved by keeping the means of corruption far away, but at other times, a nearby threat can strengthen a government. When people are worried about a danger, they pay more attention to the state's needs. Leaders must be able to raise alarm when necessary to protect the government, rather than being like a guard who fails to keep watch. Even a distant danger should be made to seem close at hand.

It's also crucial to manage the conflicts and disputes among nobles through laws, and to prevent those not yet involved from getting drawn in. Recognizing problems early is the skill of a true statesman. In both oligarchies and free states, it's important to prevent problems related to the census. If the census remains the same while the overall amount of wealth increases, it can create issues. The total amount of wealth should be compared over time, either annually in small cities or every three to five years in larger ones. If the wealth has greatly increased or decreased compared to when the census was first established, the law should adjust the census accordingly. If wealth increases, the census should be raised, and if wealth decreases, the census should be lowered. If this adjustment isn't made, oligarchies will turn into dynasties, and free states will become democracies, or oligarchies will shift into free states.

In all types of governments—whether democracies, oligarchies, or monarchies—it's important not to allow any one person to rise far above the rest. Instead, it's better to give moderate honors over a longer period rather than great honors for a short time. Most people can't handle sudden success, which corrupts them. If great honors are given all at once, they should be taken away gradually rather than suddenly. Above all, the law should ensure that no one gains too much power through wealth or connections. If someone does, they should be required to leave the country.

Since some people push for changes in order to live according to their own desires, there should be an official responsible for monitoring everyone's behavior. This person should ensure that people's behavior aligns with the character of the state, whether it's an oligarchy, democracy, or any other form of government. The state should also be cautious of those who are overly successful and assign them to public duties to keep their power in check. It's important to balance the interests of the rich and the poor by uniting them into one body and increasing the number of people in the middle class. This helps prevent rebellions caused by inequalities in status.

In every state, it's also essential to ensure that public officials aren't corrupt. This is especially important in oligarchies, where the people may not mind being excluded from government as long as they aren't being cheated. But if they suspect that public officials are stealing from them, they will be angry for two reasons: they're being excluded from power and robbed at the same time.

One way to combine elements of democracy and aristocracy is to remove financial incentives from public office. When there's no money to be made from holding office, both the rich and the poor will get what they want. Allowing everyone to share in government is democratic, while having the wealthy hold office is aristocratic. If public offices don't offer financial rewards, the poor won't want the positions since they won't make any money, but the rich will still want them since they don't need the income. The poor will focus on improving their own finances, and the majority of the people won't be ruled by those of lower status.

To prevent public funds from being misused, all government money should be distributed openly for everyone to see, and copies of the accounts should be kept in different districts. Since magistrates aren't benefiting financially from their positions, the law should provide honors for those who do their jobs well.

In democracies, the rich should be protected by preventing their land or its produce from being divided. This is sometimes done without being noticed. It would also help if the people stopped the wealthy from hosting unnecessary and expensive public events, like plays, music performances, and parades.

In an oligarchy, it's important to take care of the poor by giving them profitable public jobs. If a rich person insults a poor person, the punishment should be harsher than if they insulted someone of their own rank. Inheritance laws should also prevent someone from owning multiple estates, so wealth is more evenly distributed, and the poor have a chance to improve their circumstances.

In both democracies and oligarchies, people who don't take part in public affairs should be given equality or preference in other areas. In a democracy, this means helping the rich, and in an oligarchy, this means supporting the poor. However, the most important offices should always be filled by those best qualified for the job.

There are three important qualities that people need to have to hold the highest positions in government. First, they must be loyal to the constitution of the state. Second, they must be fully capable of handling the duties of their office. Third, they must have the kind of virtue and sense of justice that fit the type of state they are serving. Justice doesn't look the same in every state, so it's clear that there are different kinds of justice depending on the state.

But what if all these qualities don't exist in the same person? How should we choose? For example, suppose one person is a skilled military leader but has poor morals and doesn't support the constitution. Another person is just and loyal to the constitution but lacks military skill. Which one should we choose? In these cases, we should look at which qualities are rarer and more valuable. For a general, courage might be more important than virtue, since fewer people have the ability to lead an army than there are good people in general. But when it comes to managing finances or protecting the state, we should prioritize virtue because more people are capable of handling these tasks, but fewer have the necessary level of virtue.

Some might ask if a person has the ability to do their job and supports the constitution, why is it necessary for them to be virtuous? Wouldn't these two qualities be enough to make them useful to the state? The answer is no, because people who are knowledgeable and loyal often lack good judgment. Just like some people neglect their own affairs even though they understand them and love themselves, they might treat the state's business the same way.

In short, everything that the laws say is good for the state helps to preserve it, but the most important thing is to have more people who want to keep the government intact than those who wish to overthrow it. One key thing that many governments, which are now corrupt, forget is to maintain a balance. Many things that seem helpful to a democracy can actually destroy it, and the same goes for an oligarchy. People often take one idea too far. It's like a nose that's only slightly crooked can still be beautiful, but if it becomes too crooked or too flat, it stops looking like a proper nose. In the same way, an oligarchy or democracy can stray a little from its perfect form and still work well, but if it is taken to an extreme, the government becomes worse, and eventually, it might not even be a government at all.

The lawmaker and the politician need to understand what preserves and what destroys both democracies and oligarchies. Neither type of government can exist without both rich and poor people. If complete equality is forced on everyone, the government will change into something else. So, when laws that allow for inequality in wealth are destroyed, the government itself is destroyed. It's also a mistake in democracies for leaders to make the common people more powerful than the law, which divides the city into two opposing sides: the rich and the poor. Instead, leaders should encourage harmony between the classes. In oligarchies, it's wrong to support those in power when they are in conflict with the people.

The oaths taken in oligarchies should also change. In some places, people swear, "I will oppose the common people and do everything I can against them." Instead, they should swear not to harm the people.

Out of everything I've mentioned, the most important thing to preserve the state is something that is often ignored: educating children for the sake of the state. No law, no matter how wise or approved by political leaders, will work unless citizens are raised with the values of the constitution. If the government is a democracy, children should be educated for a democracy. If it's an oligarchy, they should be taught accordingly. If individual people have bad morals, the whole city will, too. But this education shouldn't cater to the desires of those in power, whether in an oligarchy or democracy. It should prepare them to lead in either type of government. Currently, in oligarchies, the children of the wealthy are raised too softly, and the children of the poor are raised too tough, with lots of physical labor. This makes both groups eager and able to cause political changes.

In pure democracies, they often act in ways that are against their own best interests because they misunderstand freedom. There are two main ideas in a democracy: first, that the people should have the most power, and second, that everyone should enjoy freedom. But they make the mistake of thinking that freedom means everyone can do whatever they want. In this kind of democracy, people think they should be able to live however they choose, as Euripides said, "according to their own desire." But this is wrong. People shouldn't see living under the government as slavery, but as protection.

I've explained the causes of corruption in different types of states and how they can be preserved.

Now, we'll talk about monarchies, how they fall apart, and how they can be preserved. In many ways, the things I've already said about other forms of government also apply to monarchies and tyrannies. A kingdom is similar to an aristocracy, and a tyranny is like a mix of the worst parts of an oligarchy and a democracy. This makes tyranny the worst form of government because it combines all the flaws of both oligarchy and democracy.

These two forms of monarchy, kingdoms and tyrannies, come from opposite ideas. A kingdom is meant to protect the best citizens from the masses. Kings are chosen either for their great virtue and noble actions or because they come from a distinguished family. A tyrant, on the other hand, is often chosen from the lowest classes because the people want someone who will stand against the elite. Most tyrants start out as demagogues, gaining favor with the people by attacking the nobles.

Some tyrannies were established after cities became large and powerful, while others were created earlier by kings who took more power than they were allowed, trying to rule as despots. Still, others came from people who were elected to important positions in the state. In the past, people sometimes chose officials for life who handled both civil and religious matters. One person was given supreme power over all the officials, and this made it easy for them to become tyrants if they wanted to. This is how Phidon of Argos and other tyrants rose to power. Phalaris and others in Ionia gained power through their roles in the state, and others, like Pansetius in Leontium, Cypselus in Corinth, Pisistratus in Athens, and Dionysius in Syracuse, came to power as demagogues.

A kingdom, as I said, is similar to an aristocracy. It is given to those who deserve it based on their virtue, family, good deeds, or power. Kings are often people who have saved their cities from slavery in war, like Codrus, or freed them from oppression, like Cyrus. Founders of cities or colonies, like the kings of Sparta, Macedon, and Molossia, also became kings.

A king's goal is to protect his people, ensuring that property owners are secure in their possessions and that citizens are free from harm. A tyrant, on the other hand, cares only for his own benefit. His main goal is pleasure, while a king's goal is virtue. A tyrant wants wealth, but a king seeks honor. Kings are guarded by citizens, while tyrants rely on foreigners for protection.

A tyranny combines all the worst features of oligarchies and democracies. Like an oligarchy, it focuses on gaining wealth, which helps the tyrant maintain his guards and live a luxurious life. A tyrant also doesn't trust the people and often disarms them to prevent rebellion. He persecutes the masses and forces them out of the city, just as an oligarchy might. Like a democracy, a tyranny fights against the nobles, either killing them or driving them into exile because they are seen as rivals.

Both kingdoms and tyrannies can fall for the same reasons that cause other types of governments to collapse. Injustice, fear, and disrespect often lead people to conspire against monarchies. Of these, disrespect is usually the strongest reason. Sometimes people plot against the ruler because they've lost their wealth or property. The end of both kingdoms and tyrannies often looks the same because monarchs have both wealth and honor, which many people want for themselves.

Some plots are aimed at killing the ruler, while others target the government itself. Personal hatred is usually the reason for plots against a ruler's life, and there are many causes for this hatred. People who are motivated by anger often don't seek power themselves but want revenge. For example, the plot against the sons of Pisistratus started because they insulted Harmodius's sister and treated Harmodius poorly. Periander, the tyrant of Ambracia, was killed because he took liberties with a boy during a drunken feast. Philip of Macedon was killed by Pausanias because Philip failed to avenge an insult Pausanias received. Amintas the Little was killed by Darda because he mocked his age. Similarly, an eunuch killed Evagoras of Cyprus in revenge for taking his son's wife.

Many rulers have been killed by those they insulted or mistreated, even when they held kingly power. For example, at Mitylene, Megacles and his friends killed the Penthelidae family because they would roam around striking people with clubs. Later, Smendes killed Penthilus for whipping him and dragging him away from his wife. Decamnichus also led the plot against Archelaus because he had been handed over to Euripides to be whipped.

Fear also causes conspiracies in monarchies, just as it does in other governments. Artabanes conspired against Xerxes because he feared punishment for hanging Darius, even though he did it on Xerxes's orders. Artabanes thought Xerxes had changed his mind and was going to pardon Darius. Some kings have been overthrown because they were despised. Sardanapalus, for example, was reportedly caught spinning wool with his wife, and his people conspired against him. Dion plotted against Dionysius the Younger because Dionysius was always drunk, and the people wanted a change.

Even a ruler's friends may conspire against him if they despise him, especially if they feel confident they won't be caught. People who think they can take over the throne also plot against rulers because they see the danger as worth the risk. Military leaders, in particular, may attempt to overthrow a king. Cyrus, for example, overthrew Astyages because he saw that Astyages's forces were weak from inactivity and that Astyages himself lived an indulgent lifestyle. Similarly, Suthes, a Thracian general, conspired against Amadocus.

Sometimes multiple reasons, like contempt and greed, drive people to conspire, as in the case of Mithridates against Ariobarzanes. Bold individuals with military honors are especially likely to lead rebellions. Their courage and strength make them ready to take on such risks.

Some people conspire against tyrants for the sake of honor and glory, rather than for wealth or power. These individuals aren't motivated by personal gain but by the desire for fame. They see taking down a tyrant as a noble act, and they want to be remembered for their bravery. Although there aren't many people like this, those who act on this principle care little for their own safety. They are willing to die for the chance to make even a small difference, as Dion did when he attacked Dionysius with just a few troops. He said that even a small victory would be enough for him, and if he died right after gaining a foothold in his country, he would still consider his death honorable.

Tyrannies can also be destroyed by powerful neighboring states. Democracies, in particular, oppose tyrannies. As Hesiod said, "a potter against a potter," meaning similar systems naturally oppose each other. This is why the Spartans overthrew so many tyrannies, and the Syracusans did the same when their state was strong. Tyrannies can be brought down from within as well, especially when people who aren't involved in the government lead a revolution. This happened to Gelon and Dionysius, who were overthrown by the people.

Two main causes lead people to conspire against tyrants: hatred and contempt. Hatred seems to be unavoidable for tyrants, but contempt is also a common cause of their downfall. Many tyrants lose power because they become lazy and weak after inheriting their position, unlike those who originally rose to power by their own strength. As a result, they become despised and vulnerable to conspiracies.

Anger often plays a role in these conspiracies. While anger is different from hatred, it can be an even stronger motivator because it doesn't rely on reason. Many rulers have been brought down because of personal insults, as was the case with the Pisistratidae and others.

In summary, the same causes that destroy pure oligarchies and extreme democracies can also destroy tyrannies because they share many of the same characteristics.

Kingdoms are rarely destroyed by external forces, which is why they tend to be more stable. However, they can still be brought down by internal problems. The two main causes of a kingdom's downfall are either when those in power cause a rebellion or when they try to turn the kingdom into a tyranny by taking more power than the law allows.

In modern times, we don't often see true kingdoms being formed, but rather monarchies and tyrannies. A true kingdom is one that people willingly submit to, giving supreme power to a ruler in times of great need. But when many people are equal, and no one stands out as being clearly better than the rest, they won't agree to be ruled. If someone takes power by force or trickery, that's a tyranny, not a kingdom.

Finally, we should talk about the causes of revolutions in hereditary kingdoms. One cause is that many rulers are naturally weak and easy to disrespect. Another is that they often act arrogantly, even though their power isn't absolute. A king's power depends on the people's willingness to obey, but a tyrant's power relies on force. These are some of the reasons why monarchies fall apart.

Monarchies are preserved in ways that are opposite to what causes their downfall. To break this down more clearly: the stability of a kingdom depends on keeping the king's power within reasonable limits. The less absolute the king's power is, the longer the government will last because the king will be less tyrannical and more on equal footing with the people. This will cause less envy and resentment from the people.

For example, the kingdom of the Molossi lasted a long time because of this balance. In Sparta, the power was divided between two kings, and moderation was introduced by Theopompus, who set up the ephors. By taking away some of the king's power, he actually extended the life of the kingdom. As he famously told his wife when she asked if he was ashamed to pass down a kingdom weaker than what he inherited, he replied, "No, I am making it last longer."

Tyrannies, on the other hand, are preserved in two completely opposite ways. One method is to delegate power among multiple people. Many tyrants have used this method, and it's said that Periander founded several of these types of governments. Another way to preserve a tyranny is to do the opposite of what preserves a healthy government. Tyrants should keep down anyone with ambition and eliminate those who refuse to submit. They should prevent people from gathering for public meals, forming clubs, or receiving education—anything that might inspire high spirits or mutual trust. Tyrants should also ensure that the people remain isolated from each other because familiarity breeds trust, which could lead to plots. To keep the people submissive, tyrants should require all strangers to be visible in public and live near the city gates, so their actions can be monitored. People who are treated like slaves rarely have noble ambitions.

In short, tyrants should mimic the practices of the Persians and other so-called "barbarians," who excel at keeping people oppressed. Tyrants should use spies to watch over everyone. For example, the Syracusans had women called potagogides who acted as spies, and Hiero would send out listeners to eavesdrop on any group discussions. This made people afraid to speak freely, and if they did, it was less likely to stay secret. Tyrants should also stir up conflict between different groups: friends against friends, commoners against nobles, and the wealthy against each other.

It's also helpful for tyrants to keep their subjects poor so they have no time or resources to organize against the government. This is why projects like the Pyramids in Egypt and the grand buildings of tyrants like the Cypselids and Pisistratids served not just as monuments but as ways to keep the people occupied and impoverished. Heavy taxes can also achieve this, as Dionysius of Syracuse did when he collected the people's wealth over five years. Tyrants should also involve their people in wars to keep them busy and dependent on their leader.

A king is supported by friends, but a tyrant can't trust anyone—not even his closest allies, since they have the greatest power to overthrow him.

A tyrant should also follow some practices seen in extreme democracies. For example, he should give great freedom to women and slaves because they are unlikely to plot against him. If treated well, women and slaves become loyal supporters of tyrants. In extreme democracies, the people also desire absolute power, which is why flatterers become important. In democracies, the demagogue flatters the people, and in a tyranny, the flatterer tells the tyrant whatever he wants to hear. Tyrants tend to surround themselves with the worst kind of people because they love to be flattered—something honorable people refuse to do. Dishonest people are also useful for carrying out evil deeds, as the saying goes, "like attracts like."

Tyrants should avoid showing favor to men of character or those who value freedom because they will naturally challenge the tyrant's authority. Instead, tyrants prefer to associate with outsiders rather than citizens, as the former are less likely to conspire against them.

These methods help tyrants maintain power, and their rule is often characterized by evil actions. However, all of these tactics can be grouped into three main goals: keeping the citizens poor and submissive, ensuring they don't trust each other, and leaving them powerless. If a tyrant can achieve these three things, his rule will be secure.

There is also another way to maintain a tyranny, which is the opposite of everything mentioned above. This method involves making the government appear more like a kingdom, while still maintaining the tyrant's absolute power. The key is to make the people think they are being ruled by a just and fair king while keeping the necessary force to maintain control. The tyrant should seem focused on public welfare and avoid spending money in ways that anger the people. He should keep careful records of income and spending, like some tyrants already do, so that he appears more like a responsible family head than a greedy ruler. The people should believe that taxes and services are collected for the good of the state, not for the tyrant's personal gain.

A tyrant should also avoid appearing harsh. He should aim to inspire respect rather than fear, and if possible, develop some political skills so his people see him as capable. He should avoid any actions that might offend others' sense of decency and should never allow those around him to act arrogantly. Many tyrants have been brought down by the haughty behavior of their wives and family members.

In terms of personal behavior, a tyrant should avoid indulging in excessive pleasures and showing off his luxuries. Instead, he should appear moderate and disciplined. People are less likely to plot against someone they see as responsible and sober rather than lazy and indulgent.

A tyrant should also make improvements to the city, so he seems more like a protector than an oppressor. Additionally, he should be seen as especially pious, which will make people less likely to believe he would commit unlawful acts. If the people think their leader is religious and respectful of the gods, they will be less inclined to criticize or rebel against him. However, this show of piety must be genuine to avoid suspicion of hypocrisy.

It's also important for a tyrant to honor and reward people of merit so that they don't believe they could be treated better in a free state. Honors should come directly from the tyrant, while any criticism or punishment should be delivered by his officials. Tyrants should avoid making any one person too powerful, especially not several people at once, as they might support each other in a rebellion. If a powerful person needs to be removed from office, it should be done gradually to avoid stirring up resistance.

Tyrants should also avoid humiliating or insulting people of honor. Just as people who value money are most upset when their wealth is taken, people who value honor are most hurt when they are publicly shamed. If punishment is necessary, it should be more like a father correcting a son than a master punishing a slave. If a tyrant does cause offense, he should make up for it by offering even greater honors to that person.

Above all, tyrants should be wary of those who are willing to risk their own lives to achieve their goals. People motivated by anger or revenge are the most dangerous because they are willing to sacrifice themselves to take down the tyrant. As Heraclitus said, "It is dangerous to fight with an angry man who will buy his victory with his own life."

A city is made up of both rich and poor people, so a tyrant must ensure that both groups are treated fairly. He should not allow either group to dominate the other. If the tyrant can win over the most powerful group, he won't need to free the slaves or disarm the citizens to stay in control. The strength of that group, combined with his own forces, will make him safe from any conspiracy.

In summary, a tyrant should try to appear as much like a king as possible. He should act as a protector of the people rather than their oppressor. By doing this, he will make his rule more honorable and less hated. Not only will this gain him the loyalty of his people, but it will also make his reign last longer. At the very least, even if he cannot be fully virtuous, he should try to appear half-virtuous.

Oligarchies and tyrannies are generally the shortest-lived forms of government. The tyranny of Orthagoras and his family in Sicyon lasted longer than most because they ruled with moderation and followed the laws in many ways. Clisthenes, in particular, was a skilled general who never lost the respect of the people. He even made his government more popular by rewarding someone who ruled against him in a judgment.

Another long-lasting tyranny was that of the Cypselids in Corinth, which lasted seventy-seven years and six months. Cypselus ruled for thirty years, Periander for forty-four, and Psammetichus for three years. Cypselus managed to stay popular and ruled without the need for bodyguards. Periander, on the other hand, ruled more like a traditional tyrant, but he was an effective general.

The Pisistratids ruled Athens for about thirty-three years, although Pisistratus himself was expelled twice. His son, Hippias, ruled for eighteen years. In total, their reign lasted thirty-three years, although it wasn't continuous.

Other notable tyrannies, like those of Hiero and Gelo in Syracuse, didn't last as long. Gelo ruled for eight years, Hiero for ten, and Thrasybulus only lasted eleven months. Many other tyrannies were even shorter-lived.

We have now discussed the main causes of corruption and the ways to preserve both free states and monarchies.

In Plato's Republic, Socrates discusses the ways in which governments change, but his argument has some flaws. He doesn't specifically address what causes the best governments to change, and he only gives a general explanation that nothing stays the same forever. He argues that human nature will eventually produce bad leaders who won't accept proper education, and in this, he's probably correct. Some people simply cannot be made into good leaders, no matter how much they are taught. But why should this kind of change happen more in the best government than in any other?

Socrates also suggests that all governments will eventually transform in a predictable cycle, from one form to another. He says a well-ordered government will first change into a Spartan-style government, then into an oligarchy, then into a democracy, and finally into a tyranny. However, he doesn't explain what will happen to a tyranny or what will cause it to change. According to his logic, all governments should eventually return to their original form, creating a continuous cycle.

In reality, tyrannies often change into something else. For example, the tyranny of Myron in Syria changed into that of Clisthenes. Some tyrannies, like Antileon's in Chalcas, turned into oligarchies. Others, like Gelo's in Syracuse, changed into democracies, and still others, like Charilaus's in Sparta and in Carthage, became aristocracies. Similarly, oligarchies have sometimes turned into tyrannies. Many of the ancient tyrannies in Sicily, like those of Panaetius in Leontini, Cleander in Gela, and Anaxilaus in Rhegium, started as oligarchies.

It's also incorrect to say that governments change simply because those in power are greedy for money. In many oligarchies, making money is not allowed, and strict laws prevent it. Yet, in Carthage, which is a democracy, money-making is considered respectable, and their government has remained stable.

It's also wrong to say that oligarchies are divided into two cities, one for the rich and one for the poor. This division can happen in any state where people don't have equal wealth or character, not just in oligarchies.

Governments can change for many reasons, and while Socrates focuses on just one—people becoming poor through luxury and debt—this is only part of the story. Oligarchies can change even when the rich grow stronger than the poor or when those who are excluded from power are treated unfairly.

Though there are many types of oligarchies and democracies, Socrates only discusses each as if there is just one form.

Book 6

We have already explained the nature of the supreme council in the state, how different councils might work, and how various officials should be managed. We've also talked about the role of the courts and what kind of court system fits different types of states. Finally, we've discussed the causes of both the downfall and the preservation of governments.

Since there are many kinds of democracies, just as there are many other types of governments, it's important to look at anything we might have missed regarding each of them. We need to give each form of government the rules and structures that best suit it and are most useful for it. We also need to examine how different types of governments can be combined, because when governments combine, they can change from one form to another, like from an aristocracy to an oligarchy or from a free state to a democracy.

I mean the combinations where, for example, the decision-making part of the government works like an oligarchy, while the court system works like an aristocracy. Or maybe only the decision-making part is like an oligarchy, while the officials are chosen like in an aristocracy. Sometimes, not every part of the government is organized according to the overall nature of that state. But first, we'll consider what kind of democracy fits a particular city and what kind of oligarchy fits a particular people. We'll also look at what's beneficial for other types of states. We need to show clearly which government is best for a particular state and how it should be established. We will also cover these topics briefly.

First, let's talk about democracy. This will help us understand its opposite, oligarchy. As we do this, we need to look closely at all the parts that make up a democracy and the things connected to it. The way these parts are combined creates different types of democracies, and that's why there are more than one kind, each with its own nature.

There are two main reasons why democracies come in different forms. The first is because the people themselves are different. In one country, most people are farmers, while in another, they might be mechanics or hired workers. If a country has both farmers and hired workers, their democracy will not only be better or worse, but also different in how it operates. The second reason we'll talk about now. The different elements connected to democracies, when combined, make one democracy different from another. Sometimes only a few elements are involved, sometimes many, and this affects how the government functions.

Anyone who wants to build a government they approve of or improve one that already exists needs to understand all these details. Most founders of states try to fit as many similar elements into their government plan as possible, but they often make mistakes, as I explained earlier when discussing how governments are preserved and destroyed. Now I'll explain the key principles and practices that every democracy needs.

The foundation of a democratic state is liberty, and people often say that only in democracy can true liberty be found. They believe liberty is the main goal of every democracy. One part of liberty is taking turns ruling and being ruled. According to democratic justice, equality is based on numbers, not on merit. Since this is seen as fair, it means the people, as a whole, should have the highest power, and what the majority decides should be final. So in a democracy, the poor should have more power than the rich because they are the majority. This is one key idea of liberty that all designers of democracies believe in.

Another is the idea that everyone should live as they like because they see this as a right that comes from liberty. They say someone who can't live as they want is like a slave. This is another basic principle of democracy. It also leads to the belief that no one should be forced to obey anyone else, except in turn, just as that person must obey when it's their turn to do so. This supports the idea of equality that liberty requires.

Since this is how the government is set up, certain rules must be followed. First, all officials should be chosen from all the people, and everyone should take turns ruling. Most officials should be chosen by lottery, except for roles that require special skills or knowledge. There shouldn't be a property requirement to hold office, or if there is, it should be very small. No one should hold the same job more than once, or only very rarely, except in the military. Most appointments should be for short terms, or as many as possible should be. The whole population should be able to judge legal cases, whether they are public issues or private contracts. For example, in Athens, the people judge officials when they finish their term and also decide on both public and private matters. The highest authority should be the public assembly, and no official should have much personal power, except in very limited and unimportant cases.

A senate is best suited to a democracy, where the whole population isn't paid for attending meetings. Without pay, the people will bring all cases before the senate, as we discussed before. If possible, there should be a fund to pay everyone who has a role in public affairs, whether in the assembly, the courts, or as officials. If that's not possible, then at least the officials, judges, senators, and assembly members should be paid, as well as those required to eat at a common table.

Just as an oligarchy is said to be a government of the wealthy and well-educated, democracy is a government run by people without high birth, wealth, or special skills. In a democracy, no office should be held for life. If any such offices remain after the government has changed to a democracy, their power should be gradually reduced, and officials should be chosen by lottery rather than election.

These ideas apply to all democracies. The key principle of democracy is that the number of people should determine equality. This is what defines a government run by the people. The rich should not have more of a say in government than the poor, and the government should not be controlled only by the wealthy. Everyone should be equal based on the number of people, as this is seen as the best way to preserve equality and liberty in the state.

Next, we need to figure out how this equality can be achieved. Should we divide the population so that 500 rich people have the same power as 1,000 poor people? Or should the 1,000 poor have the same power as the 500 rich? Or should we not do it this way? Instead, we could take an equal number from both groups to choose officials and judges. Would this be true democratic justice, or would it only reflect the rule of numbers? Those who defend democracy say that whatever the majority agrees on is fair, while supporters of oligarchy argue that the opinion of the wealthiest is what matters. They believe the government should be guided by property value.

Both views are unjust. If we follow the idea of the wealthiest, we risk creating a tyranny, because if one person happens to be richer than everyone else, then, by oligarchic logic, he should have all the power. On the other hand, if the majority's opinion always prevails, it would be unfair to the rich, since they are fewer in number, as I've already said.

To find a fair solution that both sides can agree on, we need to start with a definition of justice that works for both sides. They both agree that what most people in the state support should be established as law. But this rule should not apply fully. Since a city is made up of two groups—rich and poor—the laws should be approved by both groups, or at least by a majority from both. If they disagree, then the decision should be based on the side with the higher total wealth. For example, if there are 10 rich people and 20 poor people, and 6 of the rich and 15 of the poor agree on something, while the remaining 4 rich and 5 poor oppose it, the group with the higher total wealth should have their way. If the wealth is equal on both sides, it should be treated like a tie in a court case, where the decision is made by lot or some other method.

Even though it's hard to define exactly what's fair and just, it's easier to understand than to convince those in power to follow these principles. The weak always want equality and fairness, but the strong often ignore these ideals.

There are four kinds of democracies. The best is the one made up of people like farmers, which is also the oldest type. I call this the first kind because most people would place it first when dividing the population. The best part of this group is made up of farmers. A democracy can be formed where most people are farmers or herders, because they don't have much property and are too busy working to constantly hold public meetings. They'll spend their time on their work, not on political offices, which don't offer much reward. Most people prefer wealth to honor.

This is shown by how people in the past and even now have accepted tyrannies or oligarchies, as long as they aren't disturbed in their daily work or deprived of their property. Some of them become rich quickly, while others escape poverty. The right to vote and hold officials accountable when they finish their term will satisfy their desire for honor if they have any. In some states, even though the common people don't elect the officials, they are represented by a part of the assembly. It's enough for the people to have the power to make decisions. This should be considered a form of democracy, as it was in the past at Mantinea.

In this type of democracy, people should have the power to criticize their officials when they leave office and to make decisions on legal cases. The top officials should be elected, either based on property or skill, depending on the role. A state like this will be well-run because the best people will hold office with the approval of the people, who won't envy them. The wealthy and powerful will be satisfied because they aren't being ruled by their inferiors. They will also be careful with their power because others can hold them accountable. It benefits the state for officials to answer to others and not have total freedom to do whatever they want. Without limits, people would abuse their power.

It's clear that this is the best type of democracy because the people have the right amount of power. To create a democracy of farmers, it's helpful to have laws that limit how much land anyone can own or how close it can be to the city. In some ancient states, no one was allowed to sell their original land. There's also a law by Oxylus that forbids people from increasing their wealth through loans. We should also look at the laws of the Aphytaians, who had little land but a large population of farmers. They divided their land in a way that gave more power to the poor than the rich.

Next to farmers, the best group for a democracy is herders, as they are similar to farmers in many ways and make strong soldiers because of their lifestyle. The worst kind of people for a democracy are those who live in poverty and have no connection to virtue in their work.

These are the mechanics, tradesmen, and hired laborers. They spend their time in the city, making it easy for them to attend public meetings, while farmers, who live in the country, have a harder time getting there and are less interested in going.

In countries where much of the land is far from the city, it's easier to establish a good democracy or free state because most people will live in the country. In these democracies, even though there may be many people near the city center, no official meeting should be held without the country people present. We've explained how the first and best democracy should be set up, and this will serve as a guide for other types of democracies. In each case, the lowest class should be kept separate from the rest.

The worst kind of democracy is the one that gives every citizen a share in every part of the government. Few people can handle this kind of democracy, and it's hard to keep it stable for long unless it's well-supported by laws and customs. We've already talked about almost every cause that can destroy this type of government or any other.

Leaders of this kind of democracy try to keep it going by gathering as many people as they can and giving them citizenship, even to those born outside the city. This method works well for this kind of government, and it's what demagogues typically do. However, they should stop once the common people become more powerful than the nobles and middle class, because if they go further, the state will become disorderly. The nobles won't tolerate the power of the common people and will resent it, as happened in Cyrene. Small problems can be ignored, but when they grow large, they are harder to miss.

It's also helpful in this type of democracy to do what Clisthenes did in Athens when he wanted to increase the people's power, or what was done in Cyrene to establish democracy. This involves creating many tribes and brotherhoods, reducing private religious ceremonies, and making religious practices more public. Every effort should be made to blend the people together and break old customs.

Many things that are done in a tyranny are also useful in this type of democracy. For example, the freedom of slaves, women, and children to act as they please is useful to a certain extent. In this type of government, it's also common to let people live however they want. Many people will support such a system because it's more appealing to live without rules than to live under strict control.

It is also the job of lawmakers and those who support this kind of government not to make it overly ambitious or too perfect. Instead, they should aim for stability. Even if a state is poorly designed, it can still survive for a short while. Therefore, they should focus on preserving it through the methods we've already discussed, explaining the causes of how governments last or fall. They should avoid harmful things and create both written and unwritten laws that encourage what helps keep the state stable. They shouldn't think that what's good for a democracy or an oligarchy is making them purely one or the other, but rather what helps them last longer. However, modern demagogues, who flatter the people, cause frequent confiscations in the courts. For this reason, those who truly care about the welfare of the state should do the opposite of what these demagogues do. They should pass laws preventing forfeitures from being shared among the people or put into the treasury. Instead, these should be set aside for sacred purposes. This way, people with bad intentions will still be cautious, as the punishment would be the same, but the public wouldn't be so eager to condemn those on trial if they don't gain anything from it.

They should also ensure that the number of public trials is as few as possible, and those who bring lawsuits recklessly should be punished harshly. It's usually the nobles, not the common people, who are prosecuted. Citizens in the same state should care for one another, at the very least not treat those in power like enemies. In many of the democracies formed recently, it's hard to get people to attend public meetings unless they're paid for it. When there isn't enough public money for this, it harms the nobles. The shortfall is made up by taxes, confiscations, and fines imposed by corrupt courts, and these practices have destroyed many democracies.

So, when the state has little revenue, there should be fewer public meetings and fewer courts. However, those that exist should cover a wide range of issues but only operate for a few days. This way, the rich won't fear the cost, even if they don't get paid for attending, and the poor still receive pay. Judgments will also be fairer because the wealthy won't want to be away from their own affairs for long, but they won't mind for a short time. When there's plenty of public money, the approach should differ from what demagogues do now. Today, they distribute extra public funds to the poor. The poor take it, but soon they need more again, making it like pouring water into a leaky bucket. A true patriot in a democracy should ensure that most of the population isn't too poor, as poverty causes greed in that system. He should strive to help them enjoy lasting abundance. Since this benefits the rich too, any money saved should be set aside and then distributed to the poor in a way that helps them buy a small piece of land. If that isn't possible, at least give them enough to get the tools they need for farming or trade. If there isn't enough for everyone to receive a lot at once, it should be divided among groups or tribes.

In the meantime, the rich should pay the poor for necessary work but not be required to fund their leisure activities. This system was somewhat similar to how things were managed in Carthage, where they kept the people's loyalty by sending some of their community into colonies, which brought prosperity. It's also wise and generous for the nobility to divide the poor among themselves and give them what they need, encouraging them to work. Or, they could follow the example of the people of Tarentum, who allowed the poor to share in what they needed. This approach won over the common people. In their system, magistrates were selected in two ways: some by vote and others by lottery. The lottery allowed the people to have a role in the administration, while voting ensured good governance. The same balance can be achieved if some magistrates are chosen by vote and others by lot. This explains how democracies should be structured.

The principles discussed earlier also show how an oligarchy should be set up. To design such a state, one must consider how to oppose democracy since every type of oligarchy is based on principles that are the opposite of some form of democracy. The best type of oligarchy is the one that most closely resembles what we call a free state. In this system, there should be two different property qualifications: one high and one low. The lower class can be chosen for ordinary government offices, while the upper class provides the top officials. No one within the property qualification should be excluded from participation, and the qualifications should be set up so that the common people who meet them have more power than those who don't. People who manage public affairs should always come from the best citizens. A similar structure should be used in the second-best oligarchy. But in the worst type of oligarchy, which is closest to a dynasty or tyranny, it's much harder to maintain. As in a weak body or a leaky ship, where even small problems can cause disaster, poorly designed governments need the most care. In contrast, a well-constructed government can withstand many challenges, just as a healthy body or a well-built ship can endure more damage.

In a democracy, the number of citizens helps preserve it, as they balance the privileges based on wealth or rank. But in an oligarchy, preservation comes from regulating the various classes within society.

Most communities are made up of four types of people: farmers, craftsmen, merchants, and laborers. Those who serve in war are also divided into four groups: horsemen, heavily-armed soldiers, lightly-armed soldiers, and sailors. When a region can support many horsemen, a strong oligarchy can easily be formed, as the safety of the people depends on that force. Only those with considerable wealth can afford to maintain horses. In places where heavily-armed troops are more common, a less powerful oligarchy can be established since these soldiers tend to be wealthier but not necessarily rich. On the other hand, lightly-armed soldiers and sailors support democracy. When these groups are numerous and a conflict breaks out, the other parts of society are at a disadvantage. A solution to this problem can be learned from experienced military leaders, who always mix light troops with horsemen and heavily-armed soldiers. It's with these forces that the common people gain an advantage over the wealthy in an uprising. Lighter troops are more agile and can hold their own against horsemen and heavily-armed soldiers. If an oligarchy recruits soldiers from these groups, it's preparing for its own downfall.

Since cities consist of people of different ages, both young and old, fathers should teach their sons easy, light exercises while they are young. When the sons grow up, they should become skilled in all military exercises. Allowing the people to participate in the government should either be based on a property qualification, as mentioned earlier, or, like in Thebes, by allowing those who have stopped working in a trade for a certain period to take part, or as in Massalia, by selecting them based on merit, whether they are citizens or foreigners.

The duties of the highest-ranking officials in a state should be clearly defined to prevent the common people from wanting their jobs. When the people know what the officials have to do, they will respect them. These officials should also perform public sacrifices and build monuments to serve the state. When the people see the city adorned with these public gifts and structures, they will appreciate the stability of the government. Additionally, the generosity of the nobles will be remembered. Unfortunately, this is not the approach taken by those in power in modern oligarchies. Instead, they seek profit more than honor, which is why these oligarchies could more accurately be called small democracies.

We've now explained how democracies and oligarchies should be structured.

Next, we'll discuss the magistrates—what kind they should be, how many are needed, and their purposes. No state can exist without necessary magistrates, and it can't be happy without those who contribute to its dignity and order. Small states need only a few magistrates, while large states need more. It's also important to understand which offices can be combined and which should remain separate. First, proper officials must be appointed to oversee the markets. A magistrate should be responsible for ensuring good order in the markets since cities rely on both buyers and sellers to meet their needs. This is one of the main contributors to a comfortable life, which is why people form communities.

A second duty, closely related to the first, is to oversee both public and private buildings to ensure they are well-maintained and safe. These officials should ensure buildings don't collapse and that roads are in good condition. They should also protect property boundaries to prevent disputes. In larger cities, these responsibilities may be divided among different officials, with one overseeing buildings, another responsible for fountains, and a third in charge of harbors. These officials are called city inspectors.

A third task, similar to the previous one but dealing with rural areas, is to ensure proper care of the countryside. Officials responsible for this are called land or forest inspectors. Despite their different titles, their duties are the same as those of city inspectors.

There must also be officials in charge of managing public revenue and distributing it to various departments within the state. These officials are called treasurers or receivers. Another official is needed to record private contracts, court judgments, and legal declarations. This task is sometimes divided among many officials, but one person usually oversees them all. These officials are called clerks or secretaries.

Another vital, though unpleasant, office is that of the official responsible for enforcing judgments, collecting fines, and overseeing prisoners. This role is difficult and often unpopular, so people are usually unwilling to take it on unless it's made profitable. Even then, they may not carry out their duties properly. However, it's essential because passing judgment is pointless unless it's enforced. Without enforcement, human society couldn't function. For this reason, it's best if this office isn't handled by a single person but by several magistrates from different courts. Similarly, the collection of fines ordered by judges should be divided among different officials.

As different magistrates handle different cases, younger officials should handle cases involving young people. For cases that have already gone to trial, one person should pass judgment, and another should enforce it. For example, officials overseeing public buildings could enforce the judgments made by market inspectors. By dividing these duties, the officials responsible for enforcing laws will face less public anger, making it easier to carry out their duties. If the same person both passes and enforces judgments, they'll become widely hated, and if they handle all cases, they'll be seen as enemies of the people.

In some cases, one official holds the prisoner, while another carries out the sentence, as was done by the Eleven in Athens. It's wise to separate these roles and give them as much attention as anything else we've discussed. People of good character may avoid this job, while untrustworthy people can't be trusted with it, as they may need to be guarded themselves. Therefore, this office should never be separate from others, nor should it be continuously assigned to the same individuals. Instead, it should be taken on by young men as part of their civic duties.

These are the most necessary magistrates. Next, we have other essential officials of higher rank who must be skilled and trustworthy. These officials are responsible for the city's defense and must ensure the walls and gates are secure. They must also organize and train citizens for both war and peace. Some cities have many officials overseeing this, while smaller cities may only have one, called a general or polemarch. In larger cities, where there are horsemen, lightly-armed troops, archers, and sailors, separate commanders are often appointed for each group, with others serving under them. All of these officials work together to form one military body.

Because many magistrates deal with public money, there must be officials whose sole job is to audit them and correct any mismanagement. Additionally, there is often one official who is in charge of all the others. This person may control public revenue and taxes, preside over the people when they hold the supreme power, and summon the assembly. Sometimes this role is held by a group of officials called preadvisers, but when there are many, they're more accurately called a council.

These are the main civil magistrates required in a government, but there are also officials responsible for religious matters, such as priests and those who oversee the temples, ensuring they're maintained or rebuilt if they fall into disrepair. In some cities, this responsibility is given to one person, while in others, it's divided among many officials distinct from the priests. These officials are in charge of public worship and the sacred revenue. There are also officials responsible for overseeing public sacrifices to the state's protective gods, a task not always assigned to priests. Different states use different names for these officials.

To sum up, the various magistrates handle matters related to religion, war, taxes, expenditures, markets, public buildings, harbors, highways, and courts. There are also clerks who record private contracts and guards to watch over prisoners. Other officials ensure that the laws are enforced and advise the courts.

In especially fortunate states that have the leisure to focus on finer details and are dedicated to good order, there are even more specialized magistrates. For example, some officials oversee women, ensuring they follow the laws, while others are responsible for boys and their education. Other officials manage gymnastic exercises, theaters, and public spectacles. However, not all of these offices are necessary in every state. For example, poorer states can't afford officials to manage women since the wives and children of the poor must work, as they can't afford slaves.

Some states have three main officials with supreme power: guardians of the laws, preadvisers, and senators. Guardians of the laws are best suited for aristocracies, preadvisers for oligarchies, and senators for democracies. This concludes our discussion of magistrates.

Book 7

Whoever wants to figure out what the best government is should first understand what kind of life is the best to live. If this remains unclear, it will also be unclear which government is best. It's likely that, as long as no unexpected events happen, those who live under the best government will live the happiest lives, given their circumstances. So, we need to first figure out what kind of life is most desirable for everyone. After that, we should ask whether this best life is the same for both the individual and the citizen or if it's different. I believe I've already explained well enough what sort of life is best in my popular talks on this subject, so I think it's appropriate to repeat it here. No one has ever questioned one important point: that what is good for a person can be divided into three types—external goods, those that benefit the body, and those that benefit the soul. It's clear that all of these things must come together to make someone truly happy. No one would say that a person is happy if they lack courage, self-control, justice, or wisdom. It wouldn't make sense to say someone is happy if they're afraid of flies, would steal the smallest thing if hungry or thirsty, or would even kill a dear friend for a small amount of money. It also wouldn't make sense to say that a person is happy if they're as confused as a baby or fool. These points are so obvious that everyone agrees with them, even though people may argue over how much and what kind of virtue is necessary for happiness. Some believe that only a little virtue is enough, but when it comes to things like wealth, property, power, and honor, they try to increase them without limit. To them, we reply that it's easy to prove, based on what we learn from experience, that external goods do not create virtue, but rather, virtue helps to bring about external goods.

Now, as for whether a happy life is found in pleasure, virtue, or a combination of both, it's clear that those who are most moral and have well-trained minds enjoy more happiness, even if they aren't extremely wealthy. In fact, they are happier than those who are rich but lack morality and wisdom. Anyone who thinks carefully can see this for themselves because everything external has a limit, just like a machine. Any external good in excess can either be harmful or, at best, useless to the person who has it. But every good quality of the soul becomes even more valuable the more it is developed, if we may use the word "useful" in the same sense as "noble" when describing these qualities. It's also clear that different things bring about different kinds of outcomes, depending on how valuable they are. So, if the soul is nobler than any external possession, like the body, both in itself and in relation to us, then it follows that the best qualities of the soul are also the most valuable. Besides, it's for the sake of the soul that these other things are desirable, not the other way around. Wise people should desire external things for the sake of the soul, not desire the soul for the sake of external things. Therefore, we can be sure that the more virtue and wisdom a person has, the more happiness they will experience by living according to these virtues. We have an example of this in God, who is perfectly happy, not because of anything external but because of His own nature. Good luck, or fortune, is different from happiness because anything that isn't based on the mind comes from chance or luck. But wisdom and justice don't come from luck. This means that the city with the best government is the happiest one because it acts in the best way. No one can act well without being virtuous, and no city can do anything praiseworthy without virtue and wisdom. Whatever is just, wise, or prudent for an individual is the same for a city.

This is just an introduction, as I felt it was necessary to touch on this topic briefly, though I can't fully examine it here because it relates more to another question. For now, let's assume this: that the happiest life for a person, both as an individual and as a citizen, is a life of virtue, accompanied by the benefits that usually come with virtue. If there are those who aren't convinced by what I've said, their doubts will be addressed later. For now, let's move forward with our plan.

Now, we need to ask whether the happiness of a person and that of a city are the same or different. But this is clear enough. Anyone who believes that wealth makes a person happy must also believe that a wealthy city is the happiest. Those who think that having power over others brings happiness will think that the happiest city is the one that rules over many others. In the same way, if someone praises a person for their virtue, they will think the most virtuous city is the happiest. There are two things we need to consider here. The first is whether it's better to be a member of a community and have the rights of a citizen or to live as an outsider who doesn't get involved in public affairs. The second is what form of government is best and how the state should be organized. Should everyone have a role in governing, or just the majority, or only a few? This is a political question, and it's not directly related to the individual. The second point is the focus of my current discussion. It's clear that the best government is the one that allows everyone to act virtuously and live happily. However, some people who agree that a life of virtue is best still wonder whether an active public life or a private life of contemplation is better. Some believe that a life of contemplation is the only life suitable for a philosopher. Throughout history, the most virtuous men have chosen one of these two ways of life—either the public or the philosophical. This question is important because a wise person will naturally lean toward the better choice, both as an individual and as a citizen. Some argue that ruling over others is the greatest injustice, while others believe that political rule is not unjust but is a burden on the pleasures and peace of life. Others have the opposite view and think that a public and active life is the only life worth living. They believe that private citizens have no chance to practice virtue compared to those engaged in public affairs.

These are their beliefs. Some even argue that tyrannical and despotic governments are the only ones that bring happiness. Even among some free states, the goal of their laws seems to be to dominate their neighbors. In fact, many political systems, wherever they may be, seem to have one common goal: to conquer and rule. We see this in the laws of the Spartans and Cretans and in the way they trained their children. Their goal was to make them soldiers. Across many nations, those who have enough power to enslave others are honored because of it. This was true for the Scythians, Persians, Thracians, and Gauls. Some nations even have laws to encourage bravery. For instance, in Carthage, people could wear rings to show how many military campaigns they had participated in. In Macedonia, a man who hadn't killed an enemy had to wear a rope around his neck. Among the Scythians, during festivals, only those who had killed an enemy could drink from a special cup that was passed around. Among the Iberians, a warlike people, they put up as many pillars on a man's tomb as the number of enemies he had killed. Different nations have different customs like these, some of which are established by law and others by tradition.

It may seem absurd to some people to ask whether it's the job of a legislator to teach a state how to rule over or enslave its neighbors, whether the neighbors want this or not. How could this be the task of a politician or a legislator when it's unlawful? Something can't be lawful if it can be done both justly and unjustly because some conquests are made unjustly. In the arts, we see nothing like this. For example, a doctor or a captain of a ship doesn't use force or persuasion to get people to follow their orders. Still, many people think a despotic government is a political one. They would never allow such a government to rule over them but wouldn't hesitate to rule over others this way. They want to be governed wisely themselves but don't care if others are. However, despotic power is only justified when nature has made one group of people to rule and another to be ruled. No one should try to rule over everyone, but only over those who are meant to be ruled. Just as no one hunts people for food or sacrifice, but only wild animals that are suitable for those purposes.

Now, a city that is well-governed can be happy by itself, even if it has no contact with other states, as long as it has a good system of laws. Even if its government isn't focused on war or conquest, it wouldn't need these things. It's clear that war is only praiseworthy as a means to an end, not as an end in itself. A good legislator must carefully study their state and the nature of the people to see how they can enjoy all the aspects of a good life and the happiness that comes with it. In this respect, some laws and customs are better than others. A legislator must also think about how to deal with neighboring states, whether to resist them or offer them help.

Now, we will address those who, while agreeing that a life of virtue is best, disagree on how to live it. We speak to both sides. Some believe that all political governments are bad and that the best life is one of complete freedom, outside of citizenship. Others think the life of a citizen is the best, and that happiness comes from virtuous activity. Both groups are partly right and partly wrong. They are right in saying that the life of a free person is better than that of a slave because a slave has no honorable work. The tasks they are ordered to do have no virtue in them. However, it's wrong to say that living under any government is the same as slavery. The government of free people is as different from the government of slaves as slavery is from freedom itself, which I've already discussed.

It's also wrong to think that doing nothing is better than being active in virtuous deeds. Happiness comes from action, and many noble things come from the actions of the just and wise. Based on what we've discussed, someone might believe that the greatest good is having supreme power because that allows a person to demand many useful services from others. Therefore, such a person might think they should not give up that power but instead should seize it. They might even believe that, for this reason, a father should have no concern for his son, or a son for his father, or a friend for a friend because the best thing is the most desirable. But the best life is to be a part of the community and share in its happiness.

What these people argue might seem true if the supreme good really did belong to those who use violence to get it. But this is highly unlikely. Just because someone gains power over others doesn't mean their actions are honorable, unless they are naturally as superior to others as a man is to a woman, a father is to a child, or a master is to a slave. Once someone abandons the path of virtue, they cannot easily return to it. Among equals, what is fair and just should be mutual. This is what equality is. It's not right for equals to not receive equal treatment, nor for similar people to not be treated in a similar way. Whatever is contrary to nature is not right. Therefore, if one person in a community is superior in virtue and ability to others, then it is right for everyone to follow and obey that person. But even that person cannot lead alone; they need others to help.

If we are correct in what we've said so far, then happiness comes from virtuous activity. Both for the community and the individual, the most active life is the happiest. However, being active doesn't necessarily mean interacting with others, as some people think. Not all practical activities are about teaching others what to do. The most practical activities are often the ones that improve a person's own judgment and understanding. Virtuous activity has a goal, so it is practical. In fact, those who create the plans that others follow are said to act more than those who carry out the plans. They are superior to the workers who execute their designs. Even cities that choose not to engage with other states don't have to remain inactive. The members of those cities can interact with each other. The same is true for individuals. Otherwise, neither God nor the universe could be perfect because neither of them relies on anything external. Therefore, it is clear that the same life that brings happiness to an individual also brings happiness to the state and its members.

Now that I've finished introducing the topic and talked about different kinds of states, I'll start by saying what a city should be like if we could design it exactly how we wanted. No good state can exist without having just the right amount of what's needed. Many things are worth aiming for, but none of them should be impossible. I'm talking about the number of citizens and the size of the land. Just like a weaver or a shipbuilder needs the right materials for their work, because the better the materials, the better the final product, the same is true for the lawmaker and politician. They must aim to get the right people for the job. The first and most important tool for a politician is the number of people. They need to know how many people there should be and what kind of people they should be. They also need to know how big the land is and what kind of land it is.

Most people think a city needs to be big to be happy. But if this is true, they don't know what makes a city large or small. They often judge by the number of people living there, but they should be looking at its strength instead. A state has a goal, and its size should be measured by how well it can reach that goal, not by the number of its inhabitants. It's like saying that a great doctor like Hippocrates is better, even if he isn't a larger person, than someone bigger but less skilled. If we're going to measure a city's strength by its population, we shouldn't just count everyone living there. Cities often have many slaves, visitors, and foreigners. The real strength of a city comes from the people who are truly part of it—those who are citizens. A large number of these citizens proves that a city is large. However, a city filled with many craftsmen and few soldiers cannot be truly great, because the greatness of a city isn't about numbers but about the kind of people living in it.

This is also clear from experience. It's hard, if not impossible, to properly govern a very large number of people. In fact, in all the well-governed states, we don't find any where the rights of citizenship are given to just anyone. This makes sense because, just like the law brings order, good laws bring good order. A huge number of people can't be governed easily, unless by some divine power that rules the universe. It's true that having a certain size is important for beauty, and a city's perfection includes being large as long as it can still maintain that order.

But everything, whether animals, plants, or machines, has a proper size. When they are either too small or too large, they don't work as they should. A ship that's too short isn't really a ship, and neither is one that's too long. In both cases, it's useless. The same goes for a city. One that's too small can't defend itself, which is essential for a city. One that's too large can defend itself, but then it's a nation, not a city. It would be hard to govern such a large group. Who would want to lead such a massive crowd or speak to them without having a voice as loud as a herald like Stentor?

The first thing a city needs is a population large enough for the people to live happily in their political community. If the population grows beyond what's needed, the city can still grow, but this growth must have a limit. What that limit is will be clear from experience, and this experience comes from both the rulers and the citizens. Since it's the job of the rulers to guide the lower officials and to judge fairly, they can't make good decisions or give proper orders unless they know the character of their fellow citizens. If they don't know them well, they won't be able to manage the city well, and things will fall apart. Rulers need to avoid making hasty decisions without proper knowledge, and this will certainly happen if there are too many citizens to know personally. In addition, it will be easier for outsiders to pretend to be citizens and go unnoticed in such a large crowd.

So, it's clear that the best size for a city is one where the population is large enough to be self-sufficient but not too large to be properly governed by the leaders. This is how we should decide the size of a city.

What I've said about a city also applies to the land. The land should be enough to make the people happy, meaning it should provide them with everything they need for life. If they have all they need in abundance, they will be content. As for how large the land should be, it should be enough for the people to live comfortably with freedom and self-control. Whether I've set the right limit for the land is something we will discuss later when we talk about property and how much wealth a person needs to live well. We'll also consider how they should use that wealth. There are many disagreements on this topic, as some believe life should be strict while others believe it should be more indulgent.

Deciding the location of the land isn't hard. We should take advice from military experts for some of the details. The land should be difficult for enemies to reach but easy for the people to access. Just as I said the population should be small enough to be manageable by the rulers, the land should also be manageable so it can be easily defended.

If we could place a city wherever we wanted, it would be useful to place it near the sea. The land should be positioned in a way that it can easily support itself and receive supplies from other areas, like food, wood, and other materials the country might need.

There are some who question whether placing a city near the sea is good or bad for a well-run state. They argue that bringing in people from different backgrounds could harm the state by interfering with the laws and overwhelming the population. A large number of merchants would come and go, and this could make governing harder. But if this problem doesn't arise, then it's clear that being near the sea is better, both for safety and for making it easier to get the necessities of life. It's important for a city to be able to defend itself from enemies, both by land and sea. If possible, it should be able to defend itself in both ways, but if not, it should at least be strong where it has the most power. Being near the sea is also helpful for trading with other places when the land doesn't provide enough or has an excess of certain goods. However, a city should trade only to meet its own needs, not to supply the needs of others. Cities that open markets to everyone do so for profit, but this isn't the right approach for a well-ordered state. They shouldn't encourage this kind of trade.

In many places, cities have docks and harbors that are convenient for trade but are separated from the main city by walls or other fortifications. In such cases, if the trade brings benefits, the city will get them, but if it causes harm, the city can control it with laws about who is allowed to trade and who isn't.

When it comes to naval power, there's no doubt that a city needs a navy to some degree. This is necessary for the city itself and also for dealing with neighboring states, either to be seen as strong or to help others by land and sea. The size of the navy should depend on the city's strength. If the city is strong and can take the lead among other states, its navy should match its ambitions.

The large population that often comes with naval power isn't essential for a state, and they shouldn't be considered citizens. The sailors and soldiers in command should be free men, and the success of a naval battle depends on them. But in places with many workers and farmers, they will always have enough sailors, as we see in some states today, like Heraclea, where they man many ships, even though the city is smaller than others. This is what we should decide about the land, ports, city, sea, and naval power. As for the number of citizens, we've already discussed what it should be.

Next, we need to consider the natural qualities of the citizens. This can be seen by looking at the most well-known Greek states and other nations in the world. People in cold northern regions, like Europe, are brave but lack intelligence and the arts. Because of this, they fiercely protect their freedom, but they aren't skilled enough to conquer their neighbors. On the other hand, the people of Asia are clever and skilled in the arts, but they lack bravery, which is why they are often conquered and enslaved. The Greeks, being in the middle of these two groups, have both bravery and intelligence. This is why Greece remains free and is governed in the best way possible. If they could agree on a single system of government, they could rule the world.

This is the main difference between the Greeks and other nations. The Greeks combine both qualities, while others only have one. So, it's clear that people need to have both intelligence and bravery to follow a lawmaker whose goal is virtue. Some people say that soldiers should be gentle with people they know and harsh with strangers, but bravery is what makes a person admirable. It's the quality of the soul that we respect the most. We get angrier at friends who wrong us than at strangers, and that's why Archilaus said to himself, "Shall my friends insult me?"

The spirit of freedom and leadership comes from this type of character because courage is commanding and unbeatable. It's wrong to say we should be harsh to strangers because that's not appropriate for anyone. Those with noble character are not usually harsh, except with wicked people. When they are harsh, it's often towards friends who have wronged them. This makes sense because, when you expect a favor from someone and don't get it, you not only feel wronged but also feel the loss of what you were expecting. That's why people say, "Brothers' wars are the worst," and "Those who once loved deeply now hate deeply."

We have now mostly decided how many citizens a city should have, what their character should be, and how large and what kind of land they need. I say "mostly" because there's no need to be as exact in these matters as we would be with things that are studied by reason alone.

Just like in living bodies, where nothing is considered a part unless the whole wouldn't exist without it, it's clear that in a political state, not everything necessary to it is a part of it. Similarly, not every other group that helps make a whole can be seen as part of it. Something should be common to the community, whether shared equally or unequally, like food, land, or similar things. But when something benefits one person and not another, there's no real sense of community, except for the fact that one makes it and the other uses it. This is like the relationship between a tool and the worker who uses it. There's nothing shared between a house and the builder except the skill the builder uses to work on the house.

So, while property is necessary for states, it isn't a part of the state itself, though many types of property are alive. A city is a community of equals that aims to live the best life possible. The best and happiest life is one that involves practicing virtues perfectly. Since some people have more or fewer opportunities to engage in these virtues, this creates differences between various cities and communities. Each of them tries to achieve the best life through different means, leading to different lifestyles and forms of government.

We need to consider what things are absolutely necessary for a city to exist. We can figure this out by knowing how many things a city needs. First, the people need food. Second, they need tools because many things are required for life. Third, they need weapons to defend themselves both against their own members who might rebel and against outside enemies who might attack. Fourth, they need a source of income for the state's internal needs and for war. Fifth, and most importantly, they need religious institutions. Sixth, they need a court system to judge criminal and civil cases.

These are the things that are essential for every state. A city isn't just a random group of people coming together; they come together to secure their independence and protect themselves. Without these necessities, the city can't achieve those goals. It's essential that a city can acquire all these things. For this, it needs enough farmers to provide food, workers to make tools, soldiers to defend the state, wealthy citizens, priests, and judges to decide what's right and wrong.

Now that we've figured this out, we need to decide whether all of these different jobs should be open to everyone or if we should assign them to different groups of people. Should some jobs be reserved for certain groups, while others are shared among everyone? Not every state handles this the same way. In some states, everything is shared, while in others, only some things are. This is the main difference between types of governments. In democracies, the entire community shares everything, but in oligarchies, it's different.

Since we are discussing the best form of government, which is the one that makes the citizens happy, and since happiness can't exist without virtue, it follows that in the best-governed states, the citizens must be truly virtuous people. In these states, no one should be allowed to work in trades or commerce, as these jobs are seen as dishonorable and harmful to virtue. Citizens also shouldn't be farmers, so they can focus on improving themselves and serving the state.

As for the roles of soldiers, senators, and judges, which are clearly necessary, should these jobs be assigned to different people, or should one person do multiple jobs? This question is easy to answer. In some cases, the same person can do different jobs, but in other cases, the jobs should go to different people if they require different skills. For example, courage is needed for one role, while judgment is needed for another. In these cases, the jobs should go to different people. But when it's clear that the people who have weapons can't be forced to always follow orders, the same person should be trusted with both roles. This is because those with weapons can decide whether they want to take power or not.

The government should be entrusted to those who have both courage and judgment, but not in the same way. Young people are better suited for roles that require courage, while older people are better suited for roles that require judgment. This way, each person is given the job they are best suited for, based on their strengths. It's also necessary for these people to own land because citizens need to be wealthy. These people are the right ones to be citizens. No tradesperson should be given the rights of citizenship, nor should anyone whose job isn't considered noble, honorable, and virtuous. This follows the principle we started with: to be happy, a person must be virtuous.

We shouldn't judge a city's happiness by looking at just one group of citizens; we must examine all of them. So, it's clear that land should belong to these citizens, though they may need farmers, either slaves, foreigners, or servants, to work the land.

Of the different groups of people we've mentioned, the priests form a separate class. They aren't counted among the farmers or tradespeople because respect for the gods is an important part of every state. Since the citizens have been divided into soldiers and council members, and since proper worship must be given to the gods, it's necessary that those who serve as priests have no other responsibilities. Let this job be given to older citizens.

We've now explained what's necessary for a city to exist, what parts it's made up of, and that farmers, tradespeople, and servants are necessary for a city. But the essential parts of the city are the soldiers and sailors, and while they are different from the others, they are only occasionally different from each other.

It seems that, even in the past, philosophers who studied politics didn't realize that a city should be divided into different groups of people based on their roles. The farmers and soldiers should be kept separate from each other. This custom is still followed today in places like Egypt and Crete. In Egypt, Sesostris established this, and in Crete, Minos did the same. The practice of common meals also seems to be ancient. It was established in Crete during Minos' reign and even earlier in Italy. According to the best sources, a king named Italus in Italy, who ruled the AEnotrians, made them switch from being shepherds to being farmers and gave them new laws. He was also the first to introduce common meals, which is why some of his descendants still follow this practice.

The custom of dividing the citizens into groups likely came from Egypt, as the reign of Sesostris was long before that of Minos. Just like many other things were discovered over a long period because people needed to figure out how to survive, we should conclude that political organization also took a long time to develop. Since Egypt seems to be the oldest civilization and had laws and order before others, we should learn from their example and try to improve upon what they left out.

We've already said that land should belong to the soldiers and those who participate in the government, which is why farmers should be a separate group. We will now discuss how the land should be divided and how many farmers there should be. We don't believe that property should be entirely shared, as some have suggested. However, in the spirit of friendship, no citizen should go without the basics for survival.

It's generally agreed that common meals are appropriate in well-organized cities. I'll explain my reasons for supporting them later. All citizens should take part in them. However, it will be difficult for poorer citizens to contribute to the meals while also providing for their families. The cost of religious worship should also be covered by the entire state.

Because of these needs, the land should be divided into two parts. One part should belong to the community as a whole, and the other part should be owned by individuals. Each of these parts should be further divided. Half of the public land should be used to support religious worship, and the other half should support the common meals. Half of the private land should be on the outskirts of the country, and the other half should be near the city. This way, everyone will have land in both places, which would be fair and help the citizens work together more harmoniously, especially during times of war.

When the land isn't divided like this, some people won't care about border attacks, while others will overreact. This is why some places have laws that prevent people living on the borders from voting on matters of war, as their personal interests might make them biased.

If we had a choice, the farmers should be slaves, not from the same country and not too spirited. This would make them hardworking and less likely to cause trouble. The next best choice would be barbarian servants who have a similar temperament. Some of these slaves should work on private land, while others should work on public land. Later, we will discuss how these slaves should be treated and why it's a good idea to promise them freedom as a reward for their service.

We've already said that both the city and the land should be connected to both the sea and the mainland as much as possible. There are four main things to consider when choosing the city's location. First, the health of the citizens is the most important thing. A city that faces east and catches the eastern winds is considered the healthiest. After that, a northern location is best for winter. Next, the city's position should be good for both governing and defending in war. The city should be easy for its citizens to access but difficult for enemies to reach or capture.

The city should also have plenty of water, with rivers nearby. If there aren't any rivers, large cisterns should be built to collect rainwater, so there's enough water during a siege. Since health is so important, the first thing to consider is the city's location and position. The second thing is having good drinking water, and this shouldn't be neglected. Water is something we use all the time, and it has a big impact on our health. Both air and water affect health, which is why wise governments set aside different waters for different uses. If there isn't enough high-quality water, drinking water should be kept separate from other water used for other purposes.

As for fortifications, what works for some governments won't work for others. A high citadel is good for a monarchy or an oligarchy, while a city on a plain works better for a democracy. For an aristocracy, neither of these is ideal. Instead, it's better to have multiple strong places.

Regarding private homes, the best and most useful ones are those that are separate from each other and follow a modern design like the one Hippodamus suggested. However, for safety during war, the older style of buildings, which are hard for strangers to navigate and difficult for enemies to besiege, might be better. A city should have both types of buildings, and this can be arranged by laying them out like rows of vines. The buildings shouldn't be detached from each other throughout the city, just in some parts, so that both elegance and safety are ensured.

When it comes to walls, those who say that a brave people don't need them are holding onto outdated ideas. In fact, we often see those who take pride in this idea proven wrong. It is shameful for a people who are equal to or almost equal to their enemy to hide behind walls, but sometimes the attackers are too strong for the defenders to resist. If you don't want to suffer the horrors of war or the enemy's arrogance, it's better to take refuge behind walls. This is especially true now, with so many new weapons and machines designed to attack cities.

Choosing not to have walls is like choosing a land that's easy for enemies to invade or flattening the hills of your land. It's like someone deciding not to build a wall around their house because they don't want to be seen as a coward. But you should also consider that if your city has walls, you can choose to act as though it does or doesn't. Without walls, you don't have this option. So, it's not only necessary to have walls, but they should also serve as a defense during war and be an ornament to the city. Modern improvements should be included along with traditional methods. Just as attackers try to gain every possible advantage over their enemies, defenders should use all available means, both old and new, to protect themselves. Those who are well-prepared are rarely attacked first.

Since citizens are expected to eat together at public tables, and the city walls should have defensive towers at the right places and distances, it's clear that some of these public tables should be located in the towers. These buildings should be made to decorate the walls as well. For the temples used for public worship and the halls for the magistrates' public tables, they should be built in the right locations and close to each other. The only exception should be those temples which, by law or through oracles, must be kept separate from other buildings. These should be placed on a noticeable high point so they have a good view and are near the best-fortified part of the city.

Next to this area, there should be a large square, similar to what they call "The Square of Freedom" in Thessaly, where nothing is bought or sold. No tradespeople, farmers, or others like them should be allowed in this area unless they are called by the authorities. It would also make this area more beautiful if the older citizens performed their gymnastic exercises there. For these exercises, citizens should be divided into groups according to their age. Younger people should have officers in charge of them, while older citizens should stay near the magistrates. This setup would inspire true modesty and a sense of respectful fear in the younger ones.

There should also be another square, separate from the first one, for buying and selling. It should be placed so that goods can easily come in by both sea and land. Since the citizens include magistrates and priests, the public tables for the priests should be located near the temples. The tables for magistrates who deal with contracts, lawsuits, and similar matters, as well as those in charge of markets and public streets, should be near the square or along some main road. I mean the square where business is conducted, as the other one is meant for leisure and this one for necessary business.

The same arrangement should be followed in the countryside. The officials there, like forest wardens and land overseers, must also have their public tables and towers for protection against enemies. Temples for both gods and heroes should also be built in the proper locations, but it's not necessary to go into more detail on these points. Planning these things is not hard; it's carrying them out that's more difficult. Theory is shaped by our wishes, but the practical part depends on fortune. For this reason, we will stop discussing these subjects here.

We will now consider what number and type of people a government needs to have in order to make the state happy and well-run. There are two things that determine how excellent and perfect something is. First, the goal or purpose must be appropriate. Second, the means used to achieve that goal must fit the purpose. These two things may or may not align. For example, the goal we choose might be good, but we could make mistakes in how we try to achieve it. Other times, we might have the right methods, but the goal itself might be bad. And sometimes, we could be wrong about both the goal and the means, like a doctor who doesn't know what a healthy body should look like or how to make it healthy.

In every art and science, we need to understand both the right goal and the correct way to achieve it. It's clear that everyone wants to live well and be happy, but not everyone has the ability to make that happen. Some people lack the means either because of nature or fortune. Many factors are needed for a happy life, but fewer are needed for those with good character than for those with bad character. Some people have everything they need for happiness but fail to use it properly.

Since we are asking what the best form of government is—the one that makes a state well-run and its people the happiest—it's important to understand what happiness is. I've already said in my work on morals (if I can refer to it here) that happiness comes from the active and perfect practice of virtue. And this virtue isn't just relative to circumstances but is simply good in itself. By relative, I mean something that's necessary in certain situations. By simply good, I mean something that is good and beautiful in itself. For example, just punishments and necessary restrictions arise from virtue and are therefore virtuous, though it's better if neither the state nor any individual needs them. Actions aimed at gaining honor or wealth are simply good. The others are only useful for removing a problem, but these actions form the foundation of what's simply good.

A good person can endure poverty, sickness, and other misfortunes with a noble spirit, but happiness consists of avoiding these things. As I've already said in my work on morals, a good person considers what is good because it's virtuous as simply good. Therefore, all of this person's actions must be worthy and simply good. This has led some people to think that external goods cause happiness. But this would be like saying that playing the lyre well is because of the instrument, not the skill.

From what has been said, it's clear that some things should be readily available, and others must be provided by the lawmaker. This is why, when founding a city, we hope that many things under the control of fortune will be plentiful (because we admit that fortune controls some things). However, making a state worthy and great is not only the work of fortune but also of knowledge and good judgment. To have a worthy state, the citizens who run it must also be worthy. But since, in our city, every citizen is expected to be worthy, we need to figure out how to make that happen. It would be ideal if everyone could be worthy, not just some individuals. If one person can do something, it's better if everyone can do it.

People can be worthy and good in three ways: by nature, by habit, and by reason. First, a person must be born human, not some other animal. That means they must have both body and soul. But just being born with certain qualities isn't enough. Habit has a great impact because some things in our nature can be shaped for better or worse by habit. Other animals mostly live according to their nature, with very little influence from habit. But humans live according to reason, which only they have. Therefore, a person should make nature, habit, and reason work together. If people followed reason and believed it was best to do so, they would often act against nature and habit.

I've already said what kind of people should naturally make good members of a community. The rest of this discussion will focus on education because some things are developed through habit and others through learning.

Every political community consists of rulers and the ruled. We need to consider whether the same people should be rulers and ruled for their entire lives or whether different people should fill these roles at different times. The system of education should be based on this distinction. If people were as different from each other as we imagine gods and heroes are from ordinary men, being superior in both body and soul, then it would be clear that the superior should always rule, and the others should always be ruled. But since this isn't possible, and rulers aren't so superior to their subjects as Scylax describes kings in

India, it's clear that for many reasons, it's necessary for everyone to both govern and be governed at different times.

It's only fair that equals should have equal shares in everything. A state founded on injustice is hard to sustain. Those who want change will join forces with those who feel they are being ruled unfairly, and they will become such a large group that the rulers won't be able to control them. But it's also clear that rulers should be superior to those they govern. The lawmaker must figure out how to make this happen while ensuring that everyone gets an equal share of governing.

Nature has already given us a guide for this: she makes some people young and others old. The young should obey, and the old should rule. No young person is upset about being governed, especially when they know they will receive the same honors once they reach the right age. In some ways, rulers and the ruled are the same; in others, they are different. This means their education should be partly the same and partly different. As people say, the best rulers are those who have first learned to obey.

Some governments are set up for the benefit of the ruler, like the relationship between a master and a servant. Others are for the benefit of those who are ruled, like the relationship between free citizens. Some commands differ from others not because of the work but because of the goal. This is why some tasks, even those that seem like servile work, are not shameful for young free people to do. Many things that are commanded aren't honorable or dishonorable by nature, but the reason for doing them makes the difference.

Since we've established that the virtue of a good citizen and a good ruler is the same as that of a good person, and that everyone should first learn to obey before they command, it's up to the lawmaker to figure out how to make citizens good people, what kind of education is needed, and what the ultimate goal of a good life is.

A person's soul can be divided into two parts: the part that has reason and the part that doesn't but can follow reason's guidance. A person is considered good based on the virtues of these two parts. Of the virtues that are ends in themselves, it's easy to determine which they are based on this division. The inferior part exists for the sake of the superior, just as we see in both nature and art. The superior part is the one that has reason. Reason itself is divided into two parts: the theoretical and the practical. This division is also important here.

Actions follow the same pattern. Those that are superior should always be chosen by those who have the ability. What's most desirable is what leads to the best outcome. Life is divided into work and rest, war and peace. The goals of our actions are either necessary and useful or noble. We should value noble actions more than necessary ones, just as we value the superior parts of the soul and its actions. War exists to bring peace, work exists to bring rest, and the useful serves the noble.

A lawmaker should consider everything, including the different parts of the soul and their actions, especially focusing on the higher and nobler aspects. The same approach applies to life and its actions. People should be prepared for both work and war, but even more so for rest and peace. They should be trained to do what's necessary and useful, but even more so to do what is fair and noble. The education of children and young people should focus on these goals.

Many Greek states that are now well-governed, and the lawmakers who founded them, didn't create their laws and education systems with the best goals in mind or aim to promote every kind of virtue. Instead, they focused on what was useful and profitable. Some more recent writers have had similar views. They praise the Spartan state, showing they agree with the lawmaker who made war and victory the main goal of the government. But this thinking is wrong and can easily be proven both by argument and by looking at the facts. People like Thibron and others who wrote about the Spartan state seem to admire the lawmaker for training the citizens to endure all kinds of dangers and hardships to gain power over their neighbors.

But it's clear, now that the Spartans have no hope of holding supreme power, that they are not happy, and their lawmaker wasn't wise. It's ridiculous that they lost their chance to be honorable while they still followed their laws and no one challenged their authority. These people don't understand what kind of government reflects well on a lawmaker. A government of free people is nobler and more in line with virtue than a despotic government.

A city shouldn't be considered happy, and a lawmaker shouldn't be praised, just because the citizens have been trained to conquer their neighbors. This approach has a big problem: it encourages every citizen to seek supreme power in their own city, just as the Spartans accused Pausanias of doing, despite the great honors he received. This kind of reasoning and these laws are neither political, useful, nor true. A lawmaker should teach people laws that benefit them both in their public and private lives.

The lawmaker's goal shouldn't be to prepare people for war just so they can enslave others. Instead, the goal should be to ensure they don't become enslaved themselves. Next, the lawmaker should focus on the safety of the citizens, not on ruling over everyone else. Finally, only those who are naturally suited to be slaves should be enslaved. Both reason and experience show that the lawmaker's attention to war and all the other rules should aim at achieving rest and peace.

Many states are preserved through war, but once they gain power over others, they fall apart. Like a sword that loses its shine when not in use, these states weaken during peace. This happens because the lawmaker never taught them how to live in peace.

Since a man has the same goal both as an individual and as a citizen, it's clear that a good man and a good citizen must have the same purpose in mind. It's obvious that all the virtues that lead to rest are necessary because, as we've often said, the goal of war is peace, and the goal of work is rest. But the virtues that aim for rest and those that aim for work are both important for living a free and restful life. We need many necessities so that we can enjoy rest.

A city, therefore, needs to be temperate, brave, and patient. As the saying goes, "Rest is not for slaves." People who can't bravely face danger will become slaves to those who attack them. So, courage and patience are needed for work, philosophy is needed for rest, and temperance and justice are needed for both. These virtues are especially important during peace and rest because war forces people to be just and temperate. But the pleasures of peace and rest often lead to arrogance. People who are comfortable and have everything they need for happiness have a great need for the virtues of temperance and justice.

So, if there are, as poets say, people living in the "happy isles," these people would need a higher level of philosophy, temperance, and justice because they live comfortably with all the pleasures they could want. It's clear, then, that these virtues are necessary for any state that wants to be happy or honorable. A person without worth can never enjoy true goodness, and even less can they enjoy rest. They can only appear good through hard work and war, but during peace and rest, they become the lowest of creatures.

This is why virtue should not be cultivated the way the Spartans did. They didn't differ from others in their idea of what the highest good is. Instead, they thought this good could be achieved through a specific type of virtue. But since there are greater goods than those gained through war, it's clear that we should aim to enjoy things that are valuable on their own, rather than virtues that are only useful in war. We now need to consider how and by what means we can acquire these greater goods.

We've already said that three factors influence this: nature, habit, and reason. We've also explained what kind of people nature must produce for this purpose. Now, we need to decide whether education should begin with reason or habit because both should work together in harmony. Sometimes reason can stray from its purpose and be corrected by habit.

First of all, it's clear that, as with other things, the beginning of education comes from one source, while its end comes from another source, which is also its goal. For us, reason and intelligence are the end of nature, so our upbringing and behavior should be directed toward these goals.

Next, just as the body and the soul are two different things, the soul itself is divided into two parts: the reasoning part and the non-reasoning part. Each of these parts has its own habits: one focused on desires and the other on intelligence. Just as the body develops before the soul, the non-reasoning part of the soul develops before the reasoning part. This is clear because emotions like anger, will, and desire appear in children almost as soon as they are born, while reason and intelligence develop as they grow older. So, we must take care of the body first, then focus on the desires for the sake of the mind, and care for the body for the sake of the soul.

If the lawmaker is to ensure that children's bodies are as perfect as possible, their first priority should be marriage—when and under what conditions citizens should marry. When considering marriage, the lawmaker should think about the age and condition of both the man and the woman. The goal is for them to grow old around the same time and for their physical abilities to be in harmony. This way, the man won't be able to have children while the woman is too old to bear them, or the woman won't be able to have children while the man is too old to be a father. Situations like this often lead to arguments and disputes.

There should also not be too great an age difference between parents and children. If there is, the parent will gain no benefit from the child's affection, and the child will not receive any help from the parent's care. However, there should also not be too little of an age difference, as this can cause problems. A boy who sees his father as almost his age may not show him proper respect, and this can lead to disputes in the family.

To return to the main point, care must be taken to ensure that children's bodies meet the lawmaker's expectations. This can also be achieved through the same means. The time for producing children is roughly determined—not precisely, but in general terms. For men, this lasts until around age seventy, and for women, until age fifty. Marriage should be timed with these periods in mind.

It is very bad for children if the father is too young. In all animals, young offspring tend to be weaker, smaller, and more likely to be female. The same is true for humans. You can see this in cities where men and women marry very young; the people tend to be smaller and less well-formed. Women also suffer more during childbirth, and many die young. This is what some people think the oracle at Traezenium was referring to—not that they were gathering their crops too early, but that they were marrying too young.

Marrying too young also tends to lead to a lack of self-control, especially in women. It also prevents men's bodies from growing to their full size if they marry before they have finished growing, as marriage stops further growth. For this reason, the best age for a woman to marry is eighteen, and for a man, thirty-seven, give or take a little. When they marry at this time, their bodies will be at their best, and they will stop having children at the right time. Also, in terms of the children, they will likely be reaching their full potential just as their parents are approaching old age, around seventy.

This is the best time for marriage, but the time of year is also important. Many people already follow this idea and choose winter as the best time to marry. Married couples should also follow the advice of doctors and naturalists who have written on these topics. We will discuss the best physical conditions for this when we talk about educating children, but for now, we'll briefly touch on a few points.

It's not necessary for anyone to have the body of a wrestler to be a good citizen or to have good health or healthy children. But they should also not be weak or overly affected by hardship. They should be somewhere in the middle. A person should be used to hard work, but not too much, and not focused on just one thing like a wrestler. Instead, they should engage in activities suitable for free people. This applies equally to both men and women. Pregnant women should make sure their diet is not too limited, and they should get enough exercise. This is something the lawmaker can easily encourage by requiring them to attend daily worship of the gods who oversee marriage.

However, while it's important for the body to be active, the mind should remain as calm as possible. Just as plants are influenced by the soil they grow in, children are influenced by their mothers' emotional state.

As for whether a child should be exposed to or raised, let it be a law that no child who is imperfect or deformed should be raised. Just as we have discussed the best time for men and women to marry, we should also determine how long it benefits the community for them to have children. Just as children born to parents who are too young are physically and mentally weak, the same is true for children born to parents who are too old. While the body is still in its prime, which some poets say lasts until age fifty or a little more, children are likely to be at their best. But after this age, it's better for parents to stop having children.

Any improper relationship between a man and a woman, or a woman and a man, when either party is betrothed, should be strongly condemned. If someone is guilty of this after marriage, they should be shamed as much as they deserve for their offense.

When a child is born, their physical strength will depend largely on the quality of their food. If you study animals and observe people who are determined to raise warlike children, you'll find they mostly feed them milk because it is best suited to their bodies. They avoid giving them wine to prevent illness. The natural movements of children are also very helpful for their growth. To prevent their limbs from becoming crooked, since their bodies are still very flexible, some people even use special devices to keep their bodies straight.

It's also helpful to get children used to the cold at a young age because this strengthens their health and prepares them for the challenges of war. This is why many barbarian groups dip their children in cold rivers or dress them lightly, as the Celts do. Whatever we want to accustom children to, it's best to start them early and gradually. Boys naturally like the cold because their bodies are warm.

These are the things we should focus on first. The next stage of life lasts until the child is five years old. During this time, they shouldn't be taught anything serious, not even necessary tasks, so as not to hinder their growth. They should be encouraged to move around enough to avoid becoming lazy, and this can be done through various activities and play. Their play should not be too serious, but also not too easy or lazy.

Their caregivers should also monitor the stories they hear and the tales they are told. These should prepare them for the lessons they will learn later in life. For this reason, most of their play should imitate the things they will do when they grow older. Some people are wrong to forbid boys from arguing and quarreling because these activities help them grow. Such struggles serve as exercise for the body because the tension and strain that comes with these quarrels make boys stronger.

Their caregivers should also keep an eye on their lifestyle and the people they spend time with, making sure they never associate with slaves. Until they turn seven, children should be raised at home. During this time, they should be kept away from anything inappropriate. In fact, it is just as important for the lawmaker to remove all indecent speech from the state. If shameful words are allowed, shameful actions will soon follow, especially among young people. For this reason, they should never speak or hear anything inappropriate.

If any free person says or does something forbidden before they are old enough to join the public meals, they should be punished with disgrace and whipping. If an older person does this, they should be treated like a slave because of their dishonorable behavior. Since we are banning inappropriate speech, we should also make sure children don't see any improper images or stories. The authorities should ensure that there are no statues or pictures of such things, except for certain gods, as allowed by law. Only people of a certain age should be allowed to worship these gods, along with their wives and children.

It should also be illegal for young people to watch iambic or comedic performances before they are old enough to enjoy the pleasures of life. A good education will protect them from the bad influences of these things.

We have only briefly touched on this subject for now. Later, when we return to it properly, we will determine whether educating children is necessary, and if so, how it should be done. For now, we have only mentioned it as something important.

The tragic actor Theodoras once said something wise: he wouldn't let anyone, not even the lowest actor, go on stage before him because he wanted to be the first to catch the audience's attention. The same applies to our interactions with people and things: whatever we experience first tends to please us the most. This is why children should be kept away from anything bad, especially things that are offensive to good manners.

When children reach the age of five, the next two years should be spent watching the activities they will later have to learn. Education should be divided into two stages based on the child's age. The first stage is from age seven to puberty, and the second is from puberty until age twenty-one. Those who divide age into seven-year periods are usually wrong. It's much better to follow nature's divisions because every art and lesson is meant to complete what nature leaves unfinished.

We should first consider whether any rules are needed for raising children. Next, we should decide if it's better to make this a shared responsibility or to leave it up to individuals, as is commonly done in most cities. Lastly, we should determine what those rules should be.

Book 8

No one can doubt that the government should take a great interest in the care of young people. When this is neglected, it harms the city because every state should be governed according to its unique character. The form and habits of each government are special to it, and just as they first created it, they usually continue to preserve it. For example, the ways of a democracy create a democracy, and the ways of an oligarchy create an oligarchy. But in general, the best habits lead to the best government.

Just like in any business or art, there are things that people must first learn and get used to in order to do their jobs well. It's clear that the same is true for practicing virtue. Since every city has one common goal, education should be the same for everyone, and it should be a public responsibility, not just a private one. Right now, each person takes care of their own children individually, and they teach them whatever they want. But what children need to learn should be common to everyone. No one should think of any citizen as belonging just to them; instead, each person belongs to the whole state. Each citizen is part of the state, and each part naturally has a duty to care for the good of the whole. For this reason, the Spartans are to be praised because they pay great attention to education and make it a public concern. It is clear, then, that there should be laws about education, and it should be public.

It is important to know what education is and how children should be taught. There are disagreements about the purpose of education because not everyone agrees on what children should be taught to improve their virtues or to live a happy life. It's also not clear whether education should focus on improving reason or fixing moral behavior. Based on how education is done today, we can't say for sure whether the goal is to teach children useful life skills or to help them develop virtue and excellence. Different people defend different views.

As for virtue, not everyone agrees on what it is. Since not everyone values the same virtues equally, it makes sense that they wouldn't teach the same virtues either. It's clear that everyone should learn what is necessary. However, what is necessary for one person is not necessary for everyone. There should be a difference between what a free person learns and what a slave learns. Free people should be taught everything useful that does not make them lowly. Any kind of work or art that damages the body, mind, or character of a free person is considered lowly because it makes them unfit for the practice of virtue. This is why any art that harms the body is considered lowly, as are all jobs done for profit. These jobs take away the freedom of the mind and make it focused on money.

There are also some arts that are acceptable for free people to learn to a certain degree, but trying to become an expert in them leads to the problems we just mentioned. There is a big difference between why someone does or learns something. It is not lowly to do something for yourself, your friend, or for the sake of virtue. However, doing it for someone else can seem like the work of a servant or a slave. The way children are taught today seems to include both approaches.

There are four main things that are usually taught to children: reading, physical exercises, music, and, in some cases, painting. Reading and painting are both very useful in life, and physical exercises help develop courage. As for music, some people might question its purpose because most people use it for pleasure. But those who originally made it part of education did so because, as we have already said, nature requires that we not only work properly but also know how to spend our free time honorably. Of all things, this is the most important.

Although both work and rest are necessary, rest is more important than work. We must learn what to do when we are at rest because we should not spend our free time just playing. If we did, playing would become the main business of our lives. If this is not possible, then play is more necessary for people who work than for those who are at rest. People who work need relaxation, which play can provide. Because work brings pain and stress, play is like medicine for the mind. It gives the mind a break and brings pleasure.

Rest itself seems to be linked to pleasure, happiness, and a good life. But this kind of rest is not for those who are working; it belongs to those who are at rest. People who work do so for the sake of something they don't have yet, but happiness is an end in itself. Everyone agrees that happiness brings pleasure, not pain. However, not everyone agrees on what pleasure consists of because each person's idea of pleasure is influenced by their habits. But the best person seeks the best pleasure, which comes from the noblest actions.

It's clear, then, that in order to live a life of rest, a person must learn and be taught certain things. The purpose of this learning is the enjoyment of rest. On the other hand, the learning that prepares us for work has a different purpose. This is why the ancient people made music a part of education. It's not necessary in the way reading is for managing a household or doing something useful in public life. It's not like painting, which helps a person appreciate the fine arts. It's also not like physical exercises, which contribute to health and strength. We don't see these benefits come from music. So, music is meant to be part of how we spend our rest.

This was the intention of the people who introduced music into education. They thought it was a proper activity for free people, so they made it part of their education. Homer even writes about this when he says, "How right to call Thalia to the feast," and in other parts, he describes how Ulysses says the happiest part of life is "when at the festal board, in order plac'd, they hear the song."

It's clear that there is a certain kind of education that a child should receive, not because it's useful or necessary, but because it is noble and fitting for a free person. Whether there is one type of education or several, and how these should be taught, will be discussed later. For now, we can say that we have the support of the ancients, who included music as part of education, which shows that they understood its importance.

Moreover, it's necessary to teach children useful things, not just because they are useful, but also because they lead to other kinds of learning. For example, children should learn to read, not only because it's useful, but because it helps them gain other types of knowledge. They should also learn painting, not just so they don't get cheated when buying art or vases, but more importantly, because it helps them appreciate the beauty of the human form. Chasing after only what is profitable does not suit great and free souls.

Since it's clear whether boys should first be taught morals or reasoning, and whether their bodies or their minds should be trained first, it's obvious that boys should first be placed under the care of physical trainers to develop their bodies and teach them physical exercises.

Some states that seem to focus on their children's education put the most emphasis on wrestling, even though it can limit body growth and affect its form. The Spartans did not make this mistake. Instead, they made their children tough through hard physical labor because they believed this would make them courageous. But as we have often said, courage is not the only thing or the most important thing that should be taught. Even when it comes to courage, the Spartans may not achieve their goal.

We don't see that the most fierce animals or nations are the most courageous. In fact, it's often the gentler ones, like lions, that show true courage. Many cruel people kill and even eat other humans, like the Achaeans and Heniochi in Pontus, and many others in Asia. Some of these people are just as bad or worse than these examples. They live through tyranny, but they have no courage. We also know that the Spartans themselves, when they focused on hard labor and were superior to all others, didn't gain this superiority through their physical training. Instead, it was because they faced opponents who were not trained at all. Now, the Spartans are inferior to many other nations, both in war and physical exercises.

What is noble and honorable should be the focus of education, not what is fierce and cruel. A good man, not a wolf or any other wild animal, is the one who faces noble dangers. So, allowing boys to focus too much on these physical exercises without teaching them what's necessary makes them base and narrow-minded. They may excel in one part of being a citizen, but in everything else, they are useless.

We should not base our judgments on the past, but on what we see today. In the past, the Spartans didn't have any competition in their education, but now they do. Physical exercises are useful, and it's agreed how they should be used. During youth, it's best to focus on the gentler exercises and avoid the strict diets and harsh exercises that are often prescribed. This way, the body's growth won't be hindered. A clear sign that harsh training stunts growth is the fact that hardly any Olympic athletes have won as both boys and men. The exercises they did when young took away their strength.

After spending three years on other parts of education, starting from puberty, boys will then be at the right age to endure hard work and follow a regulated diet. It's impossible for the mind and body to work hard at the same time because they interfere with each other. The work of the body hinders the progress of the mind, and the work of the mind hinders the body.

Regarding music, we've already talked a bit about it, though not very clearly. It's a good idea to go over what we said before in more detail, which can be a starting point for others to add their thoughts. Because it's hard to clearly explain what power music has, or why we should use it. Is it for fun and relaxation, like sleep or wine? These things aren't serious but are enjoyable and help us forget our worries, as Euripides says. That's why people group together sleep, wine, music, and sometimes dancing, using them all for the same purpose. Or should we think that music helps us become virtuous, like how exercise shapes the body, and that it can influence our character so we learn to enjoy things in the right way?

Or should we say that music helps us in life and makes us wiser? Some people think this is another benefit of music. It's clear that boys shouldn't learn music just as a game, because learning isn't playing—it's actually hard work. Also, it's not right to let boys have complete free time, because stopping learning isn't good for someone who isn't fully grown. But maybe we think that boys focus on music now so they can enjoy it as fun when they become adults. But if that's true, why should they learn it themselves? Why not be like the kings of the Medes and Persians, who enjoy music by listening to others play and showing them its beauty? Because those who spend all their time studying music will be better at it than those who just learn the basics.

But if that's a reason for kids to learn something, then they should learn cooking too—but that's silly. We have the same question if music improves character: why should they learn it themselves? Can't they get all the benefits of controlling emotions or judging performances by listening to others, like the Spartans do? Because they, without learning music, can still tell what's good and bad. The same goes if music is just for fun for those who live comfortably—why should they learn it themselves instead of enjoying others' skills?

Let's think about what we believe about the gods in this matter. We see that poets never show Jupiter himself singing or playing music. In fact, we often look down on professional musicians and say only drunkards or clowns would do that. But maybe we can talk more about this topic later. The first question is: should music be part of education or not? And among the three purposes given to music, which one is correct? Is it for teaching, for fun, or to fill the free time of those who are not working? Or could all three be suitable purposes for music?

Because it seems to involve all of them. Play is needed for rest, and rest is pleasant, acting like a cure for the stress from work. Everyone agrees that a happy life must be honorable and pleasant, because happiness includes both. And we all agree that music is very enjoyable, whether instrumental or with singing; as Musaeus says, "Music is man's sweetest joy." That's why music is rightly included in all gatherings and happy lives, because it can bring joy.

From this, one might think it's necessary to teach young people music. Because all harmless pleasures not only help us reach life's ultimate goal but also serve as relaxation. And since people rarely achieve that final goal, they often stop working and turn to amusement just to enjoy the pleasure it brings. So it's helpful to enjoy pleasures like these. Some people make play and fun their goal, and maybe that goal has some pleasure attached, but not the right kind. But while people aim for one thing, they settle for another because human actions resemble their goals in some way.

Because we pursue the goal for its own sake, not for anything else that comes with it. And pleasures like these are sought not because of what comes after them, but because of what came before, like work and hardship. That's why they look for happiness in these kinds of pleasures; and anyone can easily see this. Probably no one doubts that music should be pursued not only for this reason but also because it's very helpful during breaks from work. We should also ask whether music might have another, higher purpose besides this.

And we shouldn't just enjoy the ordinary pleasure it gives (which everyone feels, since music naturally gives pleasure and is agreeable to all ages and personalities), but also look at whether it helps improve our character and our souls. And we'll easily know this if we feel our moods influenced by it. And it's clear that they are, from many examples, like the music at the Olympic games, which obviously fills the soul with excitement. But enthusiasm is a feeling that strongly stirs our mood.

Also, everyone who hears imitations feels empathy, even when they're given without rhythm or poetry. Furthermore, since music is pleasant, and since virtue means enjoying, loving, and hating the right things, it's clear that we should train ourselves to judge correctly and to take joy in good character and noble actions. But feelings like anger and calmness, courage and modesty, and their opposites, and all other moods, are best imitated by music and poetry. This is obvious from experience, because when we hear them, our soul is changed.

And someone who feels joy or sorrow from an imitation is almost in the same state as if they were affected by the real thing. So, if someone likes seeing a statue just because it's beautiful, it's clear that seeing the real person would also be pleasing. Now, in our other senses, like touch and taste, there is no imitation of character. In sight, there is a little, but these are just images of things, and the feelings they cause are mostly the same for everyone.

Also, statues and paintings don't really imitate character, but are signs that show the body showing some emotion. However, the difference isn't big, but young people shouldn't look at the paintings of Pauso, but those of Polygnotus or other artists who show character. But in poetry and music, there are imitations of character; and this is clear because different harmonies are naturally so different that listeners feel different and are not in the same mood when one is played compared to another.

For example, one kind might cause sadness and shrink the soul, like the mixed Lydian; others soften the mind and sort of melt the heart; others steady it and make it firm, like Doric music does; while Phrygian music fills the soul with excitement, as those who have studied this part of education have well described; they give examples from the music itself. The same is true for rhythm; some steady the mood, others change it; some affect us strongly, others more gently.

From all this, it's clear how much music affects our mood and how it can influence it in different ways. And if it can do this, then certainly young people should be taught music. And learning music is especially suited to them, because at their age they don't like to pay attention to things that aren't enjoyable. But music is naturally very enjoyable, and there seems to be a link between harmony and rhythm; that's why some wise people thought the soul itself is harmony, or that it contains harmony.

We will now determine whether it's right for children to be taught to sing and play instruments, which we have previously questioned. It's well known that if you want someone to be skilled in any art, it helps if they learn the practical part themselves. Because it's very hard, if not impossible, for someone to judge well what they can't do themselves. It's also very important that children have something to do that will entertain them. That's why the rattle invented by Archytas seems clever—they give it to children to play with, so they don't break things around the house.

Because at that age they can't sit still. So this toy suits babies, and as they grow up, teaching should be their toy. So it's clear that they should be taught music in a way that lets them practice it. It's not hard to say what's appropriate or not for their age, or to answer people who say this activity is low or vulgar. First of all, they need to practice so they can judge the art; that's why this should be done when they're young.

But when they're older, they can stop the practical part; they'll still be able to judge what's good in the art and enjoy it properly because of what they learned when they were young. Regarding the criticism that some people make that music is low or vulgar, it's not hard to respond if we think about how much we want those who are being educated to become good citizens to be taught in this art, and what kind of music and rhythms they should know, and what instruments they should play, because there is probably a difference in these.

That's the right answer to that criticism: we must admit that in some cases, nothing can prevent music from having some of the bad effects people attribute to it. So it's clear that learning music should never interfere with the tasks of adulthood, or make the body weak and unfit for war or government work. But it should be practiced by the young and judged by the old. For children to learn music properly, they shouldn't be involved in the parts that music experts argue about.

They also shouldn't perform pieces that are impressive because they're hard to play, and which, after being shown in public contests, have now become part of education. Instead, let them learn enough to be able to properly enjoy good music and rhythms. And not just the kind of music that all animals, slaves, and boys feel, but something more. So it's clear what instruments they should use: they should never be taught to play the flute or other instruments that need great skill, like the harp, but instead ones that will help them be good judges of music or any other learning.

Also, the flute isn't a moral instrument; instead, it stirs up the emotions and is better used when we want to excite the soul, not when we want to teach. Also, there's something about it that's opposite to what education needs: when someone plays the flute, they can't speak. That's why our ancestors rightly banned its use by young people and free citizens, even though they themselves used it at first.

Because when their wealth gave them more free time, they became more enthusiastic about virtue; and both before and after the Persian war, their noble deeds lifted their minds so much that they focused on every part of education, not just one, trying to learn everything. That's why they included the flute as one of the instruments they were to learn. In Sparta, the leader of the chorus played the flute himself; and in Athens, it was so common that almost every free man knew how to play, as shown by the tablet that Thrasippus dedicated when he was chorus leader.

But later they rejected it as dangerous, having become better at judging what helped promote virtue and what didn't. For the same reason, many old instruments like the dulcimer and the lyre were set aside, as well as those meant to give pleasure to the player and needed a delicate touch and great skill to play well. What the ancients say in the myth about the flute makes sense: that after Minerva discovered it, she threw it away.

And they're not wrong who say the goddess disliked it because it made the player's face look distorted. But more likely, she rejected it because knowing how to play it didn't help improve the mind. Now, we think of Minerva as the goddess who invented arts and sciences. Since we don't approve of a child being taught to master instruments (we'd limit that to those competing for prizes in that art; because they play not to improve their virtue, but to please listeners and satisfy their demands), therefore, we think such practice is unsuitable for free citizens; it should be limited to those who are paid to do it.

Because it often gives people low ideas, since their goal is bad. Because the rude audience member makes them change their music, so the performers who pay attention to him adjust their actions according to his movements.

We are now going to discuss harmony and rhythm—whether all types should be used in education or if only certain ones should be chosen. Also, should we give the same guidance to those learning music for education as to those who are learning it for other reasons, or is there a difference between them? Since music is made up of melody and rhythm, we need to understand the role each plays in education. Should we focus more on melody or rhythm? However, since many people, including musicians and philosophers skilled in this area, have already written extensively on this subject, we will refer those seeking detailed information to their works. Here, we will only give a general overview without going into too much detail.

Some philosophers, whose views we agree with, divide melody into three categories: moral, practical, and the kind that stirs deep emotions. Each of these types of melody is matched with a specific kind of harmony that naturally fits it. We believe music should not serve just one purpose but several—helping to teach, purify the soul, and offer enjoyment and relaxation from mental stress. I use the word "purify" here without fully explaining it but will cover it in more detail in my Poetics. Music clearly has a role in all these areas, but not all types of harmony are suitable for every purpose. The most moral harmonies should be used in education, while the more active and emotional ones can be used for entertainment or performance.

Some people have a natural passion for strong emotions like pity, fear, or enthusiasm, though the intensity of these feelings varies between individuals. In some, these emotions can be overwhelming. But we can see that sacred music can calm even those whose emotions are out of control, bringing them peace, much like a physician's treatment. This same calming effect can be seen in people who are compassionate, fearful, or overwhelmed by their emotions. Music has the power to ease their minds and bring them back to a state of calm, offering pleasure along with relief. Music that can purify the soul in this way brings harmless pleasure to everyone.

Therefore, the harmony and music performed in public settings, like theaters, should include this kind of calming and purifying quality. However, because theater audiences consist of two types of people— the educated and free-minded, and the unrefined or working-class, such as hired laborers and others like them—there needs to be some music and entertainment that appeals to both groups. Just as their tastes in life have been shaped in different ways, their tastes in music are also different. Some music caters to more base tastes, while others appreciate natural, refined harmonies. What is natural brings pleasure to everyone, so music in the theater should lean toward this type of harmony.

In education, we should use melodies and harmonies that shape good character, such as the Doric harmony, which is serious and helps develop courage. Experts in the field of music education have also supported this view. But Socrates, in Plato's Republic, made a mistake by allowing both the Phrygian and Doric harmonies while banning the flute. The Phrygian harmony has the same emotional power as the flute—it can stir up the mind and emotions. This is shown by how poets use the flute in their songs about wild, intense feelings, like in Bacchic rituals. The Phrygian harmony fits these situations perfectly.

It's widely agreed that the dithyrambic style of music is Phrygian, and experts provide many examples to prove this. For instance, when Philoxenus tried to compose dithyrambic music in the Doric style, he naturally ended up using Phrygian, because it was better suited for that purpose. Everyone agrees that Doric music is the most serious and best for inspiring courage. Since the Doric harmony sits in the middle between two extremes, it's clear that this is the type of music that young people should learn.

When teaching music, we must consider what is possible and what is appropriate. Everyone should aim for what combines both of these qualities, but it also depends on their age. For example, it's difficult for older people to sing songs that require high notes, so they should focus on gentler music that doesn't require much vocal strength. Some music experts criticize Socrates for saying that young people shouldn't learn softer harmonies, as if it would make them lazy, like getting drunk. But this is not true—these harmonies are more appropriate for those who are older.

If there is a type of harmony that is both elegant and instructive for children, it should be used—perhaps the Lydian harmony, which seems to fit this description. So, we can say that education should be guided by three principles: moderation, what is possible, and what is appropriate.

The Prince

Niccollo Macchiavelli

Chapter 1
How Many Kinds of Principalities There Are, And by What Means They Are Acquired

All states, all powers that have governed or currently govern people, are either republics or principalities.

Principalities can be hereditary, where the ruling family has been established for a long time, or they can be new.

New principalities can be completely new, as Milan was to Francesco Sforza, or they can be added to an existing hereditary state, like the kingdom of Naples, which was added to the kingdom of the King of Spain.

These newly acquired territories are either used to living under a prince or accustomed to living in freedom. They are acquired either by the ruler's own military force, by the arms of others, or by fortune or personal skill.

Chapter 2
Concerning Hereditary Principalities

I will set aside any discussion on republics, since I have written about them extensively elsewhere, and will focus only on principalities. In doing so, I will follow the order outlined above and explain how such principalities can be governed and maintained.

I state right away that it is easier to maintain control over hereditary states, where the people are long accustomed to the family of their prince, than over new states. This is because it is generally enough for a hereditary prince to follow the traditions of his ancestors and to act wisely when new situations arise. A prince of even average ability can hold onto his state unless he is overthrown by an exceptionally powerful force. Even if he is removed, when misfortune befalls the usurper, the prince is likely to regain his power.

As an example from Italy, consider the Duke of Ferrara. He would not have been able to withstand the Venetians' attacks in 1484 or those of Pope Julius in 1510 if he had not been securely established in his dominions. A hereditary prince has fewer reasons and less need to offend his subjects, which makes it more likely that he will be loved. Unless extraordinary vices cause him to be hated, it is reasonable to expect that his subjects will naturally be inclined to support him. The longer a prince's rule endures, the more the reasons and motivations for change are forgotten, because one change always sparks a desire for another.

Chapter 3
Concerning Mixed Principalities

But the difficulties arise in a new principality. First, if the principality is not completely new, but instead a part of a larger state—what can be called a composite state—the challenges primarily stem from a common problem inherent in all new principalities. People often willingly change their rulers, hoping to improve their situation, and this hope drives them to rise up against the current ruler. However, they are frequently deceived, as they later find through experience that they have gone from bad to worse. This issue is further complicated by a natural and common occurrence: a new prince must place burdens on the people who have submitted to him. He must station his soldiers there and impose countless other difficulties on his new territory in order to secure his position.

In this way, the new prince makes enemies of those he has harmed in seizing power, and at the same time, he cannot hold onto the support of those who helped him, because he is unable to meet their expectations. Moreover, he cannot take decisive action against them because he feels obligated to them. Even if a prince has a strong military, when entering a new province, he will always require the goodwill of the local population.

For these reasons, Louis XII, King of France, quickly captured Milan but just as quickly lost it. In the first instance, it was enough for Duke Lodovico's own forces to drive him out, because the people who had opened their gates to Louis, feeling betrayed in their hopes for future benefits, could not tolerate the mistreatment from the new prince. It is true, though, that once rebellious provinces are regained a second time, they are not as easily lost. This is because the prince, without hesitation, uses the rebellion as an opportunity to punish wrongdoers, remove those he cannot trust, and strengthen his position in weaker areas. Thus, to make France lose Milan the first time, it was enough for Duke Lodovico to incite unrest along the borders. But to make France lose Milan a second time, it required the combined efforts of the entire world against Louis, and his armies had to be defeated and expelled from Italy. These results occurred due to the reasons I've mentioned.

Nevertheless, France lost Milan both the first and second time. The general reasons for the first loss have already been discussed, so now we must turn to the reasons for the second and consider what resources Louis had, and what anyone in his situation would need to secure such a conquest more effectively than the King of France did.

I now say that territories which are acquired and added to an ancient state, by the one who conquers them, either share the same language and culture as the existing state or they do not. When they do, it is much easier to maintain control, especially if the new territory is not accustomed to self-governance. In such cases, to hold onto the new state securely, it is enough to eliminate the ruling family of the previous prince. The two peoples, being alike in most other respects, will live peacefully together. An example of this can be seen in Brittany, Burgundy, Gascony, and Normandy, which have been part of France for a long time. Even if there are some differences in language, the customs are similar enough that the people can live together without much difficulty. The ruler who has annexed these territories should keep two things in mind: first, he must ensure that the family of the former ruler is completely eliminated, and second, he must make sure that neither their laws nor their taxes are changed. If he does this, in a short time, the new territory will be fully integrated with the old principality.

But when a state is acquired in a region with a different language, customs, or laws, the challenges are much greater, and maintaining control requires a combination of good fortune and strong effort. One of the best ways to secure such a territory is for the prince to go and reside there. This step greatly increases the stability and longevity of the prince's rule, as it did for the Turk in Greece. Despite all the other measures he took to hold onto that state, the Turk would not have been able to keep it had he not gone to live there. By being present in the territory, the prince can observe problems as they arise and address them quickly. When a prince is not present, these issues only come to light once they have grown more serious and are more difficult to resolve. In addition, by residing there, the local officials cannot exploit the country, and the people can appeal directly to the prince for help. This not only makes the subjects more likely to remain loyal, but also gives them more reason to love the prince if he acts justly, or to fear him if they intend to rebel. Furthermore, as long as the prince resides in the new territory, any external enemy seeking to conquer it will find the task much more difficult.

Another good method for maintaining control over a new state is to establish colonies in one or two strategic locations. These colonies act as strongholds or keys to the territory. This approach is either necessary or a large number of cavalry and infantry must be kept there. Colonies, however, are much less expensive to maintain. A prince can send them out with little or no cost, and they will offend only a small portion of the local population—the ones whose lands and homes are taken to give to the new settlers. Those who are harmed in this way are left poor and scattered, so they cannot organize any serious resistance. Meanwhile, the majority of the population, who are not affected, will remain quiet and be careful not to make mistakes, fearing they could suffer the same fate as those who lost their property. In conclusion, colonies are inexpensive, loyal, and cause less harm, while those harmed by them are too weak and dispersed to seek revenge. It should be noted that men must either be treated well or crushed, because they can take revenge for minor injuries, but not for severe ones. Therefore, if a prince needs to harm someone, it should be in such a way that no fear of retaliation remains.

On the other hand, maintaining a standing army in the new territory, instead of establishing colonies, is much more costly. The entire revenue of the state must be spent on the garrison, turning the acquisition into a financial burden. Additionally, a much larger portion of the population is angered, since the presence of the garrison affects everyone. As the soldiers move throughout the territory, all the inhabitants experience hardship, and they become hostile. These people are enemies who, even if defeated in battle, can still cause damage. For all these reasons, keeping a standing garrison in the new territory is far less effective than establishing colonies.

Furthermore, a prince who controls a state with a different language, customs, or laws should make himself the leader and protector of the weaker neighboring states while weakening the stronger ones. He must also ensure that no foreign power as strong as himself gains a foothold in the region, because this often happens when dissatisfied locals invite foreign intervention due to their ambition or fear. This has occurred many times throughout history, such as when the Romans were brought into Greece by the Aetolians. In every case where foreign powers gained control, it was because local factions invited them in. The typical pattern is that when a powerful foreigner enters a territory, all the weaker states rally to him, motivated by their hatred for the ruling power. As a result, the foreigner gains their support with little effort. However, the prince must ensure that these states do not gain too much power, and with his own forces and their support, he can easily keep the more powerful factions in check, allowing him to remain the dominant ruler in the territory.

If the prince does not handle these matters effectively, he will soon lose the territory he has gained, and even while he holds onto it, he will face constant difficulties and challenges.

The Romans, whenever they annexed new territories, always paid very close attention to how they managed those lands. They sent settlers to create colonies and made sure to maintain friendly relations with smaller powers. However, they were careful not to make these smaller powers stronger than they already were. At the same time, they kept the larger, more powerful nations in check, and they never allowed any strong foreign powers to gain too much control. I think Greece offers a perfect example of this. The Romans managed to keep the Achaeans and Aetolians as allies, but they never let them become too powerful. They brought down the kingdom of Macedonia and forced Antiochus to retreat. Yet, even though the Achaeans and Aetolians had been good allies to Rome, the Romans still didn't allow them to expand their influence. And no matter how hard Philip tried to win the friendship of the Romans, they would only agree to be his allies after humbling him. As for Antiochus, no amount of influence he possessed could convince the Romans to let him hold any real power over the land. The Romans acted in these ways because they followed what every smart and cautious ruler should do—rulers who look not only at the problems right in front of them but also at potential future troubles. They understood that they needed to prepare for these future challenges with all their energy because, when you can see a problem coming, it's much easier to address it. But if you wait too long and let the issue get closer, it will already be too late to fix because the problem will have grown so much that it becomes impossible to solve. This is very similar to what doctors say about hectic fever: when the illness first starts, it's easy to cure but hard to notice. However, if too much time passes and the illness isn't treated, it becomes very obvious but extremely hard to cure. The same thing happens with matters of state—if you foresee a problem early on (which only wise leaders can do), you can address it quickly and easily. But if you let that problem grow without addressing it, it will eventually become so big that everyone can see it, and by that point, it will be much harder to fix. That's why the Romans, when they saw potential problems in the future, dealt with them right away. They didn't wait for the problems to escalate because they knew that trying to avoid a small conflict now would only lead to a bigger conflict later, which would work in their enemies' favor. The Romans preferred to handle conflicts early, even if it meant smaller battles, because they knew that war was inevitable. They believed that postponing war would only benefit others. They also wanted to fight Philip and Antiochus in Greece, rather than later facing them in Italy. The Romans could have avoided both conflicts, but they chose not to because they knew that avoiding war wasn't an option—it would only delay the inevitable and give their enemies more of an advantage. The Romans didn't subscribe to the popular idea we often hear today, that you should "enjoy the benefits of the present moment." Instead, they focused on reaping the benefits that came from their own courage and careful planning. They understood that time pushes everything forward, bringing both good and bad, just as fortune can bring both success and failure.

Now, let's take a look at France and see if they followed any of these same principles. I'll focus on King Louis XII (rather than Charles VIII), because Louis held power in Italy for a longer period, and his actions are more relevant. You'll see that Louis made many mistakes by doing the exact opposite of what he should have done to maintain control over a state made up of many different regions and people.

King Louis was brought into Italy by the ambition of the Venetians, who hoped to use him to help them gain control over half of Lombardy. I don't blame the king for taking this course of action, because when he wanted to establish a foothold in Italy, he didn't have any friends there. The actions of Charles VIII had closed every door to him. So,

Louis had no choice but to accept the alliances that were available to him. He could have succeeded in his plans very quickly if he hadn't made some critical mistakes along the way. After conquering Lombardy, Louis immediately regained the authority that Charles had lost. Genoa surrendered to him, and the Florentines became his allies. The Marquess of Mantua, the Duke of Ferrara, the Bentivogli family, my lady of Forli, the rulers of Faenza, Pesaro, Rimini, Camerino, Piombino, Lucca, Pisa, and Siena—all of them approached Louis, seeking to become his allies. At that moment, the Venetians realized how reckless their decision had been. In their attempt to gain control of two towns in Lombardy, they had allowed Louis to become the ruler of two-thirds of Italy.

Let's now consider how easily Louis could have maintained his position in Italy if he had followed the principles we've already discussed. He had many allies, and even though they were numerous, they were all weak and fearful—some feared the Church, while others were scared of the Venetians. As a result, they would have always relied on Louis for support. With their help, he could have strengthened his position and protected himself against any remaining powerful forces in Italy. But instead of securing his position, as soon as he took control of Milan, Louis made the opposite mistake. He helped Pope Alexander VI take over the Romagna, and in doing so, he failed to realize that he was weakening himself. By supporting Alexander's ambitions, he lost the allies who had placed their trust in him, while at the same time strengthening the Church by giving it even more political power. This action allowed the Church to gain greater authority. After making this huge mistake, Louis had no choice but to continue down the wrong path. He soon found himself in a position where, in order to stop Alexander's growing ambitions and prevent the Pope from gaining control over Tuscany, Louis was forced to return to Italy to deal with the situation himself.

As if it weren't enough that he had empowered the Church and lost his allies, Louis, in his desire to gain control of Naples, decided to divide the kingdom with the King of Spain. By doing this, he went from being the dominant ruler in Italy to just one of many competing powers. This gave ambitious nobles in Italy and discontented individuals in France a place to turn to for refuge and support. Louis could have placed a ruler loyal to him in Naples, but instead, he removed this ruler and replaced him with someone who would eventually turn against him and drive him, Louis, out of Italy.

It's only natural for rulers to desire more power, and they are often praised for gaining it. However, when a ruler tries to seize power in ways beyond their capabilities, they are seen as foolish and open to criticism. So, if France had the strength to conquer Naples on its own, it should have done so. But if it didn't have that strength, then dividing the kingdom was a major mistake. While Louis's decision to divide Lombardy with the Venetians could be justified because it allowed him to gain a foothold in Italy, the same cannot be said for his decision to divide Naples.

Louis made five major errors: he destroyed the smaller powers in Italy, he increased the strength of one of the major powers (the Church), he brought a foreign power (Spain) into Italy, he failed to establish a lasting presence in the country, and he didn't send colonies to secure his control. These five mistakes alone wouldn't have completely ruined him, but then Louis made a sixth error by weakening the Venetians. If Louis hadn't strengthened the Church or brought Spain into Italy, it would have made sense to weaken the Venetians. But after making those earlier mistakes, Louis should have left the Venetians strong enough to keep other powers from meddling in Lombardy. The Venetians wouldn't have allowed anyone to take Lombardy from France just to give it to them, and no other power would have dared to challenge France's hold on Lombardy if it meant giving it to the Venetians.

And if someone tries to argue that "King Louis gave the Romagna to Pope Alexander and the kingdom of Naples to Spain in order to avoid war," my response would be that, as I've already explained, making mistakes to avoid war is never wise. War cannot be avoided; it can only be postponed, and postponing it will only work to your disadvantage. If someone else argues that Louis had promised the Pope to help him in exchange for dissolving his marriage and giving the Archbishop of Rouen a cardinal's hat, I will address that issue later when discussing the importance of keeping promises.

In the end, King Louis lost Lombardy because he didn't follow the principles that successful rulers have used to gain and maintain control over new territories. There's no mystery or miracle in what happened to Louis—his downfall was predictable and completely natural. I discussed this issue with Cardinal Rouen at Nantes when Cesare Borgia (also known as Valentino), the son of Pope Alexander, had taken control of the Romagna. Cardinal Rouen remarked to me that Italians didn't understand warfare, and I responded by saying that the French didn't understand statecraft. If they had, they wouldn't have allowed the Church to grow so powerful. In fact, it's clear that France's downfall in Italy was caused by the very powers they helped strengthen—the Church and Spain.

From this, we can draw a general rule that almost always holds true: when you help someone else gain power, you are often the one who ends up being ruined. This happens because the person who rises to power, whether through cleverness or strength, no longer trusts the one who helped them get there.

Chapter 4

Why the Kingdom of Darius, Conquered by Alexander, Did Not Rebel Against the Successors of Alexander at His Death

When thinking about the struggles people face when trying to keep control of a newly conquered state, some might wonder why, after

Alexander the Great took control of Asia in just a few years and then died before he could fully settle it, the empire didn't immediately rebel. It would seem natural that such a large empire would fall apart, yet his successors managed to hold on to power, and the only real problems they faced were those created by their own ambitions.

The reason for this is that there are generally two ways that principalities, or territories ruled by princes, are governed. In one system, the prince is helped by a group of servants or ministers who only have power because the prince allows them to. In the second system, the prince rules alongside barons who gained their power through family ties, not because the prince granted it to them. These barons have their own lands and subjects, who recognize them as their rightful lords and feel a natural loyalty toward them. In the first type of government, where the prince and his servants hold power, the prince is much more respected because no one else in the country is seen as his equal. If people obey anyone else, they do so because that person is the prince's official, not because they truly feel loyal to him.

In modern times, we can see examples of both types of government by looking at the Turkish Empire and the Kingdom of France. In the Turkish Empire, the sultan is the only ruler, and everyone else is his servant. He divides his kingdom into provinces, called sanjaks, and sends different governors to rule over them. These governors can be replaced or moved whenever the sultan chooses. On the other hand, in France, the king rules alongside many lords who have been in power for a long time and are respected by their own subjects. The French lords have their own privileges, and the king cannot take those away without risking serious trouble.

When you compare these two systems, it becomes clear that conquering the Turkish Empire would be difficult, but once it's taken, it would be relatively easy to hold on to. The difficulty in conquering the Turkish Empire comes from the fact that the ruler's power is so centralized. No local princes can be persuaded to help an invader, and the sultan's ministers are loyal to him, not to their own people. Because these ministers are essentially slaves to the sultan, it's very hard to bribe or corrupt them. Even if they were bribed, they wouldn't be able to turn the people against the sultan because the people don't feel any loyalty toward them. So, if you attack the Turkish Empire, you need to rely on your own military strength rather than expecting help from the inside. However, once you've defeated the sultan in battle and his army is destroyed, there's little left to worry about. As long as the sultan's family is wiped out, there's no one else with the authority to rally the people against you, since all the sultan's officials only held power because of him.

In contrast, conquering a kingdom like France is much easier because you can gain the support of some of the local lords who are unhappy with the king. There are always people who want change and are willing to help an invader in exchange for power. These lords can help you take over the kingdom fairly easily. But holding on to it after you've conquered it is much harder. You will face challenges from both the people who helped you and those you defeated. It's not enough to simply eliminate the royal family, because the remaining lords will continue to resist you and may lead rebellions. You can't satisfy or completely eliminate all these lords, so the kingdom will eventually be lost as soon as an opportunity arises for them to strike back.

If you look at the government of Darius, the Persian ruler, you'll see that it was similar to the system used by the Turks. This is why Alexander the Great only had to defeat Darius in battle to take over his kingdom. Once Darius was killed, Alexander was able to secure the territory without much trouble for the same reasons mentioned earlier. If Alexander's successors had stayed united, they could have ruled the kingdom without difficulty because no internal rebellions would have threatened them, except those they caused themselves.

On the other hand, kingdoms like France, which have many powerful lords, are much harder to control. This is why, during Roman times, there were frequent rebellions in places like Spain, France, and Greece. These regions were filled with many principalities, and as long as the memory of these local rulers remained, the Romans could never feel completely secure in their rule. However, after the Roman Empire had ruled these places for a long time, people began to forget about their old rulers, and the Romans were finally able to maintain control without fear of rebellion. Later on, when the Roman Empire itself started to weaken, the regions were divided up among those who had gained power there, and the only rulers recognized by the people were the Romans, since the old ruling families had been eliminated.

When we consider these facts, it becomes clear why Alexander the Great was able to hold onto his empire in Asia with relative ease, while others, like Pyrrhus, struggled to maintain their conquests. It wasn't because Alexander was more skilled or capable than these other rulers, but because the structure of the territories he conquered made it easier for him to maintain control.

Chapter 5
Concerning the Way to Govern Cities or Principalities Which Lived Under Their Own Laws Before They Were Annexed

When a state that has been acquired is used to living under its own laws and enjoying freedom, there are three main ways to keep control of it. The first way is to destroy it completely. The second option is for the ruler to go and live there in person. The third way is to allow the state to keep its own laws but collect taxes from them and set up an oligarchy that will be loyal to the new ruler. This kind of government, having been put in place by the ruler, knows it cannot survive without his help and will do everything to support him. So, if a ruler wants to keep control of a city that's used to freedom, it's often easier to do so by using the city's own people to help govern rather than any other method.

Consider the example of the Spartans and the Romans. The Spartans controlled Athens and Thebes by establishing oligarchies there, but they still lost control of them. On the other hand, the Romans completely destroyed Capua, Carthage, and Numantia, and they never lost them. The Romans tried to keep control of Greece the same way the Spartans did—by allowing it to remain free and letting it keep its own laws—but they were unsuccessful. In the end, they had to destroy many cities in Greece to maintain control. The truth is, there's no safer way to keep control of a state that's used to freedom than by completely destroying it. If someone takes control of a city that is accustomed to freedom and doesn't destroy it, they can expect that city to eventually rise up and destroy them. A city like that will always use the idea of liberty and its old privileges as a rallying cry for rebellion. No amount of time or benefits will ever make them forget their former freedoms. No matter what a ruler does to prevent it, the people will never forget their past or their rights unless they become divided or scattered. They will seize any opportunity to fight for their freedom again, as Pisa did after being under the control of Florence for a hundred years.

However, when a city or state has always been ruled by a prince and the ruling family is wiped out, the people, having been used to obeying and now without their old prince, often find it hard to agree on a new leader among themselves. They don't know how to govern themselves, which makes them much slower to rebel. In such cases, it's easier for a new ruler to take control and keep them in line. But in republics, there is more energy, more hatred, and a stronger desire for revenge, which means they will never let go of the memory of their former liberty. Because of this, the safest way to handle them is either to destroy them completely or to live there and rule them directly.

Chapter 6
Concerning New Principalities Which Are Acquired by One's Own Arms and Ability

No one should be surprised if, when discussing completely new principalities, I refer to the greatest examples of both princes and states. The reason is simple: people, for the most part, walk along paths that others have already paved. They follow the footsteps of those who came before them, and though they try to imitate the actions of these predecessors, they are not always able to stick closely to their ways or match their achievements. A wise person, however, should always strive to follow in the steps of great men and emulate the best examples of leadership. Even if this person's abilities do not fully measure up to the greatness of those they are imitating, they will still come closer to success simply by aiming higher. It's like skilled archers who aim for a target that seems out of reach. Knowing the limits of their bow, they aim higher than the target, not because they expect to hit that higher point, but because aiming high allows them to reach their true target.

I say, then, that when it comes to ruling entirely new principalities, where the prince is new to his position, the difficulty of maintaining control will depend on the abilities of the person who has acquired the state. If someone rises from being a private citizen to becoming a ruler, whether through personal skill or through fortune, the challenges they face will vary according to their level of competence. Luck, or fortune, can ease some of the difficulties, but a ruler who relies less on fortune and more on their own abilities is always in a stronger position. Additionally, it is easier for a prince who doesn't rule over another state to maintain control of their own domain, because they are forced to live within their own state and focus entirely on its governance.

Let's look now at those who became princes through their own talents and abilities, rather than relying on fortune. In this regard, I would say that the most excellent examples are Moses, Cyrus, Romulus,

Theseus, and others like them. Even though Moses is often regarded as simply carrying out the will of God, he should still be admired because of the favor that allowed him to speak directly with God. Setting Moses aside for a moment, when we consider Cyrus and other leaders who founded or acquired kingdoms, we find that their deeds are no less worthy of admiration. If we closely examine their lives and actions, we see that they owed very little to fortune beyond the opportunities they encountered. Without those opportunities, their talents might have gone unnoticed. Similarly, without their extraordinary abilities, the opportunities they came across would have been wasted.

For instance, it was necessary for Moses to find the people of Israel enslaved in Egypt, oppressed and longing for freedom, so that they would be ready to follow him. It was essential for Romulus to be abandoned at birth and not remain in Alba, because only by being in such a situation could he rise to become the King of Rome and the founder of his nation. Cyrus needed to find the Persians unhappy under the rule of the Medes, while the Medes themselves had grown soft and weak from too many years of peace. Theseus, in turn, could not have demonstrated his leadership abilities had he not found the Athenians scattered and in disarray. In each of these cases, the opportunity presented itself, but it was their great abilities that allowed them to seize that opportunity and bring honor to their nations.

Those who rise to power through their own valor, like these men, often face tremendous challenges in gaining their position, but once they have succeeded, they find it much easier to maintain their rule. The difficulties they face in acquiring power often stem from the new rules and systems they must introduce to ensure the stability and security of their government. It's important to remember that nothing is harder to manage, more dangerous to carry out, or more uncertain in its success than introducing a new system of government. The reason for this is that those who benefited from the old system will naturally oppose the change, while those who stand to gain from the new system often offer only half-hearted support. This lack of strong support arises partly from fear of those who oppose the change, as they have the law on their side, and partly because people are generally resistant to accepting new things until they have had a long time to experience them.

As a result, when the enemies of change have the opportunity to attack, they do so with great determination, while the supporters defend the new system weakly, thus putting the ruler in danger. This is why, when discussing this topic in full, we need to ask whether these innovators can rely on themselves or if they must depend on others. In other words, do they achieve their goals through persuasion, or do they have the ability to use force if necessary? Those who rely solely on persuasion often fail because their efforts lack the strength to enforce their ideas. But those who can rely on their own strength and use force when needed face far fewer risks. This is why all armed prophets have succeeded, while unarmed ones have failed.

Beyond this, we must also understand that people are naturally inconsistent. It is easy to persuade them of something, but it's much harder to keep them convinced over time. For this reason, a ruler must be prepared to use force to maintain control when persuasion alone no longer works. If Moses, Cyrus, Theseus, and Romulus had not been armed, they would not have been able to establish and enforce their laws for long. This was the downfall of Fra Girolamo Savonarola, a man from our own time who tried to introduce a new order of things. As soon as people stopped believing in him, he had no way to maintain his followers' support or to bring back those who had turned against him.

Therefore, rulers who seek to introduce new systems face significant challenges, and most of their dangers arise during the process of gaining power. However, those with the necessary abilities can overcome these difficulties. Once they have triumphed over their adversaries and neutralized the threats against them, they will become secure, respected, and powerful, ensuring their success for the future.

In addition to these great examples, I want to mention a lesser-known one that still bears a resemblance to the others. This is the case of Hiero of Syracuse. Although his story may not be as grand as those of Moses or Romulus, it is still significant. Hiero rose from being an ordinary citizen to becoming the ruler of Syracuse. He did not owe his rise to fortune, but rather to opportunity, as the people of Syracuse, feeling oppressed, chose him as their leader. Later, they made him their prince. Hiero possessed such great skill, even before he became ruler, that someone once said he only needed a kingdom to become a king. After gaining power, he reorganized the military, replaced old alliances with new ones, and built a solid foundation for his rule. With his own soldiers and allies, he was able to maintain his power with ease. Though he faced great challenges in rising to power, he found it relatively easy to hold onto once he had achieved it.

Chapter 7

Concerning New Principalities Which Are Acquired Either by The Arms of Others or By Good Fortune

Those who become princes solely through good fortune, starting as private citizens, find it easy to rise but struggle to stay in power. They face few difficulties on their way up because they ascend so quickly, but they encounter many challenges once they reach the top. These are the people who gain control of a state through money or by the favor of someone else, like many in Greece who were made princes in the cities of Ionia and the Hellespont by Darius. He made them rulers to secure the cities for his own safety and glory. The same happened with emperors who, through the corruption of soldiers, rose from being private citizens to emperors. These individuals rely only on the goodwill and luck of the person who raised them to power—two of the most unreliable and unstable foundations to stand on. They also lack the necessary experience for their position because, unless they are extremely capable, it is not reasonable to expect them to know how to lead, having always lived as ordinary citizens. Additionally, they cannot maintain their power because they don't have loyal and dependable forces.

States that rise suddenly, like many things in nature that are born and grow rapidly, often fail to establish strong foundations or lasting relationships with other states. As a result, when the first storm hits, they are easily overthrown. This is what happens to people who become princes unexpectedly. Unless they are very capable and understand that they need to quickly prepare to hold onto the power fortune has handed them, their reign will be short-lived. The strong foundations that other rulers lay before becoming princes must be laid afterward by those who rise suddenly.

To illustrate the two methods of becoming a prince, through either ability or fortune, I will give two examples from recent memory: Francesco Sforza and Cesare Borgia. Francesco, through his abilities and wise actions, rose from being a private citizen to becoming Duke of Milan, and he held onto his power with ease after working so hard to obtain it. On the other hand, Cesare Borgia, who was called Duke Valentino, gained power through his father's influence, but when his father's power declined, he lost his own position. This happened even though he did everything a wise and capable person should do to firmly secure the states that were handed to him by others' efforts and fortune.

As mentioned before, if someone has not already laid their foundations, they might be able to do so later with great skill, but it will be much harder for them, and there will always be a risk of failure. If we consider the actions taken by Duke Valentino, we can see that he laid solid foundations for his future power, and I don't think it's a waste of time to discuss his efforts. In fact, I believe there is no better example to offer a new prince than the actions he took. If his plans ultimately failed, it wasn't because of any fault of his own, but rather due to an extraordinary and unpredictable stroke of bad luck.

Alexander the Sixth, Cesare Borgia's father, wanted to elevate his son's power, but he faced many difficulties, both immediate and in the long term. First, he couldn't figure out how to make his son the ruler of any state that wasn't already part of the Church. Even if he had been willing to take land from the Church, the Duke of Milan and the Venetians would never have agreed to it because Faenza and Rimini were already under the Venetians' protection. Moreover, the military forces in Italy, which could have helped Cesare, were in the hands of people who feared the Pope's growing power, like the Orsini and the Colonna families and their followers. Therefore, the Pope needed to disrupt this balance of power and create conflicts to gain control of some of their lands. Fortunately for him, he found that the Venetians, for other reasons, wanted to bring the French back into Italy. The Pope didn't oppose this; instead, he made it easier by annulling King Louis's previous marriage. As a result, the French king entered Italy with the support of the Venetians and the Pope. Once King Louis took Milan, the Pope gained soldiers from him for his campaign in the Romagna, which quickly surrendered to Cesare because of the king's reputation.

After Cesare conquered the Romagna and defeated the Colonna family, he wanted to hold onto his new territories and expand further. However, he was faced with two major problems. First, his forces didn't seem entirely loyal to him, and second, he couldn't be sure of France's continued support. In particular, he feared that the Orsini family, whose forces he was using, might not remain loyal. Not only might they prevent him from expanding, but they could also seize the territories he had already taken. He had already seen a sign of this when, after taking Faenza and attacking Bologna, the Orsini troops showed little enthusiasm for continuing the fight. As for the king of France, Cesare realized his intentions when, after he took the Duchy of Urbino, he began to move against Tuscany, only for the king to order him to stop. This led Cesare to decide that he could no longer rely on the armies or luck of others.

To address the first problem, Cesare weakened the power of the Orsini and Colonna families in Rome by gaining the loyalty of their supporters. He made these nobles his own by paying them well and giving them honors and offices. In this way, he turned their loyalty away from their former factions and toward himself. Within a few months, all their loyalty had shifted. After dealing with their supporters, Cesare waited for the right moment to crush the Orsini family itself, having already scattered the followers of the Colonna family. His opportunity came quickly, and he took full advantage of it. The Orsini family, realizing that Cesare's rise to power and the strengthening of the Church were their downfall, organized a meeting in Magione in Perugia. This led to the rebellion in Urbino and uprisings throughout the Romagna, which put Cesare in great danger. However, with the help of the French, he managed to restore his authority.

Once his power was restored, Cesare knew he couldn't leave his future to chance or trust in the help of either the French or any other foreign forces. He turned to cunning and strategy, hiding his true intentions so well that, with the help of Signor Pagolo, he tricked the Orsini into a false sense of security. He gave Pagolo money, clothes, and horses, and through these efforts, the Orsini were lulled into reconciliation, which led them right into Cesare's trap at Sinigaglia. After eliminating their leaders and winning over their followers, Cesare laid a strong foundation for his power. He now controlled all of Romagna and the Duchy of Urbino, and the people, seeing the prosperity he brought, came to support him. Since this is an important and instructive point, I believe it is worth noting for others to follow.

When the duke took control of the Romagna, he found the region under the governance of weak rulers who did not lead their people properly. Instead of ruling fairly, they exploited their subjects and caused more division than unity. The land was full of thieves, conflicts, and widespread violence. To restore peace and order, and to ensure that authority was respected again, the duke realized that a strong governor was necessary. He decided to appoint Messer Ramiro d'Orco, a man known for being swift and ruthless, giving him absolute power to do whatever was needed. In a short period, Ramiro managed to bring peace and unity to the region with great success. However, the duke soon realized that it was dangerous to allow someone to hold such immense power for too long. Ramiro had become unpopular due to his severity. To address this, the duke established a court of justice with an excellent judge presiding, giving each city representation in the court. Understanding that the harsh actions of the past might have caused the people to resent him, the duke wanted to show them that if any cruelty had been committed, it wasn't his fault, but rather the nature of the minister he had appointed. In order to clear his own name and win the people over, he took action. One morning, he had Ramiro arrested, executed, and left his body on display in the town square of Cesena with the chopping block and bloody knife beside him. The shock of this brutal scene left the people both satisfied and terrified, achieving the duke's goal of maintaining control while distancing himself from the harshness of Ramiro's rule.

Now, let's return to the situation as it was. The duke, feeling confident in his power, had armed himself and weakened the forces nearby that might have been a threat to his rule. He had dealt with the immediate dangers surrounding him and had strengthened his position. However, he now had to turn his attention to France. The duke understood that the king of France, having realized too late the mistakes he had made, would no longer support him. From that moment on, the duke began looking for new alliances and strategies to manage the French, who were involved in a campaign in Naples against the Spaniards, who had laid siege to Gaeta. The duke's goal was to secure himself against these powers, and he likely would have succeeded had Pope Alexander VI lived longer.

This was how the duke handled the present challenges, but he also had to think about the future. One of his biggest concerns was that the next pope might not be favorable to him and could try to take away the lands Alexander had given him. To prepare for this, the duke devised a four-part strategy. First, he aimed to eliminate the families of the lords he had overthrown, so the new pope couldn't use them as a reason to act against him. Second, he sought to win the loyalty of all the nobles of Rome, so he could use them to keep the pope in check. Third, he worked to build influence within the College of Cardinals. Fourth, he wanted to build enough power before the pope's death to withstand any challenges that might arise afterward. By the time Alexander died, the duke had already achieved three of these goals. He had eliminated many of the dispossessed lords, secured the loyalty of the Roman nobles, and had the largest faction within the College of Cardinals on his side. As for the fourth goal, gaining more power, he was on the way to achieving that as well. He had set his sights on controlling Tuscany, since he already held Perugia and Piombino, and Pisa was under his protection. With France no longer a threat, because the French had been driven out of Naples by the Spaniards, both sides needed his favor. He decided to make his move on Pisa. Soon after, both Lucca and Siena also fell in line, partly because of their hatred of the Florentines and partly out of fear. The Florentines would have had no way to stop him if he had continued his campaign, as he was in a strong position when Alexander died. The duke had built up so much power and reputation that he could have stood on his own, without relying on the fortune or forces of others, depending only on his own abilities.

But Alexander died just five years after the duke first took up arms. This left the duke with Romagna as the only fully consolidated part of his territory, while the rest was still up in the air. He found himself caught between two powerful enemy armies, and to make things worse, he was gravely ill. Even under these challenging circumstances, the duke's boldness and skill were evident. He knew exactly how to win over people or defeat them if necessary, and the foundations he had built in such a short time were so strong that, had it not been for the armies pressing against him or his illness, he likely would have overcome all his challenges. It was clear that the foundations he had laid were solid, as the people of Romagna waited for him for over a month. In Rome, even while severely weakened, he remained secure. Despite the presence of the Baglioni, Vitelli, and Orsini in Rome, they could do nothing to undermine him. Even though he couldn't ensure the election of the pope he wanted, he was strong enough to prevent the election of someone he opposed. If only he had been in better health at the time of Alexander's death, everything could have turned out differently. On the day Julius II was elected, the duke confided in me, saying that he had planned for every possible scenario following his father's death, and had prepared solutions for each one. The only thing he hadn't anticipated was that, when his father died, he himself would be on the verge of death.

In reviewing all of the duke's actions, I find no reason to criticize him. On the contrary, I believe that he provides an example worthy of imitation for anyone who gains power through the fortune and arms of others. The duke had a grand vision and vast ambitions, and he acted in the only way he could have to achieve them. It was not his fault that he was thwarted by the short life of Alexander and his own illness. For anyone who wishes to secure themselves in a new principality, to win friends, defeat enemies by force or deceit, be loved and feared by the people, respected by the soldiers, eliminate those who can harm them, change the old order to create something new, be both severe and gracious, and maintain alliances with other rulers so they only help with care and harm with reluctance, there is no better example to follow than the actions of this man.

The only mistake the duke made was in allowing Julius II to be elected as pope. This was a poor choice because, although he couldn't ensure the election of a pope favorable to him, he could have prevented the election of someone who would be hostile to him. He should have never permitted anyone he had wronged or who had a reason to fear him to ascend to the papacy. People harm others either out of fear or hatred. Those he had wronged, such as San Pietro ad Vincula, Colonna, San Giorgio, and Ascanio, had every reason to be concerned if they became pope. The exceptions were Rouen and the Spaniards, due to their connections and obligations to the duke. Above all, the duke should have ensured that a Spaniard was elected pope, and if that wasn't possible, he should have supported Rouen instead of San Pietro ad Vincula. Anyone who thinks that new favors can make people forget old injuries is mistaken. This is where the duke went wrong, and this misstep led to his ultimate downfall.

Chapter 8
Concerning Those Who Have Obtained a Principality by Wickedness

Although a prince may rise from a private station in two different ways, neither of which can be completely attributed to fortune or to individual ability, it is clear to me that I must not remain silent on them. Even though one of these paths could be explored in greater depth when I discuss republics, these methods still deserve attention. The two ways are: first, when someone rises to power through wicked and immoral means, and second, when a private person becomes the prince of his country through the favor of his fellow citizens. In regard to the first method, I will illustrate it with two examples—one from ancient times and one from modern times—and without delving too deeply into the subject, I am confident these examples will provide sufficient insight for anyone who might find themselves compelled to follow such a path to power.

Agathocles of Sicily became King of Syracuse not only from a private station but from a particularly humble and lowly background. Born the son of a potter, Agathocles lived an infamous life through all the shifts in his fortune. Despite his many crimes and misdeeds, he combined his wicked acts with such skill, both in mind and body, that after dedicating himself to a military career, he rose steadily through the ranks. He eventually attained the position of Praetor of Syracuse.

Once firmly established in that position and determined to make himself prince, Agathocles decided to seize power through force, relying on no one but himself. To this end, he formed an alliance with Amilcar, a Carthaginian general who was already engaged in war in Sicily. One morning, Agathocles summoned the people and senate of Syracuse to what appeared to be a discussion of matters concerning the Republic. But at a prearranged signal, his soldiers killed all the senators and the wealthiest citizens of the city. Once these individuals were eliminated, Agathocles took control of the city without any civil unrest or opposition from the populace.

Although Agathocles was defeated twice by the Carthaginians and eventually besieged, he managed not only to defend the city but also, after leaving part of his forces behind to guard it, led the rest of his army to launch an offensive against Africa. In a relatively short period of time, he was able to raise the siege of Syracuse and force the Carthaginians, now reduced to a state of extreme desperation, to come to terms. As a result, Agathocles gained control of Sicily while the Carthaginians were forced to content themselves with retaining control of Africa.

Anyone who closely examines the actions and mind of Agathocles will see that very little, if anything, in his rise to power can be attributed to luck. As mentioned above, Agathocles achieved prominence not through the favor of anyone else but through his advancement in the military profession, step by step, despite countless hardships and dangers. After gaining power, he was able to maintain his rule through bold, decisive actions, regardless of the dangers involved. However, it would not be right to call Agathocles' methods true talent, as they involved the murder of fellow citizens, the betrayal of friends, and a complete lack of faith, mercy, or religious belief. These methods might bring about the acquisition of power, but they will never bring lasting glory. Still, when considering Agathocles' bravery in both entering into and extricating himself from dangerous situations, as well as his strength in enduring and overcoming hardships, it is difficult to see why he should not be ranked among the greatest military leaders. Nevertheless, his extreme cruelty, barbarous nature, and endless wickedness prevent him from being celebrated among the most excellent and admired men. What he accomplished cannot be attributed to fortune or true genius, but rather to ruthless persistence.

In more recent times, during the rule of Pope Alexander VI, Oliverotto da Fermo provides another example of this kind of rise to power. Orphaned at a young age, Oliverotto was raised by his maternal uncle, Giovanni Fogliani. In his youth, Oliverotto was sent to serve under Pagolo Vitelli, with the aim of learning the military profession and hopefully achieving distinction. After Pagolo died, Oliverotto fought under Pagolo's brother, Vitellozzo, and quickly distinguished himself due to his intelligence and physical vigor. In a short time, he became one of the foremost men in his profession. However, feeling it was beneath him to serve under others, Oliverotto resolved to seize power for himself. With the support of several citizens of Fermo, who valued the servitude of their city more than its freedom, and with the backing of the Vitelli family, he devised a plan to take control of Fermo.

Oliverotto wrote to his uncle Giovanni, expressing his desire to visit after many years away and to see his patrimony once again. He claimed that, although he had only gained honor from his time away, he wanted to show the citizens that he had not wasted his years of service. To make his return more impressive, he planned to arrive with a hundred horsemen, friends, and followers, and he asked Giovanni to arrange an honorable reception for him. Giovanni spared no effort in fulfilling his nephew's wishes. He ensured that Oliverotto was received with honor by the people of Fermo and even hosted him in his own home. After spending several days there and carefully planning his scheme, Oliverotto invited Giovanni and the leading citizens of Fermo to a grand banquet. Once the meal and festivities were finished, Oliverotto began discussing the greatness of Pope Alexander and his son Cesare and their numerous achievements. The guests engaged in this conversation, but Oliverotto soon suggested that such important matters should be discussed in private. He led them into a separate chamber, and as soon as they were seated, armed soldiers appeared from hiding and killed Giovanni and the others.

Following these murders, Oliverotto mounted his horse, rode through the streets of the city, and laid siege to the palace where the chief magistrate resided. The terrified people were forced to submit to his rule, and Oliverotto established a new government, with himself as prince. He ruthlessly killed anyone who opposed him and solidified his control with new civil and military policies. During the year he held power, he not only secured his position in Fermo but also became feared by all his neighbors. His downfall would have been as difficult as Agathocles' had he not been deceived by Cesare Borgia, who captured him, along with the Orsini and Vitelli, at Sinigaglia. One year after committing this parricide, Oliverotto was strangled, along with Vitellozzo, who had led him in both valor and wickedness.

Some might wonder how men like Agathocles and Oliverotto, despite their countless acts of treachery and cruelty, were able to live securely in their own countries, defend themselves from external enemies, and avoid being overthrown by their own citizens. Meanwhile, other rulers who employed cruelty have never been able to hold onto power, even in times of peace, let alone in the face of war. I believe the difference lies in how cruelty is used—whether it is used effectively or poorly. Cruelty can be considered well-used—if such a thing can be said—when it is executed all at once and is necessary for securing power. Once the initial harm is done, it should not be repeated unless it benefits the people. On the other hand, cruelty is poorly used when, although it may start small, it gradually increases over time instead of being reduced. Those who use cruelty well are able, with the help of God or man, to soften its impact on their subjects, as Agathocles did. But those who misuse cruelty will never be able to maintain their power.

Thus, it is important to note that when a ruler takes over a state, he must carefully consider all the harm he needs to inflict and do it all at once, so that he does not have to repeat it every day. By inflicting harm in a single stroke, the ruler can avoid unsettling the people repeatedly, and after the initial violence, he can win their loyalty through later acts of kindness and generosity. A ruler who acts otherwise, either out of fear or due to bad advice, will be forced to keep the knife in his hand constantly, never able to trust his subjects, and they will never be able to fully trust him due to the continual harm he causes. Cruel actions should be carried out all at once so that the people experience less of the pain, while acts of kindness should be distributed gradually, allowing the people to savor them over time.

Above all, a prince must live among his people in such a way that no sudden change in fortune, whether good or bad, forces him to alter his behavior. Because if he waits until times of trouble to act, it will be too late for harsh measures to succeed, and any acts of kindness will be seen as forced and insincere. In such circumstances, no one will feel obligated to support him, and his actions will fail to inspire loyalty or gratitude.

Chapter 9
Concerning A Civil Principality

Now, turning to the other case—where a leading citizen becomes the prince of his country not through wickedness or unbearable violence, but by the favor of his fellow citizens—this is what we can call a civil principality. To achieve this, neither genius nor fortune is entirely necessary, but rather a cleverness that comes from good judgment. I would say that such a principality is gained either with the help of the people or with the help of the nobles. In all cities, there are these two distinct groups, and from this division, it naturally happens that the people do not want to be ruled or oppressed by the nobles, while the nobles want to rule and oppress the people. From these conflicting desires, one of three outcomes arises in cities: a principality, self-government, or anarchy.

A principality can be created either by the people or by the nobles, depending on who has the opportunity. When the nobles see that they cannot defeat the people, they elevate one of their own to the position of prince, so that they can use his power to fulfill their ambitions. On the other hand, when the people realize they cannot resist the power of the nobles, they will raise up one of their own as a prince, so that they can be protected by his authority. However, it is more difficult for someone who gains power through the support of the nobles to maintain his rule than it is for someone who rises with the support of the people. This is because a prince backed by the nobles finds himself surrounded by many who see themselves as his equals, making it harder for him to control them. In contrast, a prince who rises with the support of the people finds himself more alone, with few or no individuals around him who are not willing to obey him.

Additionally, it is nearly impossible to satisfy the nobles through honest means without harming others, but you can satisfy the people because their desires are more reasonable than those of the nobles. The nobles want to oppress, while the people simply want to avoid being oppressed. Moreover, a prince can never fully protect himself from a hostile population, as they are too numerous, but he can defend himself against hostile nobles, as they are fewer in number. The worst a prince can expect from an angry people is that they will abandon him. However, when it comes to hostile nobles, the prince has to worry not only about their abandonment but also about their active opposition. The nobles, being more cunning and farsighted in such matters, will always act in time to save themselves and seek favor with whoever they think will win. Furthermore, a prince must always live among the people, while he can easily do without the same group of nobles, as he can elevate or demote them at will, giving and taking away authority as he pleases.

To make this point clearer, I would say that the nobles should be considered in two main ways. First, some nobles will attach themselves entirely to your fortune and follow your lead. These nobles should be honored and loved. Second, there are those who do not attach themselves to you, and they can be handled in one of two ways. Some fail to do so because of a natural lack of courage or fearfulness. These nobles can still be useful, especially those who offer good advice. You can honor them when things are going well, and during difficult times, you don't have to fear them. However, when nobles avoid aligning with you out of ambition and self-interest, it is a sign that they are thinking more about themselves than about your success. In this case, the prince must be cautious of them and treat them as potential enemies because, in times of adversity, they will likely work toward his downfall.

Thus, a prince who gains power through the favor of the people must keep them on his side, which is relatively easy because they only ask not to be oppressed. On the other hand, a prince who rises to power with the support of the nobles, despite the people's opposition, must make it his top priority to win over the people. This can be done easily if the prince takes the people under his protection. When people receive good from a prince whom they expected to harm them, they become even more loyal to him. In such cases, the people will quickly become more dedicated to the prince than if he had originally gained power through their support. A prince can win the favor of the people in many ways, but since these ways vary depending on the circumstances, it's difficult to set hard and fast rules for this. However, I will repeat that it is crucial for a prince to maintain the people's goodwill, because without it, he has no security in difficult times.

Nabis, the prince of Sparta, successfully defended his country and his rule against the combined forces of all of Greece and a victorious Roman army. He was able to overcome this peril by ensuring he had secured the loyalty of a few key individuals. This would not have been possible had the people been against him. Some might argue using the well-known saying, "He who builds on the people, builds on mud," but this is only true for private citizens who rely on the people to save them from their enemies or from government authorities. Such people often find themselves deceived, as happened to the Gracchi in Rome and to

Giorgio Scali in Florence. But a prince who has established his power, who is able to command respect, who is courageous, and who does not lose his nerve in tough times will not find himself deceived by the people. It will become clear that he has built his foundations well.

These types of principalities are at risk when they transition from a civil government to an absolute one. Princes may rule either directly or through magistrates. When a prince rules through magistrates, his government is weaker and more vulnerable because it relies on the goodwill of the citizens who hold these offices. These citizens, especially in times of unrest, can easily undermine the government through conspiracy or open defiance. During such times, the prince may not be able to exercise full authority, because the people, having become accustomed to taking orders from the magistrates, may be unwilling to obey the prince in moments of confusion. In these challenging times, the prince may also find it difficult to trust anyone around him. The loyalty he sees during peaceful times, when people depend on the state, will not necessarily be present when the state needs its citizens. In quiet times, everyone agrees with the prince, they all make promises, and when death seems far away, they are all willing to die for him. However, in times of crisis, when the state requires their help, the prince often finds very few willing to act. This makes the situation even more dangerous because it can only be tested once.

Therefore, a wise prince must ensure that his citizens, in all situations, will always need both the state and him. If he can achieve this, he will always find them loyal and faithful to him.

Chapter 10

Concerning the Way in Which the Strength of All Principalities Ought to Be Measured

It's important to consider another factor when examining these types of principalities: whether a prince has enough power to rely on his own resources in times of need, or if he will always require the help of others. To make this clear, I believe that those princes can rely on their own resources who, through an abundance of men or money, can raise a sufficient army to face any enemy who attacks them. On the other hand, there are those who will always need the assistance of others because they cannot meet the enemy in open battle and must instead defend themselves by hiding behind their city walls.

We have already discussed the first scenario, but I will revisit it if necessary. In the second scenario, there is little more to say than to encourage such princes to strengthen and provision their cities well, and avoid trying to defend the countryside. Any prince who properly fortifies his town and manages the affairs of his subjects as we have already discussed and will continue to emphasize, will rarely be attacked without careful consideration by his enemies. This is because men generally avoid undertaking tasks that appear difficult, and it is clear that attacking a well-fortified city, ruled by a prince who is not hated by his people, is not an easy venture.

For example, the cities of Germany are almost entirely independent, owning little land outside their walls, and they obey the emperor only when it suits them. They do not fear the emperor or any neighboring power because they are so well fortified. Each city has proper defenses, such as deep ditches and strong walls, and they maintain enough artillery. Furthermore, they always store enough provisions—food, drink, and firewood—to last a year. Beyond this, they keep their people busy with work that benefits the city, providing the labor that strengthens their community and supports its economy. These cities also value military training, and they have many laws and regulations in place to keep everything running smoothly.

Therefore, a prince who has a strong, well-fortified city and has not made himself hated by his people will not be easily attacked. And even if someone does try to attack, they will likely be met with failure and shame. Moreover, because the affairs of the world are so unpredictable, it's nearly impossible for an army to remain in the field for a full year without facing some kind of disruption. If anyone argues that the people, upon seeing their property outside the city burned and destroyed, will not remain patient and will eventually forget their loyalty to the prince during a long siege, I would respond by saying that a brave and wise prince will be able to handle these challenges. He can assure his people that the hardships will not last long, instill fear of the enemy's cruelty when necessary, and skillfully manage any subjects who seem too bold or rebellious.

Additionally, the enemy will most likely burn and devastate the countryside immediately upon arrival, while the spirits of the people are still high and ready for defense. This means the prince should hesitate even less, because by the time the initial excitement has worn off and people's spirits have cooled, the damage will already have been done, and there will be no way to undo the harm. By then, the people are more likely to unite with their prince, feeling a stronger connection to him since their homes and belongings have been destroyed in the prince's defense. After all, it is human nature to feel tied to others not only by the benefits one receives but also by the benefits one gives.

Therefore, when all things are carefully considered, a wise prince will not find it difficult to maintain the loyalty of his citizens from the beginning of a siege to the end, as long as he remains steadfast in supporting and defending them.

Chapter 11
Concerning Ecclesiastical Principalities

Now we turn to the topic of ecclesiastical principalities. All difficulties concerning them arise before one acquires such a state because these types of principalities are gained either through skill or fortune. However, once acquired, they can be maintained without either of those qualities. These states are supported by the long-standing rules of religion, which are so powerful and influential that these principalities can be maintained regardless of how their princes behave. These princes are unique because they have states but do not need to defend them, and they have subjects they do not need to rule. Even though their states are not guarded, they are not taken from them, and even though their subjects are not actively governed, they do not mind. Neither do the people have the desire or the ability to separate themselves from the rule of these princes. These principalities are secure and prosperous. Since they are upheld by forces beyond human understanding, I will say no more about them, as their exalted position is maintained by God, and it would be arrogant and rash to discuss them further.

However, if anyone asks how it is that the Church has gained such great temporal power, especially considering that before the time of Alexander VI, Italian rulers, including even the smallest barons and lords, paid little attention to the Church's secular power—yet now even a king of France fears it—it would not be unnecessary to revisit this in some detail.

Before Charles VIII, King of France, invaded Italy, the country was divided among several powers: the Pope, the Venetians, the King of Naples, the Duke of Milan, and the Florentines. These rulers had two main concerns: first, that no foreign power should invade Italy, and second, that none among themselves should gain more territory. Of all these powers, the Pope and the Venetians were the most concerning. It took the united efforts of the others to restrain the Venetians, such as during the defense of Ferrara. To keep the Pope's power in check, they relied on the barons of Rome, who were divided into two factions, the Orsini and the Colonnesi. These factions were constantly at odds, and with arms always in hand, they caused unrest right under the Pope's nose, which kept the papacy weak. Even when a courageous Pope, such as Sixtus IV, came to power, neither fortune nor wisdom could free him from these challenges. Another factor that contributed to the weakness of the papacy was the short tenure of each Pope. On average, a Pope ruled for about ten years, which was not enough time to weaken one faction fully. For example, even if one Pope nearly destroyed the Colonnesi, the Orsini would rise up, and the cycle of factional rivalry would continue. This is why, in Italy, the temporal power of the Pope was not highly regarded.

Then came Alexander VI, a Pope who showed, more than any other, how powerful a Pope could become when he had both money and military strength. Through his partnership with Duke Valentino (Cesare Borgia) and the involvement of the French, Alexander was able to accomplish many things, as I have already discussed regarding the actions of the duke. Although Alexander's primary goal was to increase the power of his son, the Duke, his efforts also ended up strengthening the Church. After Alexander's death and the fall of the Duke, the Church inherited all of his efforts and became much more powerful.

Pope Julius II followed Alexander and found the Church in a strong position. It had gained control of all of Romagna, the barons of Rome had been weakened, and the factions that had once caused so much disorder were nearly destroyed, thanks to Alexander's actions. In addition, Julius found a new way to raise money that had not been practiced before Alexander's time. Julius not only continued Alexander's policies but also improved upon them. His ambitions included conquering Bologna, defeating the Venetians, and driving the French out of Italy. Julius was successful in all these endeavors, and his achievements are even more commendable because he worked solely to strengthen the Church, rather than to benefit any private individual. He also kept the Orsini and Colonnesi factions under control. Although there were still some who wanted to cause trouble, Julius maintained two key advantages: first, the great power of the Church, which he used to intimidate the factions; and second, he did not allow them to have their own cardinals, who were often the cause of disorder. When these factions have their own cardinals, they rarely remain quiet because the cardinals stir up trouble both in Rome and outside of it, and the barons are forced to support them. Thus, the ambitions of these high-ranking church officials create disorder among the barons.

For these reasons, Pope Leo X inherited a powerful papacy. If his predecessors made the Church great through military strength, it is to be hoped that Leo will make it even greater and more revered through his kindness, goodness, and many other virtues.

Chapter 12

How Many Kinds of Soldiery There Are, And Concerning Mercenaries

Having now thoroughly examined the characteristics of principalities as I initially set out to do, and having delved into the reasons why some are good and others bad, as well as the strategies through which many have acquired and maintained them, it is time to discuss the broader means of offense and defense that apply to each of them.

We have already observed how vital it is for a prince to have strong foundations. Without a solid base, a prince will inevitably face downfall. The key foundations of all states, whether new, old, or composite, are good laws and strong arms. However, since good laws cannot exist where the state is poorly armed, it naturally follows that where there are strong arms, there will also be good laws. Although laws are essential, I shall leave them aside for the moment and focus primarily on the topic of arms.

The arms with which a prince defends his state can be categorized into several types: they are either his own, or they are mercenaries, auxiliaries, or a combination of these. Of these, mercenaries and auxiliaries are not only unreliable but downright dangerous. A state that is defended by these forces will never stand firm or secure. Mercenaries are disloyal, disunited, undisciplined, and often more concerned with their own gain than with the safety of the state. They might appear brave among friends, but they will prove cowardly before enemies. They have neither the fear of God nor loyalty to their fellow men. Their destruction is merely delayed, as it is only postponed until the enemy decides to strike. In peacetime, mercenaries rob you of security, and in wartime, they abandon you to the mercy of your enemies. Their only motivation is a meager stipend, which is never enough to make them willing to sacrifice their lives for you. These soldiers are happy to serve you when there is no conflict, but as soon as war breaks out, they desert or flee from the enemy. It is not difficult to prove this point, as Italy's ruin can be traced directly to her reliance on mercenary forces for many years. While these mercenaries once put on a display of bravery among themselves, they quickly revealed their cowardice when foreign invaders arrived. This is why Charles, King of France, was able to seize Italy with "chalk in hand." The person who claimed that our sins were the reason for Italy's downfall spoke the truth, but it was not the sins they believed. It was, in fact, the failures of our princes. Since these faults lay with the rulers, they are the ones who have paid the price.

I would like to further illustrate the shortcomings of mercenary forces. Mercenary captains are either capable or they are not. If they are skilled, you cannot trust them, because they will always strive to increase their own power, often by oppressing you, their employer, or acting against your will and attacking others. If the captain is not competent, then the state will fall as expected in the usual way.

One might argue that anyone, whether a mercenary or a native soldier, will behave similarly once armed. However, I would reply that when a state must rely on arms, whether it is a prince or a republic, the prince should personally lead his army. In the case of a republic, it should send its own citizens. If one commander proves unworthy, he can be recalled, and if another proves capable, the state can secure him through laws to ensure his continued loyalty. Both history and experience have shown that states relying on their own arms have thrived, whereas those relying on mercenaries have suffered greatly. It is far easier to bring a state that is armed with foreign soldiers under the control of an ambitious individual than it is to subjugate one that is armed with its own people. Rome and Sparta, for example, remained armed and free for centuries. Similarly, the Swiss today are fully armed and completely free.

Looking back at ancient times, one of the most famous examples of mercenary soldiers is the case of the Carthaginians, who were nearly destroyed by their mercenaries after their first war with the Romans, even though the Carthaginians had placed their own citizens in command. After the death of Epaminondas, the Thebans chose Philip of Macedon as their military leader, but after securing victory for them, he stripped them of their liberty.

When Duke Filippo died, the Milanese hired Francesco Sforza to fight against the Venetians. After defeating the Venetians at Caravaggio, Sforza allied himself with them and turned against his original employers, the Milanese. Likewise, his father, Sforza, had been hired by Queen Johanna of Naples, but he abandoned her, forcing her to turn to the King of Aragon for help in order to save her kingdom. If we look to the Venetians and Florentines, they were fortunate in their use of mercenaries during their early expansions, as their commanders did not seek to overthrow them and make themselves princes. But this was more due to luck than wisdom. In the case of the Florentines, many capable captains whom they might have feared were either unsuccessful, opposed by rivals, or had ambitions elsewhere. For example, Giovanni Acuto, a notable commander, did not achieve victory, so his loyalty was never put to the test. However, it is universally accepted that had he succeeded, the Florentines would have been at his mercy. Francesco Sforza always had the Bracceschi opposing him, keeping both factions in check. Francesco set his sights on Lombardy, while Braccio focused on the Church and the Kingdom of Naples.

Let us now consider more recent events. The Florentines appointed Pagolo Vitelli, a man of great wisdom and renown, as their captain. He had risen from humble beginnings to great fame. Had he taken the city of Pisa, the Florentines would have had no choice but to align themselves with him, for they would have had no way to resist him if he chose to turn against them. If they supported him, they would have had to submit entirely to his will. The Venetians, on the other hand, acted wisely and with glory as long as they relied on their own citizens to fight their wars. Both their noblemen and commoners fought with great courage during that time. However, this was before they began seeking to expand their territories on land. Once they did, they abandoned their earlier virtues and adopted the flawed practices common in Italy.

At the beginning of their land expansion, the Venetians had little territory and an outstanding reputation, so they had little to fear from their captains. However, as they grew, they began to experience the consequences of relying on mercenary forces, particularly under the leadership of Carmignuola. Although Carmignuola had been a valiant and capable commander who led them to victory against the Duke of Milan, his growing indifference to the war made them fear he would no longer deliver further victories. They found themselves unable to dismiss him, nor could they afford to continue relying on him. To avoid losing what they had already gained, they were forced to take extreme measures and have him killed. Later, they appointed other captains, such as Bartolomeo da Bergamo, Roberto da San Severino, and the Count of Pitigliano. However, under these leaders, the Venetians experienced more losses than gains, as was evident in the Battle of Vaila, where they lost in one battle what had taken them eight hundred years to acquire. This occurred because conquests achieved through mercenary forces are slow and painstaking, while losses, when they come, are sudden and catastrophic.

With these examples now bringing us to Italy, which has been governed for many years by mercenaries, I find it necessary to delve more thoroughly into their role. By gaining a deeper understanding of their rise and how they came to dominate, we can better prepare to counteract the negative influence they've had. It's crucial to grasp that Italy recently began rejecting the authority of the empire. At the same time, the Pope gained more control over temporal power, and Italy became fragmented into numerous smaller states. This fragmentation happened because many of the large cities had taken up arms against their nobles, who, with the emperor's favor, had been oppressing them. Meanwhile, the Church was helping these cities in order to extend its own influence over political matters. In other cities, citizens themselves rose to become the rulers. Because of these shifts, Italy gradually fell partly into the hands of the Church and various republics. But since the Church was made up of clergy and the republics were run by citizens unused to warfare, both turned to hiring foreign soldiers to defend themselves.

The first to bring recognition to this practice of hiring mercenaries was Alberigo da Conio, a man from Romagna. From his military school came prominent figures such as Braccio and Sforza, who, during their lifetimes, became the most powerful military leaders in Italy. After them came a long list of commanders who have directed Italy's military affairs up until now. However, despite their supposed military prowess, the outcome of their actions has been disastrous. Italy has been trampled by Charles, plundered by Louis, ravaged by Ferdinand, and humiliated by the Swiss. The main strategy these commanders followed was to undermine the importance of infantry, solely to increase their own influence. They did this because they lived off their wages and didn't own land, which meant they couldn't support large armies. A small number of infantry soldiers didn't give them enough power, so they began to rely more on cavalry, which allowed them to maintain their influence while commanding fewer troops. As a result, Italy's armies became imbalanced, with fewer than 2,000 foot soldiers in armies of 20,000.

In addition to this, they employed various strategies to avoid both exertion and danger for themselves and their men. Rather than killing in battle, they preferred to capture their enemies and then release them without demanding ransom. They avoided night attacks on towns, and in return, garrisons didn't launch surprise raids on camps during the night. Their camps were left unfortified, without ditches or defensive barriers, and they avoided engaging in campaigns during the winter months. All of these practices were part of their military guidelines and were specifically designed to minimize effort and risks, as I've previously mentioned. Through these tactics, they have ultimately weakened Italy, leading it into slavery and earning the contempt of other nations. Their avoidance of real warfare and refusal to engage in the hardships of battle have left Italy vulnerable, both militarily and politically, to foreign powers that now dominate and exploit the region without resistance.

Chapter 13

Concerning Auxiliaries, Mixed Soldiery, And One's Own

Auxiliaries, which are another type of unreliable military force, are used when a ruler enlists the troops of another sovereign to aid in his defense, much like Pope Julius II did in recent times. When Julius embarked on his campaign against Ferrara and saw that his mercenaries were not performing well, he turned to auxiliaries, negotiating with Ferdinand, King of Spain, to provide soldiers and weapons. Although these troops may be skilled and effective in their own right, they are always a disadvantage for the ruler who relies on them. If they lose, the ruler faces defeat. If they win, the ruler becomes their prisoner, bound by their success.

There are numerous examples throughout history that illustrate this point, but I would like to highlight this recent instance with Pope Julius II, as it clearly shows the risks involved. Julius, in his eagerness to capture Ferrara, placed his entire trust in foreign troops. However, fortune intervened, bringing about an unexpected outcome that saved him from the full consequences of his poor decision. His auxiliary forces were defeated at the Battle of Ravenna, but soon after, the Swiss unexpectedly rose up and drove out the conquerors. This turn of events allowed Julius to avoid becoming a prisoner, either to his enemies or to the auxiliaries he had depended on for victory.

The Florentines made a similar mistake when they, having no army of their own, called in 10,000 French soldiers to help them capture Pisa. This decision put them in greater danger than at any other time during their troubles.

Likewise, the Emperor of Constantinople, facing threats from his neighbors, brought 10,000 Turkish troops into Greece for protection. But when the war ended, these troops refused to leave, marking the beginning of Greece's long period of subjugation to foreign rule.

Thus, any ruler who does not wish to be conquered should avoid relying on auxiliary forces. These troops pose a much greater risk than mercenaries because they come as a unified force, loyal to their original sovereign, not the ruler who hires them. Mercenaries, though dangerous, are scattered and are paid by the ruler, meaning that the person in command of them does not immediately gain enough power to overthrow the ruler. In short, the greatest risk with mercenaries is that they may be cowardly, while with auxiliaries, the danger lies in their strength and potential to overpower. Therefore, a wise ruler should always avoid relying on such forces and should instead depend on his own troops. Even if defeat is a possibility, it is better to face it with one's own army, as a victory gained with another's troops is not a true victory.

I feel compelled to mention Cesare Borgia and his actions here as an illustrative example. When Cesare first entered the Romagna, he relied on auxiliaries, specifically French troops, to capture the towns of Imola and Forli. However, it wasn't long before Cesare realized these forces were unreliable, so he switched to mercenaries, hiring the Orsini and Vitelli families. Yet, after testing these forces, he found them to be treacherous, untrustworthy, and dangerous. He eventually eliminated them and shifted entirely to using his own troops. The difference between these forces and their impact on his power and reputation can be clearly seen. When Cesare relied on foreign troops, his control was shaky. When he employed mercenaries, it was still fraught with risk. But when he depended solely on his own forces, his power grew, his reputation flourished, and his position became much more secure. He was never more respected than when people saw that he commanded his own forces and did not rely on the help of others.

Although I intended to limit my examples to recent Italian events, I cannot help but mention Hiero of Syracuse, who offers another example of the wisdom of using one's own troops. As I mentioned earlier, Hiero was placed in command of the Syracusan army, but he quickly realized that mercenaries—much like the Italian condottieri of his day—were ineffective and dangerous. Recognizing that he could neither dismiss them nor safely keep them, he had them all killed. Afterward, he waged his wars with soldiers from his own people rather than foreign troops.

I also want to recall an example from the Old Testament. When David offered to fight Goliath, the Philistine giant, King Saul gave him his own armor and weapons to use. But David, after trying them on, rejected them, saying he couldn't fight with weapons he wasn't familiar with. He chose instead to face Goliath with his own sling and stones, tools he knew well. This story perfectly illustrates the danger of relying on the arms or forces of others: they are either ill-fitting or will fail you at the critical moment.

Another notable example comes from Charles VII of France, the father of Louis XI. After Charles successfully liberated France from English control through his own efforts and good fortune, he realized the importance of having a strong, self-reliant military force. He established a system of men-at-arms and infantry, which helped secure his kingdom. However, his son Louis XI made the critical mistake of disbanding the infantry and turning to Swiss mercenaries. This decision, along with other similar errors, put France in great danger. By relying too heavily on the Swiss, Louis diminished the strength and independence of his own forces. Over time, the French became so dependent on Swiss soldiers that they could no longer fight effectively without them.

As a result, the French military became a mixed force, combining national troops and mercenaries. While this was still better than relying solely on mercenaries or auxiliaries, it was far weaker than an army composed entirely of the kingdom's own soldiers. The example of France clearly shows that if Charles VII's reforms had been continued and expanded, the kingdom would have been much more secure and potentially unconquerable.

Sadly, human wisdom often fails when dealing with situations that seem promising on the surface. People fail to recognize the hidden dangers, much like how the early symptoms of a disease can go unnoticed until it's too late to treat. This is exactly what happened to the Roman Empire. Its decline began when it started relying on foreign troops, like the Goths, to defend its territories. From that point on, the empire's strength and resilience weakened, and the power that had once made Rome great began to pass into the hands of others.

In conclusion, no state can ever be truly secure without its own military forces. Any state that relies on the soldiers of others is at the mercy of fortune and lacks the strength to defend itself when challenges arise. Wise leaders have always recognized that power based on foreign support is unstable and prone to collapse. A ruler's own forces should be made up of his own subjects, citizens, or loyal followers. Mercenaries and auxiliaries should be avoided as much as possible. The path to building a strong, self-reliant military can be found by following the principles I have laid out and by reflecting on the examples of great leaders like Philip of Macedon (the father of Alexander the Great) and the many republics and princes who have successfully armed and organized themselves. To these examples, I leave my final advice.

Chapter 14

That Which Concerns a Prince on The Subject of The Art of War

A prince should focus on nothing else but war, its rules, and its discipline. This is the most important skill for someone who rules because it not only helps those born into royalty to stay in power but also allows ordinary men to rise to greatness. On the other hand, history shows that princes who become too comfortable and neglect the art of war end up losing their kingdoms. The main reason for losing a state is ignoring this skill, while the key to acquiring one is mastering it. Francesco Sforza became the Duke of Milan through his military abilities, while his sons, who avoided the hardships of war, lost their power and became commoners. Among the many dangers that come with being unarmed, the greatest is being despised. This is a humiliation that a prince should avoid at all costs, as we will see later. There is simply no balance between those who are armed and those who are not. It's unreasonable to expect an armed man to willingly obey someone who is unarmed, or for an unarmed leader to feel safe around armed servants. There will always be distrust from one side and disrespect from the other, which makes it impossible for them to work well together. As a result, a prince who doesn't understand the art of war will not only face other misfortunes but will also fail to earn the respect of his soldiers or be able to rely on them.

Therefore, a prince should never stop thinking about war, and in times of peace, he should devote even more time to practicing it than he does during war. He can do this in two main ways: through action and through study.

As for action, the prince should keep his soldiers organized and well-trained. He should also regularly go hunting, which helps his body get used to the physical demands of war. This activity also teaches him about the lay of the land, allowing him to understand how mountains

244

rise, how valleys spread out, where plains lie, and the nature of rivers and marshes. This knowledge is valuable in two ways. First, it helps the prince defend his own country more effectively. Second, by knowing his land well, he can easily understand other territories, since the hills, valleys, rivers, and plains of one place often resemble those of another. This understanding of geography is a crucial skill for any military leader, as it enables him to plan surprise attacks, set up camps, lead troops, organize battles, and lay siege to towns in a strategic way.

Philopoemen, the leader of the Achaeans, is praised by historians for always thinking about war, even in times of peace. Whenever he was out in the countryside with his friends, he would often stop and discuss battle scenarios with them. He would ask, "If the enemy were on that hill and we were down here with our army, who would have the advantage? How should we advance to keep our troops in order? If we needed to retreat, how could we do it effectively?" He would explore every possible situation that could happen in a battle, listen to his friends' opinions, and share his own ideas, backing them up with solid reasoning. By constantly engaging in these discussions, Philopoemen made sure that no situation in war could ever catch him off guard.

In addition to physical practice, a prince should exercise his mind by studying history. He should read about the actions of great leaders from the past to see how they conducted themselves in battle, examining what led to their victories or defeats. By doing so, the prince can learn from their mistakes and follow their successful strategies. He should also find a historical figure to model himself after, much like Alexander the Great admired and imitated Achilles, or how Julius Caesar looked up to Alexander. Similarly, Scipio followed the example of Cyrus the Great, as written about by Xenophon, and he gained glory for emulating Cyrus's virtues, such as kindness, affability, humanity, and generosity.

A wise prince should follow these examples and never allow himself to become idle during peaceful times. Instead, he should work diligently to improve his resources and prepare for any challenges that may arise in the future. This way, if fortune brings adversity, the prince will be ready to face it, having already equipped himself with the necessary skills and knowledge to defend his state.

Chapter 15

Concerning Things for Which Men, And Especially Princes, Are Praised or Blamed

Now we need to consider how a prince should behave toward his subjects and friends. Although many have written on this topic, I know I may seem bold to address it again, especially since I intend to depart from the traditional views. However, my goal is to offer practical advice to those who are willing to understand it, and for this reason, I prefer to focus on the truth of the matter rather than on idealized versions of it. Many people have imagined republics and principalities that have never truly existed because the way people live is often far removed from how they should live. Anyone who tries to live up to a completely virtuous standard in such a flawed world will quickly face ruin rather than survival.

A prince, therefore, who wishes to maintain power must learn how to do wrong when necessary and know when to apply it or refrain from doing so based on the situation. Instead of imagining how a prince ought to behave, we must consider how a prince actually behaves. When people, especially princes, are discussed, they are often judged by qualities that either bring them praise or criticism. For instance, one prince might be considered generous, while another is seen as miserly. Some are viewed as bold and brave, while others appear cowardly and effeminate. Some are seen as compassionate, while others are considered cruel. One prince may be regarded as faithful and sincere, while another is known to be cunning and deceitful. These traits can go on: one may be chaste, another lascivious; one may be religious, another impious.

I understand that everyone would agree it would be praiseworthy for a prince to possess all of these good qualities. But because it is nearly impossible for a ruler to have or follow all of them, human nature being what it is, a prince must be wise enough to avoid the vices that would cause him to lose his state. He should also aim to avoid those that don't necessarily threaten his rule if he can, but when it's not possible, he should be less worried about indulging in those particular vices. In fact, a prince should not be troubled if he is criticized for certain flaws that are essential to saving his state.

Ultimately, if a prince carefully considers everything, he will see that something that appears to be virtuous may lead to his downfall, while actions that seem to be vices may actually result in his security and success. In this way, what is often viewed as a vice can sometimes be more beneficial than a perceived virtue.

Chapter 16
Concerning Liberality and Meanness

Starting with the first quality I mentioned earlier, I will say that it is indeed desirable for a prince to be known as generous. However, if generosity is practiced in a way that doesn't earn a reputation for it, it can harm more than help. If a prince is truly generous in the proper sense of the word, his efforts might not be noticed, and he could still be criticized for being the opposite. To maintain a reputation for generosity, a prince would need to spare no expense in lavish displays, leading him to exhaust his resources. In time, to maintain this image, he would be forced to burden his people with taxes or find other ways to obtain money, which would eventually make him unpopular among his subjects. As his wealth dries up, he would lose respect, and the number of people he offends would far outnumber those he rewards.

The moment any crisis arises, he will be vulnerable because of his generosity, and as soon as he tries to correct his course, he risks being labeled as miserly.

Therefore, if a prince cannot be generous without harming himself, he should not fear being seen as stingy. With careful management of his resources, he can provide for his state, defend against enemies, and embark on new endeavors without burdening his people. This will earn him the respect of many because, while he is only perceived as miserly by a small number of those who expect gifts, the broader population—whom he does not tax—will appreciate his restraint. In fact, all the great achievements we've witnessed have been accomplished by those who were considered frugal, not by those who were thought of as liberal with their wealth.

Take Pope Julius II, for instance. He gained the papacy partly because he was seen as generous, but once he secured his position, he no longer needed to uphold that image. When he went to war with the King of France, he financed these wars without imposing extra taxes on his subjects, relying instead on the wealth he had saved through careful spending. Similarly, the current King of Spain has been able to undertake and succeed in many ventures because he has not been viewed as wastefully generous. Therefore, as long as a prince doesn't need to exploit his subjects, can defend his realm, avoid poverty, and stay clear of the temptation to be greedy, he should not worry too much about being labeled as miserly. In fact, it is a vice that can help him govern successfully.

Some may argue that Caesar rose to power through his generosity, and that many others have achieved great things by being liberal with their wealth. To this, I respond: it depends on whether you are already a prince or seeking to become one. If you are already a ruler, generosity can be risky, but if you are working to rise to power, then it is crucial to be seen as generous. Caesar, for instance, sought to become the most powerful figure in Rome, and his liberality helped him achieve that goal. But had he lived longer and not reined in his spending, he would have eventually destroyed his rule.

Others might point to the fact that some princes who have led great armies and accomplished major feats have been known for their generosity. However, I would clarify that a prince either spends his own wealth, his people's wealth, or someone else's. If a prince is spending his own or his subjects' wealth, he must be frugal. But if he is spending what belongs to others, especially during military campaigns where he funds his army through looting or conquest, then generosity is useful. In these cases, being liberal with the spoils of others' wealth will make the soldiers follow him. Figures like Cyrus, Caesar, and Alexander were able to be generous without harming themselves because they were using the wealth of others. Spending what isn't yours can enhance your reputation, while spending your own wealth can diminish it.

Nothing drains resources faster than generosity, because even as you practice it, you lose the ability to continue doing so. This can lead to either poverty or a loss of respect. And if you try to avoid poverty by raising funds through unfair means, you will become hated. Above all, a prince must guard against being despised or hated, and generosity can lead to both outcomes. Therefore, it is much safer to accept a reputation for frugality, which may lead to minor criticism but without hatred, than to pursue a reputation for generosity that could lead to financial ruin and, ultimately, being seen as greedy and hated.

Chapter 17
Concerning Cruelty and Clemency, And Whether It Is Better to Be Loved Than Feared

Turning now to the other qualities I have mentioned, I say that every prince should desire to be considered kind-hearted rather than cruel. However, it is crucial that he does not misuse this kindness. Cesare

Borgia was viewed as cruel, yet his cruelty brought the Romagna under control, unified it, and restored it to peace and loyalty. When this is properly considered, one will see that Borgia was far more merciful than the Florentine people, who, in order to avoid being called cruel, allowed Pistoia to be destroyed. Therefore, a prince, as long as he keeps his subjects united and loyal, should not worry about being called cruel; because, through just a few decisive examples, he will be seen as more merciful than those who, by showing too much mercy, allow disorders to arise, leading to murders and robberies. Such acts of violence harm the entire population, while executions ordered by a prince harm only a few individuals.

For a new prince in particular, it is impossible to avoid the accusation of cruelty, as new states are full of dangers. This is why Virgil, speaking through the character Dido, justifies the harshness of her rule because her reign was new, saying: "The harshness of circumstances and the newness of my reign compel me to take such measures and protect my borders with guards far and wide." However, a prince should be cautious in believing accusations and slow in acting, avoiding fear and proceeding with calmness, wisdom, and humanity. He must ensure that overconfidence does not make him reckless and that excessive distrust does not make him unbearable.

This brings us to the question: is it better to be loved than feared, or feared than loved? Ideally, a prince should be both, but since it is difficult to unite them in one person, it is much safer to be feared than loved when one must choose. For we can say this in general about men: they are ungrateful, fickle, false, cowardly, and greedy. As long as you succeed, they are entirely yours; they will offer you their blood, property, lives, and children, as I mentioned earlier, when the need is distant. But when it comes closer, they will turn against you. The prince who relies solely on their promises and neglects other precautions will be ruined. Friendships that are bought with money and not earned through respect and greatness of character may indeed be gained but are not secure, and when you need them, they will not support you.

Men are less likely to offend someone they fear than someone they love, for love is maintained by a bond of obligation, which, due to men's selfishness, is broken whenever it benefits them; but fear is maintained by a dread of punishment, which never fails.

However, a prince must ensure that he inspires fear in such a way that he avoids hatred, because being feared while not hated is something he can endure. This is guaranteed as long as he abstains from seizing the property or women of his subjects. When a prince needs to act against someone's life, he must have clear justification and a proper reason, but above all, he must avoid taking away the property of others. People are quicker to forget the death of their father than the loss of their inheritance. Furthermore, reasons for taking away property are never lacking, for a prince who has started living by theft will always find reasons to seize what belongs to others. But reasons for taking life are harder to find and less frequent. When a prince is leading his army, and he has many soldiers under his control, it becomes absolutely necessary for him to ignore the reputation for cruelty. Without that reputation, he could never keep his army united or prepared for battle.

Among Hannibal's many great deeds, one that stands out is his ability to lead a massive army made up of men from different nations, waging war in foreign lands, without causing any rebellion against him. This was due to nothing other than his extreme cruelty, which, combined with his boundless courage, made him both feared and respected by his soldiers. Without this cruelty, his other virtues would not have been enough to achieve this. Some short-sighted writers admire his achievements but condemn the main reason for his success. That his other virtues alone would not have sufficed is clear when we compare him to Scipio, the most outstanding man of his time or perhaps of any time. Yet, Scipio's army rebelled against him in Spain, not because he lacked ability, but because of his excessive leniency, which allowed his soldiers more freedom than was compatible with military discipline. For this, he was reprimanded by Fabius Maximus in the Senate and labeled the corrupter of the Roman army. When Scipio's legate ravaged the Locrians, they were not avenged, nor was the legate punished, all due to Scipio's overly gentle nature. In fact, someone in the Senate, trying to defend Scipio, remarked that some men are better at avoiding mistakes than correcting the mistakes of others. Had Scipio's easy-going nature continued unchecked, it would eventually have ruined his fame and glory. But since he was under the control of the Senate, this weakness was concealed and even added to his renown.

Returning to the question of whether it is better to be feared or loved, I conclude that, because men love at their own will but fear at the will of the prince, a wise prince should build his foundation on what is within his control, and not on what depends on others. He should aim to avoid hatred, as I have explained.

Chapter 18
Concerning the Way in Which Princes Should Keep Faith

Everyone recognizes how praiseworthy it is for a prince to keep his word and live honestly, showing integrity in his actions. This is what most people expect of a ruler. However, history and experience tell a different story. The most successful princes, the ones who have accomplished the greatest feats, have not always been those who strictly kept their promises or were honest in all their dealings. Instead, they knew how to cleverly deceive others when necessary, and through this cunning, they outmaneuvered and defeated those who blindly relied on the prince's promises. This is not to say that deceit is always the first course of action, but it has often proven effective when handled correctly.

There are two main ways of engaging in conflict, as seen throughout history: one is through law, and the other is through force. The law is the proper domain of men, while force belongs to beasts.

Yet, there are times when the law is insufficient, and a prince must rely on force. Therefore, a wise ruler must know how to use both methods—being able to act as both a man and a beast. This concept is illustrated in ancient stories where princes like Achilles were entrusted to the care of the Centaur Chiron, who was half man and half beast. The symbolic meaning of these tales is that a prince must learn to combine the wisdom of man with the cunning of the beast in order to rule successfully. Relying on one without the other is a sure path to failure.

In particular, when a prince is forced to adopt the ways of the beast, he should aim to be both a fox and a lion. The lion is powerful and can fend off wolves, but he is vulnerable to traps. The fox, on the other hand, is clever and can avoid traps but is defenseless against wolves. Therefore, a prince must be as shrewd as a fox to recognize traps and as strong as a lion to scare off the wolves. Those rulers who rely solely on the lion's strength are often reckless and fail to recognize dangers that could have been avoided with more subtlety.

A prince should not feel bound by his word if keeping it would harm him, especially when the reasons for making the promise no longer exist. If all men were good and trustworthy, this rule would not apply. But since people are generally untrustworthy and self-serving, a prince has no obligation to be bound by promises when others do not keep faith with him. In fact, breaking a promise when circumstances change or when keeping it would be detrimental is often necessary for survival. There will always be legitimate reasons for a prince to justify not keeping his word, and history is full of examples where rulers who were adept at deception thrived while those who naively kept their promises lost their power.

One of the most recent examples of this is Pope Alexander VI. He was known for constantly deceiving others, and he made no attempt to hide this habit. He always found people willing to believe him, and despite his endless falsehoods, his schemes succeeded time and time again. He never kept his word, yet his manipulations worked because he understood human nature very well. People are simple in many ways and often prioritize their immediate needs, which makes them easy targets for deception. Alexander was particularly skilled at taking advantage of this simplicity, and his repeated success shows just how effective a well-executed strategy of deceit can be.

Therefore, it is not necessary for a prince to actually possess all the good qualities that people expect of a ruler, but it is essential for him to appear to have them. It is often more dangerous for a prince to fully embody virtues like mercy, honesty, or faithfulness, as adhering strictly to these principles can make him vulnerable. Instead, a prince should appear to be merciful, honest, faithful, humane, and religious, and in most cases, he should act that way. However, he must also be prepared to do the opposite when the situation demands it. A successful ruler knows how to adapt to changing circumstances while maintaining the appearance of virtue. This is especially important for a new prince, who will face more challenges in consolidating his power. If a prince wants to keep his state, he must be willing to act against virtues like honesty, loyalty, and kindness when necessary, though he should return to these virtues when it is safe to do so.

A prince must never let anything escape his lips that would suggest he is not all of these things—merciful, faithful, humane, upright, and religious—because his subjects and rivals alike will judge him based on what they see and hear. Appearances are critical because most people only see the surface and do not know the true intentions of their ruler. Only a few people will know a prince's real character, but they will not dare challenge the majority's opinion, which is shaped by appearances and protected by the authority of the state. This is why it is so important for a prince to cultivate an image of virtue, even if he does not always practice it in reality.

In the actions of princes, and indeed in the actions of all men, people tend to judge by the results. If a ruler is successful in maintaining power and achieving his goals, his methods will be justified, and people will praise him for his accomplishments. The means by which he achieved success will be forgotten or excused. The common people, who make up the vast majority, are more impressed by appearances and outcomes than by the details of how those outcomes were achieved. The opinions of the few who might know the full story do not matter unless they can sway the masses, and that is rarely possible.

One modern prince, whose name I will not mention, is known for constantly preaching peace and good faith. Yet, in reality, he is an enemy to both. If he had faithfully practiced what he preached, he would have lost his kingdom and reputation many times over. This shows that maintaining appearances and adapting to the realities of power are more important for a prince than strict adherence to the ideals of honesty and integrity. A wise prince understands this and uses it to his advantage, securing his rule by any means necessary while maintaining the illusion of virtue.

Chapter 19
That One Should Avoid Being Despised and Hated

Now, regarding the other traits that I mentioned earlier, I've already gone over the most important ones. For the rest, I'll address them briefly under one general rule: a prince must be mindful of avoiding actions that would make him hated or disrespected. If he manages to avoid these, he has done his part well and doesn't need to worry much about other criticisms that might come his way.

The surest way for a prince to become hated is by being greedy, taking the property of his people, or dishonoring their women. A ruler must steer clear of these behaviors. As long as their property and honor are left untouched, most people will be content. In that case, the prince only has to deal with the ambitions of a few people, which he can handle easily in several ways.

On the other hand, a prince becomes disrespected if he's seen as inconsistent, frivolous, weak, or indecisive. These are dangerous traits for any ruler, and he should avoid them as one would avoid a deadly threat. Instead, he should demonstrate boldness, strength, seriousness, and resolve in his actions. In his personal dealings with his people, he should be firm and decisive, establishing a reputation that he is not easily fooled or taken advantage of.

A prince who shows these qualities will earn the respect of his people, and a respected prince is much harder to conspire against. If people see him as a capable and strong leader, they will be less likely to rise against him. For this reason, a ruler must focus on two main areas of concern: the potential threats from his own subjects and external threats from foreign powers. He can protect himself from foreign threats by maintaining a strong military and forming good alliances. If he is well-armed, he will have strong friends, and his internal affairs will remain calm as long as his external situation is stable. Even if external conflicts arise, a prince who has prepared himself properly and followed good practices, as described earlier, will be able to withstand any attack, just as Nabis, the Spartan, did.

When it comes to his subjects, the prince should only fear secret conspiracies when things outside his kingdom are unstable. But a ruler can protect himself from these plots by avoiding hatred and contempt and by keeping his people satisfied. As I mentioned before, this is one of the most important things a prince can do. The best defense against conspiracies is to ensure that the people do not hate or despise the ruler. After all, those who plot against a prince often believe that they will win favor with the people by removing him from power. But if they know that the people support the prince, they will lack the courage to follow through, as the risks of conspiring are enormous.

History shows that conspiracies are plentiful, but very few actually succeed. This is because a conspirator cannot act alone, and must involve others. As soon as he shares his plan with another person, he puts himself at risk. The person he confides in may turn him in to the authorities in exchange for rewards or favors, because doing so is often safer and more rewarding than following through with the plot. The risks of a conspiracy are great, and only a very determined enemy or a rare, loyal friend would go through with it.

In short, the conspirator has little to motivate him aside from fear, jealousy, or anger, while the prince has many advantages on his side. The prince has the authority of his position, the laws, loyal friends, and the support of the state. When he has the goodwill of the people on top of all this, it is almost impossible for anyone to conspire successfully against him. In general, the conspirator is most fearful before carrying out his plan, but in this case, he must also fear what will happen afterward because the people will turn against him if he succeeds. The risks are simply too high.

There are countless examples of this, but I will focus on one that happened within living memory. Messer Annibale Bentivogli, the ruler of Bologna, was murdered by the Canneschi, a group of conspirators. After his death, only his young relative, Messer Giovanni, survived. However, as soon as Annibale was killed, the people of Bologna rose up and killed all the Canneschi. This was due to the loyalty the people felt towards the Bentivogli family. Even though no one from the family was left to take over, the people of Bologna learned that another Bentivogli, who had been raised in Florence and was thought to be the son of a blacksmith, was still alive. They sent for him and put him in charge of their city until Giovanni Bentivogli grew up and could rule.

From this, we can see that a prince has little to fear from conspiracies when he is loved by the people. But if the people hate him, he must fear everyone and everything. Wise rulers and well-organized states have always worked to avoid pushing the nobles into despair and have made efforts to keep the people content and satisfied. This is one of the most crucial objectives a prince can pursue.

One of the best-governed kingdoms of our time is France, which has many institutions that safeguard the king's power and security. The most important of these is the authority of the parliament. The founder of the French kingdom recognized that the nobility was ambitious and bold, and he knew they needed to be controlled. At the same time, he understood that the people feared and disliked the nobles, so he created a system to protect the people without making it seem like the king was choosing sides. He appointed a separate body to handle these issues, which allowed him to avoid accusations of favoring either the nobles or the people. This system has provided great security for both the king and the kingdom. From this, we can conclude that princes should delegate unpopular tasks to others while keeping the more rewarding actions for themselves.

Finally, I would argue that a prince should maintain good relations with the nobility, but never in a way that causes him to lose the favor of the people.

Now, some might think that the lives and deaths of Roman emperors show examples that contradict my ideas. Many of these emperors lived nobly, showing great strength of character, yet they still lost their power or were killed by conspiracies led by their own subjects. To address these concerns, I'll look at the lives of some of these emperors and explain that their downfalls happened for the reasons I've already mentioned. I will point out the key lessons to be learned from their reigns for those who want to understand the nature of leadership during those times.

To illustrate this, let's examine all the emperors who ruled after Marcus Aurelius up to Maximinus: they include Marcus Aurelius himself, his son Commodus, Pertinax, Julian, Severus, his son Caracalla, Macrinus, Heliogabalus, Alexander, and Maximinus. The main thing to note is that, while other rulers only had to deal with the ambition of the nobles or the temper of the people, Roman emperors faced an additional challenge: the cruelty and greed of their soldiers. This problem proved to be a stumbling block for many emperors, as it was difficult to satisfy both the soldiers and the people. The people preferred peaceful rulers who did not seek conflict, while the soldiers favored those who were warlike, cruel, and greedy, as these qualities allowed them to receive higher pay and plunder the people. As a result, emperors who lacked strong authority were frequently overthrown, especially those who were new to the throne. These rulers often found it easier to cater to the soldiers, even if it meant hurting the people, because they believed it was more dangerous to be hated by the soldiers than by the people. However, whether this approach succeeded or failed depended on the emperor's ability to maintain control over the soldiers.

Marcus Aurelius, Pertinax, and Alexander were all known for their modest lifestyles, love of justice, and opposition to cruelty. While Marcus Aurelius managed to live and die with honor, the other two did not fare so well. Marcus Aurelius succeeded because he inherited the throne and had the respect of both the soldiers and the people due to his many virtues. He kept both groups in check and was neither hated nor despised during his reign. However, Pertinax was made emperor against the wishes of the soldiers, who were used to the indulgent rule of Commodus and did not want to be reined in by Pertinax's strict policies. The soldiers hated him for trying to restore discipline, and, adding contempt for his old age to this hatred, they quickly overthrew him at the start of his rule.

This leads to an important lesson: a ruler can become hated not only through bad actions but also through good ones. As I mentioned earlier, a prince who wants to hold on to power is often forced to do things that may seem bad. When those who help maintain the prince's rule—whether it's the people, the soldiers, or the nobles—are corrupt, the ruler must give in to their desires. In such cases, doing what is morally right can actually be harmful.

Now, let's consider Alexander, a man of such great kindness that one of the highest praises he received was that, during the fourteen years of his reign, he never executed anyone without a fair trial. However, this very kindness led to his downfall. He was seen as weak and overly influenced by his mother, which caused him to lose the respect of the army. Eventually, the soldiers conspired against him and killed him.

On the other hand, if we look at emperors like Commodus, Severus, Caracalla, and Maximinus, we find men who were cruel and greedy. They did not hesitate to harm the people in order to please the soldiers. With the exception of Severus, all of these emperors met a bad end. Severus, however, was able to maintain power because of his remarkable strength and courage. Even though the people suffered under him, his military prowess earned him the admiration of both the soldiers and the people. The people were in awe of him, while the soldiers were kept happy. Severus serves as a prime example of how a ruler must imitate both the fox and the lion, as I discussed earlier.

Severus was cunning enough to manipulate the army into believing that they should avenge the death of Pertinax, who had been killed by the praetorian soldiers. Under this pretense, Severus led the army to Rome, claiming not to seek the throne. However, upon his arrival, the Senate, out of fear, named him emperor and executed Julian, who had been ruling at the time. After this, Severus faced two main challenges: one in Asia, where Niger had proclaimed himself emperor, and another in the West, where Albinus also sought the throne. Severus decided to deceive Albinus, pretending to share power with him by sending him the title of Caesar. Meanwhile, he focused on defeating Niger. Once he had conquered Niger and settled affairs in the East, Severus returned to Rome and accused Albinus of treachery. He eventually pursued Albinus to France, where he defeated him and seized control.

Severus exemplified both the strength of a lion and the cunning of a fox. He was feared and respected by all, yet he managed to avoid the hatred of the army. His success as a new ruler was due to his extraordinary reputation, which shielded him from any resentment the people might have felt toward his harsh rule.

Severus's son, Antoninus (Caracalla), was similarly admired for his military skills and his ability to endure hardship, which made him beloved by the soldiers. However, his extreme cruelty alienated both the people and those around him. After many acts of violence, including the slaughter of countless citizens in Rome and Alexandria, he became hated by all. Eventually, he was killed by a centurion within his own army. This demonstrates a key point: deliberate and desperate assassinations like this one are nearly impossible for a ruler to prevent, especially when carried out by someone with nothing to lose. However, such occurrences are rare, and a prince can reduce the risk by avoiding serious harm to those close to him, particularly those in his service. Antoninus failed in this regard, having previously killed the centurion's brother and threatened the centurion himself, yet he foolishly kept him in his bodyguard—leading to his own downfall.

Lastly, let's turn to Commodus, who could have easily maintained power by following in the footsteps of his father, Marcus Aurelius. However, Commodus was naturally cruel and corrupt. He focused on pleasing the soldiers and indulging their worst tendencies while exploiting the people. He undermined his own dignity by participating in gladiator fights and other demeaning activities, actions unworthy of the emperor's position. As a result, he lost the respect of the soldiers and the people, and ultimately, he was killed in a conspiracy.

Let's now talk about Maximinus. He was a very warlike man, and after the soldiers grew tired of the soft nature of Alexander, whom we've already mentioned, they killed him and made Maximinus the emperor. However, he didn't hold onto power for long, as two things made him both hated and despised. First, everyone knew he had once been a shepherd in Thrace, which people saw as humiliating. Second, after gaining control of the empire, he delayed his journey to Rome to officially take his seat, which made people view him with suspicion. On top of that, he was known for extreme cruelty, which he enforced through his officials both in Rome and other parts of the empire. This led to widespread anger because of his low birth and his brutal behavior. As a result, Africa was the first region to rebel, followed by the Senate, the people of Rome, and eventually all of Italy. His own army even turned against him when they encountered difficulties besieging the city of Aquileia. Disgusted by his cruelty and seeing that many others were against him, they ultimately killed him.

I won't go into detail about Heliogabalus, Macrinus, or Julian, as they were quickly eliminated due to their complete lack of worthiness, but I will conclude by saying that in modern times, princes don't face the same issue of needing to excessively satisfy their soldiers. Though princes still have to indulge them to some degree, this is a much smaller issue than it was in the past. Nowadays, no prince commands armies like those of the Roman Empire, which were seasoned and held great power over provinces. Back then, it was often more important to keep the soldiers happy than the people. Today, however, for almost all rulers—except for the Turkish sultan and the Egyptian sultan—it is more crucial to win over the people than the soldiers, as the people hold more influence.

The reason I exclude the Turkish sultan is that he keeps around him a permanent force of 12,000 infantry and 15,000 cavalry, and his kingdom's safety and strength depend on them. Therefore, he must focus on keeping these soldiers loyal to him, not worrying much about the general population. The same is true for the Egyptian sultan, whose power also depends entirely on his soldiers. In both of these cases, the rulers don't need to worry about pleasing the people; their soldiers are the key to maintaining their rule. But you should note that the structure of the Egyptian sultanate is different from other types of principalities because it resembles the system of the Christian papacy. It isn't exactly hereditary, nor is it a newly established principality. The sons of the previous ruler do not inherit the throne, as someone is elected to that position by those who have authority. The sons of former rulers remain nobles but don't become rulers themselves. Since this is an ancient custom, it doesn't bring the challenges that come with new principalities. Even though the prince is new, the state's framework is old, and it's designed to receive a new leader as if he had always been the rightful heir.

Returning to the subject at hand, anyone who thinks about it will see that the downfall of the emperors I've mentioned was caused either by hatred or contempt. You will also notice that, although some emperors acted one way and others acted differently, only one in each group managed to have a good outcome, while the rest met unfortunate ends. For example, it would have been a mistake for new rulers like Pertinax or Alexander to imitate Marcus Aurelius, who inherited his position. At the same time, it would have been disastrous for rulers like Caracalla, Commodus, or Maximinus to imitate Severus, as they lacked the strength and skills needed to follow in his footsteps. Therefore, a prince who is new to power should not try to copy Marcus Aurelius, but he doesn't need to imitate Severus entirely either. Instead, he should adopt the parts of Severus's approach that will help him establish his rule, while also taking from Marcus the qualities that help maintain a stable and secure state.

Chapter 20

Are Fortresses, And Many Other Things to Which Princes Often Resort, Advantageous or Hurtful?

Some princes, in order to securely hold their states, have disarmed their subjects, while others have kept their subject cities divided by encouraging factions. Some have nurtured enemies against themselves, while others have worked to win over those they distrusted at the beginning of their rule. Some princes have built fortresses, while others have torn them down. Although it's difficult to make a final judgment on all of these strategies without knowing the specifics of the states involved, I will address the topic as broadly as possible.

No new prince has ever disarmed his subjects. In fact, when new princes find their subjects unarmed, they arm them instead. By doing this, they make those arms their own, turning the people who were once untrusted into loyal followers. Those who were already loyal will remain so, and all of the prince's subjects will feel tied to him. Even though not all of the prince's subjects can be armed, those who are given arms will feel privileged. As a result, those who aren't armed won't resent the prince because they'll understand why others deserve to be trusted with weapons. However, when a prince disarms his subjects, he immediately offends them because it shows he doesn't trust them. This either suggests he believes them to be cowards or disloyal, and both interpretations create hatred. Since a prince can't remain without an armed force, he then has to rely on mercenaries. But as I've already shown, mercenaries are unreliable, and even if they were skilled, they wouldn't be enough to protect a prince from powerful enemies and dissatisfied subjects. Thus, a new prince in a new state should always give arms to his people. History is full of examples supporting this point. On the other hand, when a prince acquires a new territory, which becomes an addition to his existing state, he should disarm the people of that new land, except for those who helped him take control. Over time, even those allies should be softened and made less dangerous, and the prince should make sure that the only soldiers in the state are those from his original territory, who live close to him.

Our ancestors, who were considered wise, believed it was necessary to control cities like Pistoia by encouraging internal divisions, while maintaining control over Pisa through fortresses. They fostered divisions in their tributary cities to make it easier to manage them. This strategy may have worked in their time, when Italy's power structure was more balanced, but I don't think it applies today. Factions and divisions are never helpful. In fact, when a city is divided and an enemy attacks, the weaker faction will often side with the invader, making it easier for the enemy to take control. Meanwhile, the stronger faction won't be able to resist on its own. The Venetians, for instance, allowed the Guelph and Ghibelline factions to exist in their subject cities. They kept these factions from causing bloodshed but let their disputes continue, thinking this would keep the cities from uniting against them. However, this tactic backfired after their defeat at the Battle of Vaila, when one faction seized control of the state. This shows that encouraging factions indicates a prince's weakness. Divisions might help in times of peace, but in war, they are disastrous.

Princes, especially new ones, gain greatness when they overcome challenges and obstacles. Fortune often raises enemies against a new prince so that he has the chance to defeat them and strengthen his reputation. Many believe that a wise prince, when given the chance, should intentionally create animosity against himself, so that by overcoming it, his renown will grow even more.

New princes have often found that those they initially distrusted end up being more loyal and helpful than those they trusted from the start. For example, Pandolfo Petrucci, who ruled Siena, relied more on those he had distrusted than on others to maintain control of his state. However, this doesn't apply universally and varies depending on the circumstances. I'll only say that when a prince wins over those who were originally his enemies, they are often the ones who serve him most faithfully. They know they need to prove their loyalty and erase the bad impression they once gave. These individuals are usually more reliable than those who serve the prince with too much confidence and may become complacent. A prince who gains power through secret favors must be cautious. If the people who helped him rise did so because they were unhappy with the previous government, rather than out of genuine loyalty to him, it will be difficult to keep them on his side. If we look at examples from both ancient and modern history, we'll find that it's often easier for a prince to win over people who were content with the old government but initially opposed him, rather than those who were dissatisfied and helped him seize power.

Many princes have built fortresses to secure their rule. These fortresses can serve as protection from potential uprisings and as safe retreats in times of attack. I praise this strategy because it has been used effectively in the past. However, in modern times, we've seen princes destroy fortresses to maintain control. For example, Niccolò Vitelli demolished two fortresses in Città di Castello to keep his hold on power. Similarly, when Duke Guido Ubaldo reclaimed Urbino from Cesare Borgia, he destroyed all the fortresses in the province to reduce the threat of rebellion. The Bentivoglio family made the same decision when they returned to Bologna. Fortresses can be either useful or harmful, depending on the situation. If they help in one way, they may hurt in another. Here's how we can think about it: A prince who fears his people more than foreign enemies should build fortresses. However, a prince who fears foreign enemies more than his own people should avoid building them. For instance, the castle built by Francesco Sforza in Milan has caused more problems for his descendants than any other issue in the state. Ultimately, the best fortress a prince can have is the support of his people. Even if a prince has many fortresses, they won't protect him if his people hate him. There will always be foreign forces willing to help a population that rises up against its ruler. In modern times, fortresses have rarely been useful to any prince, except perhaps to the Countess of Forlì when her husband was killed. Fortresses helped her hold off a popular attack and wait for help from Milan, allowing her to regain control of her state. However, when Cesare Borgia attacked her, and the people sided with him, the fortresses were of little use. It would have been safer for her not to be hated by her people, rather than rely on fortresses for protection.

All things considered, I can praise both the decision to build fortresses and the decision not to. However, I criticize any prince who believes fortresses can save him while ignoring the hatred of his people.

Chapter 21
How A Prince Should Conduct Himself so as To Gain Renown

Nothing earns a prince more respect than taking on great projects and setting a good example. A good example of this in our time is

Ferdinand of Aragon, the current King of Spain. He can almost be considered a new prince because, through his fame and achievements, he went from being a minor king to becoming the most powerful king in all of Christendom. If you look at his actions, you'll find that they've all been significant, and some have been extraordinary. Early in his reign, he set his sights on conquering Granada, and this goal became the foundation of his power. He carried it out quietly at first, without fear of interference, because he kept the barons of Castile focused on the war, preventing them from noticing any changes he was making. As a result, they didn't realize that, through these efforts, he was gaining more power and authority over them. He funded his armies with money from the Church and the people, and through that long war, he built the military skill that would later define him.

Additionally, Ferdinand always used religion as an excuse to take on bigger projects. For example, he ruthlessly expelled the Moors from his kingdom, claiming it was for a religious cause. This was an admirable and rare example of using piety to justify cruelty. Using this same religious excuse, he then launched campaigns in Africa, moved into Italy, and eventually set his sights on France. His achievements and goals have always been significant, keeping the people in awe and focused on what he would do next. His actions followed one after the other in such a way that no one ever had time to oppose him.

It's also important for a prince to set remarkable examples in domestic affairs, just like Messer Bernabo da Milano did. Whenever someone did something extraordinary—whether good or bad—he would make sure to reward or punish them in a way that got people talking. A prince should always try to earn a reputation as a great and remarkable man through his actions.

A prince also gains respect when he either openly supports or opposes something. In other words, he should make it clear whether he is a true ally or a firm enemy. It's always better to take a side than to remain neutral because this will ultimately work out better. If two of your powerful neighbors start fighting, you'll need to either fear the winner or not, depending on the situation. In either case, it's always better to declare where you stand and fight hard. If you stay neutral, the winner will likely see you as an enemy, and the loser won't trust you because you didn't help. The victorious side doesn't want uncertain allies who won't help in times of need, and the losing side won't trust someone who didn't share in their struggle.

Antiochus, for instance, went to Greece at the request of the Aetolians to fight the Romans. He sent ambassadors to the Achaeans, who were Roman allies, asking them to stay neutral. The Romans, on the other hand, urged the Achaeans to join the fight. In the Achaean council, Antiochus's representative argued for neutrality. In response, the Roman representative said, "It's a mistake to think that neutrality is better for your state, because if you stay out of the fight, you'll end up as the spoils of the victor." This proves that when someone isn't your friend, they will often ask you to stay neutral, while your true allies will urge you to take a stand.

Indecisive princes tend to follow the path of neutrality to avoid immediate danger, but this often leads to their downfall. However, when a prince boldly declares support for one side, if that side wins, the victor may have the power to harm the prince but will still feel a sense of obligation and gratitude. People are rarely so ungrateful that they will turn on someone who helped them. Victory isn't always so complete that the winner can afford to ignore the need for justice. If the prince's ally loses, they may still protect him as much as they can, and together, they can wait for a chance to rise again.

In the second situation, when the outcome of the conflict doesn't concern the prince because either side winning isn't a threat, it's even wiser to pick a side. In this case, the prince will be helping one side defeat the other, which would have saved the defeated side if they had been more careful. By ensuring one side's victory, the prince can gain control over them. However, a prince should be careful not to ally with someone more powerful than himself when attacking others unless it's absolutely necessary, as I've mentioned before. If that more powerful ally wins, the prince will be at their mercy. Princes should avoid being at someone else's mercy whenever possible.

The Venetians made this mistake when they allied with France against the Duke of Milan, and this alliance led to their downfall. But when it's impossible to avoid choosing a side, as was the case when the Pope and Spain sent armies to attack Lombardy, a prince should support one of the parties for the reasons I've given.

No government can choose a perfectly safe path. Instead, they should expect to face risky decisions. In general, you can't avoid one problem without running into another, so wisdom lies in being able to choose the lesser evil.

A prince should also present himself as a supporter of talent and honor those who excel in any field. He should encourage his citizens to practice their trades without fear, whether they are involved in business, farming, or anything else. No one should be afraid to improve their property out of fear that it will be taken from them, and no one should hesitate to expand their trade out of fear of taxes. Instead, the prince should offer rewards to those who benefit the state in any way and bring honor to their city.

Furthermore, a prince should entertain the people with festivals and public spectacles at the right times of the year. Every city is usually divided into guilds or societies, and the prince should hold these groups in high regard. He should also associate with them from time to time and show them courtesy and generosity. However, he must always maintain the dignity of his position and never lower himself in any way that could undermine his authority.

In this way, a prince can gain the respect of his people while still maintaining his power and majesty.

Chapter 22
Concerning the Secretaries of Princes

Choosing good servants is very important for a prince, and whether they are good or bad depends on the prince's judgment. The first impression people have of a prince and his intelligence comes from looking at the people he surrounds himself with. If his servants are capable and loyal, the prince will always be considered wise because he knew how to pick the right people and keep them loyal. But if the servants are bad, people will have a poor opinion of the prince because his first mistake was choosing them in the first place.

Anyone who knew Messer Antonio da Venafro, the servant of Pandolfo Petrucci, the Prince of Siena, would think Pandolfo was very smart for having Venafro as his servant. This is because there are three types of minds: one that understands things on its own, one that can appreciate what others understand, and one that cannot understand anything, either by itself or from others. The first is the best, the second is good, and the third is useless. So, even if Pandolfo wasn't in the first category, he was at least in the second, because he had the ability to recognize what was good or bad when he saw or heard it. Even if he didn't come up with ideas himself, he could still see what was good or bad in his servant, praising the good and correcting the bad. This way, his servant could not deceive him and was kept honest.

There is one reliable way for a prince to judge his servant: when you see the servant caring more about his own interests than the prince's and always looking to benefit himself, that man will never be a good servant, and the prince will never be able to trust him. A servant who manages someone else's affairs should never think of himself but always of his prince, and should never focus on things that don't concern the prince.

On the other hand, to keep his servant honest, a prince should treat him well—honor him, make him wealthy, show him kindness, and share both honors and responsibilities with him. At the same time, the prince should make sure that the servant knows he cannot stand on his own. The servant shouldn't desire more honors or wealth than he already has, and the many responsibilities should make him careful about taking risks. When both the servant and the prince are like this towards each other, they can trust one another. But when things are different, it will always end badly for one or both of them.

Chapter 23
How Flatterers Should Be Avoided

I don't want to overlook an important part of this subject, which is a serious risk for princes unless they are very careful and thoughtful. This is the danger of flatterers, who are everywhere in royal courts. People tend to be pleased with themselves and are often misled by their own affairs, making it hard to avoid falling for flattery. If a prince tries to defend himself against it, he risks being seen as contemptuous. The only way to protect oneself from flatterers is by making it clear that telling the truth does not offend you. However, if everyone feels free to speak the truth, it can lead to a loss of respect.

Therefore, a wise prince should take a middle path. He should select wise men from his state and give them permission to speak the truth to him, but only about the matters he asks them about, and nothing else. He should question them about everything, listen to their opinions, and then make his own decisions. He should behave in such a way that each adviser knows the more openly they speak, the more he will value them. But beyond these trusted advisers, the prince should not listen to anyone else. Once a decision is made, he should stick to it firmly. A prince who does not do this is either manipulated by flatterers or swayed by too many differing opinions, causing him to lose respect.

I would like to bring up a modern example to illustrate this. Fra Luca, who worked for Emperor Maximilian, said that the emperor consulted no one but never got what he wanted. This happened because Maximilian did the opposite of what I recommend. He was secretive and didn't share his plans with anyone or ask for advice. However, as his plans unfolded and became known, those around him obstructed them. Because Maximilian was easily swayed, he abandoned his plans. As a result, he would undo today what he had done yesterday, leaving everyone confused about his intentions and making it impossible for anyone to trust his decisions.

A prince should always seek counsel, but only when he wants it, not when others want to give it. He should discourage unsolicited advice, but when he does ask for it, he should be a careful and patient listener. If he finds out that someone has lied to him, he should let his anger be known.

Some people think that a prince only seems wise because of the good advisers around him, but that's a mistake. There's a rule that always holds true: a prince who isn't wise on his own will never be able to take good advice. The only exception is if the prince hands over all his decisions to a single, very smart person, in which case things might go well for a while. But even then, it wouldn't last long, because eventually that adviser would take control of the state for himself.

On the other hand, if a prince who lacks experience tries to get advice from several people, he will end up with conflicting opinions and won't know how to manage them. Every adviser will look out for their own interests, and the prince won't be able to understand or manage them properly. People will always be unfaithful unless they are kept honest by force. Therefore, it should be concluded that good advice comes from the wisdom of the prince, not the other way around—the prince's wisdom doesn't come from good advice.

Chapter 24
Why the Princes of Italy
Have Lost Their States

The previous advice, when followed carefully, will allow a new prince to quickly establish himself and become more secure and stable in his position than even a ruler who has been on the throne for a long time. The actions of a new prince are scrutinized more closely than those of a hereditary one, and if they are seen to be competent, they will attract more followers and gain stronger loyalty than old family ties ever could. People are drawn to what is happening now rather than what happened in the past. When they find that the present ruler is doing well, they are satisfied and look no further. If the prince continues to meet their expectations in other areas, they will defend him fiercely. Thus, a new prince can earn double the glory by founding a principality and strengthening it with good laws, a strong military, reliable allies, and by setting a good example. On the other hand, it would be a double disgrace for a prince born into power to lose his state because of a lack of wisdom.

If we examine the rulers who have lost their states in Italy in recent times, such as the King of Naples, the Duke of Milan, and others, we will find that they all had one main weakness in terms of military power, which has been discussed in detail earlier. Additionally, some of these rulers had alienated their people, while others, who may have had the support of the people, failed to secure the loyalty of the nobles. Without these weaknesses, states that have enough strength to maintain an army would not be lost.

Take Philip of Macedon, not the father of Alexander the Great, but the one who was defeated by Titus Quintius. Although Philip did not control much territory compared to the vast power of the Romans and the Greeks who attacked him, he was a skilled warrior who knew how to win over the people and secure the loyalty of the nobles. Because of this, he was able to sustain the war against his enemies for many years. While he eventually lost control of some cities, he still managed to keep his kingdom.

Therefore, our modern-day princes should not blame fortune for the loss of their principalities after having ruled for many years. Instead, they should blame their own laziness, for in peaceful times they never considered that a change might come. It is a common flaw in human nature to fail to prepare for difficulties during calm times. When trouble finally arrived, instead of defending themselves, they thought of fleeing and hoped that the people, tired of the arrogance of the conquerors, would call them back. This strategy might work when all else has failed, but it is a poor choice to neglect every other option in favor of it. No ruler should put themselves in a position where they fall and have to hope that someone will come along later to restore them to power. That kind of rescue is neither secure nor reliable. Only those actions that depend on your own strength and courage will be trustworthy, certain, and lasting.

Chapter 25
What Fortune Can Effect in Human Affairs and How to Withstand Her

I know that many people have believed, and still believe, that the events of the world are so governed by fortune and by divine will that human wisdom cannot direct them, and that no one can help them. As a result, they argue that it is unnecessary to work hard in managing affairs and instead leave everything to chance. This belief has gained more support in recent times due to the unpredictable changes we witness every day, beyond any human foresight. Sometimes, after reflecting on this, I find myself somewhat inclined to agree with this view. However, without disregarding free will, I hold that fortune controls about half of our actions, but the other half, or perhaps a little less, is left to us to direct.

I liken fortune to a river that floods and overflows, sweeping away everything in its path—trees, buildings, and even the earth itself. Its force is so overwhelming that no one can stand against it. Yet, despite its destructive nature, this does not mean that people cannot take precautions when the weather is calm, building defenses and barriers so that, when the river rises again, its waters can be channeled safely and its force reduced. In the same way, fortune shows its power where people have not prepared to resist it, and it strikes hardest where there are no barriers or defenses to restrain it.

If you consider Italy, the epicenter of so many changes, you will see that it is an open country, lacking any true defenses. Had Italy been properly fortified and defended, like Germany, Spain, or France, the great changes that have swept through it might not have occurred or would have been less severe. This is enough to say about resisting fortune in general.

Now, narrowing the focus, we often see a prince who is successful today and ruined tomorrow without having changed his character or behavior. This, I believe, happens for reasons already discussed: a prince who relies entirely on fortune will fall when fortune changes. I also believe that a prince will succeed if his actions align with the spirit of the times, while he will fail if his actions do not. People pursue glory and wealth through different methods—some with caution, others with speed; some through strength, others through cunning; some with patience, others with urgency. Each approach can lead to success. For example, two cautious men may pursue the same goal, with one succeeding and the other failing; similarly, two men using opposite methods, one cautious and the other reckless, might both succeed. This all depends on whether their actions fit the times.

The rise and fall of rulers often result from this principle. A cautious and patient prince may thrive when circumstances suit his careful approach, but if the times change and he fails to adapt, he will be ruined. Most people cannot adapt easily, either because their nature inclines them toward a particular way of acting, or because they have always succeeded by following one method and cannot be convinced to change it. Thus, when a cautious man needs to become bold, he may not know how, and as a result, he will fail. But if he had adjusted his behavior to the times, fortune would not have abandoned him.

Pope Julius II was always impetuous in his actions, and circumstances favored this approach, so he succeeded in all his ventures. Consider his first campaign against Bologna when Messer Giovanni Bentivogli was still alive. The Venetians and the King of Spain opposed his plans, and he was still negotiating with the King of France. Despite this, Julius acted boldly, leading the campaign himself, which caused the Venetians to hesitate and the Spanish to remain passive, with the latter focused on reclaiming Naples. Even the King of France, recognizing Julius's resolve, could not refuse him because he wanted the Pope as an ally to weaken the Venetians. Julius's impetuousness achieved what no other pope could have accomplished through cautious planning. Had he waited in Rome to organize everything carefully, the French king would have found many excuses, and others would have raised many objections.

All of Julius's actions followed this same pattern, and they were all successful because he was fortunate to die before facing any contrary circumstances. Had times arisen that required a more cautious approach, Julius would likely have met with failure because he could never have changed his nature.

In conclusion, fortune is ever-changing, while human beings tend to remain fixed in their habits. As long as a person's actions are in harmony with the times, they will succeed; but when times change, and they do not, failure follows. I believe it is better to be bold than cautious because fortune, like a woman, must be controlled with force and audacity. Fortune is more likely to be commanded by those who act boldly and decisively than by those who proceed with caution. Like a woman, fortune favors the young, who are less cautious, more daring, and more aggressive in their pursuit of her.

Chapter 26
An Exhortation to Liberate Italy from The Barbarians

Having carefully considered the subject of the above discourses, and wondering within myself whether the present times were propitious to a new prince, and whether there were elements that would give an opportunity to a wise and virtuous one to introduce a new order of things which would do honour to him and good to the people of this country, it appears to me that so many things concur to favour a new prince that I never knew a time more fit than the present.

And if, as I said, it was necessary that the people of Israel should be captive so as to make manifest the ability of Moses; that the Persians should be oppressed by the Medes so as to discover the greatness of the soul of Cyrus; and that the Athenians should be dispersed to illustrate the capabilities of Theseus: then at the present time, in order to discover the virtue of an Italian spirit, it was necessary that Italy should be reduced to the extremity that she is now in, that she should be more enslaved than the Hebrews, more oppressed than the Persians, more scattered than the Athenians; without head, without order, beaten, despoiled, torn, overrun; and to have endured every kind of desolation.

Although lately some spark may have been shown by one, which made us think he was ordained by God for our redemption, nevertheless it was afterwards seen, in the height of his career, that fortune rejected him; so that Italy, left as without life, waits for him who shall yet heal her wounds and put an end to the ravaging and plundering of Lombardy, to the swindling and taxing of the kingdom and of Tuscany, and cleanse those sores that for long have festered. It is seen how she entreats God to send someone who shall deliver her from these wrongs and barbarous insolencies. It is seen also that she is ready and willing to follow a banner if only someone will raise it.

Nor is there to be seen at present one in whom she can place more hope than in your illustrious house,[1] with its valour and fortune, favoured by God and by the Church of which it is now the chief, and which could be made the head of this redemption. This will not be difficult if you will recall to yourself the actions and lives of the men I have named. And although they were great and wonderful men, yet they were men, and each one of them had no more opportunity than the present offers, for their enterprises were neither more just nor easier than this, nor was God more their friend than He is yours.

[1] Giuliano de Medici. He had just been created a cardinal by Leo X. In 1523 Giuliano was elected Pope, and took the title of Clement VII.

With us there is great justice, because that war is just which is necessary, and arms are hallowed when there is no other hope but in them. Here there is the greatest willingness, and where the willingness is great the difficulties cannot be great if you will only follow those men to whom I have directed your attention. Further than this, how extraordinarily the ways of God have been manifested beyond example: the sea is divided, a cloud has led the way, the rock has poured forth water, it has rained manna, everything has contributed to your greatness; you ought to do the rest. God is not willing to do everything, and thus take away our free will and that share of glory which belongs to us.

And it is not to be wondered at if none of the above-named Italians have been able to accomplish all that is expected from your illustrious house; and if in so many revolutions in Italy, and in so many campaigns, it has always appeared as if military virtue were exhausted, this has happened because the old order of things was not good, and none of us have known how to find a new one. And nothing honours a man more than to establish new laws and new ordinances when he himself was newly risen. Such things when they are well founded and dignified will make him revered and admired, and in Italy there are not wanting opportunities to bring such into use in every form.

Here there is great valour in the limbs whilst it fails in the head. Look attentively at the duels and the hand-to-hand combats, how superior the Italians are in strength, dexterity, and subtlety. But when it comes to armies they do not bear comparison, and this springs entirely from the insufficiency of the leaders, since those who are capable are not obedient, and each one seems to himself to know, there having never been any one so distinguished above the rest, either by valour or fortune, that others would yield to him. Hence it is that for so long a time, and during so much fighting in the past twenty years, whenever there has been an army wholly Italian, it has always given a poor account of itself; the first witness to this is Il Taro, afterwards Allesandria, Capua, Genoa, Vaila, Bologna, Mestri.[2]

[2] The battles of Il Taro, 1495; Alessandria, 1499; Capua, 1501; Genoa, 1507; Vaila, 1509; Bologna, 1511; Mestri, 1513.

If, therefore, your illustrious house wishes to follow these remarkable men who have redeemed their country, it is necessary before all things, as a true foundation for every enterprise, to be provided with your own forces, because there can be no more faithful, truer, or better soldiers. And although singly they are good, altogether they will be much better when they find themselves commanded by their prince, honoured by him, and maintained at his expense. Therefore it is necessary to be prepared with such arms, so that you can be defended against foreigners by Italian valour.

And although Swiss and Spanish infantry may be considered very formidable, nevertheless there is a defect in both, by reason of which a third order would not only be able to oppose them, but might be relied upon to overthrow them. For the Spaniards cannot resist cavalry, and the Switzers are afraid of infantry whenever they encounter them in close combat. Owing to this, as has been and may again be seen, the Spaniards are unable to resist French cavalry, and the Switzers are overthrown by Spanish infantry. And although a complete proof of this latter cannot be shown, nevertheless there was some evidence of it at the battle of Ravenna, when the Spanish infantry were confronted by German battalions, who follow the same tactics as the Swiss; when the Spaniards, by agility of body and with the aid of their shields, got in under the pikes of the Germans and stood out of danger, able to attack, while the Germans stood helpless, and, if the cavalry had not dashed up, all would have been over with them. It is possible, therefore, knowing the defects of both these infantries, to invent a new one, which will resist cavalry and not be afraid of infantry; this need not create a new order of arms, but a variation upon the old. And these are the kind of improvements which confer reputation and power upon a new prince.

This opportunity, therefore, ought not to be allowed to pass for letting Italy at last see her liberator appear. Nor can one express the love with which he would be received in all those provinces which have suffered so much from these foreign scourings, with what thirst for revenge, with what stubborn faith, with what devotion, with what tears. What door would be closed to him? Who would refuse obedience to him? What envy would hinder him? What Italian would refuse him homage? To all of us this barbarous dominion stinks. Let, therefore, your illustrious house take up this charge with that courage and hope with which all just enterprises are undertaken, so that under its standard our native country may be ennobled, and under its auspices may be verified that saying of Petrarch:

Chapter 27
Description of The Methods Adopted by The Duke Valentino When Murdering Vitellozzo

Vitelli, Oliverotto Da Fermo, The Signor Pagolo, And the Duke Di Gravina Orsini

Duke Valentino had just returned from Lombardy, where he went to clear his name with the King of France. The Florentines had accused him of stirring up rebellion in Arezzo and other towns in the Val di Chiana. He arrived at Imola, where he planned to gather his army and march against Giovanni Bentivogli, the tyrant of Bologna. He wanted to bring Bologna under his control and make it the center of his Romagnian duchy.

When the Vitelli and Orsini, along with their followers, learned of this, they became worried that the duke was gaining too much power. They feared that after taking Bologna, he would try to destroy them to become the supreme ruler of Italy. So, they called a meeting at Magione, in the district of Perugia. The meeting was attended by Cardinal Pagolo and Duke di Gravina Orsini, Vitellozzo Vitelli, Oliverotto da Fermo, Gianpagolo Baglioni, the tyrant of Perugia, and Messer Antonio da Venafro, who represented Pandolfo Petrucci, the Prince of Siena. They discussed how strong and ambitious the duke was and decided they had to stop him before his power threatened them all. They resolved not to abandon Bentivogli and to try to win the support of the Florentines. They sent messengers to different places, offering help to one group and encouragement to others to unite against their common enemy. News of this meeting spread quickly across Italy, giving hope to those discontented with the duke, including the people of Urbino, who began planning a rebellion.

Because of this unrest, some men in Urbino decided to seize the fortress of San Leo, which was under the duke's control. They did so by watching the castellan as he fortified the rock and brought timber to the fortress. When the beams were being carried across the bridge, making it impossible for those inside to raise the bridge, the conspirators seized their chance. They jumped onto the bridge and then into the fortress. After they captured it, the whole region rebelled and brought back their old duke. They were encouraged not only by the capture of the fort but also by the Diet at Magione, from whom they expected to get support.

When others heard of the rebellion in Urbino, they saw an opportunity. They quickly gathered their forces to take control of any towns that still remained loyal to the duke. They sent another message to Florence, urging the republic to join them in overthrowing their common enemy. They argued that the risk was smaller now, and they shouldn't wait for another chance.

However, the Florentines, who hated the Vitelli and Orsini for several reasons, refused to join the rebellion. Instead, they sent their secretary, Nicolo Machiavelli, to offer protection and help to the duke against his enemies. The duke, who was in Imola, was full of fear because, to everyone's surprise, his soldiers had quickly switched sides and joined the enemy. This left him unarmed and vulnerable, with war at his doorstep. But after receiving support from the Florentines, he regained his courage. He decided to delay the battle, with the few soldiers he had left, and to negotiate for peace while also seeking reinforcements. He managed to get help in two ways: by asking the King of France for more men and by recruiting soldiers and turning them into cavalry. He paid them all with money.

Despite this, his enemies moved closer to him, advancing toward Fossombrone, where they encountered some of the duke's men and, with the help of the Orsini and Vitelli, defeated them. After this occurred, the duke immediately resolved to see if he could end the conflict through offers of reconciliation. Being a master of deception, he didn't fail to make the insurgents believe that he wished for everyone who had gained something to keep it. He acted as if it was enough for him to have the title of prince, while others could hold the lands.

The duke succeeded so well in this effort that they sent Signor Pagolo to him to negotiate peace, and they brought their army to a halt. However, the duke did not stop his own preparations. He carefully ensured that he had both cavalry and infantry, and to keep these preparations hidden from others, he sent his troops in small groups to different parts of Romagna. Meanwhile, five hundred French lancers arrived to support him. And even though he found himself strong enough to seek revenge on his enemies through open war, he thought it safer and more advantageous to deceive them. For this reason, he did not stop the peace negotiations.

To ensure this, the duke made peace with them, confirming their previous agreements. He immediately gave them four thousand ducats and promised not to harm the Bentivogli. He also formed an alliance with Giovanni, and, moreover, he agreed not to force them to appear before him unless they wished to. On the other hand, they promised to return the duchy of Urbino and other places they had seized, to serve him in all his campaigns, and not to wage war or make alliances with anyone without his permission.

After this reconciliation was completed, Guido Ubaldo, the Duke of Urbino, fled once more to Venice, but not before he destroyed all the fortresses in his territory. Trusting in the loyalty of his people, he didn't want the fortresses, which he believed he couldn't defend, to fall into enemy hands, as they could then be used against his friends. However, Duke Valentino, after concluding this agreement and spreading his forces throughout Romagna, set out for Imola at the end of November, accompanied by his French cavalry. From there, he went to Cesena, where he stayed for some time to negotiate with the envoys of the Vitelli and Orsini, who had gathered their men in the duchy of Urbino to discuss their next undertaking. But since no decision was reached, Oliverotto da Fermo was sent to propose that, if the duke wished to launch an attack on Tuscany, they were ready. If not, they would besiege Sinigalia. To this, the duke replied that he did not wish to go to war with Tuscany and thus turn against the Florentines, but he was quite willing to proceed with the siege of Sinigalia.

It happened not long after that the town surrendered, but the fortress still refused to yield because the castellan insisted that he would only hand it over to the duke himself. So, they urged the duke to come in person. This seemed like a perfect chance for the duke, as being invited by them rather than coming by his own decision would not raise any suspicion. To further ease their concerns, he allowed all the French men-at-arms who had been with him in Lombardy to leave, except for the hundred lancers under the command of Mons. di Candales, his brother-in-law. He departed from Cesena around the middle of December and went to Fano. With great cunning, he managed to convince the Vitelli and Orsini to wait for him at Sinigalia, arguing that any reluctance to do so might cast doubt on the sincerity and lasting nature of their reconciliation. He assured them that he was a man who valued the arms and counsel of his friends. Still, Vitellozzo remained highly suspicious, as the death of his brother had warned him against offending a prince and then trusting him again. However, he was eventually persuaded by Pagolo Orsini, whom the duke had corrupted with gifts and promises, to stay and wait.

Before the duke departed from Fano on the 30th of December, 1502, he shared his plans with eight of his most trusted followers, including Don Michele and Monsignor d'Euna, who would later become a cardinal. He instructed them that once Vitellozzo, Pagolo Orsini, the Duke di Gravina, and Oliverotto arrived, his followers were to pair up and each pair would take responsibility for one of the leaders. These pairs were to keep their assigned men occupied until they reached Sinigalia, where the leaders were to be held under strict watch until they could be taken to the duke's quarters, where they would be seized.

The duke then commanded that all his cavalry and infantry, more than two thousand horsemen and ten thousand foot soldiers, gather at daybreak near the Metauro River, about five miles from Fano, and wait for him there. On the last day of December, the duke arrived at the Metauro with his forces. He sent a group of about two hundred horsemen ahead, followed by the rest of the infantry, which he accompanied along with the remaining men-at-arms.

Fano and Sinigalia are two cities located in La Marca, along the Adriatic Sea, about fifteen miles apart. As one approaches Sinigalia from Fano, the mountains are on the right, with the sea touching their base in some places. The city of Sinigalia sits slightly more than a bow-shot away from the base of the mountains and about a mile from the shore. On the opposite side of the city runs a small river, which flows along the part of the city walls facing Fano and the main road. Anyone approaching Sinigalia travels for a good distance along the mountainside and reaches the river that passes by the city. If they turn left along the riverbank and continue for about a bow-shot's distance, they come to a bridge that crosses the river. At this point, they are almost directly in line with the gate leading into Sinigalia, though not in a straight path, but at an angle. Before this gate, there is a cluster of houses and a square, bordered on one side by the riverbank.

The Vitelli and Orsini, having received orders to wait for the duke and honor him in person, sent their troops to several castles about six miles away from Sinigalia to make room for the duke's forces. They left only Oliverotto and his band, which included one thousand infantry and one hundred fifty horsemen, quartered in the suburb mentioned earlier. With everything arranged, Duke Valentino left for Sinigalia. When the leaders of the cavalry reached the bridge, they didn't cross it. Instead, after opening it, one group turned towards the river and the other towards the countryside, leaving a path in the middle for the infantry to enter the town without stopping.

Vitellozzo, Pagolo, and the Duke di Gravina, riding on mules and accompanied by a few horsemen, headed toward the duke. Vitellozzo, unarmed and wearing a green-lined cape, appeared deeply troubled, as if he knew his death was near. His mood, given his abilities and previous successes, caused some surprise. It is said that when he parted from his men before leaving for Sinigalia to meet the duke, he acted as if it were his final farewell. He entrusted his household and its fortune to his captains, reminding his nephews that it was not their family's fortune, but their fathers' virtues, that should be remembered. The three men came before the duke, saluted him with respect, and were received by him with apparent goodwill. They were immediately placed under the watch of those assigned to guard them.

However, the duke noticed that Oliverotto, who had stayed in Sinigalia with his troops, was missing. Oliverotto was in the square near the river, organizing and drilling his men. The duke signaled with his eyes to Don Michele, who was responsible for Oliverotto, to make sure he didn't escape. Don Michele then rode over to Oliverotto and told him that it wasn't proper to keep his men out of their quarters, as they might be taken by the duke's forces. He advised Oliverotto to send his men to their quarters and come himself to meet the duke. Oliverotto took this advice and went to see the duke. When the duke saw him, he called to him, and after Oliverotto bowed, he joined the others.

The entire group then entered Sinigalia, dismounted at the duke's quarters, and followed him into a private chamber, where the duke had them imprisoned. He then mounted his horse and gave orders for Oliverotto's and the Orsini's men to be disarmed. Oliverotto's men, being close by, were quickly dealt with. But the Orsini and Vitelli's forces, stationed farther away and sensing the doom of their leaders, had time to prepare. Remembering the strength and discipline of the Orsini and Vitelli families, they gathered themselves and successfully defended against the local forces, saving themselves.

The duke's soldiers, after stripping Oliverotto's men of their weapons, began to sack Sinigalia. Had the duke not put a stop to the looting by executing some of his soldiers, they would have completely ransacked the city. Once night fell and the chaos subsided, the duke prepared to execute Vitellozzo and Oliverotto. He led them into a room and had them strangled. Neither of them spoke in a way fitting their past lives. Vitellozzo prayed for permission to ask the pope's full pardon for his sins, while Oliverotto begged for mercy, blaming Vitellozzo for all the wrongs committed against the duke.

Pagolo and the Duke di Gravina Orsini were kept alive until the duke received word from Rome that the pope had captured Cardinal Orsino, the Archbishop of Florence, and Messer Jacopo da Santa Croce. After hearing this, on January 18, 1502, at the castle of Pieve, Pagolo and the Duke di Gravina Orsini were also strangled in the same manner.

Chapter 28
The Life of Castruccio Castracani of Lucca

Written By Nicolo Machiavelli

And Sent to His Friends Zanobi Buondelmonti And Luigi Alamanni.

Castruccio Castracani 1284-1328

It seems, dearest Zanobi and Luigi, an extraordinary thing to those who have thought about it, that nearly all the men who have achieved great things in the world and surpassed others in their time have come from lowly or obscure beginnings, or have been harshly mistreated by Fortune. Some have been abandoned to wild animals, or have had such humble origins that, out of shame, they claimed to be the sons of Jupiter or some other god. It would be tedious to list who these men were, as they are well-known to everyone, and such stories wouldn't offer much benefit to readers, so they are left out. I believe these humble beginnings of great men happen because Fortune wants to show the world that such men owe their success to her, rather than to wisdom, since she steps in when wisdom has little or no role to play in their rise, making all their accomplishments appear to be the result of her influence. Castruccio Castracani of Lucca was one such man who performed great deeds, considering the time and place in which he lived. However, like many others, he was neither fortunate nor distinguished by birth, as this story will demonstrate. It seems worthwhile to bring his memory back to light, because I've noticed in him examples of courage and fortune that make him a model for others to follow. I also believe that you should take note of his actions, as I know that of all men, you both take the greatest pleasure in noble deeds.

The Castracani family was once counted among the noble families of Lucca, but by the time of this story, their status had somewhat declined, as often happens in life. A son named Antonio was born into this family, and he became a priest in the Order of San Michele of Lucca, earning the title of Messer Antonio. He had only one sister, who had been married to Buonaccorso Cenami. After Buonaccorso's death, she became a widow, and not wishing to remarry, she went to live with her brother. Messer Antonio's house had a vineyard behind it, surrounded by gardens, making it easily accessible from various sides.

One morning, just after sunrise, Madonna Dianora, as Messer Antonio's sister was called, went into the vineyard as usual to gather herbs for the day's meal. While she was there, she heard a faint rustling among the vine leaves. Turning to look, she heard a sound resembling a baby's cry. Curious and slightly afraid, but filled with compassion, she approached and found a baby lying hidden among the leaves, its tiny hands and face visible, crying as if it were calling for its mother. Moved by the sight, she picked the baby up, brought it into the house, washed and dressed it in clean linen as was customary, and showed it to Messer Antonio when he returned home.

Messer Antonio was just as surprised and moved as his sister when he saw the child and heard how she had found it. They discussed what should be done, and since he was a priest and she was childless, they decided to raise the baby themselves. They hired a nurse to care for the infant, and they loved and raised it as their own. They baptized the child and gave him the name Castruccio, after their father.

As the years passed, Castruccio grew to be very handsome, showing signs of intelligence and good judgment. He quickly learned the lessons that Messer Antonio taught him, far beyond what was expected for his age. Messer Antonio had intended to make Castruccio a priest, planning to eventually induct him into his canonry and other church positions. All of his teachings were directed towards that goal, but Antonio soon realized that Castruccio's nature was entirely unsuited for the priesthood.

By the time Castruccio reached the age of fourteen, he had started to ignore the reprimands of Messer Antonio and Madonna Dianora and no longer feared them. He abandoned the study of religious books and instead focused on playing with weapons, finding nothing more enjoyable than learning how to use them. He also loved running, jumping, and wrestling with other boys. In all physical activities, he greatly outshone his peers, both in courage and strength. And when he did turn to books, the only ones that interested him were those that told of wars and heroic deeds. Messer Antonio watched all of this with frustration and sadness.

In the city of Lucca lived a gentleman from the Guinigi family, named Messer Francesco. He was a man of arms and stood above all others in Lucca in wealth, physical strength, and courage. He had fought many times under the command of the Visconti of Milan and, as a Ghibelline, was the esteemed leader of that faction in Lucca. Messer Francesco resided in Lucca and often gathered with others in the mornings and evenings under the balcony of the Podesta, located at the top of the San Michele square, the finest square in Lucca. He frequently saw Castruccio playing with other street children in the games I previously mentioned. Observing that Castruccio excelled far beyond the other boys, and that he seemed to hold a kind of royal authority over them, being loved and obeyed by them, Messer Francesco became eager to know more about him. After learning of Castruccio's background and how he had been raised, his desire to have the boy near him only grew stronger.

One day, he called Castruccio and asked him whether he would prefer living in the house of a gentleman, where he would learn to ride horses and handle weapons, or in the house of a priest, where he would learn only masses and church services. Messer Francesco could see that Castruccio's eyes lit up at the mention of horses and weapons, though the boy stood silent, blushing modestly. Encouraged by Messer Francesco to speak, Castruccio replied that if his master approved, nothing would please him more than to abandon his priestly studies and embrace the life of a soldier. This answer delighted Messer Francesco, and soon after, he obtained the consent of Messer Antonio. Antonio, knowing the boy's true nature and fearing he could no longer keep him in the priestly path, reluctantly agreed.

Thus, Castruccio left the house of Messer Antonio the priest and entered the home of Messer Francesco Guinigi, the soldier. It was remarkable how quickly Castruccio showed all the qualities and behavior of a true gentleman. He first became an accomplished horseman, easily mastering even the most spirited horses. In all jousts and tournaments, despite his youth, he stood out above the others. He excelled in all physical exercises, demonstrating both strength and skill. What made his talents even more admirable was his charming modesty, which allowed him to avoid offending anyone in either action or speech. He showed respect to those of high rank, modesty with his equals, and kindness to those beneath him. These virtues made him beloved not only by the entire Guinigi family but by the people of Lucca as well.

When Castruccio turned eighteen, the Ghibellines were driven out of Pavia by the Guelphs, and Messer Francesco was sent by the Visconti to support the Ghibellines. Castruccio accompanied him, leading a part of his forces. During this expedition, Castruccio proved his wisdom and bravery, earning a greater reputation than any other commander. His name and fame spread not only in Pavia but throughout all of Lombardy.

Castruccio, having returned to Lucca with a far higher reputation than when he left, did not fail to use every possible means to gain as many friends as he could, neglecting none of the strategies necessary for this purpose. Around this time, Messer Francesco passed away, leaving behind a thirteen-year-old son named Pagolo, and appointing Castruccio as his son's tutor and the administrator of his estate. Before he died, Francesco called Castruccio to his side, asking him to show the same goodwill to Pagolo that he, Francesco, had always shown to Castruccio, and to repay the father's kindness by looking after the son. Upon Francesco's death, Castruccio became the governor and tutor of Pagolo, which greatly increased his power and status. However, this rise in prominence also sparked envy in Lucca, replacing the universal goodwill he had once enjoyed, as many suspected him of harboring ambitions for tyranny. The most prominent among these was Giorgio degli Opizi, the head of the Guelph party.

Giorgio, after Messer Francesco's death, had hoped to become the leading figure in Lucca, but it seemed to him that Castruccio, with his already apparent great abilities and his position as governor, was robbing him of this opportunity. Thus, Giorgio began to plant seeds of distrust, aiming to undermine Castruccio's influence. At first, Castruccio dismissed these efforts with contempt, but later he became alarmed, fearing that Messer Giorgio might succeed in turning the deputy of King Ruberto of Naples against him, which could result in his expulsion from Lucca.

At that time, Pisa was ruled by Uguccione della Faggiuola of Arezzo, who had initially been elected as their captain but had later become their lord. Some exiled Ghibellines from Lucca were living in Pisa, and Castruccio communicated with them, seeking their help in restoring them to their homeland with Uguccione's support. Castruccio also enlisted the support of his friends in Lucca who resented the authority of the Opizi. Once the plan was set, Castruccio carefully fortified the tower of the Onesti family, stocking it with provisions and arms to withstand a siege for a few days if necessary.

On the night agreed upon with Uguccione, who had positioned his forces between the mountains and Pisa, the signal was given. Without being detected, Uguccione advanced to the gate of San Piero and set fire to the portcullis. Inside the city, Castruccio raised a great uproar, calling the people to arms and forcing open the gate from his side. Uguccione and his men poured into the town, and they killed Messer Giorgio along with his entire family and many of his friends and followers. The governor was driven out, and the government was reshaped according to Uguccione's wishes, to the detriment of the city. It was reported that over one hundred families were exiled during this time. Some of those who fled sought refuge in Florence, while others went to Pistoia, a stronghold of the Guelph party, making the city highly hostile towards Uguccione and the people of Lucca.

As it now seemed to the Florentines and the other members of the Guelph party that the Ghibellines had gained too much power in Tuscany, they decided to restore the exiled Guelphs to Lucca. They gathered a large army in the Val di Nievole and seized Montecatini. From there, they advanced to Montecarlo to secure an open passage into Lucca. In response, Uguccione gathered his Pisan and Lucchese forces, along with a number of German cavalry that he had brought down from Lombardy, and moved to confront the Florentine camp. Upon seeing the enemy approach, the Florentines withdrew from Montecarlo and set up a position between Montecatini and Pescia. Uguccione then camped near Montecarlo, about two miles away from the Florentines, and daily skirmishes between the cavalry of both armies ensued.

Due to Uguccione's illness, the Pisans and Lucchese delayed engaging the enemy in a full battle. As Uguccione's condition worsened, he retreated to Montecarlo for treatment, leaving command of the army in the hands of Castruccio. This change turned out to be disastrous for the Guelphs, who, assuming that the enemy army had lost its leadership with Uguccione's departure, grew overconfident. Castruccio noticed this and allowed several days to pass, giving the Guelphs time to strengthen their belief that the opposing forces were leaderless. He also made gestures of hesitation and didn't allow any camp supplies to be used, further giving the impression of fear.

On the Guelph side, their arrogance increased as they observed what they believed to be signs of weakness in Castruccio's army. Every day, they drew up in battle formation before his troops, challenging him. Once Castruccio saw that the enemy had become sufficiently emboldened and had understood their tactics, he decided it was time to engage them. He addressed his soldiers with words of encouragement, assuring them of certain victory if they obeyed his commands.

Castruccio had observed that the Guelphs had placed their best troops in the center of their line and their weaker forces on the flanks. In response, he arranged his army in the opposite manner, positioning his strongest soldiers on the wings and moving the less reliable men to the center. Following this strategy, he led his army out and quickly brought them within sight of the enemy, who, as usual, had lined up in their boastful manner. Castruccio ordered his central units to advance slowly, while the wings moved forward rapidly. When the battle began, only the flanks of the two armies engaged, while the central battalions on both sides remained apart, too distant to assist one another.

This tactic ensured that Castruccio's strongest troops were pitted against the enemy's weaker ones, while the best forces of the Florentines remained idle in the center, unable to help their comrades on the wings. Castruccio quickly routed the enemy's flanks, and when the Guelph center realized they were vulnerable to attack without having fought, they too fled. The defeat was total, with a heavy loss of life on the Guelph side. Over ten thousand men were killed, including many officers and knights of the Guelph party in Tuscany, as well as several princes who had come to their aid. Among the fallen were Piero, the brother of King Ruberto, Carlo, his nephew, and Filippo, the lord of Taranto.

On Castruccio's side, the loss was minimal, with fewer than three hundred men killed. Among the dead was Francesco, Uguccione's son, who, being young and reckless, was slain in the first charge.

This victory greatly enhanced Castruccio's reputation, so much so that Uguccione became jealous and suspicious of him. It seemed to Uguccione that the victory had brought him no increase in power, but rather diminished it. With this in mind, Uguccione only waited for the right moment to act. The opportunity came with the murder of Pier Agnolo Micheli, a well-known and capable man in Lucca. The murderer fled to Castruccio's house for protection. When the sergeants of the captain came to arrest him, they were driven away by Castruccio, allowing the murderer to escape. This incident reached Uguccione, who was then in Pisa, and he saw it as the perfect moment to punish Castruccio.

Uguccione sent for his son, Neri, who was the governor of Lucca, and instructed him to capture Castruccio at a banquet and have him killed. Castruccio, suspecting no ill will, went to Neri in good faith, enjoyed supper, and was then thrown into prison. However, Neri hesitated to kill him, fearing that the people would rise in anger. He decided to wait for further instructions from his father. Uguccione, enraged by his son's hesitation and cowardice, set out immediately from Pisa to Lucca with four hundred horsemen to finish the matter himself. However, before he reached Lucca, the Pisans rebelled, killed his deputy, and appointed Count Gaddo della Gherardesca as their lord. Upon hearing the news of Pisa's revolt, Uguccione chose not to turn back, fearing that the people of Lucca, inspired by Pisa's example, might close their gates against him.

Meanwhile, the citizens of Lucca, aware of what had occurred in Pisa, seized the opportunity to demand Castruccio's release, despite Uguccione's presence in the city. The matter was first discussed in private gatherings, but soon it became public, with people openly demanding Castruccio's freedom in the streets and squares. Armed and determined, the people confronted Uguccione and demanded Castruccio's release. Fearing that the situation could escalate, Uguccione freed Castruccio from prison. Castruccio then gathered his supporters, and, with the help of the people, attacked Uguccione.

Seeing no option but to flee, Uguccione escaped with his followers to Lombardy, where he sought refuge with the lords of Scala and eventually died in poverty.

Castruccio, having gone from being a prisoner to almost a prince in Lucca, handled his newfound power with such discretion that he was appointed captain of the army for one year. With this position, and eager to gain fame through military exploits, Castruccio planned to recover several towns that had rebelled after Uguccione's departure. With the help of the Pisans, with whom he had forged a treaty, he marched on Sarzana. To capture the town, he built a fort against it, which is still called Zerezzanello today. After two months, Castruccio took Sarzana. Buoyed by this success, he quickly captured Massa, Carrara, and Lavenza, and in a short time, had overrun the entire Lunigiana region.

To secure the pass between Lombardy and Lunigiana, Castruccio laid siege to Pontremoli and took it from Messer Anastagio Palavicini, who was its lord. After this victory, he returned to Lucca, where he was greeted with great celebration by the people. By now, Castruccio, seeing that it was unwise to delay any longer, sought to become the prince of Lucca. With the help of Pazzino del Poggio, Puccinello dal Portico, Francesco Boccansacchi, and Cecco Guinigi—all of whom he had corrupted—he had himself appointed lord of Lucca. He was then solemnly and officially elected prince by the people.

Around this time, Frederick of Bavaria, the King of the Romans, came to Italy to claim the Imperial crown. Castruccio, seeking to ally himself with Frederick, met him at the head of five hundred horsemen. In his absence, Castruccio left Pagolo Guinigi as his deputy in Lucca. Pagolo was highly respected because of the people's affection for the memory of his father. Frederick received Castruccio with great honor and granted him many privileges, appointing him the emperor's lieutenant in Tuscany.

At this time, the Pisans were greatly afraid of Gaddo della Gherardesca, whom they had expelled from Pisa. They turned to Frederick for assistance, and he, in turn, appointed Castruccio as the lord of Pisa. The Pisans, fearing the Guelphs and particularly the Florentines, were forced to accept Castruccio as their lord.

Frederick, having appointed a governor in Rome to manage his Italian affairs, returned to Germany. All the Tuscan and Lombard Ghibellines, who followed the imperial cause, sought Castruccio's counsel and aid, promising him governance over their regions if he could help them reclaim them. Among these exiles were Matteo Guidi, Nardo Scolari, Lapo Uberti, Gerozzo Nardi, and Piero Buonaccorsi, all Florentine Ghibellines. Castruccio secretly aimed to become the master of all Tuscany with the help of these men and his own forces. To strengthen his position, he allied himself with Messer Matteo Visconti, the Prince of Milan, and organized his city's forces and surrounding districts. Lucca had five gates, and Castruccio divided his territories into five regions, equipping each with arms and placing them under captains. This organization allowed him to quickly mobilize twenty thousand soldiers, in addition to those he could call upon from Pisa.

While Castruccio was consolidating his power, Messer Matteo Visconti was attacked by the Guelphs of Piacenza, who had expelled the Ghibellines with the help of a Florentine army and King Ruberto. Matteo called on Castruccio to invade Florentine territory, forcing them to withdraw their forces from Lombardy to defend their homeland. Castruccio invaded the Valdarno, capturing Fucecchio and San Miniato, and causing great devastation. The Florentines recalled their army, but Castruccio, dealing with other matters, was forced to return to Lucca before they could fully engage.

There lived in the city of Lucca the Poggio family, who were so influential that they had the power not only to elevate Castruccio but also to help him attain the title of prince. However, feeling that they had not been sufficiently rewarded for their services, they began to incite other families to rebel and to overthrow Castruccio. One morning, they seized their opportunity, armed themselves, and attacked the lieutenant Castruccio had left in charge, killing him. They attempted to rouse the people to revolt, but Stefano di Poggio, an elderly, peaceable man who had taken no part in the rebellion, intervened. Using his authority, he compelled them to lay down their arms, offering to act as their mediator with Castruccio to secure what they desired. The rebels, lacking better judgment, disarmed just as easily as they had taken up arms.

When Castruccio heard the news of the events in Lucca, he immediately placed Pagolo Guinigi in command of his army and hurried home with a troop of cavalry. To his surprise, he found the rebellion already quelled. Nonetheless, he stationed his soldiers in the most strategic positions throughout the city. Stefano, believing that Castruccio owed him a great debt of gratitude, sought him out. Without pleading for himself, as he saw no need, he asked Castruccio to pardon the other members of his family, citing their youth, their past friendship, and the many obligations Castruccio owed to their house.

Castruccio responded graciously, assuring Stefano that he was more pleased to find the rebellion ended than he had ever been troubled by its beginning. He encouraged Stefano to bring his family before him, saying that he thanked God for the chance to demonstrate his clemency and generosity. Trusting in Castruccio's words, Stefano convinced his family to surrender. However, once they did, they, along with Stefano, were immediately imprisoned and executed.

Meanwhile, the Florentines had reclaimed San Miniato, and Castruccio, feeling that his position in Lucca was not yet secure enough to leave, thought it wise to seek peace. He approached the Florentines with a proposal for a truce, which they were quick to accept, as they were weary of the war and eager to reduce its costs. A two year treaty was agreed upon, allowing both sides to retain the territories they had conquered.

Freed from external troubles, Castruccio turned his attention to Lucca's internal affairs. Determined not to face similar dangers again, he methodically eliminated anyone whose ambition might challenge his rule. Under various pretexts and justifications, he wiped out every potential rival—exiling some, confiscating their property, and executing those he had captured, declaring that his experience had taught him none of them could be trusted. To further ensure his security, he constructed a fortress in Lucca using stones from the towers of those he had killed or driven from the state.

While Castruccio made peace with the Florentines and strengthened his rule in Lucca, he missed no chance, short of open warfare, to increase his influence elsewhere. He believed that gaining control of Pistoia would give him a foothold in Florence, which was his ultimate goal. To this end, he formed alliances with the mountaineers and worked matters in Pistoia so cleverly that both factions in the city entrusted him with their secrets. Pistoia was, as always, divided between two factions: the Bianchi, led by Bastiano di Possente, and the Neri, led by Jacopo da Gia. Both men were secretly in communication with Castruccio, each hoping to drive the other out of the city. After many threats, open conflict finally broke out between them. Jacopo fortified himself near the Florentine gate, while Bastiano took control of the Lucchese gate. Both sides trusted Castruccio more than they trusted the Florentines, believing that he was more willing and ready to fight. They both sent to him for help.

Castruccio gave promises to both. He told Bastiano that he would come personally, and assured Jacopo that he would send his student, Pagolo Guinigi. At the agreed-upon time, Castruccio sent Pagolo through Pisa, while he himself went directly to Pistoia. At midnight, both met outside the city and were admitted as friends. Once inside, and at a signal from Castruccio, one of them killed Jacopo da Gia, while the other killed Bastiano di Possente. Their followers were either captured or slain. With little further resistance, Pistoia fell into Castruccio's hands. He forced the Signoria to leave the palace and made the people swear obedience to him, offering them many promises and forgiving their old debts. The surrounding countryside flocked to the city to see their new prince, and all were filled with hope and quickly settled under his rule, much influenced by his reputation for great valor.

Around this time, great disturbances arose in Rome due to the high cost of living, which was caused by the absence of the pope, who was residing in Avignon. Enrico, the German governor, was widely blamed for the unrest, as murders and riots occurred daily without his ability to stop them. Enrico grew anxious, fearing that the Romans might call on Ruberto, the King of Naples, who could drive out the Germans and bring the pope back to the city. With no closer ally to turn to, Enrico sent a request to Castruccio, asking for both his assistance and his personal presence in Rome. Castruccio, considering that it was in his interest to support the emperor, agreed. He believed his own safety would be at risk if the emperor lost control of Rome. Leaving Pagolo Guinigi in charge of Lucca, Castruccio set out for Rome with six hundred horsemen.

Upon his arrival, he was received with the highest honors by Enrico. Castruccio's presence quickly restored respect for the emperor's authority, and without bloodshed or violence, peace was restored in the city. A large part of this success was due to Castruccio, who sent large supplies of grain from the area around Pisa by sea, thus relieving the food shortage that had caused much of the trouble. After disciplining some of the Roman leaders and warning others, order was voluntarily restored to Enrico's rule. Castruccio was showered with honors and was made a Roman senator. This title was bestowed upon him with great ceremony. He wore a richly brocaded toga, embroidered on the front with the words: "I am what God wills," and on the back: "What God desires shall be."

During this time, the Florentines, angered that Castruccio had taken Pistoia during the truce, began to devise ways to incite the city to rebel, believing it would be easy to achieve in his absence. Among the exiled Pistoians living in Florence were two prominent men, Baldo Cecchi and Jacopo Baldini, both of whom were willing to face danger. These men maintained contact with their friends in Pistoia, and with the help of the Florentines, they entered the city by night. After expelling some of Castruccio's officials and partisans, and killing others, they succeeded in restoring Pistoia's independence.

When Castruccio received this news, he was furious. He quickly took leave of Enrico and hastened toward Pistoia. Upon hearing of his return, the Florentines, aware that he would waste no time, decided to intercept him in the Val di Nievole. They believed that by doing so, they could block his route to Pistoia. Gathering a large army of Guelph supporters, the Florentines marched into Pistoian territory. Meanwhile, Castruccio reached Montecarlo with his army. Learning of the Florentines' position, he chose not to engage them in the plains of Pistoia or wait for them in the plains of Pescia. Instead, he planned a bold attack in the Pass of Serravalle. He believed that, despite having only twelve thousand men compared to the Florentines' thirty thousand, success would guarantee his victory. Although he trusted in his own abilities and the bravery of his troops, he hesitated to meet the Florentines in open battle, fearing they might overwhelm him with their numbers.

Serravalle is a castle located between Pescia and Pistoia, positioned on a hill that blocks the Val di Nievole. It lies just beyond the pass, which is narrow and steep in some areas, while generally rising gently but still remaining narrow, especially at the summit where the waters divide. Here, twenty men side by side could hold the pass. The lord of Serravalle, Manfred, a German, had been allowed to remain in possession of the castle even before Castruccio became lord of Pistoia. The castle was considered neutral territory, unclaimed by either the Lucchese or the Pistoians, as neither side wished to displace Manfred as long as he remained neutral and made no commitments to anyone. The castle was well fortified, and Manfred had maintained his position there for these reasons.

Castruccio saw that possessing this castle would give him a significant advantage in his conflict with Florence. Knowing this, and having a close friendship with a resident inside the castle, Castruccio arranged for four hundred of his men to be secretly admitted the night before the attack on the Florentines, with the castellan to be killed.

Castruccio, having prepared everything, needed to ensure that the Florentines continued with their plan to move the war away from Pistoia into the Val di Nievole. Thus, he did not move his army from Montecarlo, allowing the Florentines to proceed. They hurried on and set up camp beneath Serravalle, planning to cross the hill the next morning. Meanwhile, Castruccio had seized the castle during the night, and, marching his army silently from Montecarlo at midnight, reached the base of Serravalle. At dawn, both Castruccio's forces and the Florentines began ascending the hill simultaneously.

Castruccio sent his infantry up the main road and dispatched a troop of four hundred horsemen along a path to the left toward the castle. The Florentines, unaware that Castruccio had seized the hill and the castle, sent forward four hundred cavalry ahead of their main army. To their complete surprise, they encountered Castruccio's infantry. So close were they upon the enemy that they barely had time to lower their visors before being attacked. The Florentines, unprepared and caught off guard, faced a well-prepared enemy who assaulted them with such vigor that they struggled to hold their position, although a few managed to break through.

When the sounds of battle reached the Florentine camp below, confusion erupted. The narrow pass caused the cavalry and infantry to become entangled, and the captains could not move their men either forward or backward. Amid the chaos, no one knew what should or could be done. In short order, the Florentine cavalry engaged with Castruccio's infantry were either scattered or killed. Due to their unfortunate position, they were unable to defend themselves effectively, despite their desperate resistance. Retreat was impossible, as the mountains flanked them on both sides, their enemies blocked their way ahead, and their own forces pressed from behind.

Seeing that his forces had not yet dealt a decisive blow, Castruccio sent one thousand infantry to join the four hundred horsemen stationed at the castle, ordering them to strike the Florentine flank. They carried out the attack with such ferocity that the Florentines were unable to withstand it. Soon, they broke ranks and fled in full retreat, defeated more by the difficult terrain than by the strength of their enemy. Those in the rear fled toward Pistoia, spreading across the plains, each man seeking only his own safety.

The defeat was total and bloody. Many captains were taken prisoner, including Bandini dei Rossi, Francesco Brunelleschi, and Giovanni della Tosa, all prominent Florentine nobles. Many Tuscans and Neapolitans who had fought alongside the Florentines, sent by King Ruberto to support the Guelphs, were also captured. When news of the defeat reached Pistoia, the citizens expelled the Guelph supporters and surrendered the city to Castruccio.

Castruccio did not stop at Pistoia. He took control of Prato and all the castles on both sides of the Arno plains. He then advanced his army to the plains of Peretola, just two miles from Florence. There, he stayed for several days, dividing the spoils of war and celebrating his victory with feasts, games, horse races, and foot races for both men and women. To commemorate the Florentines' defeat, he even minted medals.

During this time, Castruccio attempted to bribe some citizens of Florence to open the city gates at night, but the conspiracy was uncovered. Those involved in the plot, including Tommaso Lupacci and Lambertuccio Frescobaldi, were captured and beheaded. The Florentines, deeply anxious after their defeat and despairing of preserving their liberty, sent envoys to King Ruberto of Naples, offering him control of the city. Recognizing the immense importance of maintaining Guelph power, Ruberto accepted their offer. He agreed to receive a yearly tribute of two hundred thousand florins from Florence and sent his son, Carlo, to the city with four thousand horsemen.

Shortly after this, the Florentines experienced some relief from the pressure of Castruccio's army, as he was forced to abandon his positions near Florence and march on Pisa to suppress a conspiracy. This rebellion was led by Benedetto Lanfranchi, one of the most prominent men in Pisa, who could not tolerate seeing his homeland under the control of the Lucchese. Lanfranchi had planned to seize the citadel, kill Castruccio's supporters, and expel the garrison. However, in any conspiracy, secrecy requires few participants, while execution requires many, and in seeking more supporters, Lanfranchi approached someone who betrayed the plot to Castruccio. This betrayal cannot go without harsh condemnation of Bonifacio Cerchi and Giovanni Guidi, two Florentine exiles living in Pisa, who were involved in the plot's exposure.

As a result, Castruccio captured Benedetto and had him executed, along with many other noble citizens, whose families he sent into exile. Castruccio now realized that both Pisa and Pistoia were deeply disaffected, and he dedicated considerable thought and effort to securing his hold on these cities. This preoccupation gave the Florentines an opportunity to regroup their army and await the arrival of Carlo, the son of the King of Naples. Once Carlo arrived, they decided to act swiftly, assembling a massive army of over thirty thousand infantry and ten thousand cavalry, having called upon every Guelph in Italy for assistance. They deliberated whether to attack Pistoia or Pisa first and concluded that Pisa was the better target, especially considering the recent conspiracy. They believed that once Pisa fell, Pistoia would quickly follow.

In early May 1328, the Florentines launched their campaign, swiftly capturing Lastra, Signa, Montelupo, and Empoli, before advancing to San Miniato. When Castruccio learned of the enormous army the Florentines were sending against him, he remained unshaken. He believed that Fortune was now preparing to grant him control of Tuscany, confident that his enemies would fare no better than they had at Pisa or Serravalle. Castruccio gathered twenty thousand infantry and four thousand cavalry and marched to Fucecchio, while he sent Pagolo Guinigi to Pisa with five thousand infantry.

Fucecchio was strategically stronger than any other town in the Pisan region, situated between the Arno and Gusciana rivers and slightly elevated above the surrounding plains. The Florentines would be unable to prevent supplies from reaching it without splitting their forces. Furthermore, they could not approach the town either from Lucca or Pisa without putting themselves at a disadvantage. If they attempted to attack Castruccio, they would find themselves caught between his two armies, the one under his own command and the other under Pagolo's. Alternatively, they would need to cross the Arno to engage directly with his forces, a risky maneuver.

To tempt the Florentines into this dangerous course of action, Castruccio withdrew his men from the riverbanks and positioned them beneath the walls of Fucecchio, leaving a wide stretch of land between his army and the river.

The Florentines, after taking San Miniato, convened a war council to decide whether to attack Pisa or engage Castruccio's army. After weighing the challenges of both options, they chose to face Castruccio. At that time, the Arno River was low enough to be fordable, though the water still reached the shoulders of the infantrymen and the saddles of the cavalry. On the morning of June 10, 1328, the Florentines initiated the battle, sending forward several cavalry units and ten thousand infantrymen. Castruccio, who had already formulated his plan and knew exactly what to do, immediately attacked the Florentines with five thousand infantry and three thousand cavalry, not allowing them to emerge from the river before charging them. He also sent one thousand light infantry up the riverbank and another thousand down the Arno.

The Florentine infantry, weighed down by their armor and hindered by the water, struggled to scale the riverbanks. Meanwhile, the cavalry, having crossed in small numbers, made the crossing more difficult for others by disturbing the riverbed, which became bogged down with mud. Many horses toppled over with their riders, and others became stuck, unable to move. Seeing the difficulties their troops were facing, the Florentine captains pulled their men back and moved them further up the river, hoping to find a less treacherous crossing point and more suitable banks for landing.

However, when they reached the bank, they were met by the forces Castruccio had already dispatched, who, armed lightly with bucklers and javelins, unleashed a fierce barrage of projectiles at the faces and bodies of the Florentine cavalry. The horses, spooked by the noise and wounds, fell into confusion, trampling each other in the chaos. A fierce and desperate battle erupted between Castruccio's men and the Florentines who managed to cross. The Florentines fought to establish a foothold on the banks to make room for their comrades still in the water, while Castruccio's troops strove to drive them back into the river. Both sides fought with equal determination, encouraged by their captains. Castruccio rallied his men by reminding them that these were the same enemies they had defeated at Serravalle, while the Florentine captains scolded their troops, urging them not to let the many be defeated by the few.

The battle dragged on, with heavy losses and exhaustion on both sides. Recognizing that the fight had lasted long and both sides were near their breaking point, Castruccio sent a fresh unit of infantry to the rear of his engaged forces. He then ordered his front lines to open their ranks as if they were retreating, with one part turning to the right and the other to the left. The Florentines, thinking they had gained an advantage, rushed forward to occupy the space. However, exhausted from battle, they could not hold their ground when they encountered Castruccio's reserves and were soon driven back into the river.

Meanwhile, the cavalry on both sides had yet to gain any decisive advantage, as Castruccio, aware of his disadvantage in cavalry numbers, had instructed his commanders to focus on defense rather than offense. He knew that once he defeated the Florentine infantry, he would be able to quickly deal with the cavalry. His strategy worked. When he saw the Florentine army pushed back into the river, he ordered the rest of his infantry to attack the enemy cavalry. His forces, armed with lances and javelins, along with their own cavalry, launched a furious assault on the Florentine cavalry, quickly routing them.

The Florentine captains, seeing how difficult it was for their cavalry to cross the river, had attempted to send their infantry lower down the river to flank Castruccio's army. However, the steep banks were already fortified by Castruccio's men, making this maneuver futile. The Florentines were completely defeated at all points, and barely a third of their forces escaped. Castruccio once again emerged victorious and covered in glory.

Many Florentine captains were taken prisoner, while Carlo, the son of King Ruberto, along with Michelagnolo Falconi and Taddeo degli Albizzi, the Florentine commissioners, fled to Empoli. Although the spoils of war were significant, the slaughter was far greater, as is often the case in such battles. Of the Florentines, 20,231 men were killed, while Castruccio lost only 1,570 men.

But Fortune, envious of Castruccio's glory, took his life at the very moment when she should have preserved it, thereby ruining all the plans he had worked so long to bring to fruition—plans that only death could have stopped. Castruccio had been fully engaged in the battle all day, and when it ended, despite being exhausted and overheated, he stood at the gate of Fucecchio to welcome his returning soldiers and personally thank them for their efforts. Ever vigilant, he also watched for any signs of the enemy attempting to recover from their defeat, believing it was the duty of a good general to be the first to mount his horse and the last to dismount.

While standing there, Castruccio was exposed to a wind that often rises at midday along the banks of the Arno, a wind notorious for being unhealthy. Though he felt chilled, he paid little attention to it, as he was used to enduring such discomforts. However, this chill would prove fatal. That night, he was struck with a high fever, which worsened so quickly that the doctors realized it would be the cause of his death. Knowing his end was near, Castruccio called Pagolo Guinigi to his side and spoke to him as follows:

"If I had known that Fortune would cut me off in the midst of my path to the glory promised by all my successes, I would have worked less, and left you, if not a larger state, at least one with fewer enemies and dangers. I would have been content with ruling Lucca and Pisa alone. I wouldn't have subjugated the Pistoians or provoked the Florentines with so many offenses. Instead, I would have made both peoples my allies. I might not have lived longer, but I would have lived more peacefully, and I would have left you a state that, while smaller, would have been more secure and established on a stronger foundation.

But Fortune, who governs human affairs, did not grant me the foresight to recognize this from the beginning, nor the time to correct it. You've heard, as many have told you, and I have never hidden it, how I entered your father's house as a boy—without the ambitions that every noble heart should possess—and how he raised me and loved me as if I were his own son. Under his guidance, I learned to be valiant and to seize every opportunity Fortune offered me, as you yourself have witnessed. When your good father passed away, he entrusted you and all his possessions to me. I have cared for you with love and expanded your estate with the devotion I owed him.

In order that you would inherit not only the estate your father left but also what my fortune and abilities have gained, I never married. I didn't want the love for my own children to conflict with the loyalty I owed to your father's. So, I leave you a vast estate, of which I am proud, but I am deeply concerned because I leave it to you unsettled and insecure.

You now have Lucca, but its people will never be satisfied under your rule. You also have Pisa, where the people are fickle and unreliable. Though they may submit to control for a time, they will always resist serving under someone from Lucca. Pistoia, too, is disloyal, torn by factions and still bitter towards your family due to the wrongs we recently inflicted on them. You are surrounded by the Florentines, whom we have harmed in countless ways but not entirely defeated. They will rejoice more at the news of my death than they would if they gained all of Tuscany.

You cannot rely on the Emperor or the princes of Milan—they are distant, slow to act, and their help comes far too late. So, you must depend on your own abilities, the memory of my valor, and the prestige this latest victory has brought you. If you use it wisely, it will help you make peace with the Florentines, who, after suffering this major defeat, should be more willing to negotiate. While I sought to make them my enemies, believing that war would bring me power and glory, you have every reason to make them your allies. Their friendship will provide you with both security and advantages.

In this world, it is crucial for a man to know himself and understand the limits of his own strength and resources. A man who knows he is not suited for war must learn to govern through the arts of peace. It would be wise for you to follow my counsel, and in doing so, you will enjoy the fruits of my life's work and the dangers I have endured. You will succeed easily if you learn to trust what I have told you is true. And you will owe me a double debt, for I have not only left you this realm but also taught you how to keep it."

After this, the citizens of Pisa, Pistoia, and Lucca who had fought alongside Castruccio came to him. As he recommended Pagolo to them and had them swear their loyalty to Pagolo as his successor, Castruccio passed away. He left behind a cherished memory among those who knew him, and no prince of that time was ever loved with such devotion as he was. His funeral was marked by every sign of mourning, and he was buried in San Francesco in Lucca. Fortune did not favor Pagolo Guinigi as she had favored Castruccio, for Pagolo lacked the abilities of his predecessor. Not long after Castruccio's death, Pagolo lost Pisa, then Pistoia, and struggled to retain control over Lucca. This city remained under the Guinigi family until the time of Pagolo's great-grandson.

From what has been related, it is clear that Castruccio was a man of exceptional abilities, measured not only against the men of his own time but also those of earlier eras. He was taller than average, perfectly proportioned, and of a gracious presence. He greeted people with such charm and warmth that few ever left his company displeased. His hair was reddish, and he wore it short above the ears, going without a hat regardless of rain or snow. Castruccio was delightful among friends but formidable to his enemies, just to his subjects, and cunning with those who betrayed him. He was willing to defeat others through deceit if necessary, believing that it was victory, not the means of achieving it, that brought glory. No one was bolder in facing danger, and few were more prudent in extracting themselves from difficult situations.

Castruccio often said that men should attempt everything and fear nothing, claiming that God favored the strong, as the weak are always punished by the strong. He was known for his sharp wit, often biting but always courteous in his responses. Just as he didn't expect indulgence in his way of speaking, he didn't take offense when others spoke sharply to him. Many times, he calmly listened when others were bold with him. For example, when he once paid a ducat for a partridge and was criticized by a friend, Castruccio responded, "You wouldn't have paid more than a penny." The friend agreed, and Castruccio replied, "A ducat means much less to me than a penny does to you." Another time, he spat on a flatterer to show his contempt. The flatterer, unbothered, remarked, "Fishermen endure the sea's waters to catch a few small fish, and I let myself be drenched in spittle to catch a whale." Castruccio heard this with patience and even rewarded the man.

Once, a priest told Castruccio that living so lavishly was a sin. Castruccio replied, "If that's a vice, then you shouldn't indulge so extravagantly at the feasts of our saints." On another occasion, he saw a young man blush as he left a brothel and said, "You should be ashamed when you go in, not when you come out." When a friend handed him a complicated knot to untie, Castruccio quipped, "Fool, do you think I want to undo something that was tied with so much difficulty?" He also remarked to someone who claimed to be a philosopher, "You're like dogs, always chasing after those who will feed you the best." The philosopher responded, "We're more like doctors, going where we're most needed."

Once, while traveling by boat from Pisa to Leghorn, Castruccio was alarmed by a sudden storm. Someone with him mocked his fear, saying they weren't afraid at all.

Castruccio, known for his sharp wit, once responded to someone mocking his fear of a storm by saying, "I'm not surprised you aren't afraid—every man values his soul according to what it's worth." When asked what one should do to gain respect, he advised, "When you go to a banquet, be sure not to seat one piece of wood upon another," suggesting that one should avoid acting foolishly. To someone boasting about having read many things, Castruccio replied, "A wise man knows better than to boast about remembering much." When another bragged that he could drink heavily without getting drunk, Castruccio quipped, "An ox can do the same."

Castruccio had an intimate relationship with a woman, and when a friend criticized him for being taken in by her, he replied, "She hasn't taken me in—I've taken her." Similarly, when scolded for enjoying fine foods, he asked, "Do you spend as much as I do?" When the critic admitted spending less, Castruccio retorted, "Then you're more miserly than I am gluttonous."

At a supper hosted by Taddeo Bernardi, a wealthy citizen of Lucca, Castruccio was shown into a beautifully adorned room. He spat on the floor, and when Taddeo was disturbed, Castruccio calmly said, "I didn't know where else to spit to offend you less." When asked how Caesar died, he replied, "God willing, I will die the same way."

One evening, while dancing and socializing with ladies, a friend remarked that it was beneath someone of his rank to behave so. Castruccio responded, "He who is considered wise by day won't be thought a fool at night." A man once threw himself to the ground in a desperate plea for a favor. When Castruccio rebuked him, the man replied, "You force me to act this way, for your ears are in your feet." Amused, Castruccio granted him double the favor he had requested.

Castruccio often said that the path to hell was easy since it was downhill and traveled blindfolded. When asked for a favor by someone using too many words, he said, "Next time, send someone else to make your request." After enduring a long-winded oration, the speaker apologized, saying, "Perhaps I have tired you." Castruccio replied, "Not at all, I didn't listen to a word."

Of a man who had been a beautiful child and grew into a fine adult, Castruccio remarked, "He's dangerous—he first took husbands from their wives, and now he takes wives from their husbands." To an envious man who laughed, Castruccio asked, "Do you laugh because you're successful, or because someone else is unfortunate?"

While under the care of Messer Francesco Guinigi, a companion asked Castruccio, "What will you give me if I let you strike me on the nose?" Castruccio answered, "A helmet." When criticized for executing a citizen of Lucca who had helped him rise to power, Castruccio responded, "People misunderstand—I didn't kill an old friend, I killed a new enemy." Castruccio often praised men who intended to marry but then decided against it, comparing them to sailors who planned to set sail but wisely chose not to when the time came. He was always surprised that while men would tap and inspect an earthen or glass vase to check its quality before buying, they would choose a wife based only on her appearance.

When asked how he wished to be buried after his death, Castruccio replied, "With my face downwards, because I know that once I'm gone, this country will be turned upside down." On another occasion, someone asked if he had ever considered becoming a friar to save his soul. He responded that the thought had never crossed his mind, as he found it odd that someone like Fra Lazerone could end up in Paradise while Uguccione della Faggiuola would go to Hell.

Once, when asked when a man should eat to maintain his health, Castruccio said, "If the man is rich, he should eat when he is hungry; if he is poor, then whenever he can." Observing one of his gentlemen being laced up by a family member, Castruccio remarked, "I pray God you let him feed you as well."

Upon seeing a house with a Latin inscription that read, "May God preserve this house from the wicked," Castruccio quipped, "Then the owner must never go inside." While passing by a small house with a disproportionately large door, he commented, "That house will fly through the door."

In a discussion with the ambassador of the King of Naples about the property of exiled nobles, a disagreement arose. The ambassador asked Castruccio if he feared the king. Castruccio replied, "Is your king a bad man or a good one?" When the ambassador said the king was a good man, Castruccio responded, "Then why should I fear a good man?"

I could recount many more stories of his sayings, both witty and profound, but I believe the examples already given are enough to demonstrate his remarkable qualities. He lived for forty-four years and, in every sense, was a true prince. Though surrounded by the many signs of his good fortune, Castruccio also wished to keep reminders of his hardships close by. The manacles that once bound him in prison can still be seen today, fixed to the tower of his residence, placed there by him as a lasting testament to the days of his adversity.

In his lifetime, Castruccio was not inferior to figures like Philip of Macedon, the father of Alexander, or Scipio of Rome. He died at the same age as they did, and without question, had Fortune placed him in Macedonia or Rome instead of Lucca, he would have surpassed them both.

Thank You for Reading

Dear Reader,

We hope this timeless classic has sparked your imagination and enriched your literary journey. Now that you've turned the final page, we want to share a vision for the future of reading—one where every classic you've ever wanted to explore is at your fingertips, in a format that best suits your life.

We'd like to invite you to gain immediate, unlimited digital & audiobook access to hundreds of the most treasured literary classics ever written—along with the option to secure deluxe paperback, hardcover & box set editions at printing cost. Together, we can spark a new global literary renaissance alongside our small, independent publishing house called "The Library of Alexandria."

Thousands of years ago, the Library of Alexandria stood as a beacon of knowledge—until it was lost to history. We aim to reignite that spirit of preservation and discovery right now, in the modern age—only this time, it's accessible to all, in every language and every format.

Picture a world where every timeless classic, novel, poem, or philosophical treatise is not only available to read but also updated for today's readers—modernized, translated into any language or dialect, and ready to enjoy in any format you choose, whether that is in an eBook, audiobook, paperback, or deluxe hardcover & box set version a printing cost.

By joining our movement to rebuild the modern Library of Alexandria, you become part of an unprecedented mission to offer:

- **Unlimited Audiobook & eBook Access to the Greatest Classics of All Time**

  Instantly explore thousands of legendary works, from Plato and Shakespeare to Jane Austen and Leo Tolstoy. All are instantly ready to read or listen to, giving you a complete literary universe at your fingertips.

- **Paperback & Deluxe Editions at Printing Costs:**

  Purchase any title in a paperback, deluxe hardbound, or deluxe boxset edition at printing costs, shipped right to your doorstep. Curate your personal library of Alexandria with editions worthy of display—crafted to last, designed to captivate, and delivered straight to your door.

- **Modern translations for Contemporary Readers in all languages and dialects**

  Discover a vast selection of classics reimagined in clear, current language—no more struggling with outdated phrases or obscure references. Next to the original versions, we aim to offer translations in as many languages and dialects as possible.

  As we continue our translation efforts and add new languages, readers everywhere can connect with these works as if they were written today. By bridging linguistic divides, you're contributing to ensuring that these timeless stories become more meaningful, accessible, and inspiring for people across the globe.

- **Your Personal Library of Alexandria:**

  Over the months and years, you'll curate a unique physical archive of classics—each volume a testament to your taste, curiosity, and love of knowledge. It's not just about owning books—it's about curating a cultural legacy you'll cherish and pass down for generations to come.

- **Join a Global Literary Renaissance:**

  Your support fuels an ongoing mission: allowing us to reinvest in offering deluxe print editions (including special boxsets) at their true cost, broaden the range of available formats and translations, and extend the reach of these works to new audiences worldwide. By joining today, you're not just preserving a legacy of masterpieces; you set in motion a powerful wave of literary accessibility.

  We are more than a publisher—we're a movement, and we can't do it alone. Your support lets us scale our mission, preserving and reimagining history's greatest works for tomorrow's readers.

Become a Torchbearer of knowledge.

Thank you for picking up this book and allowing us into your literary journey. As you turn the pages, know that you're part of something larger: a global effort to keep these stories alive, share their wisdom across borders and generations, and spark a true cultural revival for the modern era.

If this resonates with you—please consider taking the next step by visiting:

www.libraryofalexandria.com

With gratitude and a shared love of knowledge,

The Modern Library of Alexandria Team

Visit:

www.libraryofalexandria.com

Or scan the code below:

www.ingramcontent.com/pod-product-compliance
Lightning Source LLC
Chambersburg PA
CBHW011403010726
47495CB00009B/2764

9 781806 294510